AN ASHLEY PARKER NOVEL

PLAGUE
NATION

DANA FREDSTI

TITAN BOOKS

PLAGUE NATION
Print edition ISBN: 9780857686367
E-book edition ISBN: 9780857686398

Published by Titan Books
A division of Titan Publishing Group Ltd
144 Southwark St, London SE1 0UP

First edition: April 2013
10 9 8 7 6 5 4 3

Dana Fredsti asserts the moral right to be identified as the author of this work.

Visit our website: www.titanbooks.com

Did you enjoy this book? We love to hear from our readers.
Please email us at readerfeedback@titanemail.com or write to us at Reader Feedback at the above address.

To receive advance information, news, competitions, and exclusive offers online, please sign up for the Titan newsletter on our website: www.titanbooks.com

A CIP catalogue record for this title is available from the British Library.

Printed and bound in the United States.

Praise for PLAGUE NATION

"If you like your heroines smart and sassy and kick ass capable, Ashley Parker has what you need. And *Plague Nation* is exactly what the zombie genre needed."
    JOE MCKINNEY, Stoker Award-winning author of FLESH EATERS and INHERITANCE

"*Plague Nation* is a rollicking zombie thriller packed with action, chills, and biting humor. Brava!"
    JONATHAN MABERRY, *New York Times* bestselling author of PATIENT ZERO, FIRE AND ASH, and DEAD OF NIGHT

Praise for PLAGUE TOWN

"In *Plague Town*, Dana Fredsti has created something truly unique in the world of horror fiction – a cool, hip zombie apocalypse novel. With crisp writing, a cast of memorable characters, and tons of undead combat action, it's a zombie lover's literary dream. When the dead rise, I'll want the Wild Cards by my side."
    ROGER MA, author of ZOMBIE COMBAT MANUAL

"One of the Top Ten Zombie Releases of 2012."
    BARNESANDNOBLE.COM

"A gruesomely good read that has me panting for the next book in the series. As hard to put down as a swarm of zombies. When's the next one?"
    KAT RICHARDSON, bestselling author of the GREYWALKER novels

"Fredsti's writing is razor sharp as her heroes fight off the horde while fighting their attraction for each other."
    STACEY GRAHAM, author of THE ZOMBIE DATING GUIDE

"*Plague Town* is a fast-moving zombie tale that reads like a blast of energy. If you like zombie apocalypse stories, this is a must read!"
LOIS GRESH, *New York Times* Best-Selling Author of BLOOD AND ICE and ELDRITCH EVOLUTIONS

"Dana Fredsti has created a world as familiar as our own back yard and populated it with recognizable people we care about... and zombies. *Plague Town* will have you turning pages fast... and checking the locks on all the doors."
RAY GARTON, author of LIVE GIRLS AND SEX and VIOLENCE IN HOLLYWOOD

"As adorable an end of the world as you're liable to get... a brisk, witty ultraviolent romantic gurlventure..."
GINA MCQUEEN, author of OPPOSITE SEX and APOCALYPSE AS FOREPLAY

"Chills and thrills for that season when you're looking for—chills and thrills!"
HEATHER GRAHAM, author of HALLOWED GROUND and the FLYNN BROTHERS TRILOGY

"Not only is the prose good, but it's seasoned with a dash of steamy romance and an excellent sense of originality and pacing... it survives the zombie apocalypse in style."
MISPRINTED PAGES

"More action than season two of *The Walking Dead*."
HORROR TALK

"Revoltingly gory in just the right way, and I'll be picking up the sequel when it rolls around." HOUSE OF GEEKERY

"Read it—I zombie dare you. Fun, fast, read."
AFFAIRS MAGAZINE

BOOKS BY
DANA FREDSTI

THE ASHLEY PARKER NOVELS
Plague Town
Plague Nation
Plague World

Murder For Hire: The Peruvian Pigeon

The Spawn of Lilith

To my cousin,
Staff Sergeant Nick Fredsti

with the 82nd Airborne, killed in
action in Afghanistan while serving his
country, and his sister, Sarah Fredsti,
one of the bravest people I know.

PROLOGUE

"And now for some more bad news. Ready?"

Egg Shen, *Big Trouble in Little China*

BELLEVILLE, WISCONSIN

Bart shuffled out onto the front porch to collect the morning paper, cursing when he saw that their idiot paperboy had once again managed to pitch it nowhere near the house. Instead it lay in a pile of slush in the middle of the front yard, meaning he would have to get his slippers soaking wet to get the damn thing.

Grumbling, he made his way carefully down the slippery steps, moderately grateful that Belleville was experiencing a relatively mild winter, and it wasn't actually snowing any more. Early November in Wisconsin wasn't always so gentle. Even so, the sky was a solid gray layer of clouds.

Bart managed to retrieve the paper without mishap, and turned to go back into his house, but paused as he noticed a pile of newspapers on Lucy Swenson's front stoop. His first thought was how come the little shit of a paperboy had managed to get his neighbor's papers right up against the front door.

Then he frowned. Why hadn't Swenson picked up her paper? Bart counted at least three in their plastic bags, lying in the half-melted snow on the cement porch.

No, this wasn't like Swenson at all. Hell, Bart could set a timer by her daily routine. Porch light off at 6:30 a.m., step outside at 7, always wearing a scowl that frightened small children... Pick up her paper. Grumble something under her breath—usually about the neighborhood dogs ruining her yard. Go back inside and slam the door. She only reappeared when Belleville's lone postal carrier delivered her mail, and harangued him about all sorts of crap that had nothing to do with the postal service.

Porch light on at 6 p.m. sharp—even in the summer.

With this last thought, Bart realized his neighbor's porch light was still on. No, that wasn't right. Could she have fallen and hurt herself? As much as he disliked Lucy Swenson, the cantankerous old bitch was still his neighbor. And in a place as small as Belleville, people looked after one another.

"Well, shit."

Bart sighed and pulled his terrycloth robe tightly around him, retying the belt in a secure knot before carefully making his way onto his neighbor's property, avoiding piles of muddy slush. Even so, the cold wind gusting across the yard penetrated both robe and flannel pajamas, sending an unwelcome chill straight through his bones.

As he approached the porch, Bart's eyebrows shot up as he peered at the mailbox mounted to one of the porch supports. It was stuffed to overflowing. A chill tickled his spine that had nothing to do with the wind.

Careful to avoid patches of ice on the cement steps, Bart navigated his way to Lucy's porch and rapped on the front door.

"Miss Swenson?" He'd known his neighbor for years, long enough to call her by her first name, but she'd have a conniption fit if he did it. He knocked again, more vigorously. "Miss Swenson?"

He held his breath, and thought he heard something. Bart pressed his ear to the door. It was a thumping sound, followed by a noise as if something was being dragged across the floor.

"Well, shit."

He went around the porch until he'd reached the living room window. His view inside was obscured by snowy white eyelet curtains, with hardly any space between the panels. The interior of the house was dark. He thought he saw something moving inside, but it was hard to tell.

"Miss Swenson—you okay in there?"

He heard a low moan. It didn't sound good.

That decided him. Putting his shoulder to the door and a hand on the doorknob, he pushed and twisted at the same time. The door opened easily, and Bart stumbled, practically falling inside the front hallway. He caught himself, his right knee screaming at the unexpected twist. The pain, however, was quickly overwhelmed by the stench that wafted through the house, like an overflowing port-a-potty in the heat of summer. Slipping, Bart fell to his knees into a puddle of viscous black fluid. He began choking on the thick smell, his gorge rising even though he hadn't even had his first cup of coffee.

Something was dead in here.

Trying not to panic, he pulled himself to his feet, ignoring the ache in his joints and trying to ignore the foul black goo that now coated the knees of his pajama bottoms and the hem of his robe. Slow, stumbling footsteps sounded in the living room to the right of the front hall.

"That you, Miss Swenson?" he said hopefully, covering his nose and mouth with one hand.

The hair on the back of Bart's neck rose. Something was really wrong here, and he realized the best thing he could do was leave. Right now. But his conscience wouldn't let him do so without one last try.

"Miss Swens...?" Bart's voice broke in the middle as another low, guttural moan sounded. The footsteps drew closer, lurching across the living room.

Bart stumbled backward. His gut screamed at him to get the hell out, go home, call the cops and lock his house up. Just do it now.

He turned toward the front door, feet slipping again in the stinking black goo that covered the hallway floor. His outstretched hand hit the edge of the door, inadvertently sending it slamming shut on his fingers. He stifled a gasp of pain and fell again to his knees.

The footsteps rounded the corner of the living room as Bart clutched at the doorknob, slimy hands giving little grip. Finally it turned in his hand, and he might have made it out if he hadn't paused to look back.

It was Lucy Swenson, several days dead, but somehow walking even as black fluid and blood oozed out of her mouth, nose, and eyes—dead milky corneas framed by bloody yellowed whites. Her housecoat was filthy, and stuck to her body grotesquely. And she stunk, plain and simple.

"Well, shit."

CHAPTER ONE

We generally don't believe anything bad will happen to us. Things like earthquakes, tsunamis, and zombie apocalypses happen to *other* people. We all firmly believe this... until suddenly that first bastard bites us on the ass.

Then that feeling of security is shot to shit, never to return.

I, for one, resent the hell out of this fact.

My fellow wild cards and I stood outside Licker Up—yeah, really—a poor man's BevMo!, and its sister store Partyrama. "One stop shopping for your party needs!" They were situated in a cluster of interconnected shops on Palm Street.

Located at the south end of Redwood Grove, Palm was considered the main drag of the town's "industrial district." In other words, stores and offices built in that utilitarian saltine cracker box style that clashed with the "quaint" building code imposed on the rest of the community. There were no residences other than a rundown trailer park at the end of the street, and whatever homes were tucked into the woods outside the actual town limits.

The weather was unusually clear, a brisk wind having

swept out the coastal fog that usually shrouded the town. Instead, sunshine filtered through the trees and reflected off the windows. The downside was that without the cloud cover, the crisp November air was butt-ass cold. Gusts of wind managed to insinuate themselves under our clothing and Kevlar, and standing still wasn't helping the situation. I stomped my feet and blew on my hands, wishing Gabriel—our team leader—would get his butt in gear and tell us what to do.

Captain Gabriel was a member of the *Dolofónoitou Zontanoús Nekroús*—usually called DZN, for obvious reasons—an ancient organization dedicated to protecting mankind from the undead. The DZN enlisted members from all walks of life, including various armies and other agencies worldwide. Think *The X-Files* under the auspices of the U.N.

Gabriel was also in charge of this "chickenshit operation," as Tony liked to call it, so we were waiting on his orders.

We gonna kill some zombies, or what? I rubbed my hands together briskly.

"How come we're out here in the butt end of nowhere?" Kai grumbled. Guess I wasn't the only one getting impatient. As usual, he radiated an attitude that said, "I'm cuter than a young Will Smith and I know it." While I had to admit that he made riot-gear chic look pretty damn good, I always found it a toss-up whether to admire his looks, or dropkick him in his admittedly well-toned ass.

Gabriel gave Kai what my dad used to call the "hairy eyeball."

"There are still zombies trickling in from the quarantine perimeter," he said, "probably drawn to the activity in town. The remaining teams are sweeping the outlying areas with the help of incoming military assistance, now that we can risk letting other soldiers inside the quarantine zone."

"About time," Tony muttered.

We all shared his resentment—at first, when the quarantine zone was established, the potential for an uncontained outbreak was too high to risk sending in more personnel. Which really sucked for those of us stuck inside to fight the zombies. The Powers-That-Be had only just started sending in reinforcements to help us clear out the remaining ghouls, because some of the soldiers who'd been inside the zone from the beginning had gotten sick, *without* being bitten. They were the ones who'd received the not-so-thoroughly tested vaccine for Walker's, the *Flu de Jour*.

Gabriel may not have had wild card hearing, but he wasn't deaf. The look he shot Tony was way past irate. He turned away without saying a word and stalked down the block, yanking out his two-way radio.

I watched his cute butt every step of the way. If Kai made swat chic look good, Gabriel rocked it like a runway model.

"What crawled up his ass and died?" Tony said. Four heads turned and looked at me—everyone but Sergeant Gentry, who looked in the opposite direction. He was shooting for the "I am invisible" approach.

"Oh, don't even *try* and pin this on me," I growled. "Gentry, tell them this is *not* my fault."

Gentry was a baby-faced Army sergeant who'd been fighting zombies with the DZN's Zed Tactical Squad—ZTS—even before he'd been bitten and discovered his own immunity. He just shook his head.

"Sorry, Ash, but I'm staying out of this, for the sake of our friendship and my continued health."

Tony snickered. Not surprising since he had a solid case of hero worship for Gentry. The lieutenant wielded a mean flamethrower, and held his own with Tony and Kai when they started batting around movie quotes like the ROTC's answer to *The Big Bang Theory*.

"Wuss," I muttered. Not that I could really blame

him, seeing as Gabriel was his direct superior. Then I turned back to the others.

"Not that it's any of your business," I said, "but Gabriel and I, well, we haven't… er… *seen* each other since we fought the swarm."

Tony nodded sagely. His tongue piercing clicked against a tooth. Tall enough to play for any basketball team, he'd gone from an irritating punked-out teenager to a slightly less irritating zombie-killing teenager—and done it in record time. The metal ball in his tongue was only one of the multiple piercings Tony had sported when I'd first met him. But he'd learned the hard way that dangling pieces of metal didn't mix well with zombies.

"Classic case of Pon Farr," he said. "Get him back to Vulcan, stat!"

"Damn straight," Kai said, nodding his head in agreement. "The dude needs to get laid."

"Is there anyone here but me who thinks this conversation is totally inappropriate?" I looked entreatingly at Mack. "Come on, man, back me up here." A fifty-something mailman, Mack wore an expression that reminded me of a mournful hound dog. Unfortunately I could tell by the way his blue eyes shone with mischief that I wasn't gonna get the support I wanted.

"Tony has a point, Ashley," he said. "It's your job to make sure our fearless leader has an outlet for his stress."

That elicited a snort from Lil, an eighteen-year-old Arts major and my roomie during the current quarantine. She giggled, then looked at me guiltily.

I sputtered in outrage.

"So what, I'm some kind of human stress ball now?" I demanded. Even as the words escaped my mouth, I knew they were a bad choice.

"Well, you *are* his main squeeze," Mack replied. His straight face lasted all of five seconds until Tony, Kai, and Lil all dissolved into fits of laughter that made me want to smack them. Repeatedly.

Not wanting to add fuel to the fire, I settled for a mega-watt glare, then stomped off down the sidewalk after Gabriel to find out exactly what his problem was.

Gabriel and I had been sniping at each other since we'd met as student and teacher at Big Red, before the zombie shit hit the fan. Well, technically he was a teacher's assistant, a self-righteous vegan, and I was a happy little caffeine and sugar junkie omnivore. The sexual tension had developed somewhere between my surviving being bitten by zombies, and my transformation into a wild card—a person immune to the zombie virus. That tension had culminated in some hot, sweaty sex that hadn't as yet been repeated—despite what the rest of the team thought.

I'd hoped all of the sniping was over with, especially after we'd fought together—and almost died—defending the university against a zombie swarm.

I guess I was wrong.

In many ways my ex—okay, *dead*—boyfriend Matt had been a lot easier to deal with. Matt had been uncomplicated. Give him sex and praise on a regular basis and he'd been a happy camper. A far simpler, and definitely more rewarding relationship than I'd had with my ex-husband.

Gabriel, who I found a lot more compelling, was nowhere as easy to keep satisfied. Hell, I didn't know if he even wanted me to try.

I just wanted an adult relationship with mutual respect, intellectual compatibility, and lots of hot sex. Hell, at this point I'd settle for a steamy round of cuddling. Not that I was likely to get any of it, now that Gabriel was back in douche mode.

* * *

He was still talking on the radio when I caught up to him, so I leaned against a building next to the alley that separated Licker Up and Partyrama. He was spewing a string of Byzantine military phrases, and I rolled my eyes as I eavesdropped.

See, being a wild card not only meant enhanced physical abilities and a whole world of super-cool weapons. To my dismay, I'd heard more acronyms, code words, and pompous jargon over the last few weeks of rapid-fire training than in my previous twenty-nine years. That's even if you included the hours I'd been forced to watch the Military Channel with my ex-husband—it was the only way I could spend any "quality" time with him.

Gabriel finally signed off with some variant on "Tango Whiskey Foxtrot." Frowning, he thrust his radio back in its holster and turned to me.

"Did you need something, Ashley?" he demanded.

Ouch. Not the friendliest tone I could have asked for, all things considered.

"Well," I said, choosing my words carefully, "I was kind of hoping you'd tell me what exactly is the reason for that very large stick you've currently got shoved up your ass."

Okay, maybe not so carefully.

Gabriel's brows lowered over a pair of denim-blue eyes as his frown went—to use meteorological parlance—from an F1 to an F2. Before he could snap my head off, however, I kept talking. I'm good at that.

"Because the rest of the gang is talking about it, and they're all blaming me for not helping you relieve your tension on a regular basis."

Unfortunately I'm not always so good at filtering what comes out of my mouth. From the look on Gabriel's face, we just skipped F3 and headed straight to F4, destroying all of the trailer parks in a hundred-mile swath.

"Oh, that's just great," he snapped. "What is this,

high school? Am I supposed to give a shit about who's sleeping with whom?"

"That's not exactly the point," I said carefully.

Seriously, I really was being careful this time.

"Then what exactly *is* the point?" He folded his arms and glared down at me.

"The point is that you're acting like an athlete on the verge of 'roid rage and—" I took a deep breath and put a hand on his arm. "And I'm worried about you."

"Well, don't be," he snapped, jerking his arm away. "I don't have time for this juvenile shit, okay?"

He might as well have slapped me across the face. I felt my cheeks flame as hurt and anger duked it out with humiliation for dominance. Anger won.

"You know that song 'I Might Like You Better If We Slept Together'?" I shook my head. "Well, not so much."

Gabriel glared at me for a split second then turned without another word and stalked back down the sidewalk toward the entrance to the shops. I'd be damned before scurrying after him like some sort of slave girl, so I stayed where I was, fuming silently.

It didn't last long, though.

The unmistakably nasty stench of the walking dead gave me just enough warning to dodge to one side as a zombie lurched out of the alley and lunged at me. It used be a waitress at the local Spanky's Coffee Shop, her nametag and the tattered remains of what used to be a retro pink uniform tipping me off. Just like Flo used to wear in *Alice*. Its face looked like it had been pressed onto a hot grill, with strips of blistered flesh peeling off. I was tonight's special.

My M4 was still slung across my shoulder and my blades were sheathed, so like an idiot I was caught empty-handed. Luckily there are a bunch of ways to kill a zombie, if you're creative. I grabbed a trashcan lid and hefted it.

"Just pick up a lid, Sid," I sang quietly to myself. "Give it a whack, Jack." I smashed the edge of the lid against the zombie's head, the metal leaving a dent in its skull. I swatted it a few more times for good measure, finding it very therapeutic after dealing with Captain Jerk.

"Do it again… er… Len."

Finally Zombie Flo crumpled to the ground.

"Until it drops dead."

So sue me. I'm not a lyricist. But I *am* a kick-ass zombie killer.

"Can I take your orwdah?" I intoned in my best Schwarzenegger.

"Talking to yourself?"

"*Shit!*" I yelped. The unexpected sound of Lil's voice made me jump almost as much as Zombie Flo had. I recovered quickly, though, and pointed to the zombie. "Nope. Talking to her."

Lil looked down at the twice-dead corpse and gave a quiet little sigh.

"I knew her," she said. "Mom and I used to go to Spanky's for lunch, and—" She stopped, swallowing hard. I immediately enfolded her in a hug.

Lil's mom had been out of town when the whole zombie plague had hit, but she'd evidently made it back before the quarantine had been imposed around Redwood Grove and the surrounding area. Lil and I had found her car outside their apartment building. Not knowing her mom's fate weighed heavily, and the cracks in Lil's already fragile emotional state grew a little bigger with every day. The only time she seemed happy was when she was cuddling with her cats, or killing zombies. I understood the cat thing—they were a connection to her old world. But the homicidal tendencies? Those worried me.

Often I joked that she was like a lethal Care Bear in her combat gear, but it was true. All wide green eyes and cuddly curves, Lil turned into a gleeful slaughter machine when faced with the walking dead. Now, however, she was just an eighteen-year-old who missed her mother.

I missed mine, too, but at least I knew both my parents were alive and well up north in Lake County. Lil didn't even have the comfort of closure.

"Let's go take care of business before Gabriel comes looking for us," I suggested. Giving her one last squeeze, I let go and took a step back.

She nodded, wiping her eyes with the back of one hand. I pretended not to notice.

"Yeah… I heard him yelling." Lil snuck a quick peek at me. "Are you okay?"

It was my turn to nod.

"Yup," I said, "just pissed off." And also worried, but I didn't want to go into that right now, or even think about it. I'd already been caught by surprise once today because of shit with Gabriel. I didn't intend to let it happen again. I smacked Lil lightly on the shoulder.

"Let's go hunting."

That brought a smile to her face. I tried not to worry.

We joined the rest of the gang in front of Licker Up. Gabriel had returned, but I didn't bother looking at him.

"We doing two teams on this?" Mack asked. Gabriel nodded.

"Mack, Gentry, Lil, you take the office complex across the street," he said. "Ash, Tony, Kai, check out the stores on this side of the block."

"What about you?" Oops… almost forgot we were pissed at each other.

He hadn't. He just ignored my question and walked away. My face burned just like the good old days, when he was just a self-righteous jerk, giving me grief when I showed up late to class. I made a face at his retreating back and Lil giggled, then tried to turn it into a fake cough when Gabriel turned and shot a dark glance our way.

Immature? Yeah, I totally cop to it. But it was better that than throwing a punch at the back of his head— which was my other impulse.

I turned to the rest of my team, unsheathing my

tanto. While my modified katana was shorter than the traditional blade, the even shorter tanto was a better choice for close quarters encounters. Less chance of accidentally slicing one of my fellow wild cards if things got hairy. And the M4? We may have been immune to the zombie virus, but a stray round ricocheting off a hard surface could still kill us.

Tony had what I referred to as "Thor's Wee Hammer," a small but lethal sledgehammer that was his weapon of choice, while Kai hefted his favorite crowbar.

"Time to *pahty*," Tony said, adding his own *Ahnold* impersonation to the day.

Kai grinned and the two clanged their respective weapons together. They had bonded early on during training, and were pretty much inseparable. The term "bromance" could have been invented just for them.

Lucky me. I got to be third wheel on today's date.

CHAPTER TWO

We entered Licker Up through the front door, which was ajar. I took point, hitting the light switch as I stepped in. Even with the bright sunshine outside, the interior of the store was gloomy—not enough windows to let any real light in. Tony and Kai followed close on my heels.

Broken bottles lay scattered on the floor, their contents blending together in a brew that smelled like the afterhours of an especially rowdy frat party, thankfully minus the vomit. Still, it made my eyes water.

"What a waste," Kai said, kicking a broken bottle of Maker's Mark.

"Plenty still left, bro." Tony hefted a still sealed one and tossed it to Kai.

I gave them both a look.

"Later, okay?" Truth to tell, I was tempted to grab one of the many unopened, unbroken bottles of booze myself. And maybe I would, to enjoy it after we were safe back at Patterson Hall. With that thought in my head, I tucked a bottle of a forty-dollar Napa Cabernet into my knapsack. If the owner of the store turned up alive, I'd settle my account later.

Other than the broken bottles, Licker Up looked clear. No gouts of blood, smears of viscera, or random body parts. It was a refreshing change. We went aisle to aisle, wincing at the smell of way-overripe cheese in a cooler that had long since lost its power.

"That is *ripe*, señor," muttered Tony.

As soon as he spoke, a creaking noise drew our attention to the back of the store.

Holding a finger up to my lips, I made my way as quietly as possible to a small hallway that had three doors off it, each bearing a little plastic sign labeling them restroom, office, and stockroom. The three of us stood quietly, and listened.

All was quiet.

I cracked open the restroom door, reluctantly taking a deep inhalation. I got a whiff of an ammonia-based cleanser that seared my sinuses, but no *Eau de Zombie*. Letting the door close, I turned toward the office and gestured to Tony, who smirked and strolled over to the door, opening it with a casual air that made me want to punch him. A familiar urge, that.

While he checked out the office, I went over to the stockroom door and pressed my ear against it. I didn't hear anything, but for some reason my Spidey senses were tingling.

Not satisfied, I knocked.

"Hello?"

A moan sounded from behind the door. Suddenly something started scratching and pounding on the other side. Stepping back, I looked at Kai, jerking my chin in the direction of the commotion. I backed further away, giving him room, and he kicked the door inward.

The smell of rotting flesh immediately assaulted my nostrils. Doing my best to ignore it, I slipped inside, and found a male zombie in a red Licker Up vest sprawled on the floor, knocked there by the door's impact. Even in the gloom I could see that pieces were missing from its face, neck and arms, and the remaining flesh was a greenish-gray with black goop oozing from the wounds.

Before it could get to its feet, I stepped in and thrust the tip of my tanto into its left eye socket. It only stopped when it reached the back of the skull. Then, putting my foot against its shoulder, I shoved hard as I pulled the blade out. A lovely sucking sound accompanied my movement.

Yuck.

"He's been chewed on pretty good," Kai observed.

I nodded. "Which means he either got bitten and crawled in here to die, or—"

There was a crash, and three zombies stumbled out from behind the shelves stacked high with cases of hard liquor, beer, and wine—two of them in store uniforms, and a young woman in bloodstained jeans and a T-shirt proclaiming "I'm a Princess," the words outlined in rhinestones.

No, you're a zombie, I thought, giving her a permanent frontal lobotomy. Does it make me a bad person to admit I kind of enjoyed it? I mean, unless you're Honey Boo-Boo, who the hell would wear something like that?

While I took care of Princess Z, Kai dispatched the other two zombies with several skull-shattering blows to their craniums, using his crowbar with a casual aplomb that spoke of a lot of repetition. Suddenly a wave of self-consciousness swept over me. It brought my own callousness close to home.

"Doesn't it worry you that we're getting used to this?" I asked, wiping my blade on the leg of my pants.

Kai shrugged.

"I'd rather get used to it," he said, "than need a therapy session every time we have to put one of these things down. And maybe if one of these people'd known what to do, they'd still be alive, you know?"

He had a point, but it still bothered me that killing had become so routine. I looked at the floor and shook my head. There was no easy answer to any of this. Maybe normal emotional responses had to be tossed out the window when the dead walked the earth... But it still sucked.

Kai and I checked out the rest of the stockroom, finding puddles of blood and bits of flesh, but no more bodies, ambulatory or otherwise. Tony was waiting for us in the hallway, flipping through an old Licker Up newsletter. Irritated, I smacked it out of his hands.

"Hey!" he protested.

"Did it ever occur to you we might've needed your help in there?"

He shrugged. "I didn't hear any screams."

This time I clipped him on the back of his head.

"By the time you hear them, it might be too late."

BELLEVILLE, WISCONSIN

Bart's corpse twitched. At first just a finger or two—all that were left on his mangled hands—before a ripple shuddered through his body as though it had been hit by an invisible electric current.

What was left of his neighbor chewed on a piece of his intestines, causing them to unspool from Bart's gutted abdomen as he staggered to his feet.

A gust of wind blew the front door open and the sound of children's voices and laughter drifted inside, catching his attention. The two zombies made their way outside into the chill November morning, Bart's intestine linking them together like rotting mountain climbers.

Laughter turned to screams in no time at all.

CHAPTER THREE

The rear exit led to the end of the alley, with Partyrama's back entrance right across the way. The alley was clear, and the door unlocked. But I tried not to get optimistic.

Partyrama was a typical tchotchke store, with merchandise divided into sections for holidays, themed parties, and weddings. The first thing we saw was the "Hold Your Own Luau!" aisle, with plastic leis, tiki torches, brightly colored dishware, and tropical themed cutouts. Next to that was a "Princess Party" aisle, sporting everything you needed for precious royalty between the ages of three and thirteen. "Pirate Cove" themed stuff was right next to it.

Kai stooped over and picked something off the floor.

"Eye-patch, anyone?"

Our footsteps crunched on scattered plastic beads from a fallen display. An end cap of frothy net tutus lay toppled to one side.

"Nothing will remain but the bare earth soaked in putrefying flesh!" Tony picked up one of the tutus, then shook his fist skyward.

"*Hell of the Living Dead*," Kai said, sounding bored. "Try again."

I rolled my eyes. The boys were playing "name that zombie movie" again. We'd watched a slew of them, ostensibly as part of our training. *Hell of the Living Dead* had featured a mercenary doing a soft shoe routine with a green tutu slung over his neck, just before getting ripped to pieces by third-world zombies.

Tony frowned, and thought about it for a moment.

"'He took a poo and it stank,'" he offered.

"*Dead Set*," Kai responded, without missing a beat. "Pippa." He shook his head again. "Next you'll be all 'ein, zwie, die' and expect me to be stumped."

"Can you two please focus on the job at hand?" I snapped. "Like, checking to make sure there aren't any zombies wandering around?"

Kai delivered a snappy salute in my direction.

"You got it, Ash." Spinning on his heels, he wandered off down the St. Patrick's Day aisle, crowbar dangling loosely from one hand.

"Jeez frickin' Louise," I muttered to myself.

"Don't worry, Ash." Tony patted me condescendingly on the shoulder. "He'll be fine. You just need to chillax, y'know?"

I smacked his hand.

"No, I *don't* know. And you can tell me to chill, or you can tell me to relax. Do *not* friggin' tell me to 'chillax'!"

Tony pouted. "Hey, we totally kicked ass against the swarm at Big Red. So how can a few stragglers be a problem?"

"Weren't you listening? Professor Fraser said this shit could be going nationwide. Maybe even global." He was really starting to piss me off.

Tony shrugged. "We'll deal with that if and when it happens."

I narrowed my eyes.

"Let me paraphrase one of your favorite movies, Tony, with words you can hopefully understand. Don't get cocky."

As I stalked off down the Pirate Cove aisle, I heard him mutter, "Yeah, whatevs."

I swear, I was gonna kill him, if a zombie didn't take

care of his cocky ass first. He and Kai could drive a saint to homicide, and I was *far* from sainthood. *Gabriel must hate me*, I decided. *Why else would he stick me alone with both of them at the same time?*

Suddenly Kai's voice broke through the stillness.

"Ash! X-Box! Check this shit out!"

Instantly the urgency in his words had me running down the aisles, pulling my tanto out of its sheath, Tony close on my heels. We found him in "Miscellaneous Party Fun," hunkered down by a display of—

"Silly String?" I stared at him in disbelief.

"Why didn't you say so in the first place?" Tony slapped a hand against his forehead. "Now if we only had a wheelbarrow and a holocaust cloak…"

Kai grinned. "You killed my father, prepare to die."

I restrained the urge to shove a can of the stuff down each of their throats. Taking a deep breath, I turned to Kai.

"What, may I ask, is so awesome about Silly String?"

"Navy ordinance disposal teams used it in Iraq to find trip wires," he replied. "Spray some of this shit, it catches on one of the invisible wires, and there you go."

"Great," I said. "But zombies don't set trip wires."

"It's also highly flammable." Kai tucked a couple of cans into his knapsack and held one can aloft dramatically. "Light a match near this shit and you've got zombie barbecue."

"Seriously?"

He nodded.

"Yup. Couple of kids at a party found out the hard way." He looked at the can, examining the ingredients. "I'm surprised it's still even for sale."

Something crashed to the floor in the back of the store. All three of us straightened up, staring back into the shadowed depths of the Wedding section, where something moved clumsily towards us. We heard the plaintive moan about the same time as the graveyard stench hit us.

"I got this." Kai darted behind the counter and snatched up a cigarette lighter. Before I could smack it out of his hand, he pressed the button on the Silly String and clicked the trigger on the lighter, sending a jet of flaming string toward the corpse that was lurching in our direction. Its tattered clothing quickly went up in flames.

Just great.

"Oh, shit," Kai said. *Zombie flambé* still staggered in our general direction, rebounding off the shelves and igniting a bunch of Pretty Princess tiaras.

Shoving Kai out of my way, I moved forward and thrust the business end of my tanto into one of its eyes. It crumpled to the ground and I proceeded to stomp out the flames on both zombie and the tiara display before they spread any further. The smell of scorched plastic mingled with the stink of burnt, rotting flesh.

I glared at Kai.

"No more Silly String."

"You got it." He tossed the can and lighter aside.

"What the hell is going on?"

The three of us turned as Gabriel strode down the aisle toward us, his expression reflecting the pissed-off tone of his voice.

Swell.

"Kai was demonstrating the efficacy of Silly String against the enemy... sir." I kept my voice as neutral as I could, but I guess the sarcasm of the "sir" snuck through my limited acting ability, because the look Gabriel shot us could have started another fire.

"I can't believe you three." He shook his head in disgust. "Can't you take things seriously, even for a few minutes?"

Tony and Kai exchanged sheepish looks. I, on the other hand, walked straight up to him until we were toe-to-toe, and glared up at him.

"In case you haven't noticed, *sir*—" I didn't even try this time "—we have a dead zombie here, which would intimate that Team A takes our mission *very* seriously. The fact that Lando chose to utilize an unorthodox weapon would show that he's capable of thinking outside the box, if the occasion necessitates it."

Out of the corner of my eye I saw Kai and Tony look at me with new appreciation as I piled on the bullshit. Gabriel, on the other hand, did not look impressed.

"The occasion didn't necessitate it. This was just sloppy work."

Since I actually agreed with him, I kept my mouth shut. But that didn't stop me from chanting "douche" over and over in my head.

"Is that clear?" He glared at the three of us.

The Wonder Twins nodded. It hurt my neck and my pride to do so, but I did the same.

"Good," he said. "We're done for the day. Debrief in Room 217 in an hour. Don't forget to mark the doors." Turning on his heel, Gabriel strode out of the store without a backward glance.

This time I didn't even appreciate the sight of his retreating butt; I just wanted to plant my foot on it and push hard. *Really* hard.

I couldn't believe that three days ago he and I had engaged in hot monkey sex, and then fought the zombie swarm. Together. At some point between our victory and now, something had gone wrong. Or, more specifically, something had definitely gone fubar with Gabriel. Maybe it was his meds, maybe something else, but whatever it was I didn't know whether to be worried or pissed off. So I went for both.

"Sorry, Ash." Kai put a hand on my shoulder. He sounded sincere, so I resisted my first impulse to shrug it off.

"Yeah, okay." I turned and faced him. "Just… no more shit like the Silly String, okay?"

Kai and Tony both nodded, expressions too solemn for comfort. But at least they were trying.

Mika studied her reflection in the window that separated the pharmacy from the rest of the drug store. She nodded slightly, approving of the shine of her long glossy black hair and the contrast between her olive-toned skin and lush red lips, courtesy of Cover Girl's "Desire" lipstick.

Then she looked past her reflection out into the store, and sighed.

"What's wrong?" Emmet, one of her fellow pharmacists at the Sacramento Street Walgreen's, took a swig of his fourth Coke of the morning. He averaged two per hour, and it showed in the comfortably expansive stomach that lurked under his white coat.

"Check out the line," she said.

Emmett hoisted himself out of his chair and peered around Mika at the dozen or so people snaking down the medications aisle, at least half of them coughing, sniffling, or sneezing. He groaned, and then sat back down.

"What, did the entire San Francisco Financial District get sick at once?" he said. "Tell me these people aren't all here for vaccines."

Mika held out the sign-up sheet. All twenty-four slots were filled, each one with a check indicating the flu vaccine.

"This is just the top sheet," she said. "Every reservation is full, and we have walk-ins."

"Well, slap my ass and call me Sally." Emmett shook his head. "Guess Walker's Flu came to visit."

Mika giggled as she always did when Emmett used one of his incomprehensible Mid-western expressions. Tossing her hair over one shoulder, she looked at the clock.

"It's five till ten," she pointed out. "We should start."

Emmett heaved a sigh worthy of the drama queen he was.

"Right, then. No rest for the wicked."

Mika smirked. "You must not sleep too much."

"Funny girl." He hauled himself up again. "How about you get the first two victims, and I'll grab more vaccines so we're stocked for the day."

Swigging the last of his Coke, Emmett went into the stockroom, heading straight for the refrigeration units that held the various vaccines the drugstore chain was authorized to dispense. He skimmed over shingles, polio, and Japanese encephalitis, wondering yet again why the shipping and receiving clerks never put things in alphabetical order. TB... rabies... and the unit dedicated to flu vaccines. Emmett opened it, and found himself staring at empty shelves.

"Well, shit on a shingle." He put a hand on one hip, and glared at the shelves. *"Kenny! Kenny, you in here?"*

Kenny—one of the two shipping and receiving clerks and, as Emmett always said, skinny as a drink of water—sauntered around the corner.

"What can I do you for, Em?" he asked.

Emmett rolled his eyes.

"First of all, don't call me Em. I am not Dorothy's aunt, got it?"

Kenny stared at him blankly.

"Who's Dorothy?"

Emmett opened his mouth to answer, then shook his head.

"Never mind. Your lack of cultural awareness isn't my problem. What is my problem, however, is the fact we appear to be out of flu vaccinations, and I've got a line of people running half the store, all wanting one."

"No prob." Kenny vanished back around the corner, reappearing minutes later with a cart piled high with cardboard boxes, all labeled "Keep Refrigerated!" Brandishing a box-cutter like a switchblade, he sliced the top box open and pulled out a hard-sided styrofoam container, sliding the top half off to reveal small boxes filled with little vials.

Emmett took one of the boxes.

"What happened to the rest of the stock?"

"Got a message from corporate, telling us to pull 'em 'cause we were getting this new batch in."

"Why? The others were well under the expiration date."

"Heck if I know." Kenny shrugged. *"I just work here."*

"Alrighty, then." Emmett tucked the box under his arm,

gave the clerk a little salute and headed back into the store. It wasn't his business if corporate wanted to waste money and toss out perfectly good drugs. Time to go shoot up a bunch of local venture capitalists and bankers.

CHAPTER FOUR

"What the hell is he doing here?"

I was tired, I was grouchy, and my blood sugar was beyond low. The last person I wanted to see sitting across from me in Patterson Hall's cafeteria was Dr. Albert— my childhood physician, flu vaccine researcher, and the man responsible for the zombie plague.

Judging from their expressions, I gathered that Tony, Mack, and Gentry—the three other wild cards at the table—all felt the same way I did.

"I said, why is he here?" I repeated.

Dr. Albert peered at me reproachfully over his plate of pasta and salad, his pinched features and graying red hair reminding me of a ginger-haired were-rat. Only a day or so ago, he'd been practically suicidal after finding out the Redwood Grove zombie outbreak was his fault, and that it might have gone nationwide.

Desperate to discover the cure for Walker's Flu, Dr. Albert had helped falsify test results for his vaccine, in the hopes of making a buttload of money. As it was, the vaccine reacted to a normally dormant variant of a retrovirus present in about ten percent of the population. This caused a nasty but manageable flu bug to mutate into the walking death.

Thanks a hell of a lot, doc.

Yet here he was, sitting at the same table as several

wild cards, each of whom had risked their lives to try and stop the spread of the virus he'd unleashed. Hell, one of us had died in the attempt. So much for his emotional I.Q.

I turned to Simone Fraser. Back when I was just a student at Redwood Grove College—"Big Red" for short—she was my teacher for "Pandemics in History." I'd come to learn she was a long-time member of the *Dolofónoitou Zontanóús Nekroús*—which for some reason she liked to say without abbreviating it. I considered her my mentor.

"Seriously, Simone, why is he here?"

Simone looked up from her dinner and sighed.

"He needs to eat, Ashley." She was clearly not in the mood for confrontation.

Well, tough shit.

"Seems to me he could eat in a locked room somewhere." I slammed my tray of food on the table hard enough to bounce a few French fries off my plate.

My fellow wild cards muttered in agreement, all of us having nearly died, and then risked our lives more than once, all because of what Dr. Albert's greed had unleashed.

I took an unnecessarily vicious bite of my hamburger, channeling Nomi from *Showgirls*. Sure, Dr. Albert had been my doctor since, like, forever, but somehow that made me even angrier. It was like finding out that it had been Dr. Mengele who'd done all those pap smears.

"I don't see how he can eat," Tony growled, tongue-stud clicking against the bottom of his teeth in agitation.

"I have to agree," Mack chimed in. "I mean, if it was me, and I'd found out that I'd engineered Armageddon, I think I'd have a little trouble keeping my dinner down. Not to mention what this could do to future vaccination and immunization programs. Those are too important to lose, all because one man screwed up." Strong words, coming from Mack—he was usually the one who tried to keep the peace.

"Good point," I said, "although it may be moot if zombies take over the world."

Gentry gave an almost imperceptible nod, keeping quiet. One of the soldiers sent into the quarantine area around Redwood Grove at the beginning of the outbreak, I guess he was used to having to keep his mouth shut in bullshit situations. I, on the other hand, felt no such constraints.

"Exactly," I said. "Not to mention the fact that what he did *has* to be illegal. So why hasn't he been locked up?"

Dr. Albert clucked indignantly.

"Ashley, after all the years I've been your doctor, I can't believe you're saying this," he said.

Simone cut in before I could blast him.

"Dr. Albert hasn't been locked up because, regardless of the ethics inherent to his previous decision, he still may be the only person alive who is capable of finding a cure."

This matter-of-fact answer took the steam out of my self-righteous anger.

"Oh." I tried to think of something else to say. *Nope, that's all I've got.*

"Oh, indeed." Simone nodded, brushed a stray strand of honey blonde hair out of her face, and rubbed the back of her neck as if it hurt.

If not for the fact that the dead were already walking the earth, I would have taken this as a sign of the coming apocalypse. Simone *never* had stray strands of hair. Calm, composed, and well groomed, she always looked as if she'd strayed from some forties movie where the women all wore trumpet skirts and silk blouses, and styled their hair in chignons. She could have been anywhere between forty and fifty, and if I'd been casting her life story, it would've been a toss-up between Cate Blanchett and Helen Mirren.

To see her fraying around the edge—both emotionally

and physically—reminded me that we were in some seriously deep shit.

With that sobering thought, I turned my attention back to my hamburger. Glancing around, I wondered briefly where Kai was. Probably still cleaning up. When it came to grooming, Kai was like a cat—minus the inappropriate spot cleaning.

As if on cue, Mr. Perfect sauntered in, hair still damp from his shower, looking as pleased with himself as the Old Spice Guy. He filled a tray in record time and plonked himself in between Tony and Mack, barely letting his ass hit the seat before attacking his food.

"Hungry?" I grinned at him.

He shoveled in a forkful of pasta by way of reply.

Like our senses, wild card appetites were revved a few notches above normal. Luckily our metabolisms were equally hyperactive so we wouldn't, as Tony put it, "do a Kilmer."

Mack looked around.

"Where's Lil?"

"She's eating in our room," I answered. "Spending some quality time with the cats. She's not in the mood for socializing about now."

Mack nodded. He understood, and worried about Lil as much as I did. Her mother hadn't been with the survivors we'd rescued from the basement of a local church, or among the far too many corpses scattered around town. By the time we'd returned to Big Red, her killing glee had dissipated into quiet depression. It was just as well she'd opted out of communal dinner. Sitting across from the man who might be responsible for her mother's death wouldn't have helped her already fragile emotional state.

Gabriel was MIA, too. He'd vanished right after the debriefing in Room 217.

I had no idea how he felt about Dr. Albert. On one hand, the man was responsible for almost turning Gabriel into a mindless zombie, or at very least a sentient flesh-eater. On the other hand, Dr. Albert had also synthesized the antiserum that kept Gabriel's condition in check.

I was distracted from my dark thoughts as Nathan and Jamie joined us at our table. Nathan Smith—I was *still* convinced that was an alias. Tall, dark and perpetually cranky, he had some sort of secret past with Simone, back when he was a member of a Special Forces unit. He never elaborated on which unit, and I guess it didn't really matter. There was still a *Moonlighting* level of sexual tension between them—enough to make Kate and Sawyer look like kindergarten playmates.

A badass with a ton of weapons—some legal, and others not so much—Nathan's house could have been featured in *Survivalists' Homes and Gardens*. He'd saved Lil and me when we'd broken protocol and gone after Lil's cats, and then saved all of the wild cards when we'd been on the run from a shitload of hungry zombies.

Good times.

Jamie had been Simone's teacher's assistant in "Pandemics in History," before the zombie shit had hit the fan. She was a veritable gothic Tinkerbell, with her Hot Topic clothes, petite build, and screaming pink hair. The torch Jamie carried for Simone lit her up like a solar flare whenever they were in the same room. Until she realized I didn't want to be teacher's pet, so to speak, she'd tried more than once to eliminate me with her laser stares of death. For whatever reason, though, she seemed to take Nathan's presence in her stride. Go figure.

Jamie sat down across from me, next to Simone, while Nathan took the "dad's" seat at the head of the table. I smiled at them both. Simone, on the other hand, made a point of smiling at Jamie and ignoring Nathan. It was fascinating to watch two adults behave with all the finesse of hormonal high school students. I gave them a week before they either did the deed or killed each other.

I looked down at my plate, which was sadly empty. Time for a refill.

There were five soldiers ahead of me in the serving line. I recognized two of them from the fight against the swarm. We exchanged friendly and respectful nods. The other three were new faces. One of the newbies gave his buddy a nudge when he saw me. His friend, a burly twenty-something with "bad attitude" written all over him, whispered something back, including the words "prime," "ass," "pussy," and "get me some of that."

Guess no one had warned them about wild card hearing. I smiled a not too nice smile, and took a step forward.

"Would you like to say that a little louder?" I asked cheerfully.

Bad Attitude looked at me, his grin getting wider.

"Don't think I was talking to you," he said, tossing his friend a glance.

"Yes, but you were talking *about* me." I shook my head. "That's very rude, you know."

The two soldiers who'd fought the swarm took several sensible steps back. One of them shook his head.

"Oh man, Jeeter, you are so screwed," he said.

Jeeter? Seriously, is that even a name? Bad Attitude grinned, looking me up and down.

"That's what I'm hoping for."

I was never in the mood for this sort of shit. But today? Less so than usual. And I was just looking for a reason to go medieval on someone's ass.

Before I could do anything, however, Nathan strode up to the soldiers, grabbed the two offenders by their forest-camo shirtfronts, and lifted them up in the air a few inches. Then he pulled them in close, so he could look them both in the eye.

"I hear shit like that coming out of your mouths again about Ms. Parker or *any* of the women at Big Red, I'll feed you to the zombies myself." He gave them each a bone-rattling shake and let them go. "Got it?"

"Yes, sir!" yelled the first one.

"Jeeter" gave a resentful mutter.

"What was that, soldier?" Nathan asked. He stepped in a little closer, towering over his target and grabbing another handful of shirt.

"Nothing… sir," Jeeter responded. A more grudging "sir" has never been uttered.

"Nothing?" Nathan looked down at him. "It better have been 'Yes, sir,' Private, or I will let this woman have her way with you, and I can guarantee you that you will not enjoy it."

Guess I wasn't the only one itching for someone's ass to kick.

"With all respect… *sir*," Jeeter said, "I'd like to see her try."

Nathan and I exchanged glances. I smiled and he let go of the soldier with an abruptness that saw the little snot weasel sprawled on the ground. His buddy backed away from him. Maybe the look in my eyes scared him.

Smart kid.

I walked up to the fallen soldier and held out a hand.

"Want some help?" For a second or two I thought he was gonna back down. Unfortunately, or fortunately—it depended on how you wanted to look at it—stupidity and testosterone got in the way.

"Yeah." He looked me up and down. "Why don't you just shut that dick sucker and—"

The heel of my palm hit the bridge of his nose, in and out like a piston. He yelled, eyes watering in pain, and swung his fist toward my face. I sidestepped, grabbing his wrist with one hand, shoving the palm of my hand in between his shoulder blades, forcing him to the ground.

One broken nose (his), a dislocated shoulder (also his) and a bruised knuckle (mine, ouch) later, I left my new friend sprawled on the linoleum for someone else to deal with. It took all of ten seconds.

Nathan looked over the results of my handiwork.

"I'm glad you didn't break anything important," he said.

I shrugged.

"Didn't want him out of commission for too long."

"That's very thoughtful of you," he said. "But I didn't mean him. Make sure you ice those knuckles."

I grinned, stepped up to the front of the line, and loaded up my plate with seconds. We went back to the table, where Simone eyed us with equal parts amusement and disapproval.

"Do you really think that was the best way to handle the situation?" she asked.

I shrugged apologetically.

"It seemed like a good idea at the time."

Nathan also shrugged, but without any hint of apology.

"Little shit learned a lesson, right? And maybe next time the new recruits will treat the wild cards with some respect."

"And women in general, of course," Simone added.

"Of course," Nathan agreed.

"Plus it was fun to watch," Tony chimed in.

"Totally," Kai agreed. "There's something about a hot chick beating the crap out of a guy in uniform."

Nathan chuckled.

"Can't argue there, Lando." Lifting his bottle of whatever microbrew he was drinking, he toasted in Simone's general direction. "Damned hot."

We all turned expectantly, but Simone remained silent. Her cheeks were bright red, though.

Oh, to have been a fly on the wall when they first met.

* * *

"Welcome to the Gateway to Hell."

Jackson stood at the entrance to Semetei Air Base, a huge grin on his sunburned face. He was your quintessential California surfer, all shaggy blond hair, long overdue for a regulation cut, and he had a laid-back nature unusual for someone in this particular line of work. He and the rest of the team had arrived at Semetei 24 hours ahead of Nathan, who'd had to go through an extra day of debriefing for reasons he still thought were bullshit.

Like its larger counterpart, Manas Transit Station, Semetei was a popular stopping point for all US military personnel coming to and leaving Afghanistan. Both had good recreation facilities that allowed coalition forces from all branches a comfortable way station between assignments.

Jackson gave Nathan the tour of the various buildings, including spacious barracks, dining hall, gymnasium, library, and chapel, all well-appointed.

Nathan raised an eyebrow.

"I'm not seeing the 'hell' part here."

"That comes when you leave," Jackson said. They walked out of the chapel and paused at the entrance. Some sort of altercation was going on across the way, involving a couple of flyboys and a woman in an indeterminate uniform of khaki skirt and blouse that still managed to make her look like a centerfold. Even from a distance, it was obvious the flyboys appreciated the woman's charms as much as Nathan did. They stood in her way as she tried to walk past, and it was just as clear that she didn't appreciate their "compliments."

"Who's that, Jackson?" Nathan nudged his buddy. *"The blonde over there."*

Jackson snorted.

"That, my friend, is Simone Fraser. And let me just tell you, there are cold fish in the Arctic that'll give you a warmer reception than she will."

"Really?" Nathan said absently, still staring across the

distance as one of the flyboys put a hand on her shoulder. There was a blur of motion, and the flyboy's arm was twisted up behind his back, the woman's knee pressed into his spine as he was forced to eat tarmac.

Jackson just rolled his eyes as if to say *I told you so.*

"Really," he echoed. "Trust me when I say you do not wanna go there."

Yeah, I really do, Nathan thought, but he held his tongue.

The next day, when he saw Simone Fraser heading toward the library, he didn't hesitate. Deciding to intercept her, he stepped in front of her just enough to make her pause, but not enough to come across as predatory.

"Excuse me," he said.

She stopped, raising a perfectly arched brow as she turned a cool, sea-green gaze in his direction.

"Yes?"

"I'm new here, and was hoping you could answer a very important question." Nathan gave her his most charming smile, one he'd been told could have convinced a nun to give up her celibacy.

The eyebrow arched a bit higher.

"And what would that be?"

Nathan leaned in for the kill.

"Who do I have to shoot to get a decent cup of coffee around here?"

Her lips quirked.

"No one," she replied without a hint of humor. "We have a Starbucks."

"Damn," Nathan said.

She gave him a look, a half smile playing around her mouth.

"You sound disappointed."

"I am."

"You enjoy killing that much?"

Nathan cocked his head to one side and gave her a look.

"No," he replied. "I prefer Peet's."

Her smile widened, exposing straight, pearly-white teeth.
"So do I."

Nathan grinned and offered his arm.

"Care to join me for an espresso anyway?"

She tilted her head to one side in a way that would have been coquettish on most women, but just seemed natural for her.

"I would be delighted, Lieutenant…?"

"It's Captain… Captain Smith. But you can call me Nathan."

"I'm Simone." She took his arm. "Simone Fraser."

"I know."

"Oh, really?"

He grinned at her.

"I believe in doing my research."

"Good," she replied. "So do I." She looked him up and down, frank appreciation in her gaze. "Shall we start with coffee?"

Ooh, boy, thought Nathan.

"Sure. And maybe you can tell me a little bit about this place, since you've been here for a while."

"I'd be happy to, Captain… Nathan."

It turned out she wasn't kidding.

"—geologists refer to this area as the 'Pamir Knot,' specifically the mountains of Kyrgyzstan and the countries it borders."

"Really?" Nathan took a hefty slug of his Depth Charge, relishing the rocket fuel rush as the caffeine hit his bloodstream. Five packets of sugar and a hefty dollop of cream didn't hurt either, although according to his ex-wife, men drank their coffee black.

Screw that. He liked his cream and sugar.

"Kyrgyzstan is a small country, but it was an extremely important outpost along the Silk Road, facilitating the historic exchange of goods, ideas, and even technologies between the

East and West. It was also the launching pad for the Golden Horde of Genghis Khan and other nomadic armies."

"Uh-huh..."

He liked the sound of her voice, rich and musical, cream and honey even with her matter-of-fact manner of speaking. It made the constant flow of words enjoyable, instead of irritating.

"Of course, the geographic location, smack dab in the middle of Asia's great landmass, makes it extremely chilly at night, even in the summer, so—"

"I'll wear my long johns."

Simone looked at him quizzically.

"I'm lecturing, aren't I?"

"A little bit." He smiled to take any sting out of his words.

"It's a bad habit of mine, I'm afraid." She sipped her cappuccino, color high in her patrician cheekbones.

"I'm guessing you're a teacher."

"It's rather painfully obvious, isn't it?" she said. "I'm sorry."

"Don't apologize. I'd have killed to have a teacher like you in high school."

She laughed. "Try college." Responding to his surprised expression she added, "I'm older than I look."

"So what's a college professor doing at a military base in Kyrgyzstan?"

"Research." She smiled at him over the rim of her mug, those startlingly green eyes wide and ingenuous.

CHAPTER FIVE

I'd hoped to have a chance to talk to Gabriel before going to bed but he was nowhere to be found, and I was just too tired to go hunting for him. Besides, it was painfully obvious he wasn't interested in dealing with me. Hey, I could take a hint. I didn't have to like it, but I could take it.

So I decided to retreat to the room I shared with Lil to lick my metaphorical wounds, and make sure Lil was doing okay. Or at least as well as could be expected. I was an only child so I didn't have any experience dealing with the angst of a younger sibling, let alone the sort of shit she was going through.

The elevator smelled like bleach and antiseptic, that very special fragrance of decontamination that we all went through after any encounter with the walking dead. I'd gone through an entire case of body butter and facial moisturizer in the last few weeks.

I could see light bleeding from under the bottom of the door to our room, which meant Lil was either still awake or had fallen asleep while reading. I'd found her sacked out once or twice, a book flopped face down on her chest.

Cracking open the door, I peered around the edge to find Lil awake and reading the Brooks *Zombie Survival Guide*. Her cats Binkey, a long-haired brindle tabby, and Doodle, a glossy black short-hair, were keeping her company. Binkey was coiled around the top of her head like a whiskered fur hat, while Doodle snuggled against Lil's side, head buried in her armpit. Both cats were hefty, bringing to mind furry blimps. We'd almost lost our lives retrieving them from Lil's apartment in Redwood Grove. Only Nathan's timely intervention had prevented us from becoming zombie chow.

Still, I'd do it again to give Lil something to fight for, and bring a smile to her face.

She looked up, and I could see that her sea-green eyes were red-rimmed with recent tears. I crossed the room and sat on the edge of her bed.

"You okay?"

She shook her head. Binkey opened one eye and yawned.

"You know you will be, though. Right?" I offered.

She gave me a wan smile.

Binkey stretched and patted Lil on the face with one paw as if in agreement, before coiling back up in a ball.

"See? Binkey says so." I gave my feline ally a scritch on the head, making sure to pet Doodle, too, just in case he was paying attention.

I wasn't sure if it was better or worse to see Lil go from gleeful slayer to this less manic but totally depressed state. Lately there didn't seem to be much of an in-between, and I didn't know if it was the continued emotional strain of not knowing what had happened to her mother, or something else. I'd started thinking of Lil as the little sister I'd never had. We looked enough alike to be related, both of us with green eyes and brown hair, although mine was a few shades darker. She had a lot of hair, that girl, like a fairy-tale princess.

"I'll be okay," Lil said, staring off at the wall. "As soon as I find Mom."

Not knowing what else to say, I patted her on the shoulder, got up, and went into the bathroom to brush my teeth.

As I reached for the toothpaste, I knocked a pill bottle off the sink. The lid popped off and a tablet skittered on the tiles behind the toilet. Grumbling, I scooped up the pill and put it back in the bottle, making sure the lid was screwed on tightly this time. I glanced at the label—it was Clozapine, prescribed to Lil. Something else she'd retrieved when we'd gone to her apartment for Binkey and Doodle.

I brought the bottle with me when I left the bathroom and shook it.

"Lil, you're almost out of these. Do we need to get you more?"

She glanced up from her book. "Nah, no big deal."

"Are you sure?" I must have sounded doubtful, because Lil abruptly threw her book down on the bed and sat up, dislodging both cats. Okay, Doodle just rolled a few inches down the pillow and went back to sleep, while Binkey looked up, yawned and jumped off the bed in search of food.

"I'm sure!" she snapped. "I can handle it. It's none of your business anyway, okay?"

Whoa. I held up my hands in a "no trouble here" gesture. "Easy, girl," I said. "I'm just gonna put these back in the bathroom, okay?"

"Fine!"

Obviously it wasn't.

"Look, I'm not trying to be nosy," I said. "I just worry."

"Well, *don't.*" With that, Lil retrieved her book, threw herself back on the bed, and cracked it back open. "I'm fine, okay?"

That was up for debate, but now was not the time. Without another word I went back in the bathroom and put the pills in the medicine cabinet, telling myself it would be okay. I mean, she wasn't popping pills and going on about needing her "dolls." That was a good sign, right?

When I came back out, Lil was sitting up, hugging

her knees to her chest with both arms, staring at me remorsefully.

"I'm sorry, Ashley." She sounded miserable.

I sighed and sat down on my own bed.

"It's okay."

"No, it's not." Lil sniffled, wiping her nose on one sleeve. I handed her the box of Kleenex we kept on our nightstand.

"Even if I say it is?"

Lil shook her head.

"Especially then. You're too nice to me. All the time." She blew her nose, quietly. "Even when I don't deserve it."

I shook my head, failing to hide a smile.

"You're easy to be nice to," I said truthfully. "And you've got plenty of reasons to be upset. You should let yourself. Okay?"

Lil burrowed her head against her arms and knees. Binkey gave a plaintive meow and bumped his head against her back.

"But it's not okay for me to take it out on you. I mean, that's what Gabriel is doing, whatever's wrong with him. He's taking it out on you." Wise words from a eighteen year old.

"Trust me when I say that you have a long way to go before reaching Gabriel's current level of asshat behavior." I shot her a grin. "You're not even in his league."

Lil gave a shaky laugh and propped her chin up on her knees. Then she looked serious.

"Do you think it's his meds?"

"I don't know." I shrugged. "Could be. Or maybe it was finding out this shit has spread out of the quarantine zone. Could be that's upped his stress level, so he's permanently set in jerk mode." Even as I said it, I felt bad. So I hastily added, "In which case I'll give him at least a partial 'get out of jail free' card." I looked at

Lil and grinned again. "Same with you, kiddo. No one should have to put up with the shit you're dealing with."

Lil jumped out of bed and gave me a bone-crunching hug.

"You're the best, Ash."

Binkey jumped off the bed in a huff, giving me a look as he made his way into the bathroom. It was obviously my fault he'd been disturbed. A loud, vigorous scratching followed his disappearance—another way for him to express his opinion.

I hugged her back as the pungent odor of cat poop wafted out into the room. Lil and I both winced.

"I'll go scoop that out," she said, waving a hand in front of her nose.

"Good idea," I said, grabbing a handy bottle of citrus room deodorizer and giving a generous spray. The result was orange-scented cat shit. "You might want to re-think his diet, too."

Maybe I'll see if I can find Gabriel, after all.

We needed to have a heart-to-heart.

CHAPTER SIX

I didn't want Lil to think Binkey was chasing me away—
even if it was partly true—so I told her what I had
decided to do. Then I went looking for Gabriel.

He wasn't in his room on the first basement level,
where our living quarters had been set up. There was a
chance he was in the med ward. But not even my desire
to speak with Gabriel could get me to venture further
down into that house of horrors, with all the people
dying of zombie bites and the experiments being done
on the undead specimens in the labs. Oh, for the naïve
days when I was just a student. Before I learned that
the DZN had top-secret research facilities in an equally
secret sub-level of Patterson Hall.

I was fully expecting to find a Bat Cave on campus,
one of these days.

So I headed for the main floor where the lecture halls
were, ending up in front of Room 217, where Simone
had taught her courses. The door was cracked open and
the lights were on, and as I drew closer it was easy for
me to pick up the sound of voices coming from the room.
I stopped, not wanting them to know I was there.

"So, what have you heard?" Nathan's tone held
barely concealed impatience.

There was a pause before an answer came. It was
Simone.

"The news isn't good," she said. "Confirmed sightings in all the locations where Dr. Albert's vaccine was sent for testing." There was silence for a moment, then she continued. "We're still waiting for the reports from more distant locations. Who knows what tomorrow will bring?"

Eavesdropping is a time-honored method of acquiring information you otherwise wouldn't be privy to. And it wasn't like I *meant* to stumble across their conversation. Therefore I felt very little—if any—guilt.

"What are you doing about it?" This was Nathan.

I peeked through the crack in the door just in time to see Simone shoot Nathan a look that should have shriveled his man bits. They were both at the front of the lecture hall. She was standing by the lectern as if preparing to teach a class, while he leaned against the "command central" table that Paxton usually occupied during our briefings and debriefings.

"Are you referring to me personally," she asked testily, "or the *Dolofónoitou Zontanóus Nekroús*?"

"I consider you interchangeable." Nathan crossed his arms and stared at her.

"They've already sent people to each of the locations, to attempt damage control before the general populace can become aware of the situation."

Nathan snorted. "General populace. No one talks like that unless they're on the BBC."

Simone glared at him. "Not everyone is limited to words of one or two syllables, Captain Smith."

I held a hand over my mouth, trying to hold back my amusement. Something about watching the two of them was just too much fun, even given the undeniably serious situation. They were like overly erudite junior high school students. Ones that had been kept back a decade or so.

"Fine, Henrietta Higgins." Nathan walked to the other side of the lecture area, then back again, pacing like an irate puma. "So how is the grand scheme working?"

"It's becoming increasingly difficult to keep things

under wraps," Simone admitted, looking uncomfortable. "A few of the smaller, more isolated locations have been quarantined using similar cover stories as the Ebola outbreak we used for Redwood Grove."

I could almost hear Nathan rolling his eyes as he responded.

"How many escaped laboratory monkeys do you people think the—" He did the most sarcastic finger quotes I'd ever seen "—*general populace* will buy before they begin to catch on?"

"We're not using Ebola for each cover story," Simone snapped. "Throw in the words 'terrorist plot,' and enough people are willing to accept it. That buys us some time." She didn't sound too happy about it, though.

"Wow," Nathan said with a smirk. "The DZN and the military really think your average citizen is pretty stupid, huh?"

"No doubt there are plenty of conspiracy theorists like yourself who will be questioning the stories, and coming up with even more fanciful explanations than a zombie outbreak." Simone's snippy tone could've cut through paper. "More often than not, those work in our favor."

"What about the towns that aren't isolated?" Nathan countered. "What will you use as an excuse under those conditions? 'Oh, we're just filming an episode of *The Walking Dead*. Would you like to be extras?' That should do it."

Wow. Nathan watches Walking Dead?

"You watch *The Walking Dead*?" Simone said. "I'd have thought you were more the type for The History Channel, or perhaps old *Star Trek* marathons."

"Know your enemy," Nathan replied. "After Kyrgyzstan, there wasn't a lot on the subject that I didn't read *or* watch. I also watch *Game of Thrones* and *The Borgias*. Those help me understand the DZN."

There was a long pause, and I wondered if Simone was taking a few deep breaths while contemplating homicide. When she finally spoke, however, her tone was nothing I'd heard from her before.

She sounded scared. And if Simone sounded scared, that meant things really were bad.

"They're still looking into solutions. For now, they can play it off as necessary precautions taken against a possible pandemic of Walker's Flu. But that will only hold for so long, especially if we can't bring things under control. Martial law is the next logical step."

"And then come the helicopter gunships, napalm, cluster bombs, and artillery, right? Tactical air strikes, anyone?" He paced back and forth, frustration and anger radiating off of him with each step.

"Don't forget the tactical nukes."

Shit. I nearly jumped out of my skin. The voice, worthy of a Shakespearean actor, came from directly behind me.

"Excuse me, Ashley." Colonel Paxton smiled, an expression that always looked out of place on a man with a face like a tragedy mask.

I wondered if there was a penalty for eavesdropping. The colonel seemed like a fair man, but after Lil and I had gone AWOL to rescue her cats, he'd pretty much told us that if we stepped out of line again, he'd lock us up. The way he'd said it, I didn't doubt he'd carry out his threat. For all that he looked like some comic book character named Master Thespian, he was someone to take seriously.

It was hard to get a handle on him. I thought he was one of the good guys, as far as it went, but the older I got, and the more I paid attention to politics and the news, the less inclined I was to trust anyone to do the right thing for the right reasons. Especially anyone with power.

At the sound of Paxton's voice, Simone and Nathan looked up and saw me standing in the doorway with a blatantly guilty expression on my face. I knew better than to try for the innocent routine. I haven't been able to carry that off since I was, oh, five years old.

"Ashley," Simone said politely. "Won't you sit down? Given what you've likely heard, you might as well join the conversation." Her tone was hard to read, but I was probably in for a world of hurt, one way or the other.

I gave Paxton a sideways glance. He responded with a little "after you" gesture, so I went in and sat in the front row of seats.

As I usually did in most situations, I decided that the best defense was a good offense.

"So, is there any chance of containing this?" I asked.

Simone gave my question some thought before replying.

"For an organization as secretive as the *Dolofónoitou Zontanoús Nekroús*, it's quite large and has many members in branches of the military and government worldwide. So we're doing what we can to stem the outbreaks… quietly."

"That's only realistic within one or two small towns and you know it, Simone," Nathan growled impatiently. "There've already been videos on YouTube, and reports from the smaller news outlets."

"Yes, but the current popularity of zombies in the various media has played to our favor," Simone argued. "Any doubters are assuming that it's a gimmick, or hysteria."

"But only to a point." Nathan shook his head. "The *Dolofóni* can only blame things on designer drugs like Bath Salts, or play it off as student film projects, for a limited amount of time. Eventually word is going to spread, and some sort of overt action will be needed. Maybe even demanded."

"They're not really talking tactical nukes yet, are they?" My voice sounded small in the large room.

"Not yet." It was Paxton who answered my question. "It's easier to consider that as a viable option when dealing with a small and relatively isolated community such as Redwood Grove. Collateral damage is limited because of the geography. For larger, more populated areas, however, the sort of public outcry that would result from, say, San Francisco being bombed, would be a PR disaster for the administration."

"Can't have that, can we?" Nathan muttered. Paxton ignored him and continued.

"Besides, at what point would that even work? Do it too soon, and you risk outraging the American public—and the rest of the world, for that matter. Who knows how they'll react. Wait too long, though, and what's the point? The problem will have spread past the point of containment."

Well, that just sucks.

"Containment only works when the numbers are relatively small, and the geographical logistics are favorable." Simone shook her head. "We were lucky with Redwood Grove. If one can call this sort of devastation 'lucky.'"

Nathan snorted.

"Like you were lucky in Kyrgyzstan?"

That got my attention. The "glare" switch lit up in Simone's eyes again.

"Not *nearly* as lucky as we were in Kyrgyzstan," she replied.

"Kyrgyzstan?" I looked expectantly from Nathan to Simone and back again. Colonel Paxton seemed to suddenly find his fingernails very interesting.

Simone gave something that sounded like a cross between a cough and a sigh.

"I suppose there's no reason not to tell her."

Nathan shrugged.

"Fine by me," he said.

CHAPTER SEVEN

KYRGYZSTAN MOUNTAINS

Through a sniper scope, Nathan watched the small group of Kyrgyz tribesmen as they made their way up a trail that would make mountain goats think twice. They reached a plateau and the ruins of an ancient fortress, and then headed toward a rocky outcrop. Nathan's vantage point, a few hundred feet above in another pile of ruins, provided him the perfect cover to watch their progress without fear of being seen.

According to Intel, there were Scythian burial mounds in the area. Most were under the waters of Lake Issyk Kul, but some still lay nestled in the crevices and canyons of the surrounding mountains. So it was possible that these really were tribesmen after valuable artifacts buried in the mounds. Or they could be Mujahideen on their way to a hidden bunker in one of the many caves honeycombing the area.

From the furtiveness of their progress and the well-worn Kalashnikovs slung across their shoulders, along with the odd RPG-7, Nathan was betting on the latter. One of them even had an Enfield, its stock wrapped in fabric, cradled under one arm. Most of them were also lugging long canvas bags on their backs. More weapons, maybe.

Hunkering down behind the cover of a crumbling stone wall, Nathan downed a handful of almonds and dried apricots, followed by a few swigs of bottled water, watching as the tribesmen reached the outcropping of rocks. He adjusted the scope for a better look at their destination, taking in the tangle of brush that hung over what looked like an indentation in the mountain itself, blocked with boulders of various sizes.

It had been a stroke of luck, finding the scope. He'd picked it up off a discarded Dragunov he'd found in the ruins, the barrel burst. Whoever had fired it hadn't checked for blockages. Given the amount of grit, mud, and sand in this country... not too smart. Although considering the fact that he'd managed to drop his binoculars on the climb up, he wasn't one to judge.

At least not much.

One of the tribesmen, the one carrying the Enfield, barked out a few words in Kyrgyz. The men carrying the canvas bags unslung them, pulling out what looked like pry bars, and set to work heaving the boulders away from what had to be an entrance to one of the many caves honeycombing the region.

"Gotcha, you bastards," Nathan muttered. He took another pull of water and continued to watch the activity across from him and below.

One of the men paused in his work, leaning down and picking something off the rocky ground. He held it up for closer inspection, then gave a sharp yell, dropping it as if it'd burned his fingers. Enfield Man snapped at him, his irritation obvious to Nathan even from a distance.

Enfield Man jerked his head at the boulders still obscuring the now obvious cave entrance. The other man shook his head and backed away from whatever he'd dropped to the ground.

Nathan adjusted his focus, honing in on the object.

"Move the fuck to the right, okay?" he muttered. Enfield Man's dusty shoes were in his line of sight. The fellow obligingly—if obliviously—took a step to the right before hunkering down to examine the discarded—

What the fuck?

—foot.

Nathan shook his head, then looked back through the scope.

A human foot lay in the dirt, bone sticking out of the ragged edges of flesh where an ankle should have been attached. As desiccated as it was, it was clear that something had been chewing on it.

Enfield Man stumbled backward, shouting frantic orders to the men using the pry bars on the boulders blocking the cave entrance. His shouts were clearly audible to Nathan, and from what little Kyrgyz knew, he recognized the word "stop."

Even as the orders were shouted, one of the men succeeded in toppling the largest boulder out of the rocky jigsaw puzzle, jumping back as the rock smashed to the ground, revealing a gaping black hole. The man turned to his compatriots with a triumphant yell—

—which cut off abruptly as several pairs of hands, as desiccated as the foot, reached out of the darkness, seized him by his face, throat and chest, and dragged him over the remaining boulders that still partially obscured the cave mouth. He'd vanished into its depths before his compatriots could do more than gape in horror.

A sound, maybe the wind, rose in the air.

Enfield Man's face contorted in genuine fear as he shouted to his men, gesturing toward the hole and the boulders. Nathan bet that he was saying whatever was Kyrgyz for "close that fucking hole back up again!"

What the hell is in that cave?

Several of the men had actually started to try and hoist the large boulder back into its former place when people started clambering slowly out of the cave. Mostly men, but a few women as well, robes hanging in tattered shreds from emaciated frames, faces something out of a horror film—almost skeletal, dried black fluid outlining their mouths, although several had dark red smears on down their chins. But the eyes were the worst. The corneas were filmed over like those of a cadaver, and the whites were a ghastly yellow, streaked with red.

At any other time Nathan would have appreciated the sharp focus of the scope he'd found. Now he just wondered what the hell these poor bastards had contracted. Christ, he thought. What kind of screwed up government shuts its diseased citizens in a fucking cave?

The tribesmen who were trying to shove the boulder back in place scattered, letting the thing drop onto the ground. It rolled against one of the people crawling out of the cave. Although he couldn't hear the crunch of bones as the boulder pinned the man against the cliff wall, Nathan had no doubt that pretty much everything in the poor bastard's body had just been crushed. Only his head and one arm were still visible.

Except—

He was still moving.

Nathan stared in disbelief as the pinned man opened and closed his mouth, arm reaching out toward the tribesmen as if imploring them to set him free. One of the tribesmen stumbled back against the boulder, and the trapped man immediately seized his robes and yanked the fellow toward him in what seemed like an impossible feat of strength.

The man screamed and pulled away, leaving a swatch of his robe in the trapped man's hand as he plowed into another one of the cave's escapees—one of the few women in the group. She grabbed him by the shoulders as if to steady him… and then took a bite out of his right trapezius. His scream rose to an agonized pitch, cut off by the explosive percussion of a shot fired from the Enfield rifle, straight into the woman's skull.

The bitten tribesman fell to his knees, hands clutching the bleeding wound on his neck as Enfield Man took aim again… and blew a hole in his compatriot's head.

Things happened fast after that.

Gunfire mixed with the sounds of agonized screaming and the rising moans of the creatures from the cave, blending into a hellish concert that echoed off the mountain walls. Nathan watched as more emaciated people staggered out of the cave, and the tribesmen fired on them. He watched as bullets struck shoulders, guts, arms, and merely staggered the targets back a few steps… before they lurched forward again.

Enfield Man kept shouting something and pointing to his head, lifting his rifle to then put a round through the skull of a man so emaciated, it didn't seem possible that he was mobile.

The man immediately fell on his knees, then did a face plant on the ground.

He didn't move again.

Still the other tribesmen fired wildly into torsos and limbs, fear overcoming discipline as the cannibals from the cave continued to advance and overwhelm them. Thrashing, screaming bodies were borne to the ground, blood flowing as their attackers tore chunks of flesh with teeth and hands.

Those tribesmen who tried to retreat down the path created their own log jam, effectively trapping them until they found their way blocked by yet more cannibals, who continued to pour out of the cave in a steady flow.

Nathan was frozen, his hands clamped around the scope as he watched the horror unfold. He thought he might be in shock. And wasn't that a laugh. Jackson would rag on his ass six ways from Sunday if he found out.

Enfield Man was the last tribesman standing, wedged in between the mountain wall and the fallen boulder, making every shot count. When his gun ran out of ammo, he grabbed an AK47 from one of his fallen compatriots and opened fire in full auto, spraying bullets into the advancing horde, still aiming at their heads. Some fell as the projectiles hit their targets, enough that it looked like the guy might have a chance.

Then the man pinned by the boulder snagged Enfield Man's shoulder with his free hand, taking his attention just long enough for several attackers to reach him. One grasped the AK47's barrel in a claw-like hand. Another clutched at the tribesman's robes, while the third grabbed an arm and promptly took a bite out of it. Enfield managed to get off one more round of ammo before he was borne to the ground.

Still unable to move, Nathan watched as the attackers proceeded to devour the fallen men. And as he did so, the partially-devoured tribesmen started moving... and staggered to their feet.

"Jesus..."

It was barely more than a mutter under his breath, so what happened next had to be a coincidence. One of the cannibals suddenly turned away from the body he was eating and looked up at the ruins where Nathan was crouching. Those milky eyes seemed to stare straight at him.

Nathan's fingers unclenched and the scope dropped to the ground with an impossibly loud clatter. Even without the scope, he could see the figures turn toward the sound and start lurching their way in his general direction.

This is majorly fucked up right here.

Something scuffed up dirt and pebbles behind him. Nathan jerked around fast and hard enough to hurt his neck just as teeth fastened onto his left arm, and the smell of putrefying flesh assaulted his nostrils.

He screamed—the first time in his adult life he'd done so. A chunk of his arm tore away under the teeth of his attacker, and Nathan threw himself to the side, a shoulder scraping hard against a section of crumbling wall. He looked up in time to see an emaciated figure lurching toward him, with the same yellow whites and filmed-over corneas as the cannibals from the cave. Its teeth were coated with fresh blood, a gobbet of flesh and fabric hanging from the mouth.

Nathan fumbled for his firearm, but before he even managed to unsnap the holster, a gunshot cracked and a messy hole appeared in the thing's head. It thumped against the wall, its slide down to the ground leaving a trail of stinking black fluid on the stones. It lay unmoving, Nathan's flesh still clenched between its teeth.

He stared at the corpse, clutching his wounded arm with one hand. It hurt, burned like a motherfucker. His ears rang from the close proximity of the gunshot and if he hadn't been in shock before, he sure as hell was now. 'Cause he couldn't be seeing a freshly killed corpse with flesh rotting off its bones, skin on its face so desiccated that it might as well be a mummy.

"Nathan?"

He turned bleary eyes toward the sound of Simone's voice, seeing her standing in the entrance to the ruins wearing fatigues and holding a handgun in one hand. Somehow her presence here didn't surprise him, even though it should have. He watched as she ran across the clearing, concern clearly etched on her features as she dropped to one knee next to him.

"Were you bit?"

"Huh?" Nathan couldn't quite focus on the question. His arm felt as if there was acid running through it. No, make that acid lit on fire.

Simone's attention focused on his arm. She gave an indrawn hiss.

"Oh, no…"

"Not… so bad," Nathan managed.

Cool hands touched his face.

"You're burning up."

"You're pretty hot yourself," Nathan mumbled, inordinately pleased with his cleverness.

"And you're delirious."

"With love for you, ba—" Pain coursed through him, cutting off his words. Something sharp penetrated his arm above the bite. Almost immediately a blessed numbness chased the pain away, Simone's face vanishing as his consciousness toppled down a very dark rabbit hole.

"He seems to be fighting off the infection."

"Will he make it?"

"I… think so. I… I hope so."

He woke up a few times, but consciousness never lasted more than a few minutes before another shot sent him spiraling back into fever dreams and unimaginable pain. A few times he thought he heard Simone's voice, but he never stayed awake long enough to verify.

She was there when he finally did wake up, a few days later. He felt good. Really good. Probably too good to be real, which meant he would probably die in a day or so from some sort of infection. In the meantime, though, the soup and crackers Simone set down in front of him smelled better than any meal he could remember.

She sat quietly at his bedside while he ate. When he finally finished eating, he wiped his mouth with the napkin she provided, set it down on the empty tray, and looked Simone straight in the eye.

"You gonna tell me what happened out there?"

"You tell me," she countered.

He rolled his eyes, not in the mood for the banter. "Please do not pull this psychoanalysis shit on me, Simone. I know what I saw. I just want to know what the hell it was."

"Sick people, Nathan." She looked away, then turned back to him with an almost defiant glare. "Quarantined, rightly or wrongly, like the lepers on Molokai."

"So you're saying they had leprosy?"

An almost imperceptible pause.

"Something like that."

"You're lying." Nathan knew from the brief flash of guilt in her eyes that he was right.

Simone gave a shuddering sigh. She got up and looked out into the hallway, then shut the door to Nathan's room and turned back to him.

"Look. I can't talk about this. The organization I'm involved with... it's about as black ops as you can get."

Nathan stared at her coldly.

"Are the dead coming back to life?" Even as he said it the words sounded absurd. But real.

"What part of 'black ops' did you not understand?"

"Are the dead coming back to life?" he repeated.

"I can't answer that," she replied. "And even if I could, if something like this got out, do you have any idea what sort of panic it would cause—even without the religious implications—if rumors of the dead coming to life were made public knowledge?"

"That would be a 'yes' then," he said.

Simone shook her head and left the room.

* * *

Nathan didn't try to get any other information out of Simone. He let her take blood samples and monitor his vitals, but refused to say more than the absolute minimum required to facilitate his return to health. Their relationship died a quick death in an atmosphere of mutual distrust.

"So how did you control the outbreak?" I felt like a kid at story time—in Stephen King's house.

"A very rare instance of the divergent political and religious factions in the area working together against a common foe," Simone said. "The most difficult part was convincing the locals not to shut the infected up in the caverns."

"What about the installation? How did you keep things a secret from all the incoming and outgoing military personal?"

Nathan snorted. He did that a lot.

"They shut it down, of course. Some bullshit story about how the U.S. and Kyrgyzstan governments couldn't agree on the new rental terms."

"That, actually," Simone said, "was true."

Nathan shot her a look.

"So zombies had nothing to do with it?" he countered.

"I didn't say that." Simone glared at him.

"So why didn't you tell him he was a wild card?" I asked, fascinated by this glimpse into their past. It was better than a soap opera, especially considering how pissy the two behaved when they were in the same room.

Nathan made a sound between a snort and a laugh. For variety, I guess.

"Professor Fraser wasn't telling me anything she didn't have to," he said.

I marveled at how Simone managed to look down her nose at him despite being shorter by a good half foot. He glowered back at her. I wished they'd just sleep together and get it over with.

"Captain Smith was one of the first people to show immunity to the virus."

"Then why didn't you tell him the truth about the zombies? It's not like you kept it a secret from the rest of us after we got chomped."

Simone hesitated before she responded.

"Back then we only recruited people into the *Dolofónoitou Zontanóus Nekroús* after several years of observation. Paranoia was high—"

"I'll say," Nathan muttered. Simone ignored him.

"—and secrecy was paramount. Higher authorities than I judged Captain Smith, and deemed him to be a potential security risk because of certain maverick tendencies displayed in previous missions." She glanced over at Nathan before continuing.

"Had Captain Smith been less hostile and more cooperative—"

"In other words, a happy little lab rat."

"—we might have learned more at the time. And perhaps eventually recruited him into the organization."

"Not likely," Nathan said.

"As it was," Simone continued, "the Army retrieved him. Before we could take any steps, his term of service was up, and he vanished from the military's radar."

Nathan shrugged.

"No one would tell me the truth. Not much incentive to stick around, and *lots* of reasons to disappear. So I left—actually a little bit before I was supposed to." Simone looked irritated that that little revelation. "Did my own research, and figured out what was what."

"Couldn't you have gone to prison for deserting?" I asked.

"If they'd found me, yeah." Nathan's tone implied that it would have been a long shot. From what I'd seen of him, I didn't think his confidence was misplaced.

"Why aren't you in prison now?" I asked. "Is there a statute of limitations for desertion?"

"Special dispensation for extraordinary circumstances." Nathan grinned.

I had enough food for thought to keep me up all night.

"And now, young lady," Colonel Paxton said, making me wonder if he could read minds, "you need to get some sleep before tomorrow's work. Bright and early, you know!"

CHAPTER EIGHT

Morning seemed to come extra early the next day. I had to wonder if Colonel Paxton had set the alarms back.

Even after two cups of coffee, liberally laced with cream and honey, I was tired, heavy-lidded, and irritable when we pulled up to one of the last places in Redwood Grove where we had to search for zombies—and possible survivors. Back when the swarm had hit, you couldn't swing a bat without hitting one of the undead. Now we had to go digging. But letting any of them slip through, well, it simply wasn't an option.

The Redwood Trailer Heaven trailer park, located past a cul-de-sac at the end of Palm Street, should have been an idyllic location, all nestled in the redwoods. But zombie apocalypse notwithstanding, if there was a contest for the most cliché white trash neighborhood in America, I'd nominate Trailer Heaven in a heartbeat.

Rows of double-wides sagged on concrete block foundations, shabby and derelict. At least twenty or thirty trailers stretched back into the woods, on either side of a roughly paved road running vertically through the middle, and another bisecting it horizontally. Smaller dirt roads ran parallel in between the rows. Cars—mostly older models—hugged the sides of the trailers, a few under canvas lean-tos, some also on concrete blocks. The ground was littered with trash, including a truly frightening number of Pabst Blue Ribbon cans.

There was a stiff breeze, and the sound it made in the trees was loud enough to be annoying. Every now and then it would die down, then pick up again, rattling the empty beer cans.

"Let's start at the far end," I said after a moment's thought. "When Team B shows up, they can start at the entrance, and we'll meet in the middle. Kai, let 'em know, okay?" He pulled out his radio and proceeded to do so.

It would have been safer to work in teams, one person opening the door and staying safely behind it, while the other stood back dispatched the zombie with a bullet to the head, but we had a lot of ground to cover, and I trusted Tony and Kai's ability to handle whatever they came across. Unless they ran into some more Silly String.

"Let's go." I nodded to Tony. "Kai, we'll see you back there."

Kai nodded as Tony and I unslung our M4s and threaded our way between trailers to the far end of the park.

I took the one at the furthest point, nestled against redwoods on two sides. Some care had been taken with landscaping around it, planters with herbs and flowers bordering the edge of the trailer. The plants still thrived, even in the face of forced neglect, the damp weather making it easy to be a lazy gardener in Redwood Grove.

Ascending the steps to the front door, I listened carefully, trying to discern sound above the banshee howl of the wind. It was difficult, even with my enhanced senses, which picked up everything equally. So I cautiously opened the door, the creak of fog-rusted hinges loud enough to wake the dead. I took a step back and waited.

Nothing.

Stepping inside, I took a big old sniff. I smelled rotting food mixed with a musty smell of an enclosed space that hadn't been aired out in over two weeks.

Nothing pleasant, but after the crap I'd smelled around the undead, stenches were relative.

A quick scan of the interior from front to back revealed nothing more than the fact that its inhabitants had enjoyed the fine taste of cheap beer in large quantities, Domino's pizza, and preferred Big Bob's banana-flavored condoms as their birth control of choice. The box was sitting out on the bedside table. I hoped they survived to have many more banana splits.

Okay, just grossed myself out.

I used my extra-broad black Sharpie on the door, and moved on.

The next trailer was an eBay seller's wet dream, with scads of Hummel figurines and Smithsonian collector's plates displayed on doilies, all against a background of flocked pink wallpaper. It was like being trapped inside a tchotchke-stuffed Pepto-Bismol bottle. But at least there were no signs of body parts.

I made another black check with satisfaction, and started to relax as I moved to trailer number three. Maybe Trailer Heaven's residents had made it to a safe house, like the church or the fire station. Maybe the person who'd collected all those precious figurines, and the complete *Star Trek: The Next Generation* collector's plate series, was secure at Big Red with the rest of the survivors. I hoped this was the case, even if I thought Hummel figurines were as tacky as velvet paintings of Elvis.

Smiling at the thought, I opened the door to the third trailer without bothering to listen or knock.

My bad.

Rotting hands seized my arm and the front of my vest, yanking me inside before I could do more than yelp with surprise. My eyes watered as a wave of putrid stench rolled over me, and I found myself up close and personal with two zombies—a tall, skinny male wearing nothing but a pair of BVDs that had probably been gross before their occupant had died, and a female with a bouffant of lacquered red hair, skinny jeans on a frame that couldn't be called skinny even with chunks of flesh missing, and a shredded skin-tight tank top that exposed a major muffin top stomach and one sagging breast. One arm was gone, leaving a mess of blood, gristle, and chewed flesh in its place. There was a hole where the other breast had been.

Both zombies gripped my arms and torso, pulling me toward them with relentless hunger and threatening to dislocate my shoulders as they played a mindless tug-of-war. The woman's mouth gaped open, a foul smell wafting out of it as she leaned in toward my neck.

No you don't, bitch.

Yanking my arm free from her grip, I shoved my forearm under her chin as she tried to take a chunk out of me, in the process losing my grip on the M4, which clattered to the floor. Mr. Underwear hooked his fingers into the front of my vest and yanked me toward him, knocking my arm loose and giving the female zombie ample surface to bite. Luckily its teeth couldn't penetrate the armored pads on my forearm. Even if I was immune to infection, I didn't particularly want to have another chunk of my flesh ripped out.

I slammed my right forearm into the female zombie's head, sending it flailing backward into the kitchen. Its feet skidded on a floor coated with an indefinable mix of blood, rotted food, and goo that I didn't want to think about. Then it slammed head first into one of the kitchen cupboards.

But the impact wasn't hard enough to take Ms. Zombie of Wal-Mart out of commission. It slowly and relentlessly managed to find its way back to its feet as I kicked the male zombie in the kneecap, feeling the patella shatter beneath the impact. It didn't register pain, but the right leg buckled as it still grappled with me, trying to use my vest as leverage to pull me to its gaping, reeking mouth.

There wasn't enough Listerine in the world to cure this zombie's halitosis.

I kicked its other kneecap, stomping as hard as I could with the heel of my boot. That leg crumpled, as well, but it still clung to my vest with both rotting hands, and the sudden weight sent me toppling forward on top of the suddenly prone zombie. My hands plunged into the thing's torso with a truly gross popping sound, as if I'd punctured the world's nastiest balloon. The thing just moaned and gnashed its teeth as it tried to pull my face close enough to bite.

I'd had enough of this shit.

Giving a scream of disgust and fury, I pulled my hands out of its viscera, entwined my fingers together and went "Hulk, smash!" on its ass. I slammed both fists into its head with all my not inconsiderable strength. The skull, already weakened by decay, shattered beneath the blow. I followed up with another double-fisted strike, then burrowed one hand into the brain, fingers stiff, until I'd scrambled the sucker in its shell.

The thing stopped moving and its hands finally gave up their death grip on my vest, flopping to the ground with a meaty thump.

Meanwhile, Ms. Zombie had regained some traction and pulled herself back toward me across the gore-streaked floor as I struggled to a sitting position, scooting back until I was propped up against a wall. I stared at the thing, hating and pitying it at the same time.

There was something almost hypnotic in its dead eyes and slow, relentless crawl. It wouldn't stop. I knew that. I could get up, leave the trailer, and it would try its best to come after me. And that was what freaked me out the most, realizing that "you can run, but you can't hide" could be the world's new rule if we didn't stop this plague in its tracks.

"Right, then."

I stood up, grabbed a cast-iron pan from the counter,

pausing to get a solid grip through all of the goo, and slammed it down on Lady Wal-Mart's head. It only took one blow to drop the zombie in its tracks, but I gave it a second whack for good measure. And then a third because I wanted to punish someone... something... for fucking up my world so completely. The zombie was the closest thing at hand.

And they wouldn't let me beat the shit out of Dr. Albert.

I tossed the pan to the floor, the sound clattering almost unbearably loudly in the small confines of the trailer. Brains and other viscous innards smeared my hands. I staggered over to the sink, hoping to wash up a bit, but stopped short at the sight of scum-crusted water. Bits of ancient food rose up to the surface to tell the tale of a nasty-ass clog that lay beneath. The thought of dipping my fingers in there, or getting hit by backsplash if I turned on the faucet, didn't sit well with my already unhappy stomach.

So I wiped my hands best as I could on a relatively clean dishtowel, dropping it over the female zombie's face as I limped to the back of the trailer. My heart dropped when I saw a bag of Pampers on the hallway floor. Immediately regretting all the dead baby jokes I'd ever told, I reluctantly opened the bedroom door.

A small crib stood under one of the windows, shut tightly against the chill air of a northern California autumn. Standing inside it on unsteady legs, clutching the bars of the crib with pudgy grayish-blue fingers, was a baby in a blood-splotched blue onesie. It couldn't have been more than a year old when it died. It still had thick curls of white blond hair framing its face. Adorable fat baby cheeks had been lost to the beginnings of decay. I recognized the signs of Walker's Flu—black fluids, now dried, trickling from the mouth, eyes, and nose, and noticed that the only blood on the baby's skin was around its mouth. I winced as I realized what had happened to its mom's missing breast.

The baby made a low rattling noise in its throat, a sick parody of a normal infant's gurgle.

At least he hadn't known the horror of being torn to pieces by his parents, no matter how sick he'd been. Poor little guy.

I found a clean spot on my sleeve, and wiped some moisture away from under my eyes. I'd seen a lot of horrible things since this whole mess began, but somehow the sight of this baby, long past his feeding time, hit hard.

"I don't even like kids," I told it, angrily dashing more tears away. It mewled at me, little mouth opening and closing as if suckling on a phantom bottle. I hardened my heart, drew my tanto, and did my job.

But it really sucked.

CHAPTER NINE

I stumbled out of that trailer like a prisoner released from a month of solitary. Fresh air had never smelled and felt so good. I nearly tripped on a hose coiled up next to the stairs, followed the end to a faucet and turned the water on, gratefully rinsing as much gore off my face and hands as possible. I wiped off the larger clots from my clothing, but nothing short of an Olympic pool full of hot water and bleach would even begin to decontaminate them.

Kind of pointless, considering my day of fun-filled extermination wasn't even close to finished yet.

"You okay, Ash?"

I glanced up to find Kai, looking as clean as he had when we'd started out that morning.

"Yeah." I gave my hands one more quick rinse. "Just reached my viscera limit, y'know?" A tiny involuntary shudder rippled through me as the baby's undead face flashed through my mind.

"You sure you're okay?" Kai touched my shoulder. "You look kinda white."

I looked at his hand, the color of coffee with a splash of milk, as it rested on my shoulder.

"You being racist, Lando?"

Kai gave me a look.

"Don't change the subject. What's up?"

"Seriously, I'm okay." I don't know why I was so

reluctant to tell him about the baby. Maybe I was afraid he'd make a joke out of it. And if he did, I'd have to kill him.

"If you say so," Kai said doubtfully. "But girl, you sure are a mess."

"Only compared to you, Mister Clean."

He grinned. "I'm like rubber, you're like glue. Zombie shit bounces off me and sticks to you."

Maybe it was the adrenaline rush, but that struck me as hilarious. I started laughing, a deep belly laugh, and couldn't stop. Kai's grin grew wider and he broke into laughter, as well. It was one of those "once you start, you can't stop" situations where your stomach hurts, but you still can't stop.

"Glad to know you two are having so much fun."

The voice of our increasingly snarky fearless leader dumped a bucket of ice water on our shared hilarity. Kai and I both looked up to see Gabriel giving us his patented "we are not amused" look.

Wonderful. Just what I need.

"I'll just go check out the next trailer." Kai's hand dropped from my shoulder and he vanished across the lane.

Gabriel walked up to me, looking beyond me to the trailer I'd just left.

"Did you check out this one?" he demanded.

"Yeah."

"Red or black?"

It took me a moment to figure out what he was talking about, and then I realized I'd forgotten to mark the door. I pulled out my red Sharpie and made three large hatch marks on it.

"Next time try keeping your mind on the job instead of your teammates," he said flatly.

That was it.

"I just had to kill a baby, okay?" I took a step toward him, clutching my Sharpie so tightly it hurt. "I had to put it down like a little rabid puppy. So cut me some slack if I take a few minutes to collect myself, and excuse the fuck out of me if I can still find something to laugh about after that."

Running out of words, I threw the pen in frustration. It hit Gabriel on his chest and bounced right back at me. I grabbed it in mid-air and we glared at each other.

"Nice catch." The corners of his mouth twitched.

"Thanks."

The tension between us practically crackled. He turned to leave, then stopped and looked back at me.

"Are you okay to keep going?" His bearing was stiff, and his tone overly formal.

I nodded with equal stiffness, then looked at him closely, noting the telltale dark circles under his eyes and the faint beads of moisture on abnormally pale skin.

"Are you?" I asked.

"Yeah." He patted his pocket. "I'm due in a couple of hours."

"Maybe you should take it now."

Gabriel hesitated. "Maybe I will."

Then he left me to my job.

CHAPTER TEN

With every trailer we cleared, it got easier to tell when zombies were inside the next one. Thanks to the ruckus, they were agitated now that they realized tasty treats were close by, and the sound of moans and rattling hinges made it obvious that, when the door was opened, one would be springing out like a decayed Jack-in-the-Box.

By the time we'd finished clearing the area, I'd personally dispatched around a dozen of the undead, all of them trapped in their former homes. They were rattling around like marbles in tin cans, unable to figure out how to escape, and lacking the motivation or strength to knock out a window or bust through a door.

Our teams met up in the middle of the park, on the brilliantly named "Middle Lane." Lil ran over to me, her pint-sized pickaxe and clothes equally spattered with all sorts of nasty goo.

"I killed at least ten!" She grinned up at me, eyes alight with a glee I found disturbing. I wasn't sure if I should pat her on the head with a "That's nice, dear," or sign her up for psychotherapy. Before I had a chance to decide, Tony plunked himself in between us, Thor's Wee Hammer dripping with gore.

"That's nothing," he boasted. "I took out at least that many in the first two rows."

"Piker," Kai said. "I had one trailer with six."

"And I killed ten with a single blow," I muttered, wondering when our search-and-destroy missions had turned into a game of one-upmanship.

All three looked at me blankly. Classic fairy-tale fail.

"They're young," Mack said, giving me a pat on the shoulder.

There was a trailer set back in the trees off to the right side of the park. It was somewhat nicer than its neighbors, with a covered porch running around the front. A sign proclaimed it as the manager's office, and there was a bell to ring for help.

"Anyone got that one yet?" Gabriel gestured to the trailer.

I hadn't. I looked at Tony and Kai, who both shook their heads. Same with Team B.

A flash of irritation passed over Gabriel's face. He suppressed it with a visible effort, and I sincerely hoped he got his meds soon.

"Okay, you guys take a break," he said. "I'll get this one."

Gravel and redwood chips crunched beneath his feet as Gabriel walked over to the trailer. He had his hand on the door handle when his radio squawked. He stopped in mid-turn and answered it. I did my best to eavesdrop, but between the howling wind and Lil, Tony, and Kai boasting about their kills, even my wild card hearing didn't suffice.

Whatever the message was, it didn't look good. Gabriel's face went all grim and tense.

"Change of plans," he said. "One of the other search-and-destroy teams found something. They want us over there ASAP. I need to talk to Professor Fraser before we go, so one of you go check out the trailer, okay? It seemed quiet."

Kai stepped forward before Lil or Tony had a chance to volunteer.

"Allow me," he said, unhooking his crowbar.

"Hell, no," Tony said. "This one's mine."

"That's not fair." Lil frowned. "You both had more kills than I did."

Kai grinned. "Race you." He and Tony darted forward, Lil hot on their heels as the three jockeyed for position.

Mack nudged me, following Lil with anxious eyes.

"You know, Ash, I'm worried about her. I know we have to kill these things, but she really seems to enjoy it."

"It stops her from thinking about her mother," I said. "She has to have something to take out her anxiety on, so I guess we have to look at it as therapy."

Really gross therapy.

Kai and Lil elbowed each other out of the way, inadvertently giving Tony the lead. Mack and I watched their antics with a sort of fond disapproval. Gabriel and Gentry ignored them, too busy conferring about the news that had come over the radio. I still wondered what had stopped Mr. Freeze in his tracks.

"You have any kids?" I asked Mack.

He shook his head.

"Nope. And this is why."

We grinned in mutual understanding.

It looked like Tony would reach the door first, by virtue of his long stride, but Kai did a body check as Tony hit the porch stairs, slowing them both down and giving Lil the opportunity to bob and weave in between the two. She would have made it, if Kai hadn't seized the back of her Kevlar vest, pulling her up short as she reached for the doorknob. He dodged around her and slammed his palm against the door in triumph.

"First!"

"No fair!" Lil gave Kai a solid whack on one shoulder, knocking him to one side. Tony joined the fray and the three jostled one another like puppies fighting over a toy. None of them noticed as the door swung open and something long and metallic protruded from the gap.

It took me a split second to place the object—it was the barrel of a shotgun. But the delay was a split second too long. My shout of warning echoed simultaneously with the deafening percussion of the shotgun being fired.

Kai flew backward as if punched in the gut by a giant fist. I heard the *kachunk* of another round being chambered. Even as Kai's back hit the railing that ran the length of the porch, another shot ripped out. I saw the top of Kai's head vaporize in a mist of blood, brains and flesh. His body cracked through the railing and thudded to the ground below.

"Man down!" I recognized Gentry's voice even as I screamed Kai's name, my cries mingling with Tony's and Lil's.

Someone barreled into me, arms wrapped around my waist and knocking me to the ground even as another shotgun blast ripped through the air where I'd been standing.

A shriek of fury rose above the wind, a wordless battle cry.

"Lil?"

I lifted my head, only to have it shoved back down by whoever knocked me ass over teakettle in the first place.

"Stay down!"

It was Gabriel. He lay on top of me, his body shielding mine. I was torn between frustration that he wouldn't let me go to Lil, and gratification that his first instinct had been to protect me.

Two more shots shattered the air. I heard Tony give a holler, then sounds of fists hitting flesh, bodies slamming against hard surfaces.

Gabriel loosened his hold and stood up. I scrambled to my feet, barely conscious of his helping hand. I pulled away and dashed toward the trailer, dimly aware of Tony and Lil, wrestling with someone just inside the door. They could handle it.

My first priority was Kai.

He'd landed on the ground between two large hydrangeas and at first all I saw was an arm stretched out, as if trying to escape the tendrils of blood trickling out from a larger puddle. Time slowed down as I took one, then another step forward until I could see his entire body. I focused on his other arm, bent awkwardly under his torso. I wondered if it was broken.

That has to hurt, I thought vaguely.

But it would heal fast. Kai was a wild card.

My mind refused to process any possibility beyond serious injury. He'd been wearing his Kevlar vest so depending on the type of round fired, maybe he was just badly bruised, maybe a few ribs broken. At the worst some internal injury that could be dealt with, given his accelerated healing abilities. As for the second shot, head injuries bleed a lot. He'd probably just been grazed. At any moment he'd pop up and say something like "I'm fine, Ashley, I ran it under a cold tap!"

Yeah, I was in serious denial right up to the point I looked down at his corpse. His eyes were open, staring lifelessly up at the sky, the top of his head a mangled mess. Not even a wild card could recover from the wounds he'd received.

"Oh, no."

I turned to find Mack standing next to me, his eyes reflecting my own feelings. He put a hand on my shoulder and I clutched it like a lifeline.

Handsome, cocky, irritating… good-natured Kai.

Gone in the space of a few seconds.

I heard more commotion on the porch as Gabriel and Gentry thudded up the stairs into the trailer. A shotgun lay across the threshold of the trailer door, its blood-spattered stock facing outward. Tony continued to curse up a blue streak. Someone else wailed incoherently—it was a woman.

Lil. Is she hurt too?

No, it wasn't Lil. The voice was too deep.

"Stand down!" Gabriel's voice rose above the cursing and the wailing. "Tony, stand down!"

Sounds of more scuffling and cursing.

I looked up to see Gentry pulling Tony out of the trailer, one arm locked around his neck, the other gripping the back of his collar. Gentry spun him around so he faced the yard, away from the door, still holding on to him. The precaution was unnecessary, though, because Tony looked down and saw his friend. He pushed away from Gentry and stared at the mangled mess of shattered skull and brains, blood pooling where the top of the head should have been.

I've always made fun of characters in movies who raise their fists to the sky and scream "Nooooo!" after some tragic event. But I wasn't laughing as Tony fell to his knees and gave a primal scream that combined raw grief, devastation, and rage. It rang in my ears, and pierced my heart.

I clutched Mack's hand even tighter, tears spilling down my cheeks as I willed time to run backward so Kai would still be alive, and all the stupid carelessness would be erased. Time, however, callously stayed just where it was.

Lil emerged from the trailer, the light of battle in her eyes. It was extinguished when she saw Tony. She walked slowly to the edge of the porch, locking gazes with me.

"Kai?"

I shook my head, and Mack held out his other arm. Lil let out a strangled sob and stumbled down the steps into his comforting embrace.

Gentry reached down to help Tony to his feet, but Tony slapped his hands away and stumbled up on his own, hanging onto the section of railing next to the broken gap left by Kai's fall. His breath came in harsh gasps as he gripped the wood so hard I could see his knuckles go white.

Gabriel came out of the trailer, half leading, half supporting a short, skinny person dressed in grungy jeans, and an oversized and equally filthy plum-colored down jacket, the hood totally obscuring the face. The person barely came up to Gabriel's chest. I couldn't tell if it was a man or a woman.

A low growl was the only warning Tony gave before lunging for them. Gabriel immediately shoved the stranger behind him, inserting his bulk as a protective barrier just as Tony slammed into him. The force knocked Gabriel to the ground. The person gave a high-pitched scream and lurched back against the trailer wall, curling up into a small ball. Tony reached out, murder on his face, but Gentry—always Johnny on the spot—grabbed him just before his clenched fists connected.

Mack, Lil, and I ran up the stairs, Mack heading straight for the shooter, although for what purpose, I wasn't sure.

Still Tony fought, swearing and screaming as tears rolled unheeded down his face. It took the rest of us— Lil and me hanging onto his arms, Gabriel tackling him around the legs, while Gentry got him in a chokehold— to subdue him to the point where he finally stopped fighting. His muscles still quivered with unspent fury.

Gentry loosened the chokehold enough to let him catch a breath.

"You gonna stand down?"

Coughing, Tony nodded, but his body and voice still vibrated with barely contained anger as he spat out, "Why are you stopping me? This motherfucker killed Kai. Shot his head off." He glared in the direction of the huddled figure, now hidden behind Mack. "We were here to rescue you. What the fuck, asshole?" His voice broke.

"It's a woman, Tony," Mack said softly. He very gently pulled back the hood of the killer's down jacket, revealing a matt of filthy, snarled hair that might be blonde when clean. Hard to tell under the grease and dirt.

Gabriel nodded, still holding onto Tony's legs.

"I was trying to tell you, X-Box."

Tony flinched at the nickname.

I don't know why this took us all by surprise, but it did. Mack pushed some of the matted hair back, revealing a softly rounded profile, skin as filthy as the hair, but definitely a woman somewhere in her mid-to-late thirties. She flinched away from his careful touch. The one eye we could see was puffed shut, the flesh purpled and bruised around it. Blood ran from her nose, which looked broken.

"It's okay," he said. "I'm not going to hurt you. None of us are going to hurt you."

She continued to whimper, shaking inside the oversized coat.

"Oh, jeez…" I felt all the fight go out of Tony in that instant, as if someone had pressed the "purge" button on his adrenaline. He stared at the bruised and battered face, then at his hands. I could see it the moment it truly hit him that he'd caused the damage to her face and god knows what to the rest of her body.

"Oh, man."

He shook his head, his tone bewildered and anguished as he asked, "Why did you kill him? I… We were here to rescue you. He was gonna help you. Why would you kill him?"

The woman didn't respond, giving no sign that she even had heard him. Mack continued to try and reassure her, but she didn't look at him either, just cringed and whimpered. She had to be crazy or deaf or—

I looked sharply at the woman's right ear, poking through hanks of greasy hair. "Earplugs. She's wearing earplugs. She can't hear us. Probably didn't hear Kai, just saw the door opening and freaked."

Mack gingerly removed the right earplug, grimacing as he tossed the nasty little wax-encrusted piece of yellow foam away. "Can you hear me, ma'am?"

Clapping her hands over her ears, the woman shrieked, the sound like a siren that rose and blended into the howls of the wind. Startled, Mack stumbled backward.

"Dontwannahearthemdontwannahearthemdontwanna hearthem…" she chanted, running the words together in a non-stop stream. It was an invocation to keep the horrors at bay.

"She couldn't hear us." Mack knelt back beside her and put an arm around the woman. "You don't have to hear them, it's okay. Shhh, it's okay."

Tony took another look at the woman's battered face, stepped off the porch to kneel next to his friend's corpse, put his hands over his face and started to cry.

CHAPTER ELEVEN

Gentry and Lil comforted Tony while Mack stayed with the woman, who finally stopped chanting when Mack retrieved her filthy earplug and let her put it back in.

I did a quick check of the interior of the trailer, finding a shitload of paperback romance novels, a pile of mail telling me the woman's name was Judy Thomas, and the corpse of a young boy, head partially missing, lying on the floor of what had been her office.

So much for happily ever after.

Sorrow for Kai's loss mixed with an unwanted compassion for his murderer and the sad story that corpse told. I didn't want to feel sorry for her, but it was hard not to.

I walked outside where Mack still sat with her.

"Her name is Judy," I said flatly.

Gabriel and Lil returned with the SUV. Kai's body was put in the back, and Gentry guided Tony into the back seat. Lil sat in the front passenger seat, staring out at nothing. Gabriel saw me and got out of the driver's seat, coming around the front of the truck to meet me as I came down the steps.

"Did you tell Simone—" I stopped, swallowed the lump in my throat and continued, "Did you tell her about Kai?"

"Yeah." He ran a hand through his hair, causing it

to stick up in places. I suppressed the urge to smooth it back down, knowing it wasn't appropriate and that it wouldn't be appreciated. "Nathan's on his way here to pick me up to handle the other situation. Can you drive the Hummer back to Big Red?"

"Probably," I said doubtfully. "But shouldn't Gentry do it? He's clocked time behind the wheel, and I haven't."

"I want Gentry with Tony, just in case..." Gabriel nodded toward Judy. "Last thing we want is him going batshit on her in a moving vehicle."

"I think he'll be okay," Mack said as he came down the steps, arm around the stricken woman. "I saw his face when he realized what he'd done to her already. He's not going to do anything else. He knows she didn't mean to do what she did."

I thought he was right. Tony didn't even register when Mack loaded Judy into the SUV and climbed in next to her.

Gabriel reached out and touched my shoulder.

"Are you okay?"

I shook my head.

"No. You?"

"Not even close."

We looked at each other for a moment, so much needing to be said without the time or the place to say it. I satisfied myself with a quick touch to his face as he gave my shoulder a squeeze.

"Did you—"

He nodded.

"Took them when I radioed Simone." He paused, then added, "It's helping."

A very small weight lifted off the collection that was hanging out in my chest.

At that moment Nathan's monster truck came barreling down the road, his face impassive behind the windshield. I wondered how many friends he'd seen buried in his lifetime, and if it still hurt him now.

Gabriel gave my shoulder another squeeze, this one so hard it almost hurt.

"Get them back safely."

"Where are you and Nathan going?"

A shadow passed over his expression.

"A weekend home up on Ridge Crest, one of the expensive ones. One of the other teams found a survivor, but there's something wrong with him." He looked at me. "It might be Jake."

A vision flashed into my mind—a man sobbing as he chewed pieces of flesh from his wife's face. Then a quick fast-forward to him ripping a chunk out of Kaitlyn's shoulder as she tried to help him.

"I want to go with you," I said suddenly.

"No."

"Why not?"

"I need you to drive the Hummer back, make sure they make it safely."

"Gentry can drive," I said again.

Gabriel scowled and turned away. I grabbed his arm.

"I was there when we found Jake the first time. I know what he looks like. You only got a glimpse of him, and Nathan hasn't seen him at all. I got a good close-up when he was—" I stopped myself before adding "—ripping his wife's lips off with his teeth."

I could see Gabriel fighting with himself, wanting to say no, but knowing I was right.

"I need to do this," I said. "Please. Otherwise I'm going to think about all the ways I could have stopped what happened to Kai from happening."

"If that was anyone's fault, it was mine," he said.

"No." I shook my head. "That's bullshit, and you know it. Tony and Kai were my team, under my command. You were right about what you said yesterday. We weren't taking things seriously, and it got Kai killed."

"Ash…"

I held up a hand.

"I don't want to hear it right now. If you really want to make me feel better, let me go with you now."

I sat between Gabriel and Nathan in the front seat of Nathan's black monster truck, grateful for a chance to be near Gabriel without having to do more than shut my eyes and enjoy the warmth of his body. I would probably have drifted off to sleep, except for Nathan's uncanny ability to ram the gearshift into my left thigh every time I started to go under.

Nathan didn't say much. I guess he already knew what went down with Kai. Gabriel didn't say much either. It was a silent thirty-minute drive to our location.

We pulled into yet another cedar chip-paved driveway that led to a small yet expensive looking vacation "cabin" up in the mountains. Another military Hummer and an ambulance were parked in the expansive driveway, four armed soldiers standing guard out front. A carved wooden sign reading "Mountain Haven" decorated the lintel above the front door. Clumsily carved grapevines decorated the wooden posts at the foot of the stairs.

I nudged Nathan on the arm.

"Isn't this near your place?"

"Other side of the summit," Nathan replied. "This is the popular side. One of those microclimates perfect for growing Pinot or Cabernet or some other winey shit. Mine's on the side that gets the worst of the wind. Keeps the amateur winemakers and the tourists out of my hair."

I almost smiled at the thought of unsuspecting tourists, intent on wine-tasting, showing up at Nathan's uninviting compound and demanding his best "winey shit." The smile didn't make it past a mental snapshot of Kai.

We got out of the truck and all four soldiers immediately saluted. Gabriel returned the salute.

"Where is he?"

"Inside, sir." The private nodded. "He's been subdued and contained."

"Any other civilians?"

The soldier swallowed.

"Yes, sir. One still alive."

"That's good, right?" I asked, but got no answer.

We went inside.

I recoiled as the smell hit—an olfactory assault made up of blood, meat, and yet more rotting flesh. Whatever happened here had been beyond bad.

Unlike the trailers, this vacation getaway was decorated in what I thought of as Mountain Man chic, furniture made of logs, lots of dark plaid fabrics, and trophy heads on the wall. A giant flatscreen TV took up most of one wall, a pile of DVDs was scattered on the table and floor below. Someone had been having a *Lord of the Rings* marathon. What didn't fit the decor were the smears and puddles of blood—dried, gelatinous, and fresh—on the walls, furniture, and hardwood floors. A man sat on the couch, hands cuffed behind his back, head hanging forward. Three soldiers surrounded him, two on either side and one holding a gun on him from behind the couch. All three looked as green in the gills as the two out front.

I couldn't blame them. Even after the trailer park cleanup, the smell in the cabin was enough to make my stomach churn.

"Ashley, can you verify the identity of the prisoner?" Gabriel nodded toward the man on the couch.

I stepped forward, already certain I knew who he was. "Jake?"

The man raised his head and smiled at me, bloodstained lips, gums, and teeth even more disturbing because the smile was genuine.

"Hi there," he said. "Do I know you? I must if you know my name, right?"

I nodded, trying to hide my revulsion.

"Yeah. We met at Big Foot's Revenge a few days or so ago." I didn't mention that he'd been sobbing over the remains of his wife and kid at the time, even as he'd been nibbling on them. It looked like he still had on the same pair of gore-encrusted jeans and blue flannel shirt he'd been wearing when we'd found him.

Recognition lit his face, a face that had no doubt been pleasantly handsome before he'd been bitten by a zombie and turned into a half-deader, thanks to another mutation of the zombie virus. He had to eat human flesh, preferably still living, in order to stop his own body from rotting. The plus side? His brain still functioned, memories intact.

Which wasn't such a plus if you couldn't stop yourself from eating your family and friends. Unlike Gabriel, Jake didn't have a handy dandy antiserum keeping the contagion at bay, so he'd turned on his wife and son after they'd taken refuge in a cabin. I'd have felt sorry for the guy if he hadn't been at least partially responsible for Kaitlyn's death.

This is getting to be a nasty habit.

I shoved the morbid thought away.

"That's right," he said. "You were going to take my wife and son to a doctor, right?"

"Yeah, that's right," I said.

"But you left me there." He looked confused. "Why did you leave me?"

"You hurt our friend, Jake." I hunkered down in front of him. "Remember? You bit her."

"Oh, that." He shrugged. "I was hungry. Can't blame a man for being hungry, can you?"

I saw the soldier behind him tighten his grip on his firearm, index finger itching to pull that trigger. I shook my head "no" and he glared at me.

"Begging your pardon, Ma'am," he said, "but you haven't seen what this crazy bastard did here. We have every cause to put him down like a mad dog."

"He's right, you know." Nathan came back out of the kitchen. He looked ill, an expression totally out of place considering his normal unflappable—if cranky—personality.

"He kept them alive while he was eating them, one piece at a time," the soldier continued. "Stopped them from bleeding out with tourniquets, but didn't do anything about infection. Nothing to stop the pain. Just… sliced pieces off like they were shawarma on a spit."

"Shawarma." Jake nodded in agreement. "I've always wanted to try shawarma." He giggled. "Guess I have to wait till the end of the movie."

Two people in Hazmat suits came out, carrying a body bag that looked only partially filled. I swallowed, willing myself not to throw up.

"You say one of them is still alive?"

"Yeah. If you can call it that." Nathan swallowed, hard. "The medics had to sedate her before she'd stop screaming."

"He needs to die!" The soldier with the itchy trigger finger stepped forward, only to be straight-armed by Gabriel.

"We have to take him back to Big Red," he said sternly. These were the first words Gabriel had spoken since he'd asked me to identify Jake. I almost didn't recognize his voice, it sounded so… dead.

Nathan nodded, but he didn't look happy.

"Agreed. They'll want to run tests. Simone always wants to run tests."

I looked down at Jake, who sat there giggling, rocking back and forth.

"If we're lucky," Nathan added, "they won't use any anesthetic."

The medics brought out the other victim on a stretcher, a woman in her early forties with short brown hair plastered to her skull by sweat and blood. The medics had draped a sheet over her body; it settled in unnatural divots and indentations already soaking through with blood and other fluids. Even in repose, her expression showed the nightmare she'd just survived. I wondered if there were enough sedatives in the world to give her a dream-free sleep.

"Did he do anything else to them?"

"No," Nathan replied. "Our friend here isn't interested in sex. Just food."

"I'm hungry," Jake chimed in. "Is it tea time? I already had elevenses." He giggled again and the soldier standing in back of the chair suddenly reversed his firearm and slammed the butt into the back of his skull. Jake's eyes rolled up in his head and he slumped forward, falling face first onto the floor.

No one moved to pick him up.

"I'm sorry, sir." The soldier, who didn't look old enough to order a beer in public, stared straight ahead, barely holding it together. I could see him starting to crack open at the seams. I didn't blame him. No way any kind of training could prepare someone for this.

"If you hadn't done it, I would have," I said.

Nathan gave the soldier a sympathetic look.

"Just don't do it again. We need him alive."

A muscle twitched in Gabriel's jaw as he stared at Jake's prone body. I could only imagine what he was thinking. That—but for Dr. Albert's antiserum—would be his fate.

I wanted to sit down, but couldn't find a chair or section of couch that wasn't liberally soaked in blood, so I settled for perching gingerly on the edge of the stone hearth. I almost instantly regretted my decision when I looked in the fireplace and saw charred bones mixed in with the ashes and half-burned chunks of wood.

"We're done here," Nathan said, sitting down next to me.

"What next?" I didn't really want an answer.

"We take this son-of-a-bitch back to Big Red and find out what the common denominator is between him and Gabriel. Then we try and figure out what, if anything, they both share with the wild cards." He slung an arm around my shoulder and gave me a rough hug. I didn't know what to do with it.

"And if we're lucky," he continued, "maybe Dr. Albert and Simone can actually figure out a cure for this whole shitstorm."

CHAPTER TWELVE

The sun was setting as we drove up the access road to Big Red. The last of the day's light reflected off the windows of the outer buildings of the campus just beyond the defensive perimeter of Mount Gillette and the Slinky of Doom, nicknames I'd come up with during a more frivolous moment.

The former was a mini Great Wall of China made out of some military grade shaving cream that hardened to the consistency of Silly Putty when exposed to air. It could be employed quickly, and made for an effective barrier against the walking dead as long as their numbers weren't too great.

The Slinky of Doom was my nickname for the accordion-style razor wire set in front of Mount Gillette, loops of the stuff meant to entangle rotting limbs long enough for the perimeter guards and snipers to dispatch them with clean shots to the head.

A gap had been made in the perimeter during the swarm attack, designed to funnel the zombies into a killing chute of flames and gunfire. That gap now provided access into and out of the campus, and was guarded 24/7, two trucks parked on either side of it. Guess we were safe unless a rogue biker gang came along and wanted to get into the mall.

Jake sat in the back of the Humvee, handcuffed and

flanked on either side by two soldiers, neither of whom looked happy to be near him. He was still groggy from the blow to the head, and thankfully quiet as we drove through the gap. The setting sun cast eerie shadows on his bloodstained face.

As we rolled through the quad toward Patterson Hall, I thought of the first time the wild cards had faced the zombies as separate teams. It had been Gabriel, Lil, Kai, and me on our team... and we had kicked zombie ass.

I shut my eyes, forcibly willing the tears to stay back a little while longer, taking comfort in the warmth of Gabriel and Nathan on either side of me. No way I wanted to cry with Psycho Jake there.

We pulled up outside of Patterson Hall, next to the military ambulance that was already parked in front. The soldiers quickly dragged Jake out of the back, none too gently, supporting most of his weight between them.

"Where are we going?" he asked.

"Disneyland," I said without a hint of humor.

"Good. I like Disneyland. Shanna and I took Tyce there last year. Good times." He smiled at me, a genuinely sweet smile even more disturbing than the psycho cannibal he'd become. "I'm going to see them now, right?"

God, this is so fucked up. Chalk up another war crime to lay at Dr. Albert's doorstep.

"Right," I said, forcing myself not to choke on the word as the two soldiers led Jake up the stairs, and from there to the lab facilities below.

Gabriel put a hand on my shoulder.

"You okay?" he asked yet again. I started to nod, but then lurched away from his hand, making it as far as the bushes before losing the contents of my stomach.

Tears streamed down my face as my stomach heaved again and again, until there was nothing left. I fell onto my knees, light-headed, dry-heaving and sobbing until I thought I'd pass out.

"Just breathe, Ash…" Gentle hands pulled my hair back from my face, and rubbed my back until the spasms passed. A water bottle appeared in front of me. I gratefully took a swallow, then another. I wanted to brush my teeth. I focused on breathing some more, had another sip of water and looked up.

"Thanks."

Gabriel helped me to my feet, keeping an arm around me when I staggered, still dizzy from all the vomiting.

"They'll be waiting for us, after we clean up," he said. By "they" I knew he meant Simone and Colonel Paxton.

"Is… are… will the other wild cards be there?" My voice rasped. It hurt to talk.

"Yes." Gabriel handed me the water bottle. This time I drank deeply, pretty sure it would stay down. "They'll need to be debriefed."

I sighed, a great shuddering sigh. That was something I was *not* looking forward to.

"What's going to happen to Jake?" I asked.

"Quarantine, and tests. Maybe his blood will give us another key to figuring out how to stop this thing."

"What about that poor woman he… the one that's still alive?" I shuddered again, this time from the sheer horror of what Jake's victims must have suffered.

Nathan spoke up from nearby. I hadn't realized that he was there.

"Simone will take care of her," he said.

"They won't take her to the labs, though, will they?" The last thing that poor woman needed was to wake up in the midst of Eli Roth's vision of a mad doctor's laboratory. If she weren't already totally crazy, that would drive her over the edge for sure. As far as Jake went, I didn't think he could go any further on the road to Crazy Town. Clearly, he was already there.

"No," Gabriel said. "I'm sure Professor Fraser will see to it that she has a private room, as soon as it's certain she's not infected."

Whether or not she would ever be completely sane again was another question.

I swallowed some more water, rolled my shoulders a couple of times to get the kinks out, nodded, and headed inside. I wanted to get the debriefing over with so I could go find a quiet corner and grieve for Kai in private. Then maybe I'd have the emotional fortitude to go find Lil and be strong for her. But first I'd need some time to be weak, all by myself.

The rest of the wild cards were already seated at the front of the auditorium. They seemed diminished, sunken into themselves with grief. Mack sat next to Lil, a comforting arm around her shoulders, while Tony huddled by himself in a seat by the wall halfway to the back of the room. Gentry sat a few seats away from him, close enough to be there if needed, but leaving enough room to give him his own space.

I'd liked Gentry from day one, and his emotional intelligence continually impressed me. He burst any preconceived stereotypes I'd ever had of your average military grunt.

Nathan and Gabriel went up to sit at the "command central" table with Simone and Colonel Paxton. I sat on the other side of Lil, giving her hand a brief squeeze to let her know I was there. She didn't respond. Mack's resemblance to a mournful hound dog was more marked than ever, his eyes red with unashamed tears, everything sagging with grief.

Tony didn't even look up at our entrance, just stared straight ahead at nothing. I wanted to hug him, but knew better than to try.

We all sat there in silence for a minute. I looked at Simone, surprised and disturbed to see her looking as if she'd aged ten years. She was dressed and groomed as impeccably as ever, but her eyes were swollen. The contrast between her grass-green irises and bloodshot whites was startling.

After all the things she's seen—must *have seen over the years, it still gets to her,* I realized. Somehow, that made me afraid—maybe for all of us.

Even Paxton looked… well, he always looked sad, given his weird-ass mask of a face, but if that wasn't genuine sorrow I saw in his eyes, he was a damned fine actor. Somehow, though, he also looked pissed off. And when he finally spoke, his voice thrummed with barely suppressed anger.

"So, what happened out there?"

Gentry started to speak, but Paxton raised a hand to cut him off.

"I've already received your report, Sergeant Gentry. I'm interested in hearing from the rest of the wild cards." He looked around the room, his gaze landing on each of us, as penetrating as a laser beam. I felt judged as his gaze hit me. Tried, judged, and convicted before I'd said a word.

"Ashley?"

Shit.

"What happened?"

I took a few seconds to think about it, trying to figure out if there was any sort of "right answer" to explain what had happened. We'd all fucked up, dropped our guard. Even though Mack and I had worried about their behavior, when Tony, Kai, and Lil had dashed off to check that last trailer, we hadn't done anything to stop them. Our passiveness was as much at fault as their cocky carelessness. Even Gabriel had been operating at less than his best, especially given his irrational behavior of late.

"Well, Ms. Parker?" Paxton stared at me, waiting for my response.

I gulped, *so* not wanting to be the one to say what needed to be said.

"We got careless." I felt rather than saw Tony flinch at my words. "*All* of us. We didn't stop to think about the fact there might be something or someone other than zombies that could hurt us." I paused, unable to think of anything to add that might mitigate our part in Kai's death.

The room was quiet.

"Anyone else have anything to add?" he asked. The quiet turned into a dead silence—the difference between an attentive classroom and a tomb.

"No?" Paxton stood up and paced back and forth in front of the table a couple times before coming to a stop in front of it. "Then I have something to say. Everyone dies. We are in the equivalent of a wartime situation. Unexpected variables come into play. Shit, as they say, happens."

Okay, so maybe he was going to cut us some slack after all.

"But what happened to Kai?" He shook his head, and I knew we were about to get hammered. "His death should not have happened." His gaze swept across the room again, the disappointment and anger in it like shards of white-hot shrapnel. "It was pure carelessness. Horseplay instead of professional behavior." Lil gave a choked sob next to me. I didn't dare look at Tony.

"And if even *one* of you had been paying attention, this might have been prevented." His Shakespearean voice added extra weight—and guilt—to his words. He paused again, and then continued. "*Might* have been prevented. Perhaps, and perhaps not. We have no way of knowing how else this situation might have unfolded had you all been at the top of your game, instead of *playing* games."

Ouch.

"I want all of you to think about this." His voice softened marginally. "You are wild cards. You're not invulnerable, but you've been given enhanced senses, and an immunity to whatever causes the dead to resurrect. You can fight in situations no one else can survive, without fear of infection. And your blood holds at least part of the answer to what could be the ultimate cure to what is arguably the greatest threat our civilization has ever faced." Then the softness disappeared, making me wonder if it ever was there.

"To squander these advantages is inexcusable. You are among our greatest assets."

"Kai wasn't a fucking *asset*."

We all looked up as Tony uncurled from his ball of misery and stared at Paxton with real hate.

"He was a person, and he was my friend."

I looked at Paxton, wondering how he'd respond.

"You're right, Tony. Kai wasn't just a wild card, and I don't just mourn his death as if he was a lost weapon. But in my position, I'm forced to think of these things on the most basic and practical levels, because that's my job. It doesn't mean I don't respect—and feel—your loss."

I had to give him credit. What he said made sense.

Tony didn't reply.

"So think about this tomorrow when you go back out," Paxton added. "This isn't just about you. It's not even about the survival of Redwood Grove. This is about the survival of the human race." He stopped, and looked around the room. "Any questions?"

There weren't any.

"Well, then." Paxton sat back down behind the table. "I am truly sorry for your loss. I know you lost not only a teammate, but also a friend. Do his memory proud, and don't let this happen again."

Now don't do it again.

I had to stifle a majorly inappropriate giggle as the line from *Life of Brian* made an unfortunately timed hit-and-run through my brain. Paxton shot me a look and I turned the sound into a cough, then dug my nails into my thighs.

* * *

"Sir, are you ready to order?"

Griffin looked up at the hip, twenty-something waitress who was standing in front of him. She looked somewhere past his left ear, avoiding eye contact. Typical waitress-slash-whatever-the-fuck, perfectly suited to work at a trendy wine bar in Santa Monica.

Too cool for school, this one. So he turned on the charm.

"What do you recommend, love?" The endearment could have been offensive, but just a little hint of an accent turned it into something acceptable.

"Um… what do you like?" she asked.

Griff smiled more broadly.

"Now that is an open question."

He looked directly into her eyes before giving her body a slow up-and-down, briefly admiring the long—and thankfully not too skinny—legs displayed by her short black skirt, and breasts that were either fake or cleverly displayed in Victoria's Secret's most miraculous of bras. Her face was generic Hollywood starlet—collagen trout pout, perfect little nose, and a deliberately casual mane of the best blonde dye job her salary could buy.

Her most attractive—and genuine—features were her eyes, dark brown and framed with thick lashes. So he focused on those, giving her the full benefit of his own undeniably seductive hazel ones. Those eyes, combined with the kind of accessible bad boy looks that women loved, had yet to let him down.

He could sense both her discomfort, and her arousal.

Both reactions turned him on.

"But let's just start with wine…" He looked at her nametag. "Mandy, is it?"

He settled on a Zinfandel from Paso Robles, flirting with Mandy enough to ensure an extra large pour. Then he settled back to enjoy people-watching from his patio seating.

It'd been a long time since he'd had the luxury of watching anyone who wasn't wearing standard prison orange.

* * *

Mandy's shift ended at 10 p.m., and there was no question that Griff would "walk her home." He did just that, to a little mother-in-law cottage behind a Craftsman-style bungalow on Fourth Avenue. He walked her all the way into her bedroom, where their clothes went flying and they killed several bottles of wine in between bouts of ferociously kinky sex. Mandy had a seemingly bottomless chest of sex toys, and Griff took it as a point of pride to test out every one of them.

Hours later, both lay exhausted on Mandy's bed, its memory foam mattress abused into amnesia. Griff reached out and poured the last dregs of very expensive Pinot Noir, savoring the aroma before drinking. He could swear his senses were more… well… sensitive since he'd rejoined the real world.

"Mmmm…" Mandy gave a little purr of satisfaction, her eyes glazed with wine, satiated lust, and exhaustion. *"You are something, you—"* A sharp cough cut off the rest of her sentence.

Sitting up, she reached for a bottle of Perrier on the bedside table, but another coughing fit hit before she could grab it. Griff stretched a lazy arm over her and snagged the Perrier, waiting until her coughing subsided before offering it to her.

"Thanks." She took a sip, then another.

"You okay?" he asked.

"I don't feel so good."

Griff looked at her. Mandy's corneas were now yellow, shot through with red streaks, like bloody egg yolks.

"You don't look so good, love." She didn't. Fucking unappetizing, if the truth be told.

She started coughing again, this time doubling over with the force of the spasms. Dark fluid trickled out from the corners of her mouth, as her eyes widened in fear and pain.

"I don't—" The cough turned into retching, gouts of viscous black liquid spraying over the white down comforter. Griff raised an eyebrow and got out of bed, taking the wine glass with him.

"Call nine-one—" Mandy vomited again, her eyes now leaking blood.

"I think it's too late for that, love." Griff sipped his wine and watched as she went into convulsions, her entire body wracked with spasms, until one last back-breaking shudder engulfed her frame.

And then she stopped breathing.

Griff finished his wine and set the glass on the bedside table. Calmly putting on his clothes, he wandered into the small kitchen, had a glass of water, and pulled a carving knife from a block on the counter. It was a cheap-shit knife set, but it would have to do.

A thumping sound from the bedroom alerted him. He turned in time to see Mandy's reanimated corpse fumble its way through the bedroom door, once-brown corneas now corpse-white in the center of that bloody sea of yellow.

A shame, *he thought*. Ah, well.

"Come here, love," Griff said softly, raising the knife.

Never let it be said that he didn't take responsibility for his actions.

CHAPTER THIRTEEN

We held a memorial service for Kai in the quad early the next morning.

The weather was gray and foggy again, as if in sympathy. Everyone stood in a semi-circle under a tall redwood, the wild cards at the front of the group. The turnout would have gratified Kai—it would have confirmed that he was every bit as popular as he thought he was.

Egotistical little shit, I thought affectionately.

I figured at least eighty or so people showed up, both military and civilians, even the ones who'd given us the stink-eye when we'd first started fighting the outbreak. Shades of X-Men, right? But after we'd taken out the swarm, many of them had started treating us like heroes and, more importantly, human beings. Kai's death proved we were just as vulnerable as they were.

Jamie was there, eyes brimming with tears as she gave me a hug before going to stand near Simone. Colonel Paxton gave a short but eloquent eulogy. He talked about Kai's bravery, and sacrifice for the greater good, but how ultimately nothing was worth the loss of Kai's life. I agreed with "nothing being worth the loss," but how getting killed by "friendly fire" contributed to the greater good, well, that was beyond me.

I guess it was better than saying that Kai's death was

a tragic mistake and an utter waste, which was closer to the truth.

Paxton asked if anyone else wanted to say a few words, but no one took him up on it. We were all too shell-shocked. Lil and Tony were both emotional wrecks, but Lil was much easier to deal with because she accepted whatever affection and comfort she could get. Mack and I took turns letting her cry on our shoulders, with Nathan filling in as grief counselor now and again, in his own gruff way. He had a soft spot for Lil, and generally reserved his least sarcastic moods for her.

Tony, on the other hand, shrugged off any attempts to comfort him. His attitude toward the rest of us was beyond hostile, almost as if he hated us—and probably himself—for being alive. He seemed especially pissed off at Mack, because Mack had defended Kai's killer, and he couldn't forgive that yet.

My guess was that he also couldn't forgive himself for beating up on a woman, even if he hadn't known what he was doing at the time. It was a truly fucked up, complicated guilt cocktail served to someone far too young.

And I kind of understood. Personally, I didn't know where Mack got his endless well of compassion, because even though it had been an accident, I still couldn't help but feel angry—at the woman, and at Kai and the rest of us for getting sloppy, letting our guards down, and turning a very serious mission into a stupid game.

The only person who could get near Tony was Gentry, maybe because of the geeky bond he'd formed with Tony and Kai from day one. Whatever the reason, the rest of us backed off in unspoken agreement and let Gentry take point on this particular mission. We were barely holding together as it was, and didn't need the emotional collateral damage.

* * *

Unfortunately, *death* didn't take a holiday.

We went out the next day, Nathan joining us this time. We were down to six wild cards.

Technically Simone was one of us, but she didn't exactly count because Paxton wouldn't authorize her to go on any sort of combat outings. Her knowledge of the zombie contagion was too valuable, and most of her time was spent working in the lab with Dr. Albert. Gabriel counted as a sort of half wild card, because he couldn't get infected again if he was bitten, and he could kick major ass even without the enhanced abilities.

Gentry and Nathan seemed to be the least potentially explosive combination for Tony, leaving Lil, Gabriel, and me to work together. Lil's killing exuberance was unusually subdued, which wasn't necessarily a bad thing.

We found a small pocket of zombies in the forest, and managed to get the job done quickly and quietly. Too quietly. A week earlier, if you would have told me I'd miss the irritating antics Tony and Kai always pulled, I'd have laughed and made you watch *Phantom Menace*— repeatedly, eyes propped open à la *Clockwork Orange*.

But now I'd have gladly sat through hours of their dueling Jar Jar Binks impersonations, just to see Kai alive again.

On the upside—and I desperately needed *any* kind of upside—Gabriel's mood shifts were less extreme again, and I no longer felt as if I was constantly navigating a minefield strewn with nails. Whenever I thought about how he'd covered me with his own body, just to protect me from harm, I felt all warm and fuzzy.

And maybe just a little bit turned on.

* * *

Two days after the funeral, we cleared an exclusive enclave of expensive vacation homes resting along the top of a ridge that lay between Redwood Grove and the ocean. We had military backup this time—a team of six men and women working with us to sweep the nooks and crannies of the surrounding woods. The sweep shook loose a few zombies, emaciated and pretty much incapacitated, but no survivors.

I was beginning to wonder why we were obsessing about the quarantine area around Redwood Grove, when from the reports that were coming in, this thing was popping up in other parts of the country. Then I remembered my parents, who lived up in Lake Country, and redoubled my efforts.

I also wondered if more wild cards had cropped up in the other areas where Dr. Albert's deadly vaccine had been tested. If so, did they have military backup, or were the people inside those quarantine areas just shit out of luck—left to survive or die on their own? I wanted to ask someone all of these questions, preferably Simone, but she wasn't available. She and Dr. Albert were spending every spare minute in the lab working toward what I assumed was a cure.

Although knowing Dr. Albert, he might just be working on building a better, faster zombie.

I was determined to talk to someone, though, so that night, when Lil fell asleep earlier than usual—wiped out from the physical and emotional drain of the last few days—I decided it was safe to go out for a while. I left her in our room, guarded by two very fat felines, one on either side of her head, and ventured into the quiet hallway.

It was time to take an exceptionally grouchy bull by the horns, and corner Gabriel in his lair. After all, Gabriel was part of the DZN's inner circle, so he should be able to fill me in on a few details—such as when we were going to stop dicking around in Redwood Grove. I wanted reassurance that the plague hadn't spread anywhere near my folks' ranch, and that they were still safe.

Mostly I wanted to know that we weren't wasting our time.

Of course, I had other reasons for seeking out Gabriel instead of, say, Nathan or even Colonel Paxton—although truth be told, Paxton definitely intimidated me. It was time to end the ambiguity about our relationship once and for all. Gabriel either wanted me, or he didn't. If there were insurmountable issues, just because he might turn into a flesh-eating nut job, then I needed to hear him say it. Or if he'd simply lost interest, I'd rather know, so I could move on and stop feeling like the heroine of a really twisted Lifetime movie. *My Son, My Love, My Zombie.*

The hallways were thankfully clear. Not that anyone would care, but there was something so… juvenile about trying to make my way unnoticed into Gabriel's room. I felt like a teenage girl at summer camp, sneaking into the boys' dormitory, padding on the cheap linoleum in my bare feet, blue flannel pajama bottoms and white tank top.

His door was shut, but I could hear music coming from underneath the door. Some really cheesy New Age crap, like…

Oh.

Wow.

Yanni?

I took a deep breath, then rapped sharply on the door. I heard a distinctly irritated sigh. Guess he was really rocking out.

The door opened a crack, revealing one of Gabriel's denim-blue eyes.

"Ashley." He stared at me, without opening the door any further.

I waited a polite few seconds before saying anything. "Can I come in?"

"Um…" He scratched his head, looking distinctly uncomfortable.

I rolled my eyes.

"Look, I'm not after your virtue or anything here. I just want to talk."

"Oh," he said. Then, after a few more seconds, "Okay."

He opened the door just wide enough for me to enter. I enjoyed the unaccustomed sight of him in sweat pants and a black tank top, just tight enough to show off his pectoral muscles.

Why can't I find a nice, non-neurotic guy to drool over?

The room was even more Spartan than the one I shared with Lil, lacking the homey touch of a fragrant cat box. There was a CD player—the source of the auditory pain—and a stack of books on a little desk next to his bed. They all looked academic—not a potboiler among them.

Since he hadn't offered me a seat, I decided to take the initiative and plunked myself on the edge of the mattress, a basic twin. Barely large enough for one person, let alone two. Not that I cared, right?

"What did you want to talk about?"

I raised an eyebrow. His clueless levels were unusually high, but I didn't have to start with the pesky personal stuff.

"So this thing has spread to other towns, right?" I said. "Wherever Dr. Crazy Pants sent the vaccine for testing?"

"Uh, right." He sounded surprised, as if he'd expected me to proposition him. "From what we're hearing, there have been more outbreaks."

"Have they found any other wild cards?"

Gabriel leaned over and turned the volume down on the CD player, and I was tempted to thank him for that act of mercy.

"I don't know." He leaned against the far wall and folded his arms in what some might call a protectively defensive gesture. "I don't think so. At least none that I've heard about."

"So how come we're still dicking around in Redwood Grove, instead of going to help them? The kind of stuff we're dealing with now could be handled by regular army, couldn't it?"

Gabriel sighed, the sound more weary than exasperated.

"Our primary goal at this time is to ensure a secure base of operations, from which Dr. Albert and Professor Fraser can work on a cure." It could have come straight out of the manual, and he knew it.

"Okay, seriously here. You're telling me there's no place else in the world that's as secure and high-tech as Big Red?" I paused to let that sink in. "I mean, wouldn't they be better off in a place that hasn't been crawling with flesh-eating vermin lately?"

"They would," he agreed. "But there isn't one—all of the outbreaks are geographically linked with other medical and research facilities currently equipped to deal with the contagion."

I looked at him sharply.

"That can't be a coincidence."

"It could be." Gabriel stared straight ahead. "But I don't think it is. And neither do Professor Fraser or Colonel Paxton."

Shit.

"That can't be good. Right? I mean, there's no way this is a coincidence. We're talking some sort of deliberate conspiracy here. Someone who knows about the DZN and the virus. Someone who *wants* it to spread."

Gabriel was silent. His expression said it all, though. He thought he'd said too much already. He'd suck as a poker player.

I had another thought.

"Or did they send the vaccine to places where the DZN has research facilities, to see if they *could* contain the outbreaks? Like a test or something."

Or…

I stopped, not sure if I should voice my thoughts. Gabriel looked at me, probably struck by my sudden and uncharacteristic silence.

"What?" he said.

It was my turn to remain silent. Hopefully I had a better poker face than Gabriel.

"Ash, you've got something on your mind. Say it."

Okay, guess not.

"If whoever did this knows about the wild cards, and about Jake and…" I trailed off.

"People like me and Jake." Gabriel's tone was carefully neutral.

I nodded.

"If they know, then maybe they want to find more of us, for some reason. And are willing to kill a shitload of people to do it."

Gabriel pushed himself away from the wall.

"But why? I mean, we all know the value of the wild cards. But someone like Jake… or like me?" He frowned. "What would be the point?'

"Maybe they want to develop some sort of super-duper-über soldier."

Gabriel snorted.

"Okay, fine," I grumbled. "It's a cliché plot device any way you look at it, but clichés exist for a reason, y'know." I stood up and started to pace. The more I thought about it, the more convinced I was that I was on the right track. "Someone out there thinks it's a good idea. And worth the collateral damage."

Then another thought occurred to me. I stopped.

"They don't attack him. Jake, I mean. But why not? Why weren't there zombies clawing to get inside at Bigfoot's Revenge? Or up on Ridge Crest?"

"They think he's one of them," Gabriel said flatly.

"Then why do they attack you?" He shot me a look, and I hastily added, "I mean, you have the same condition, right?"

"The antiserum. As long as I take it, I'm still human." Gabriel's voice was bleak as he added, "Unless it stops working."

I really didn't want to ask my next question, because I

was ninety-nine percent sure I already knew the answer. But I asked it anyway.

"Do you think… I mean, is that a possibility?"

"Yes." He sat on the edge of the bed, his shoulders slumping in a way I'd never seen before. "Both Professor Fraser and Dr. Albert feel that the antiserum is losing its efficacy, at least in its current dosage."

I sat down next to him.

"So they'll up the dosage, right?"

"Yes, for now." He looked at me. "But what happens when *that* dosage stops working? And how much of it can I even take, without inducing some sort of fucked up side effect?"

"Are there any side effects?" I asked.

He shrugged. "You've seen some of them, when the drug starts to wear off. Irrational outbursts of anger, extreme mood swings, overreacting to situations and people." He stared at the floor. "You used the term 'roid rage the other day. I guess that describes it pretty well."

I nodded slowly, as sudden light was shed on his recent erratic behavior.

"And you didn't have these reactions on the lower dosage?"

"No," Gabriel replied.

"You're not going to turn into Jake, you know. You're just not like him."

"Not yet."

"You won't be." I spoke with an assurance that I almost believed. "I don't think you have it in you to lose control like that. Jake went crazy. He had no frame of reference for what happened to him, to his family, or the world." I looked him in the eyes.

"You do."

"That doesn't change the reality of what could happen to me if the serum runs out, or stops working."

I thought about the implications.

"Would it… does it have to be fresh?" I asked. "Could

you stockpile it, so there's no chance of it running out?"

As soon as I asked the question, I knew it was a bad idea.

"What does it matter?" Gabriel turned toward me, moving violently enough to make me stand up and take a step backward. He stood up, too, and grabbed my shoulders, glaring down. "The thought of having to eat *any* living creature is bad enough. But a person? And yet, that part of me is starting to crave it... knowing that one of these days I could be looking at you, wanting to kiss you, wanting you... and suddenly that desire could turn into literal hunger."

He gave me an uncompromising look.

"If I ever turn into that," he said, "I need to know that you will kill me."

I stared up at him, speechless. His fingers dug into my shoulders hard enough to hurt.

"I don't want to lose you, Ash... but even more, I don't want to lose myself. And if I hurt you, I've lost everything. Promise me."

"I... I promise." His grip relaxed.

"But only if there's absolutely no hope for a cure," I added.

And his grip tightened right back up again. *Ouch.*

"Not good enough," he said. "No conditions."

"Tough shit," I said. "It'll have to do, because that's my final word on it."

"Damn it, Ash, it's not your choice to make!"

"Yeah, actually it is." Wrenching away from his grip, I turned and slammed a hand against the wall, leaving a slight dent in the cheap plaster. "If there's no hope, then I will kill you myself. But as long as there's a chance you can be cured, I will *not* let you go." I turned to face him again. "Tell me you wouldn't do the same thing in my place."

That shut him up. Which was a good thing because I don't know what I would have done if he'd said something like, "Hell, no, I'd cap you in a heartbeat."

I hunkered down in front of him.

"Gabriel... listen. I believe in you. And I'll do anything I can to help you. But I won't kill you unless I know for certain that you're beyond help." I paused for effect. "That is, unless you continue to act like a total douche. Because if you do, then I'll have to kill you just on principal."

His lips twitched as part of him tried to smile, while the asshat half of him did its best to stop him.

Asshat lost as Gabriel made a sound somewhere between a growl and a laugh, and grabbed me, pulling me down onto the bed where he tipped me over onto my back and lay on top of me, hands cradling my face.

And just like that, the tension between us vanished, and Gabriel was back. The stranger with the psycho stick up his butt was replaced with the man I'd come to care about—despite the fact he could be a self-righteous jerk.

"I always find myself stuck between wanting to kiss you or strangle you," he said.

"I vote for the former. I'm not into that kinky Midnight Sun stuff."

"Good," he replied. "Me neither." He kissed me, tasting all minty fresh and delicious, and I wrapped my arms around him, pulling him as close to me as possible. Who knew how long this would last? For all I knew, he'd be back in douche mode tomorrow and treat me like... well, like he used to treat me when we'd first met. So I wanted to enjoy every second of closeness I could get, with or without the hot monkey love.

Although "with" would be nice.

For the moment, though, I had to be content with some hot monkey kissing and cuddling before eventually falling asleep spooned up against Gabriel, my back to his chest. One of his arms was firmly wrapped around me. I felt safe when I was with him, a sensation now so rare that I treasured it like the world's last box of See's chocolates.

"Do you think they're open?"

Gary rolled his eyes. This was the umpteenth time Laura had asked the question, and he was ready to end their first date right now. Sure, she was hot. Smokin' hot, and if the rumors were accurate, smokin' hot *and* accessible.

But none of the rumors had mentioned her type-A personality, or the need to double- and even triple-check things like addresses, closing times, and directions. Or her annoying habit of asking the same question a bunch of times in less than an hour.

But there was the smokin' hot factor, still weighing heavily in her favor, so Gary took yet another deep breath to help him stay patient long enough to make it through the evening and get laid.

"Yes, they're open," he said cheerfully. *"I go to this place at least once a week, and they haven't changed their hours in five years."*

"Did you call ahead?"

Gary nearly told her to go fuck herself, but common sense and the sight of a shapely thigh extending from her short-short skirt toned down his response to a strategic lie.

"Yup, sure did."

It was a good move. Laura sat back in the passenger seat, a satisfied expression on her face. Gary grinned to himself. If that was all it took, he'd lie his way right into her panties.

So he turned off the 1, waiting for oncoming traffic to clear before making the turn. Normally he would've barreled across the street, but Laura probably wouldn't appreciate the whole adrenaline rush he enjoyed by dodging death. Not that there was a lot of traffic. He'd heard something about a freeway closure south of Eugene, some sort of industrial chemical and an overturned truck. That would explain it.

The fog seemed thicker, once they turned onto the subsidiary road that led to Captain Jack's Crab Shack. The Shack itself was set back a ways, with a gravel parking lot cutting into

one of the many marshy sloughs in the area. The owners—
Captain Jack and family—caught fresh crab out in the cold
northern Pacific water off Humboldt County, and sold it daily,
steaming it at the Shack and then packing it in ice. During the
height of crab season, you could get it for $2.99 a pound. Now,
a few weeks on the downward side, it was $4.99 a pound, still
a bargain.

Gary had a loaf of fresh sourdough, butter, and several
bottles of inexpensive chardonnay back at the apartment. The
plan was to take the fresh crabs back with them, eating them
while they watched movies. He had Direct TV and figured he'd
score more points by letting Laura pick the flicks. If he was
really lucky, and the rumors were true, the wine would do its
job and he'd be spared too much chick-flickage before getting
down to business.

He was so busy contemplating the possibilities that he
nearly missed the driveway in the heavy fog. Swearing, he did
a sharp swerving turn into the parking lot, tires crunching
on gravel as Laura gave a little scream and held onto the "Oh
Jesus" handle with an unnecessarily white-knuckled grip.

Drama queen, Gary thought.

There were several other cars in the parking lot, including
Jack's ubiquitous Crab Truck, a white serial-killer style van with
a sliding door and blacked out windows. The giant red crabs
painted on all sides of the van, along with "Captain Jack's Crab
Shack" in big, black letters, made it the perfect front. After all,
no self-respecting homicidal maniac would run around with his
address and phone number on display, would he?

Gary pulled in next to the Crab Van and turned off the
engine.

"See, I told you they'd still be open," he said, trying not to
sound smug.

The Shack was an open-air structure constructed like an
extra large fruit stand, with roll-down metal shutters to seal it
off at night. But they were still open, a single bright light bulb
hanging from the center of the ceiling, casting a warm glow
against the fog that drifted through the air.

"I don't see anyone inside." Laura gave a sniff as she unclenched her fingers from the handle.

"Amy's probably cleaning up something in back," Gary said, deciding that whether or not he got laid, Laura's nitpicky negativity wasn't going to make it worth a second date.

Unless she's freaky good in bed. Then he'd reconsider the issue.

"Who's Amy?"

"Captain Jack's daughter. She usually works Sunday through Wednesday nights, but both her mom and brother came down with that flu bug, so she's working mega-overtime."

"You really do come here a lot, don't you?" Her tone somehow made it sound like a bad thing. But he ignored it, opened the car door, and stepped out into the parking lot, his sneakered feet abnormally loud on the gravel as he walked around to the passenger side and opened the door for Laura, lending her a steadying arm as she wobbled on impractical but totally sexy black boots with spiky three-inch heels. They made the ten-foot walk to the wooden floor of the Shack slow going, but Gary didn't mind.

And by the way Laura snuggled against him, he didn't think she was hating it either.

"It's really quiet out here." Laura shivered and Gary tightened his arm around her.

"Not a lot out in this area," he said. "It's hard to even hear the traffic from the highway. Usually you can hear crickets and birds, though."

"Not tonight," she observed. And she was right. It was totally quiet, except for the sound of their shoes on the gravel and the occasional moan of a foghorn in the distance.

"Amy?" he called. His voice was muffled and oddly flat, as if the word had been swallowed by the mist.

They reached the Shack, Laura's heels finding much sturdier purchase on the wooden flooring. She stayed firmly pressed up against Gary anyway.

"Amy?" he repeated.

They stepped further into the Shack, where several huge

chest-like freezers hugged the walls. There was a counter with several scales, and a huge industrial sink with a hose attachment for cleaning the crabs if customers chose to have them backed— at an extra buck per crab—before taking them home.

Laura wrinkled her nose in distaste.

"Ugh, it stinks in here."

Gary couldn't argue. The place always smelled like dead crabs, and he had to admit the odor seemed especially pungent this evening, with an emphasis on "dead." Maybe one of the freezers had gone and died, 'cause something had gone majorly off.

The rear door was open, too. Out back there was an outdoor cooking range big enough to fit four large pots for boiling the live crabs as they came in. That way the more tenderhearted customers didn't have to see the dirty deed being done, and could enjoy the tasty crab-flesh with a clear conscience.

"Amy?" Gary tried yet again. Once again, the low moan of the foghorn was the only response.

Okay, now this is kind of weird. *Water dripped steadily from the hose, which dangled off the counter so the water trickled onto the floor, leaving a dark, slowly expanding puddle. Several crabs lay on the counter, the back of one peeled off as if someone has been in the middle of cleaning it, and been interrupted.*

"Maybe she's out back," he suggested, as much for his own benefit as Laura's. The truth was that he was pretty creeped out by now. "The door's open. I bet she's boiling up the last of the day's catch."

"Maybe we should just leave."

"Without our crabs?" He grinned at her. "No way. If she's not here, I'll just grab a couple, and pay her next time."

"But—"

"Just stay here," he insisted. "I'll be right back." Quickly, before he could change his mind, Gary strode toward the back door—only to have first one foot and then the other slip out from under him with a suddenness that left him no time to catch himself. He landed with a bone-jarring thud on his tailbone, and lay there for a minute, groaning in pain.

"Are you okay?" Laura click-clacked her way across the wooden floor, stopping short a foot away. "Oh my god, what is that?" She stared at the floor.

Gary managed to stop groaning long enough to turn his head and see the pile of gelatinous offal he'd slipped on. At first he thought it was discarded crab guts, and yeah, there was some greenish yellow goo and what he thought were crab lungs there. But crabs didn't have intestines, ones that were leaking shit all over the floor, and pieces of bloody meat and…

Is that a finger?

Gary scrabbled backward, every movement sending a bolt of pain up his tailbone.

The foghorn sounded again, louder than before. Closer. Like, outside the back of the damn Shack, for fuck's sake. Gary stared at the open doorway as the foghorn let out another plaintive moan, this time right outside the door.

He heard Laura scream, registered the sound of her heels clacking on the wood as she ran out the front door of the Shack, leaving him lying on the floor as Amy crawled in through the back doorway, dragging herself in with her fingertips, one eye hanging from its stalk over a shredded cheek. Chunks were missing from her neck and bare arms, and blood covered the Captain Jack's logo on her formerly white tank top. Even worse, though, was the fact that only half of Amy followed her into the room, bits and pieces dragging behind her in tattered, bloody ribbons of flesh and viscera.

She stank of shit and rot and the ocean at low tide on a hot day. Her formerly brown eyes were bluish white and focused entirely on Gary. She moaned again, just as an actual foghorn sounded off in the distance, and as other plaintive moans drifted in from the slough in back of the Shack.

"Oh fuck no way, no fucking way." Gary skittered backward on his ass, hands, and feet, ignoring pain and the sticky warmth under his palms. He backed up into the sink, screaming as his head made contact with the hose nozzle that was dangling over the edge. As soon as he realized what it was, he used the hose to pull himself to his feet, just as what was left of Amy dragged itself close enough to touch his shoe with one mutilated hand.

He screamed then, his voice almost as high as Laura's had been, and ran out of the building into the parking lot. He was vaguely aware of figures sloshing through the muck toward the Shack, their moans growing louder by the second.

Laura lay in a heap on the gravel, holding one of her ankles and crying. Gary thought there might be bone sticking through the side of it. She saw him and reached up one perfectly manicured hand toward him, pleading.

"Gary, help me!"

He ignored her, scrabbling in his pockets for his car keys as he ran around the Crab Van to his car. The driver's side door was unlocked—no reason to lock it here. Which meant he had just enough time to open the door as a sodden, stinking thing reached for him out of the fog. He used the door as a barrier, but felt clammy fingertips graze his face. Throwing himself into the car, he slammed the door shut after him, hitting the automatic lock button just as something else fell against the passenger door, wet hands slapping at the window. Several other figures moved past the car into the parking lot.

Tough shit, Laura.

Gary got the key into the ignition first try—pretty fucking good, considering how badly his hands were shaking. The engine roared to life and he hit the lights, illuminating a few dozen bodies shambling out of the foggy slough.

He didn't bother to look behind him as he threw the car into reverse and hit the accelerator, pedal to the metal, gravel spewing out from under the tires. He may have heard Laura screaming as he sped out of the parking lot, but he didn't look back then, either.

CHAPTER FOURTEEN

I was at my parents' house in Lake County, sitting in the living room with the huge stone fireplace my dad had fallen in love with when they'd gone house shopping. It was big, like something you'd expect the witch from Hansel and Gretel to have in her gingerbread cottage.

My dad kept adding logs to an already blazing fire. I was roasting hot, sweat pouring from my face and body, and I kept asking him to open a window and stop adding wood to the blaze. They both just smiled at me, though, and tossed on more big chunks of redwood until I could barely breathe.

I woke up with a start.

Gabriel's arm was still holding me against him. But something was wrong. The sense of safety was replaced by burning eyes. My head throbbed, it hurt to swallow, and a wave of nausea hit as I struggled to sit up.

I smelled smoke.

Oh, shit.

I grabbed Gabriel's arm and shook it. He muttered in his sleep, but didn't wake. I threw off his arm and struggled out of the bed, my already leaden limbs entangled in the blankets. I literally tumbled out of the bed, hitting the thinly carpeted floor hard with my knees.

"Gabriel!" I shouted, and the effort hurt my throat.

He mumbled something again and burrowed deeper under the covers. The smell of smoke increased. Was it my imagination, or could I see it curling through the air?

How the hell can he still be asleep?

Struggling to my feet, I seized the edge of the blankets and yanked them down away from him and all the way off the bed. He sat up, jolted awake, and glared at me.

"What the hell, Ash?" he demanded.

"I smell smoke!"

The look of irritation immediately vanished as Gabriel rolled out of bed and stood up, all in one smooth motion. He sniffed the air.

"I can't smell anything. Are you sure?"

"Yeah, I'm sure."

He didn't bother with any more questions. We knew from experience that my sense of smell was better than his. We both scrambled for our clothing.

"If I can't detect it yet," he said, "it might be something small."

At which point, with the kind of comedic timing envied by sitcom writers everywhere, the fire alarm went off. The clarion call of disaster sent a new surge of adrenalin through my body.

"Head upstairs to the courtyard," Gabriel said as he pulled on a pair of camo pants and a dark green T-shirt. "Gather anyone you can along the way."

"Lil," I said. "I need to get her first, and help her with the cats, get my weapons. Then we can both help evacuate."

Gabriel didn't even try to argue with me. Points for a learning curve there.

I ran to the door, poking the handle cautiously to make sure it wasn't hot to the touch. It was still cool, so I opened the door without further ado and dashed into the hallway, barreling around the corner to the section that housed the wild cards. Hanging a tight left, I ran straight into Mack. He was already dressed.

He steadied me with one hand as another door opened and Tony stuck his head out, bleary-eyed from interrupted sleep.

"Is it a drill?" he asked, cringing at the sound of the alarm. I knew how he felt—sometimes enhanced senses were a pain.

Mack shook his head before I could say anything.

"Can't you smell the smoke?" he asked. "I don't think this is a drill."

"It's not," I said shortly. "Go to the courtyard, get everyone you can out along the way. The soldiers will do the rest."

Tony nodded and vanished back into his room, presumably to get dressed. Of course, being a quintessential teen, there was every possibility he'd crawl back into bed and go back to sleep. I made a mental note to check before leaving the building.

Mack nodded toward the stairwell door.

"Look."

Smoke was seeping out from under the bottom of the door. I ran over and tested the handle, which was still cool to the touch. Cautiously I cracked the door, coughing when a plume of acrid smoke hit me in the face. I waved a hand in front of my nose and did a quick check, up and down the stairwell. The lower levels were hazy with an ever-thickening cloud, while the floors above were still relatively clear.

I shut the door and turned to Mack.

"It's definitely coming from one of the floors below," I said.

"Good. We should have plenty of time to clear the civilians from this level." He took off to help with the evacuation process. Knowing Mack, he'd stay inside until every last person was safe, or until one of us dragged him out of the building.

A thin haze was definitely visible on our floor by the time I got to the room I shared with Lil. I opened the door to find her already dressed and frantically trying to bundle the cats into their carrier. Neither feline was cooperating, with Binkey holed up under my bed and Doodle doing the classic stiff-legged claw against the doorframe of the carrier. It would have been funny, if the situation weren't so serious.

Lil looked up at my entrance, her tense expression relaxing into relief when she saw me.

"I'm so glad you're here," she said. "I can smell smoke, Ash. I could smell it before the alarm went off."

"Me, too," I said, giving her a quick one-armed hug. "Were you with Gabriel?"

I nodded, figuring there was no point in being coy.

"There's a fire somewhere in the building, on one of the lower levels," I said, helping her lever Doodle into the carrier. "Let's get the kids out of here, and then we can help with evacuation. Grab some food for them, and I'll see if I can get Binkey."

Lil nodded, grabbing a bag of dry cat food and her childhood toy Lambie-Pie, a threadbare stuffed lamb. She crammed them into a duffle bag along with her favorite pickaxe and M4, while I wriggled under my bed and tried to grab the cat.

Binkey, normally a mellow marshmallow, swatted me with an angry paw. I hissed with the unexpected pain of five sharp claws ripping bloody furrows in my hand.

"Son of a…"

I narrowed my eyes and grabbed the little bugger by his scruff, dragging him out from under the bed as he howled in outrage. *Ungrateful furball.*

"Ready?" I asked Lil. She nodded and opened the door to the carrier just wide enough for me to stuff him inside. Lil slammed the door shut and latched it securely as both cats started up a chorus of the damned. They'd done the same thing when we'd liberated them from Lil's old apartment in Redwood Grove, and the sound had attracted the attention of every zombie in a five-mile radius. At least tonight we didn't have to worry about the Z factor.

"Here." I handed Lil the duffle bag, helping her sling it over her shoulder. "You take the kids outside, and stash them someplace safe."

"What about you?"

"I'm going to help with the evacuation," I said, retrieving my own M4 and swords from the closet.

"You'll be careful, right?" Lil's eyes were wide and worried as Binkey and Doodle continued to howl.

"I will *totally* be careful," I replied, rooting around in the closet for my ammo pouch and extra cartridges.

"Promise?"

I stopped what I was doing, my attention caught by the naked vulnerability in Lil's voice. Gone was the slightly crazed zombie-killing goddess of death. In her place was just a frightened girl who didn't want to lose anyone else she cared about. Dropping my weapons, I crossed the room and gave her a fiercely protective hug.

"I promise."

"Okay." She hugged me back, her face pressed against my shoulder. When she stepped away, her expression was suddenly fierce. "Don't you leave me, Ashley."

I grinned at her.

"No way am I leaving you on your own with the banshee twins. Now get the hell out of here!"

She slung the duffle bag over her shoulder, hefted the cat carrier filled with at least thirty pounds of feline, and dashed out the door. I heaved a sigh of relief, knowing I'd be able to focus much better with Lil and the kids out of danger.

Stepping out into the hallway, I waited until I saw her vanish up the stairs, then went back into our room to retrieve my weapons and change into fighting gear. As I did so, I formed a mental picture of the lower floors. If the fire had started in the labs, it meant the research subjects could be loose. And by "research subjects" I wasn't talking lab rats. I was talking zombies. I'd been down there once when Colonel Paxton's predecessor had tried to blackmail me into joining the wild cards by showing me my ex-boyfriend turned zombie.

There'd been around a dozen ghouls in cages, with more strapped to tables. There were also a number of lab techs. Hopefully they'd already made it out, but if they hadn't… if their subjects had gotten loose, I needed to be ready for battle.

I ran back into the hallway toward the stairwell, passing Mack and a group of civilians he was leading out of the building.

"Any more of them?" I asked.

"Tony's got another group," Mack replied. "I think we've pretty much cleared this floor, and the military is handling the med ward below."

"Have you seen Simone?"

Mack shook his head.

"You get everyone you can off this floor," I said.

"What about Lil?"

I gave him a reassuring pat on one shoulder.

"She's out, along with the cats," I said. "I'm going to make sure Simone is safe."

Mack nodded. "Be careful."

I laughed. "It's my job, right?"

"Right." He gave me a quick one-armed hug.

We hit the stairwell. Mack and his group headed up, and I ran down the cement stairs into a slowly thickening cloud of ominously dark, acrid smoke, the smell noxious and chemical. It left an oily residue on my skin, making me wonder what kind of toxic cocktail was burning in the lab.

Could the infection be transmitted via the remnants of cremated zombies, à la O'Bannon's *Return of the Living Dead*? I shuddered at the thought, and not just because that movie started the whole "braaaa-i-nsss" craze. It'd been wrong about that part, so hopefully it hadn't gotten the whole infected rainfall thing right, either.

That would suck.

I coughed as I got another good whiff of the nasty-ass smoke when I reached the landing above the labs. The smoke further down was even thicker, and remembering that most people died of smoke inhalation, I knew I couldn't risk going down another flight of stairs without any protection, even if it was just a damp cloth to drape over my head. Besides, I doubted this stairwell would get me where I wanted to go. Access to the labs required following a path of labyrinthine complexity through the med ward.

I shuddered at the thought. Last time I'd been in the med ward had been to watch a bunch of soldiers—including Gabriel—try to subdue my boyfriend-turned-zombie amid a bunch of people who were tied to cots and dying from a hideously painful disease involving lots of blood and black fluids oozing from various orifices. You know, the kind of memories that lead to major PTSD. I'd managed to avoid the nightmares so far, most likely because I'd been too busy training and fighting to give them a chance to take root.

Either that, or I was amazingly resilient.

Or shallow as hell.

Whichever it was, I still didn't want to go back into that particular circle of hell. But if there was even a *chance* that Simone was down there, maybe injured or trapped... Well, I didn't see that I had much of a choice.

A quick hand on the stairwell door told me it was safe to open. Stepping through, I found myself in the middle of a chaotic rush of military and medical personnel, dashing in and out of the med ward, some with arms full of medical equipment and supplies, others pushing wheeled dollies to the elevator at the far end of the corridor. I'd seen *Towering Inferno* so I wouldn't want to trust an elevator in the middle of a fire, but since they were going up instead of down, the risk of it stopping on the wrong floor probably wasn't an issue.

Smoke drifted lazily through the hallway, the acrid chemical smell becoming stronger by the minute. I looked for a familiar face, hoping to see Simone, but most of the people dashing back and forth were wearing protective gear, some with full-on Level 4 biohazard suits, and others just in protective face masks and hoods with breathing apparatus.

As I'd hoped, they were evacuating the civilians. I recognized Judy from the trailer park, huddling against a soldier in protective face gear, her eyes rolling, showing the whites like a crazed horse. Guess she hadn't been infected, but her sanity levels clearly still needed a refill.

There were other folks with what looked like minor injuries—broken limbs and such—being helped out, but I didn't see anyone with Walker's symptoms, which made me wonder what was happening to the patients in the med ward. Some of the men and women there had been bitten, and were under observation to see if they were immune to the infection. Like me.

I grabbed one of the med techs as she ran past with an armful of syringes and bags of IV fluid.

"Have you seen Professor Fraser?" I asked. She shook her head, frantic to get out of the building.

Tough shit, lady.

"Are you sure?" I grabbed the front of her hazmat suit.

"I… she… she was in the lab, I think." She nodded back over her shoulder.

"How long ago?" I demanded. "When did she go there?"

"I don't know, maybe a few hours?" She tried to push past me, but I held onto the suit, ready to rip a hole in it if need be.

"Did you see her come back up? This is important."

I gave her a little shake for emphasis. "She's the one trying to come up with a cure for this shit, remember?"

"I—I don't think so. No, I haven't seen her."

"What about Dr. Albert?"

She shook her head again, clearly frantic to get the hell out of Dodge. I let go of her suit and she scurried past me toward the elevator.

Shoving my way through the hallway, I ignored the attempts by several soldiers and medical personnel who were trying to corral me toward the elevator, and elbowed my way through to the med ward doors. Pushing through, I was met with a Dante-esque vision of hell.

Trying to steady myself, I took a deep breath—and instantly regretted it, as I took in another lungful of smoke mixed with the thick, rich stench of blood, shit, and rotting flesh, overlaid with the smell of burning chemicals, plastic, wood and who knows what else. There was another set of double doors at the far end of the room, and I saw black smoke pouring through the cracks between, under and over them. They were the ones leading into the lab. I needed to find something to cut the amount of crap I was inhaling, or I'd end up with shriveled raisins for lungs.

Patients in varying stages of the zombie infection were still strapped to their cots, some unconscious, others in too much agony to notice the chaos and smoke. But a few, those still in the earlier stages, were all too aware of what was happening. They screamed for help, for release from the straps that held them to their beds, even as they hacked up gouts of black fluid and blood, their throats even more irritated by the smoke. But no one paid any attention to their screams. The techs and soldiers were busily piling supplies onto carts and wheeling them out of the room.

No one stopped to help the patients.

They couldn't just leave them to die… could they?

I grabbed a passing soldier by the arm.

"What's being done to evacuate these people?" He tried to shrug my hand off, but I easily maintained my kung-fu grip, pulling him closer. "Answer the question!"

I could tell he was young, even under his mask, and totally terrified.

Tough shit, dude. It was becoming a litany.

"W—we can't take them w—with us," he stammered. "They're infected."

"So you're leaving them here to burn?"

He shook his head. "No, w—we…"

Before he could answer, a shout went up from the far end of the room. The doors burst open and smoke poured in, along with several zombies in advanced stages of decay. Slices of flesh were missing from various parts of their bodies, cut away with surgical precision instead of being ripped out with teeth. The test subjects had gotten loose, which meant god-knows-what for the people who'd been working in the lab.

Like Simone.

Panic broke out. Most of the soldiers and civilians ran for the exit, dropping whatever they were carrying. One soldier gestured toward the forms still strapped to the cots, and two others immediately started up the rows, systematically putting bullets in the heads of each of the infected patients, moving down the line with a calm efficiency a robot would envy.

Two others held their positions and began shooting at the approaching zombies.

My grip loosened as I stared in horrified disbelief. The soldier took advantage of my lapse in attention and pulled away, dashing out the doors before I could stop him.

Two more bullets, two more dead patients. The lucky ones were too far gone to realize what was happening, but those close to me strained against the straps holding them to the cots, shrieking as they realized what was being done.

I couldn't let this happen. It was murder—a cold, calculated death squad in action. I started to unsling my M4, only to have someone grab my wrist from behind in a grip stronger than my own. I turned, ready to go medieval on the person's ass.

"Don't," Nathan said. "You can't stop it."

His voice was oddly muffled, and I stopped fighting. He was wearing one of the fire-evac hoods or masks or whatever they were called, the upper half of his face visible through clear plastic. He had a bulging duffle bag slung over one shoulder.

"It's wrong."

"I know," he replied. "But it's either that, or leave them here to burn to death. They're going to die no matter what. You know that."

"But these ones..." I gestured to the three patients closest to us. A little boy no more than six years old, a girl barely into her teens, and a heavy-set man in his forties, all hellishly aware of the situation. "They might make it. They could be wild cards, right?"

Nathan shook his head.

"They're past that point." He handed me a smoke hood. "Here, put this on." I didn't ask where he got it. Nathan and his seemingly endless bag of tricks and supplies were like Mary Poppins and her carpetbag.

I took the hood and put it over my head. Nathan made a few adjustments and suddenly I could breathe freely again.

"Come on," he said.

I hesitated as through the clear plastic of the hood, I locked eyes with the little boy lying on the cot. His expression was pleading with me to do something.

"I—"

I heard a loud crack and a small hole punctured the boy's forehead. His eyes glazed over even as his expression still begged me to save him.

"I'm sorry," I whispered, even though he could no longer hear me. A sob wrenched through me, and my eyes burned with unshed tears and residual smoke. I looked up and saw the soldier who'd fired the shot, walking slowly toward the little boy he'd just killed. He lifted his head, and even through the protective mask I could see horror and grief in his eyes. I wondered if he'd ever be able to come back from this night as a sane and functional human being.

I knew I'd never forget, and I wasn't the one who'd had to pull the trigger.

"Come on." Nathan grabbed my arm and pulled me toward the far door. With his other hand he hefted some fancy handgun from his personal armory. Part of me appreciated the fact that he didn't ask what I was doing there, or tell me to evacuate. He knew why I was there, because he was on the same mission—find Simone and get her to safety.

As we walked, he coolly shot at the oncoming zombies, each shot finding its way into the skull of a walking corpse. I followed, happy to have someone else take the lead about now. I unsheathed my katana, reasoning that I could clean up anything Nathan missed.

Not that Nathan missed much.

Charred, blackened corpses continued to stumble through the door as he and I reached it, dodging the last few fleeing civilians as we did so. The smell of burnt flesh mixed with decay, as if someone had tossed rotting meat onto a BBQ. Cooking didn't make zombies smell any better, and not even the chemical stench in the air could mask it.

Nathan capped the two lead zombies in their heads. They fell to the ground, creating a stumbling block for the ones behind them. I could see more through the gap in the door, at least half a dozen in the hallway beyond. I wondered how many had been in the lab when the fire broke out, and how many of those had managed to make their way up a level, much less any further.

"How the hell did they get out of the lab?" Nathan growled, echoing my line of thought. We didn't have time for speculation, though, as an extra crispy zombie pushed its way through the door. Nathan didn't waste a round on it, instead bashing in its Kentucky Fried head with the stock of his rifle.

I dodged past him into the hallway and decapitated another smoked ghoul, so charred that its original sex was unidentifiable. Several more trailed behind it, each one more burned than the last. Nathan and I dispatched them quickly, heading down the hallway toward a door on the left that should have been shut, but was now standing wide open.

What the fuck? I thought. *The door's been wedged open.* Sure enough, a small piece of metal kept it from swinging shut on its own.

Smoke poured out of the stairwell that led to the floor below. Flames were visible now, far below, moving up the stairs—along with more zombies, each one looking sorrier than the one before it. All I could think was that if the zombies were this badly damaged, could any humans have survived?

"We have to hurry," Nathan said, and he pushed past me, bashing another zombie's skull in with one thwack of his rifle stock. "If anyone's still alive down there, they don't have much time left."

I nodded, and the two of us transformed into whirlwinds of zombie destruction, making our way down the stairwell. I hoped Nathan had an access badge or the security code for the door that led into the lab. Otherwise we were shit out of luck.

The formerly sterile antechamber was filled with smoke, its white walls smeared with blood and bits of flesh. Several lab techs sprawled on the floor, their HAZMAT suits shredded along with their bodies.

A discarded fire extinguisher lay next to one of them. Nathan scooped it up just as that particular corpse started to stir. Without missing a beat, he smashed the tech in the head, but the force of the blow was cushioned by the HAZMAT hood.

Nathan jerked his head at me.

"Take care of this, would you?"

I stabbed down with my blade, using extra force to penetrate the hood and the zombie's skull. I did the same thing—preemptively—to the other fallen techs, knowing it was just a matter of time before they got back up, too.

Nathan, in the meantime, used the fire extinguisher on the flames that were licking at the edges of the wide-open double doors, also wedged open with hunks of metal. Someone wanted this fire to spread, which meant that someone had set it on purpose. *Great.* As if zombies weren't enough, we had a frickin' arsonist on the loose—and on the payroll.

Through the double doors it was a hell of flame and smoke. I could see several figures staggering around, whatever clothing they had long since burned off. The metal tables were all empty, the restraining straps no doubt burned into ash. Even through the smoke I could see that the holding pens in the back of the room were empty, their metal doors slung open.

Fire burned in places I wouldn't have thought could catch, like the metal tables and cement floor. It licked up the walls, reaching hungrily for the ceiling. The smell of melted plastic, chemicals, and what smelled like gasoline seeped through the mask's protective filter, and the heat from the fire was nearly unbearable.

We didn't have much time.

"Simone!" Even muffled by the mask, Nathan's voice rang out over the low roar of the flames.

Was it my imagination, or did someone answer? Even with my enhanced hearing, I couldn't be certain.

"Did you hear that?" I said.

Nathan shook his head.

"Not sure." He yelled Simone's name again, the word ending in a series of rattling coughs that sounded like they hurt. The masks weren't meant for this sort of exposure—they were designed to get someone to safety, and quickly.

Why isn't the sprinkler system kicking in?

I was ready to go back the way we came and get the hell out of there when I heard, very faintly, someone call for help, followed by a dull thumping on a hard surface.

"Someone's alive in there," I said.

But I needn't have bothered saying anything; Nathan had heard it, too, and was already spraying foam from the extinguisher to clear a path through the flames. I took the initiative and ran ahead, silently praying that we weren't collectively hallucinating.

Two flaming zombies staggered toward me, and even as I dispatched them with my katana, I found myself giggling. The phrase "flaming zombies" conjured some very politically incorrect images in my mind. I blamed the smoke inhalation and kept moving, honing in on a closed door to the left, in between the dissection tables and the holding pens. Melted paint bubbled on its surface.

A lone zombie clawed at the door, slowly sinking to the ground as the flames that engulfed it finally ate through its connective tissue. Nathan sprayed more foam, clearing a path for me to reach the door. I pistoned the heel of one foot into the foot of the zombie's skull, then kicked it out of the way.

Without bothering to do the "is it hot?" test, I just grabbed the handle.

Shit!

Yes, it was hot, and I'd have blisters. The door also didn't budge. I looked up and noticed a lock and hasp on it. The lock was engaged, and there was no key in sight.

"Nathan, it's locked!"

"Stand out of the way."

I did, and Nathan charged the door, hitting it dead center with his right shoulder. The wood shuddered, but didn't give way.

"My turn," I said, then sent my right heel into the door with a side kick. Nathan followed up with a kick of his own.

The wood began to give way.

We kept kicking until we'd cleared a hole large enough to reveal a fairly roomy supply closet. Lying on the floor, with a cloth pressed over her face was Simone, coughs wracking her body as more smoke poured into the space. Her white lab coat was spattered with gore, blood oozing from what looked like a bullet hole in her right arm.

Nathan immediately pushed past me, impatiently yanking large chunks of wood out of his way, clearing enough space for us to get inside. He dumped his duffel bag on the floor and extracted another evac hood. Pulling the cloth out of Simone's hands, he started to tug the hood over her head, but she resisted, pulling it away as another coughing fit wracked her body.

Nathan held her until it passed, then spoke to her.

"Simone, can you hear me?"

She nodded weakly.

"You have to put this on," he said. "There's too much smoke and shit in the air here for us to get you out without it."

"These…" Simone pulled a blue bag from behind her, one of those soft insulated coolers. What sounded like bits of glass were clinking together inside of it. "Take—"

"I have it." Nathan took the bag from her and set it off to one side. "Now put this on." Simone reached for the mask, trying to help pull it on with fingers unable to complete the motion. Her eyes rolled up in her head.

"Shit," he said. "Help me, Ash."

"What about that?" I nodded at the wound on her arm.

"It'll wait. We have to get her out of here before she asphyxiates."

I held Simone steady as Nathan pulled the evac hood over her head as gently as possible. I snuck a quick look at his expression. If ever a man's feelings for a woman were evident, it was at that moment.

Blazing heat beat against my back as ribbons of flame dripped from the ceiling, which in turn started to melt like wax from a candle. The walls may have been cement, but the ceiling was made of acoustical tiles, probably with a crawl space up above. I saw sprinkler heads up there. Why the hell didn't they activate?

Another chunk of tile fell onto the floor, hitting a patch of liquid that immediately flared into a wall of fire in between two metal tables and the path leading out of the lab.

"Nathan…"

"Here." He shoved the fire extinguisher at me, hoisting a now unconscious Simone in the classic fireman's carry, duffle bag once more slung over his shoulder. "Clear us a path."

Sweat poured down my face under my mask as I shoved my katana into its sheath so I could handle the extinguisher and pointed the nozzle at the base of the flames. Squeezing the lever, I swept the nozzle from side to side… but nothing came out. The damn thing was empty.

We are so screwed.

As if to emphasize how screwed we were, another section of ceiling plummeted to the ground near the exit, connecting with another wide ribbon of flame and creating a nice little ring of fire. I consciously willed Johnny Cash to get the hell out of my brain as it wilted from the heat. The double doors to the antechamber were now completely blocked, the air shimmering like a desert mirage.

"Can we make it?" I looked at Nathan, who didn't appear to feel the weight that was draped over his shoulders. My eyes and lungs burned, even with the protection. If we didn't get Simone out of here immediately, she would die.

"We have to try."

"Wait." I dashed into the closet and grabbed a couple bottles of water. The plastic was tacky to the touch. Unscrewing the lids, I dumped the contents over him and Simone.

"Let's go," I said, tossing the bottles aside.

Nathan sprinted into the flames, vanishing through them into the antechamber. I heard the thud of his footsteps on the metal stairs. They'd make it.

Good.

I started after them, then noticed the bag Simone had pushed at us, still sitting on the floor. If it was important enough for her to protect, I'd bring it out. Slinging it over my shoulder, I took a couple of steps, only to have a blast of heat send me scuttling back into the closet for momentary refuge. I needed another bottle of water to give me some degree of protection. I grabbed for one, but my fingers sunk into the plastic, the water pouring out and evaporating onto the floor.

I scanned the room, trying to breathe through the increasing smoke and heat. The evac hood had pretty much done its job—and then some—but I couldn't expect it to do any more.

Another section of ceiling tile, larger than any before, fell right in front of the exit. Fire and smoke billowed up, obscuring the rest of the room. I laughed, and then started coughing, then choking as my fire-evac hood gave up the ghost and started letting the toxins in.

The coughing continued, leading into full on hacking as I tried to bring up the crap that was infiltrating my system before it could kill me. But the shit poured in faster than I could void it.

Sorry, Lil, I thought, remembering the promise I'd made to her.

My head throbbed as I slumped to the floor. I closed my eyes.

Damn. I really hadn't expected to die today.

SAN FRANCISCO

Tiffany made her way carefully out of the ladies' room at the Royal Bank, trying to ignore the fact that each step on her Steve Madden heels felt like she was navigating a tightrope. She'd only had three… or maybe four gin and tonics. Hard to keep track during happy hour.

Hell, who wants to keep track during happy hour, right? *Especially with a hot date like Geo.*

Tiffany stifled a laugh. Okay, that had to be a fake name, 'cause who would, like, name their kid after a car, right? At least they hadn't named him Mini. That thought set her giggling again as she rounded the corner to the stairs that led back up to the restaurant.

Fucking stairs. *There should be a law against having the restrooms up or down stairs from the bar. It was a liability issue, a lawsuit waiting to happen—booze and stairs, especially when combined with high heels. Seriously, like, how many women her age going out on hot dates were going to wear flats, right?*

Someday she'd be able to afford Jimmy Choos and Manolo Blahniks. Full price, no more remnant sales. Until then, eBay and the less expensive designers were a girl's best friend.

As she wobbled her way up the wooden stairs, Tiffany thought she heard… was that screaming? Usually Tuesday nights in the Financial District weren't that rowdy, even during happy hour.

She neared the top of the stairs and almost ran right into an attractive brunette, with two men right behind her. One of them was one of the waiters, a real hottie. Tiffany had flirted with him during many a happy hour. He'd always been friendly, but disinterested. Now he couldn't follow this other woman fast enough.

What the hell did a brunette have that she didn't? Tiffany glanced down and sneered. The other woman was wearing flat-heeled boots with her black skirt and red sweater. Heels would have made the outfit.

"Turn around and go back down."

It took a few seconds for her to realize the woman was speaking to her.

"Huh?" Tiffany said. "My date's waiting for me."

"Don't go in there—it's not worth it," the woman snapped. "You don't want to see—"

Ri-ight… Tiffany shook her head, making herself a little dizzy, and shoved past the trio. Going back into the restaurant, she left them to run down the stairwell and disappear from sight.

"Whatever." If they want to get all kinky, that's their problem.

She tottered her way toward the front of the restaurant, where Geo waited for her at her table. Some sort of ruckus was happening at the bar, a fight maybe. She heard shouts and swearing in Irish accents. Definitely a bar brawl.

What the fuck?

As Tiffany neared the table, she saw another sitting woman on the bench seat next to Geo, looking like she was giving him the King Kong of hickeys.

Oh, bring it on, bitch.

She didn't stop to think—just marched over to the table, grabbed the woman by the shoulder and snarled at them.

"What the fuck? I'm gone for five minutes and you think you can just—"

The woman turned around, chunks of red meat falling from her gaping mouth. Her eyes looked blind or something, yellowed whites shot through with veins of blood, the corneas milky white and just wrong.

For a heartbeat, Tiffany wondered if Geo had spiked her

G&Ts. This has gotta be a hallucination. Then the nightmare bitch who'd stolen her seat grabbed her wrist and bit into it, and the agonizing pain convinced her it was all too real.

CHAPTER FIFTEEN

Something wet and cool dripped onto my arm.

First just a few drops, and then a steady stream.

My head throbbed as I forced my eyelids open to see water pouring down from a sprinkler head right above me.

I sat up, pushing the nausea and pain back so I could pick myself up off the supply closet floor. Bleary-eyed, I looked across the lab and saw a path to the doors, water pouring down from a few operating sprinkler heads around the room. Flames still licked across the floor and walls, but the water held them back from taking over the entire lab, and even extinguished the fire in spots.

Okay. Time to go.

I staggered out of the closet and into the room, still carrying Simone's precious bag and breathing as shallowly as possible. I tried to stay under the working sprinklers until I made it past the antechamber, back into the stairwell leading up to the med ward.

The smoke was still thick and toxic when I hit the stairs and with every step it felt like I was weighed down with lead. My eyes watered from the acrid fumes, making it almost impossible to see. Even with the protective hood, each breath seared my lungs as I pulled myself up the stairs by the railing, vaguely aware that the heated metal was crisping my hand. I did my best to ignore the corpses that Nathan and I had dispatched, and which now were draped on the stairs.

Crunch.

Ugh. Kind of hard to ignore it when you step into the middle of a flash-fried rotted corpse.

Just when you think things couldn't get any grosser.

Fuckin' zombies.

Why couldn't it have been an outbreak of, say, bunnies or French bulldogs? Then we'd just have to deal with lots of inoffensive pellets, or drool.

"Zombies… zombies, it must be zombie-e-ees," I sang softly and off-key, as I neared the landing.

More water poured down onto my head, as if I had my own little rainstorm following me wherever I went. Sort of like Pig Pen and his perpetual cloud of dirt.

Oh god, I need oxygen…

When I reached the top of the stairs, I quickly retraced my steps down the hallway and back to the med ward. Most of the fire damage had been sustained at the far end, where the smoldering zombies had staggered through the door. As they'd collapsed onto the nearest cots, the flames had ignited the bedding and created more charred corpses… ones with bullet holes in their heads.

It was just wrong.

Even more wrong was the merrily burning fire and thick cloud of smoke that now danced through the med ward. I was just too damn tired to fight my way through another gauntlet of flame and smoke, so I headed down the hallway away from it. Smoke had spread down this way, but the flames hadn't, making it a friendlier option even if I had no clue where it went.

It had to go somewhere, right? I mean, who would build a hallway that dead-ended? Well, aside from Jigsaw or some other psycho killer.

Luckily for me the hallway led to a door with a nice big green exit sign above it. That led to another staircase, one that deposited me on the ground floor of Patterson

Hall, outside at the rear of the building. Stumbling past a few startled looking people, I fell to my knees on the grass next to the sidewalk. Dropping Simone's bag to the accompaniment of the sound of bits of glass clinking together, I ripped the hood off and coughed up no end of black gunk, with deep wracking coughs that felt like my internal organs were passing through my throat.

"Ashley?"

A familiar voice said my name, and hands fell on my hunched shoulders, firmly patting my back until the coughing spasm had passed.

"Here, have some water."

A plastic water bottle touched my lips, and I gratefully took a swallow, rinsing out my mouth—which tasted like the granddaddy of all ashtrays. I spit before taking another mouthful and swallowing. The cool water hurt going down, but it also tasted like smoky ambrosia.

"How are you feeling, Ashley?"

I looked up to find none other than Dr. Albert peering down at me with what looked like genuine concern on his rodent-like face.

"I'm just swell," I said, then started giggling again, the smoke inhalation and near-death experience making me giddy.

"Yes, have some more water." The doctor held the water bottle up again. "Your enhanced metabolism should kick out the effects of the smoke very quickly."

Oh, goody. I shut my eyes as the world spun around me.

"Dizzy," I muttered, and my eyelids felt like lead, coated with concrete.

"Just sit still for a few minutes and—what?"

The "what"—uttered on a rising note—was followed by a dull thump. The sound of flesh hitting flesh.

I forced my eyes open in time to see two male figures dressed in black, their faces covered with dark balaclava masks, dragging Dr. Albert's prone body off into the darkness. I heard another one just in time to stop him from smacking my head with what looked like a policeman's baton.

Fuck you, I thought, and grabbed the asshole's forearm as he brought the baton down toward my unprotected noggin. Lurching to my feet, I reversed the path of the baton, so that it landed on my attacker's head with a solid *thunk* on his skull.

He collapsed bonelessly to the ground.

I grabbed the baton and staggered after the two assailants who were dragging Dr. Albert off toward a dark-colored van parked in between Patterson Hall and the adjacent building. I heard the sound of an engine revving, and did my best to hurry up my pace, trying to ignore my pounding head and lurching stomach.

A sliding door opened on the passenger side of the van and someone inside reached out to help drag the doctor into the vehicle. I threw myself forward, smashing one of his abductors on the head with the leading end of the baton, then whipping it around to clock the other man solidly on the chin with the butt end.

The guy in the van gave a shout of surprise, letting go of Dr. Albert and grabbing for a gun on the floor. I kicked out as hard as I could, knocking the firearm out of his grasp, sending it spinning onto the ground just as Dr. Albert collapsed onto the concrete sidewalk, oblivious to the battle being fought over his prone body.

Another totally inconvenient coughing fit wracked my body, doubling me over as the man in the van stumbled out. He swung a fist, catching me with a glancing blow to my chin, followed by another blow to the back of my head. That one sent me down to the ground again, still coughing.

Fuck you, I thought again, exhaustion making me repetitive. I lashed out with a roundhouse kick as the man reached for the fallen firearm, catching him squarely in the back of the knees, sending him sprawling to the ground on top of Dr. Albert's unconscious body. I waited until he tried to stand up, then thrust one heel into his head in a fairly lazy yet effective side kick, knocking him out.

One of the would-be kidnappers I'd thumped with the baton leapt into the van as the motor roared. It surged forward, careening into a bush before slamming into reverse, the right back tire running over the guy I'd put down with my side kick. I grabbed Dr. Albert's limp body and yanked him clear as the van accelerated forward, then careened back again.

This time right in my direction.

I threw us both into the bushes, pulling Dr. Albert underneath the low hanging branches and off to the side. The van barely missed us, its rear bumper smashing through the bushes right next to us and into the brick wall of the building behind. The driver once again accelerated, the van's tires squealing as it shot forward, veered to the left, and took off down the narrow path.

Guess whoever was driving decided it was better to get the hell out. Fine by me—I was pretty much done for the evening.

As I sunk back to the ground, I heard footsteps pounding in my direction, voices shouting. My head pounded, sinuses totally clogged. I would have killed for a Neti pot about now.

CHAPTER SIXTEEN

"Ashley?"

I opened my eyes and looked up to see Mack hovering over me. Good. If Mack was there, I knew I could rest.

"You okay, hon?"

I nodded.

"Yup. But make sure these assholes don't go anywhere." I gave a general wave I hoped was in the right direction.

"It's okay," Mack said in that soothing storyteller voice of his. "They're not going anywhere."

"Good," I said. "Then they can tell us what the hell is going on."

"Well, no, they can't." Mack helped me back to my feet, supporting me as I swayed back and forth unsteadily. "One's dead, and the other doesn't look like he'll be waking up any time soon."

"Dead?"

"Yup."

"Did I do it?" I didn't think I'd hit *that* hard. Not that I was sorry.

"Only if you were driving whatever ran over his face."

Euwww.

"Ashley!"

Lil came barreling around the corner of Patterson Hall, with Gentry and Gabriel close behind. Gabriel's face looked garishly white beneath a coating of soot. Lil reached me first, the impact of her hug nearly knocking me back to the ground. She hung onto me with the strength of a very determined limpet.

"You're okay," she said, her tone fierce, almost angry.

"Told you I would be, didn't I?" I gave her a feeble hug back.

Gabriel put an arm around me.

"You alright, Ash?"

"I got the black lung, Pop." I gave a weak but genuine cough.

Gentry snorted, even as he was helping Dr. Albert to his feet. I gave him a weak smile, wishing Kai and Tony were there to share the *Zoolander* moment. The grin slid from my face as I remembered that Kai would never share another quote.

"Those men!" The doctor had regained consciousness, and was struggling to sit up. "They were trying to kidnap me!"

"They would have gotten away with it, if not for us darn kids." I started giggling again, which led to another coughing fit. Gabriel offered me a bottle of water, keeping a firm arm around my shoulders. I leaned against him and sipped from the plastic bottle.

"Why would anyone want to kidnap *you*?" Lil looked at Dr. Albert as if he were a particularly stinky turd.

"Probably for the same reason they set fire to the lab, and tried to kill Simone." We all looked up to see Nathan striding toward us, face and clothes coated with soot. Damn, but that man had a knack for dramatic entrances.

"They—" Dr. Albert swallowed hard. "Someone tried to kill Professor Fraser?"

Nathan looked at him impassively.

"They shot her then locked her in a closet to burn to death," he said. "If that qualifies as attempted homicide, then yes."

"Is she okay?" I managed to get out three words

without coughing again. *Yay for me.*

"She's a wild card." Nathan patted me on the shoulder. "The bullet wound will heal, and she'll have a sore throat for a day or so—like you and me—but she'll be fine."

"That's good news." Dr. Albert's tone sounded strained. "Did she say anything? See who did it?" I looked at him and his gaze skittered away from mine. If he wasn't hiding something, he was doing a good job of disguising his lack of guilt.

Something in Nathan's expression told me he wasn't entirely convinced of Dr. Albert's sincerity either, but he chose to answer the question anyway.

"Yeah. About a half-dozen guys in fire-retardant gear stormed the lab, killed everyone they could. Simone was shot, but made it to the supply closet. They rigged the exits so that even if she got out, the fire would take care of her. Then they either destroyed or stole all of the vaccine supplies, tissue samples, and data that has been assembled to date.

"With Simone dead and the doctor MIA, our chances of stopping the plague would be crippled."

"But why would anyone do that?" Lil asked, the look on her face genuinely confused.

Nathan's expression softened when he looked at her.

"I'm going to take a wild guess that they want what Simone and the good doctor have been working on and don't want anyone else to have it," he said. "It would take months—maybe years—for us to catch up again. Even with backup, we'd have lost everything that was in their heads."

"'So who did this?" I had to ask.

Nathan walked over to one of the sprawled bodies and pulled off the balaclava that covered the head and face to reveal a young man.

"Recognize him?"

It's Old Man Johnson, I thought, and giggled quietly.

"That's Rollins." Gentry stared down at the body. "He joined the Zed Tactical Squad last month. I trained him."

"So it was an inside job," Mack said.

Lil narrowed her eyes and glared at Dr. Albert.

"Maybe you planned it," she said.

"M-m-me?" Dr. Albert stuttered with outrage, either real or well contrived. "Why would I destroy my own work?"

I thought about it, then answered for her.

"Maybe to hide your major-league fuck-up of setting loose the zombie bug in the first place? Seems like decent motivation to me."

"Ridiculous!" Dr. Albert snapped. "All of my notes, all of my research…" He swallowed hard, his voice bleak as he continued, "I would never destroy it. It's my life's work."

Strangely enough, I believed him, simply because his ego was so huge that I couldn't imagine him allowing his work to be burned. But then, on the other hand, if the information and samples had been stolen, secreted away to another location…

"But it wasn't all destroyed, right?" My voice was hard as I left the shelter of Gabriel's arm and walked over until I was face-to-face with my childhood doctor. More or less, considering I was at least six inches taller.

"So who's to say the whole kidnapping scenario wasn't faked to spirit you out of here, so you could work on, say, a new improved super-zombie bug somewhere else?"

Dr. Albert looked at me with what I could swear was genuine hurt.

"Ashley Parker, I've been your doctor since you were an infant," he said, his voice faltering. "How you could believe I'd do something so heinous—"

"Um… Walker's vaccine without any real testing?" I stared at him, refusing to feel guilty for his tender feelings.

"Fine!" His face reddened as hurt evaporated in a wave of self-righteous indignation. "Yes, I knew the results of the tests for Walker's vaccine were falsified, and I did it to speed up distribution, but only in select, controlled environments, and only because Walker's had the potential to cause a pandemic that would surpass the Spanish Flu as a global disaster."

"I guess it's a good thing we only have the walking dead to worry about now," I shot back.

"Yes, we do, and I am committed to finding a cure!" He looked around at all of us, not finding a sympathetic face among the group. "You must believe me!"

He was genuinely distressed—even frightened, that much was certain. But I couldn't shake the feeling he knew or suspected more about the fire than he was letting on.

"Everything is gone?" I could tell Gabriel was working hard to keep his voice carefully neutral.

Nathan nodded.

"Yeah," he said. "They were thorough."

Gabriel stood frozen in place, and it was as if he'd stared into the face of Medusa. I hurried back to his side.

"Gabriel, what—"

Then it hit me.

His antidote. The magic potion that kept him stable. He looked at me, naked despair breaking through his carefully guarded expression.

"Ash, without the antiserum…" His voice trailed off. We both knew what would happen without it, and so did everyone else in the immediate vicinity.

"Can you make more?" I rounded on Dr. Albert, jarring him from his own little world of self pity. He blinked, looking like a cross between a startled owl and a confused rodent.

"More of the Walker's vaccine?"

I wanted to smack him across the head for being so obtuse.

"More of the antiserum that's keeping Gabriel human."

"With the proper ingredients and equipment, of course." He sounded indignant that I'd even had to ask. The man went from defensive to arrogant with amazing rapidity. "Although without my notes, or a sample of the serum, it will require time."

"How *much* time?"

"A week, maybe two. I don't know, precisely."

I looked at Gabriel again. His expression made it clear that he didn't have that much time.

I shook my head in denial.

"There's got to be *something* you can do, right?" I glared at Dr. Albert, the urge to whack him a good one increasing by the minute. "You made the stuff, you can make more."

"It's not that simple," Dr. Albert snapped back impatiently. "If I had a sample of the antiserum, it would cut the time down substantially, but I'd still need the proper equipment, and supplies to synthesize more. Those no longer exist on this campus!"

Frustrated, I stomped away from him and nearly tripped over the insulated tote I'd rescued from the lab, my right foot catching in the strap. I stumbled, but kept my balance even as my forward momentum dragged the tote forward about a foot.

Glass clinked inside of it.

My anger was suddenly replaced with a flare of wild hope. Hardly daring to breathe, I pulled my foot away from the strap, dropped to my knees, and unzipped the top of the bag with trembling fingers. Jumbled inside were maybe a few dozen little liquid-filled glass vials, sealed with colored metal caps. Broken bits of glass testified that there'd been more of them before my mad dash out of the lab.

Instantly Nathan covered the ground between us. Gabriel was just a step behind.

"Is that the bag Simone had with her?" Nathan demanded.

I nodded mutely, my throat constricted by an overwhelming combination of hope and fear as I handed him one of the vials. I looked over to see the same emotions mirrored on Gabriel's face. I wanted to give him a reassuring smile, but couldn't make my facial muscles cooperate. I was too damned scared.

"Dr. Albert, would you please take a look at this and tell us what it is?" Nathan said.

Coming out of his self-centered fog, Dr. Albert approached somewhat cautiously, as if expecting me to bite him or something, but as soon as he saw what Nathan held, he had eyes for nothing but the vial.

"Did this come from the lab?" he asked as Nathan dropped the vial into the doctor's outstretched hand.

"It did."

"Are there more?"

Nathan pointed at the bag, and Dr. Albert's eyes lit up.

"Marvelous!" he said. "Simply marvelous!"

I couldn't take it any more.

"Is it Gabriel's antiserum?" I said.

"No, no, it's a sample of the last version of the cure we synthesized. This is a real stroke of luck!"

My hope plummeted faster and harder than Wile E. Coyote falling off a cliff.

"Are you sure?"

"This one has a red cap, see?" He held up the vial to show me. "Gabriel's serum has blue caps."

I scrabbled in the bag and pulled out one of the vials with a blue lid. "Like this?"

"Oh, yes. That's right." Dr. Albert smiled. "Blue lid."

I let a Matrix joke go unsaid as I shut my eyes for a brief second, clutching the vial tightly in my hand.

"So now you need…"

"A laboratory with the proper equipment," he replied,

"and ingredients to make more."

"Is there anything suitable nearby?"

"Professor Fraser would have a better idea of location than I would," he said, "but I expect there's something within a few hundred miles, yes." He reached for the insulated tote, but I was faster and snatched it up. I wanted to personally make sure it was delivered to Simone.

Not that I didn't trust Dr. Albert or anything.

Oh, wait, I *didn't* trust him. *Silly me.*

I stood up and handed the bag to Nathan.

"Can you make sure this gets to Simone?"

"I can take it to her," Dr. Albert huffed.

"No need," Nathan said, throwing the strap over his shoulder.

"But I'd like to see exactly what's in there," Dr. Albert responded. "It *is* my work, after all!"

Nathan raised an eyebrow.

"I thought you and Simone were working on this stuff together."

"Well, yes, technically, but it's still based on *my* original work."

I'm sure your mother would be very proud, I thought, and gave the doctor a false smile.

"Well, she trusted Nathan and me to get it safely out of the lab, and I'd personally feel better if one of us handed it back to her." I turned. "Right, Nathan?"

"Absolutely."

Dr. Albert sputtered indignantly, but even his ego wasn't strong enough to go face-to-face with Nathan.

I went to Gabriel, who still seemed to be in a state of paralysis. Taking one of his hands, I pressed the vial against his palm.

"There are at least a dozen of these in that bag, maybe more," I said softly. "How much time does that buy us?" I used "us" deliberately, looking him in the eye and silently daring him to contradict me.

He held onto the vial for a few seconds, as if he had to convince himself it was real. Then he swallowed, gave a long exhale and answered.

"I'm up to two a day." He paused. "I can do one, if I have to, but it's not optimal."

"So two a day, if we want you bearable, and one if we don't mind dealing with you in jerk mode."

Gabriel gave a short laugh.

"Something like that."

"Then we have around a week to find what we need." I nodded to myself. "We can totally do this."

"You don't give up, do you?"

I shrugged.

"What's the point? You wouldn't let me give up when the swarm had us surrounded, and here we are, still alive. Besides—" I grinned up at him "—you know I'll still like you, even if you aren't vegan, right?"

He laughed again, this time more genuinely, then drew me to him in a hug as fierce as Lil's had been. I clung to him as sirens sounded in the distance, growing closer by the moment.

GRAND LEDGE, MICHIGAN

"Shit."

Gage stared fixedly towards the northeast side of the Grand Ledge Railroad Bridge, trying to penetrate the gloom. The November skies had been gray with the threat of rain, even before the sun started to fade. Now shadows merged together, making it impossible to tell how many figures lurked on the tracks.

"Why won't they go away?" Stacy's voice rose in a shrill pitch that matched the whistling of the wind above the Grand River.

"Shh!" Gage held up a hand, dropping his voice to a whisper. "They're there... but so far they don't seem too

interested. Chris, what about the other side?

"They're still there." Chris's voice was hoarse from coughing, his mild cold of the past two days now settled deep into his chest. "And they definitely are interested." He fell silent, then added, "We are so fucked."

The three of them had been at the theater's fundraising dinner. Chris and Stacy, both bit players at the Spotlight Theater, were currying favor with the management by filling in as wait-staff while Gage, who currently had a sweet fight choreography gig, fulfilled his duty by looking dashing in full-on cavalier costume and flirting with the wealthy patrons.

Gage also had been flirting outrageously with Stacy as she served "ale and foin wine, good sair" at the big oak bar. She looked hot in her peasant wench get-up, with one of those vest thingees that made her boobs pop up on display. Chris, on the other hand—in obligatory doublet, tights, puffy shirt and breeches, while carting around platters of roast chicken and prime rib—had flirted pretty heavily with Gage.

Gage didn't mind. He was an equal opportunity horndog.

When the initial attack occurred, people thought it was part of the entertainment. Gage had recognized some of them as fellow actors, others as patrons of the Spotlight Theater and residents of Grand Ledge. He knew a lot of them, and assumed they wouldn't hurt anyone. He truly believed that until the moment the theater's resident leading lady and diva bitch tore a chunk out of her leading man.

Things had gone to shit after that—a total chaos of screams, ripping flesh, and blood.

Somehow Gage had ended up behind the old barn that housed the theater. He was there with Chris and Stacy, the three of them hiding from the carnage taking place a few hundred yards away, blocking their escape route to the parking lot. Gage had grabbed a spare awning pole and Chris had done the same, while Stacy had bundled up a table's worth of food and drink in one of the damask tablecloths. Whatever the impulse that inspired her to do so, it at least partially made up for her whining.

Moving as quietly as they could, they'd ended up on the abandoned railroad bridge halfway over the river, thinking that if they crossed it, the other side would somehow be miraculously free of carnage. Their hopes had been dashed, however, when they'd reached the halfway point, only to see a slender figure stumbling onto the trestle from the northeast side. What looked like a teenage boy was pulled back by a half dozen or so shambling freaks. They ripped him to pieces, devouring him in front of their eyes.

They were thankful for the darkness, which hid the details.

When they'd turned to retrace their steps to the southwest side, a cluster of ghouls from the Spotlight Theater stood there waiting for them. At least a dozen had followed the three in their flight along the riverside path.

If the dead had been more agile, they'd have been fucked right from the start. But the first few that tried to cross didn't have the coordination to navigate the railroad ties and fell partway through, legs dangling through the gaps, unable to go any further. Beyond that point, many of the ties were missing altogether, and their ghoulish pursuers were completely incapable of balancing on the narrow rails.

That didn't stop the zombies from trying to reach their potential meal, however. Some fell into the river sixty feet below, and were carried off by the current. A couple even managed to make it past their trapped compatriots, to shamble and crawl toward the trio.

Gage and Chris used the awning supports to shove them off the side. It wasn't hard to do, but there seemed to be a never-ending stream of them on either side of the river, all wanting to try their luck. There were too many clustered together for the three of them to try and make a break for it. Gage considered climbing down the trestle and dropping into the river, but this time of year the water level was only about four feet deep and the likelihood was too great that he would break a leg or an arm on the rocky riverbed.

So they stayed on the bridge, hoping the things would go in search of easier prey.

They didn't.

Periodically some of the creatures would wander off, distracted by something in the darkness. But they were replaced by others, and the way to safety was never entirely clear.

Sleep was impossible except in short shifts. After nearly forty-five hours, the three were exhausted and in real danger of hypothermia. Gage knew they wouldn't last another night.

They'd run out of the fruit, cheese, and crackers Stacy had scavenged. They used the threadbare tablecloth to cover their bodies in an attempt to stave off the deadly effects of the cold fall weather. There were still two bottles left of Three Buck Chuck Syrah, but the water was gone, so dehydration was a real danger.

It was mightily tempting to just drink the wine, get shit-faced, and forget about the flesh-eating ghouls.

Stacy shivered again. The peasant blouse, bodice, and full skirt were made of cheap cotton and gauze, and not nearly warm enough. She'd wrapped the extra material from the skirt around her shoulders, but that left her legs susceptible to the icy drafts coming off the river below.

"Mom told me to wear my thermal underwear, you know," she said as the sun started to go down, and the wind kicked up even more. *"I swear, I'd give up all of my Victoria's Secret G-strings for my long johns right now."* Her teeth started chattering.

Gage grinned at her.

"Keep talking about your G-strings," he said. *"That'll keep me warm. Won't do much for poor Chris there, though. Chris, you want me to talk about my Calvin Kleins?"*

"At this point, I think I'd get more excited over a bag of apple cider donuts and hot coffee from the Dairy Mart." Chris broke into a coughing fit that sounded as if it was ripping his chest apart. The sound carried across the river to either side of the bridge and moans filled the air, blending with the wind.

"Christ, that hurts." He thumped his chest, face flushed with the heat of fever.

"Not as much as it'll hurt if those things get a hold of you." Gage pointed as yet more creatures began moving across the bridge from the northeast.

"Fuck." Chris shifted into position, pole held at the ready. His arms trembled with the effort. "I don't know how much longer I can do this."

Stacy began to sob, the sound exhausted and hopeless.

"Me, either." Gage turned as more moans sounded from the southwest. He decided that, if they survived the night, he would risk the drop into the river. A cider donut sounded really good about now.

CHAPTER SEVENTEEN

The sirens heralded fire trucks from Santa Rosa, about an hour or so south of us. They'd been passed through the quarantine barricades, and DZN and ZTS personnel were on hand as the firefighters put out the flames. Then our guys moved in immediately to remove all traces of bodies—zombies and human alike—before they could be too closely examined.

Nevertheless, some of the firefighters likely spotted more than they should have. I'd have bet a month's pay they were under some sort of über-secret federal gag order to prevent them from talking about what horrors they might have seen. And I knew firsthand the kind of nightmares they'd be having.

The laboratory was totally destroyed. The med ward, while not as badly devastated, had suffered major smoke damage. The rest of Patterson Hall, while relatively unscathed on the upper floors, stunk of smoke and chemical residue. So we had to move.

We'd need living quarters, a mess hall, and lab facilities. None of the other academic buildings were equipped with all that shit in one building, so everyone was moved to the nearest on-campus dormitory, one of the buildings we'd cleared out when the swarm had hit.

All potential sources of infection—blood-soaked linens and clothing, body parts, and so on—had been incinerated along with the corpses, both dead and undead. The walls and furnishings were scrubbed with disinfectant, so the pungent aroma of bleach still hung in the air of the second-story room Lil and I commandeered. In fact, it was a bit of a relief when Binkey and Doodle put their own distinctive olfactory marks on it.

The dorm had its own kitchen, so supplies scavenged from Patterson Hall could be stored and refrigerated. A lot of the foodstuffs were still kept in the student union, so we weren't in danger of running out of food or drink any time soon, with or without provisions brought in from outside the quarantine zone. We even had medical supplies, thanks to quick-thinking personnel and their evacuation of the med ward.

What were missing were any patients or test subjects. They had been incinerated, along with whatever bits and pieces of zombies and other corpses were left after the fire. We'd also lost half a dozen innocent people, most of them lab techs unfortunate enough to be working late hours the night of the assault. It was sheer luck that we hadn't lost Simone. Or Jamie, for that matter, who'd left the lab to get some sleep an hour before the fire was set.

I found this out from Simone herself when I went to visit her first thing the next morning.

"There are fifteen doses of Gabriel's vaccine in the bag," Simone said, looking elegant as ever despite the bandage covering her upper torso, and the fact she was wearing a hospital gown. We were in the new and distinctly unimproved med ward, set up in the common room of the dorm building. Her hair hung unaccustomedly loose past her shoulders, and she wore minimal makeup, but somehow still managed to convey the same cool composure she always had.

"So we have about a week to do this, right?" I said, sitting in a chair by Simone's bedside. Jamie was perched in a chair on the other side of the bed.

"You might have a few days more," she replied, taking

a sip from a mug of hot tea and grimacing. "I don't know why Dr. Albert insists on giving me tea instead of coffee. I don't really like tea." She eyed the mug with distaste. "Herbal, no less."

"Would you like me to get you something stronger?" Jamie jumped to her feet.

"That would be lovely." Simone smiled up at her assistant, the kind of smile that could move mountains. She was always so composed that the sudden sincere smile was as unexpected as the sun coming out after a week-long storm. Jamie was up and out of the room in seconds. I tried to hide my own smile.

"Finally." Simone heaved a contented sigh. "That girl is convinced that I won't heal unless she's by my side for every step of the process."

"She's, ah... very devoted," I said diplomatically. I wondered if Simone had any idea just how devoted Jamie really was, but now wasn't the time or place to ask. "So you were saying…"

"Erm, yes. Ideally Gabriel should have one dose of vaccine in the morning, and one at night. He can get by on one per day, but we'll see a definite deterioration in his impulse control, cognitive ability, and judgment."

"In other words, 'roid rage." I said.

"An accurate description." Simone took another grudging sip of tea, looking as dissatisfied as she had with the first.

"Dr. Albert said you'd know where the closest lab facility would be," I noted.

"That would be UCSF in San Francisco. There's also a smaller one in Arcata, but we received word that Humboldt County was severely compromised within the last twenty-four hours, and they're having trouble holding the quarantine. Besides, it's not nearly as well equipped as I'd like."

I had to ask.

"I'm not surprised that UCSF is better equipped than

Arcata, but… why were you here at Big Red? I mean, why not set up the main DZN shop in a bigger facility, in the first place?"

She gave me a wan smile.

"Because if things go badly south with our research, it's better to have it happen in a controlled environment with a relatively small population. We use the larger, more centrally located facilities for research with a lower risk potential."

"How many of these facilities *are* there?"

Simone looked at her teacup, as if reading the future in the bottom.

"A minimum of one in every state," she admitted. "At least there were."

"And the rest of the world?"

"Depending on size, geography, and cooperation of the government in question, there's at least one per country."

I was silent for a moment, taking in just how fucking global the DZN was.

Kind of like the Scientologists.

Aloud I asked, "Are all the locations where the vaccine was sent places where the DZN has facilities?"

"No." Simone looked pensive. "Not all of them, but enough to convince me it's not coincidence. But other towns chosen to receive the vaccine seem to have been picked at random. Whoever chose the locations to test the Walker's vaccine…" She stopped, looking distinctly troubled. "Well, they were either very short-sighted, or have an agenda I can't even begin to fathom."

Something about her tone told me she had indeed started to fathom it, but didn't want to discuss the matter. Fine with me. I was more interested in the immediate problem of keeping Gabriel human. That would also keep me distracted from the fact my parents were in Lake County, less than two hundred miles from Humboldt.

At least the mountains acted as a natural barrier.

"So we're looking at a trip over the Golden Gate Bridge," I said.

"Colonel Paxton and I believe it's the best option at this point, yes," Simone agreed.

"Then we should get going, right?"

Simone looked up at me.

"I realize you have a personal stake in this, Ashley."

"I—"

She held up a hand, and I fell silent.

"You don't have to justify yourself to me or to anyone else. Just be aware that you may have to make choices down the road that will be made much more difficult by your relationship with Gabriel." She looked down again at her teacup. "Trust me when I say I know of that of which I speak."

"You still have the hots for Nathan, don't you?"

"I don't—" she began. "That is…"

I just looked at her, not even bothering to raise an eyebrow. Didn't need to.

"Is it that obvious?" she asked.

I couldn't help it—I laughed.

"Jeez, Simone, you guys are like something out of—" the first thought that occurred to me was Ron and Hermione in Harry Potter, but I thought better of it and said "—out of a Katherine Hepburn and Spencer Tracy flick."

"Bless you for using that comparison, and not something like *Twilight*…" Simone gulped down the rest of her tea, cheeks flushed with what I could only assume was embarrassment. "But yes, you are correct in your assumption. And because of that attachment, I don't always trust my instincts. The urge to protect can override common sense and the ability to make the best decisions for everyone involved. The big picture gets lost amidst the personal details. And in this case, the big picture is all we dare consider," she added. "While other labs possess backup files based on our research, I don't believe there is anyone else who is as close to an answer as Dr. Albert… and me." She looked down, sipped at the nearly empty cup of tea, and set it down with a grimace.

"Unless we can replicate our laboratory conditions, and quickly, the point may become moot," she said. "We daren't allow the plague to spread beyond the point of no return. The results—well, they're entirely *too* easy to envision."

I eyed her narrowly.

"There's something you're not telling me, isn't there?"

"And I used to have such a good poker face." She studied her hands before looking me in the eyes. "We've had reports of Walker's in several neighborhoods of San Francisco, including the Financial District, North Beach, and SoMa. I have every reason to believe Dr. Albert's vaccine was introduced into the city."

"But that's—" I stopped, unwilling to even consider the ramifications.

"Insanity? Yes." She stopped for a moment, and then continued. "If our intelligence is correct, San Francisco is the first major urban center to have been infected."

"You think it was done deliberately?"

"We don't know."

"But there's no way they can keep an outbreak in San Francisco a secret," I said. "All it'll take is one person with an iPhone and a YouTube account."

"One person wouldn't present a problem," Simone replied. "It would be dismissed as a joke. They're trying for a quarantine, but in reality, I think evacuation procedures are already being put into place."

Evacuate to where? I wondered. *Sausalito?*

I didn't pursue that line of thought, though, because something in Simone's attitude hinted at yet more bad news. "There's something else, right?"

She sighed.

"Ashley, every day that passes reduces Gabriel's resistance to the virus in his body. He's gone from needing half a dose of the antiserum every twenty-four hours to one dose, then to two, all within the space of the last two weeks. There's no telling how quickly the twice-a-day dosage will become ineffective. So every second counts at this point."

"I get that," I said.

"I'm not sure that you do." Simone reached out and took one of my hands in hers. "The way the zombie virus works is insidious. It's essentially a retrovirus that sets off the zombification process. In Gabriel's case, there's a... a glitch in the process that stops him from turning completely. The antiserum Dr. Albert has developed from Gabriel's blood—and that of the wild cards—has factors that attach to the enzymes that cause the subject to change. The problem in Gabriel is that, although the enzymes are being rendered ineffective, the virus itself is replicating at an exponentially increased rate."

I kept silent, hoping she was leading up to something I could understand more completely.

"The virus is determined to win," she said. "It's aggressive and doing its best to overwhelm the positive effects of the antiserum. He will continue to need increased dosages until it stops being efficacious. Gabriel might have a week, or he might have less. We just don't know."

"So we need to leave right away," I replied. "No sense in waiting."

"Pretty much, yes. But you also need to be aware of the possibility that he could become dangerous. And you'll need to be ready to deal with that eventuality, if it happens."

"We could restrain him, if it comes to that."

"And you'll need to take Dr. Albert with you."

Great, I thought.

Not.

"Can we trust him?" I asked.

"I hope so," she answered. "I truly hope so."

I looked at her.

"Wow, you sure know how to reassure a person, don't you?"

"I'm not trying to reassure you, Ashley," she said without a hint of humor. "I'm trying to prepare you."

"Couldn't you reassure me just a *little* bit?" I asked wistfully.

She smiled at that.

"Would it help you to know that I have full confidence in your ability to deal with any situation you might encounter?"

"Um, kind of not really."

Simone laughed, and then started coughing. It looked like it hurt. I handed her a bottle of water from the bedside table, waiting until she swallowed some and the coughing fit subsided before asking the sixty-four-thousand-dollar question preying on my mind.

"What happens if he does flip, before we can make more antiserum? Is there any coming back from this?"

Simone was quiet for a minute.

"Oh, Ashley, I just don't know. We tried treating Jake with the same serum that's kept Gabriel's condition from worsening, but he didn't respond to it. Whether or not that's because of his specific physiology, or because his condition is too far gone…" She squeezed my hand and repeated, "I just don't know."

"Then we'd better get going about now." I stood up, leaned over, and gave her a quick hug. "I'll make sure this happens."

Simone hugged me back.

"I know you will. And I'll help you as best I can, every step of the way."

"Slightly better at the reassuring part there." I turned to leave, then something else occurred to me.

"Did Jake die in the fire?"

"We don't know. We had him confined in a separate room off the lab. The door was closed and locked at the start of the evening. When they checked after the fire was out, the door was open. His remains haven't been positively identified as of yet."

I shut my eyes. Okay, there was a good chance he'd either died in the fire, or was part of the "samples" that were stolen. The latter was bad, but better than if he'd escaped. We already had zombies—the last thing we needed was a Dahmer Mini-Me loose on campus like some sort of eighties horror villain.

Before I could say anything else, the door opened and Jamie came back in, bearing a tray with a carafe of coffee. Simone's expression transformed into pure bliss as Jamie poured her a cup, the aroma wafting through the air.

Who was I to interfere with this moment? I left, determined to get things moving as soon as possible.

CHAPTER EIGHTEEN

As it turned out, I'd just left Simone's room when I ran into one of Paxton's ZT squad members. The same guy I'd whomped the shit out of, point of fact. He still had a healthy shiner on his left eye.

"Jeeter, right?" I said.

He stepped back at least a foot. *Ooh, points for flinching.* I tried not to smile, but damn me if he hadn't deserved everything he'd gotten.

"Colonel Paxton has asked all of you wild things—"

"Wild cards."

He nodded energetically. "Yeah, that's it. Wild cards. He wants you to report to the quad, ASAP."

"Thanks."

He turned to go, stopped, then turned back again.

"I heard about what you did, going down to the lab." He hesitated, then added, "That took some real balls."

"Um… thank you?"

"And I'm sorry for being a dick the other night, ma'am."

Wow. Had anyone bet me this guy would apologize, it was a bet I would have taken in an instant, and lost.

"Er… apology accepted."

He gave me a sharp salute and limped off down the hallway. I almost felt bad about his injuries.

Almost.

Changing course, I headed outside and toward the quad, walking through a quiet, not quite deserted campus. There were some soldiers out and about when I reached my destination, but few civilians. Most of those preferred to stay indoors. I wistfully remembered what it was like during normal times: dozens of students strolling about, clutching lattes and snacks from one of the campus coffee kiosks, or lounging on the grass or perched on cement benches scattered across the large rectangle, the inevitable hacky sack players showing off their skills or lack thereof.

I missed it all.

The last time I'd seen it crowded was on our first mission as wild cards, when the quad had been seething with the walking dead. I preferred the hacky sack players.

The rest of the gang was already assembled on the far side of the quad, next to the library. Nathan, Gabriel, and Paxton were deep in conversation. The rest were sitting, Tony a few feet apart from everyone else, still obviously determined to isolate himself.

There were also two zombies, an adolescent male in a hoodie and a nearly nude older female, shoved up against the wall of the library, each with a collar hooked to a capture pole being manned by a couple of Hazmat-geared soldiers. Both looked as if they'd been turned at the beginning of the outbreak. The smell was horrific, even from a distance, and the stench only got worse with every step I took in their direction.

"Where did these come from?" I asked Gentry, just because he was the closest person to me, and because Gabriel was still in the kaffeeklatsch with the big boys.

"They were brought in a little while ago by one of the ZTS teams." Gentry waved a hand in front of his nose. "They were locked in the basement of a house near the edge of the quarantine zone, probably a few weeks ago. So they're pretty ripe."

"What's up with the poles and shit?"

He shrugged.

"Nathan's idea."

"That could be a good or a bad thing," I commented to no one in particular.

"Attention, people!" Colonel Paxton's resonate voice caught all of our attention. He was one man who would never need a microphone. He didn't need to say it more than once, either—everyone gave him their full attention. Even Tony.

Gabriel looked up and saw me. He looked good, without the sallow skin tone I'd come to recognize when the zombie bug was coursing though his system without the antiserum to combat it. I smiled and in return got a partial lift of the corners of his mouth. That was good enough for me, under the circumstances.

"I'm not going to waste any time," Paxton said. "You know our lab was destroyed, and most of the materials either burned or stolen by the same people who set the fire."

Last week on Zombocalypse…

"Dr. Albert and Professor Fraser were working on a cure for the plague, as well as making an antiserum to keep Captain Drake's condition from worsening." He nodded toward Gabriel. "We have a limited supply of this serum. And more importantly, we need to secure a new base of operations—one with the materials and equipment necessary to continue this work."

Mack raised his hand, and Paxton nodded in his direction.

"Why can't the military just fly in more equipment and supplies to Redwood Grove?"

Paxton nodded again, this time in acknowledgment.

"Good question. Under normal circumstances this is exactly what we would do. But there is nothing normal about the current events. Every hour brings more news of infection, and each new outbreak requires that more of our resources be deployed to put out these fires. We simply don't have the time to rebuild the lab facilities. And we don't have the luxury of moving our operations without first securing the new location.

"We are on our own," he said flatly. Then he paused, looking around at all of us for what looked like maximum dramatic effect. Or maybe I was just being bitchy. His next words, however, drove all snarky thoughts out of my head.

"San Francisco is our best bet—perhaps our only one, given the urgency of our situation—but it has been badly compromised," he announced. "Under the guise of flu shots, the vaccine was introduced into drugstores in the city proper, and possibly on the Peninsula and in the East Bay. While the number of actual zombies reported has so far been minimal, the number of potentially infected persons is high."

"How bad is it?" Mack asked.

"Few enough cases and enough media damage control that any national news is still reporting it as a potentially lethal flu outbreak."

"What, no Ebola this time?" I muttered.

Paxton gave me a fairly lethal Hairy Eyeball. I shut up.

"This situation can't hold," he continued. "Already the hospitals are overwhelmed with Walker's patients and people with bite wounds. It's only a matter of time before the zombie population explodes. If we're lucky, you'll reach your target before that happens. More than ever, it's absolutely essential that the lab there is fully functional as soon as possible."

He paced back and forth as he continued.

"The military is setting up a quarantine zone, blocking access to all the bridges in the area, and shutting down the 280, 101, 580, 80, 24 and 1 freeways. You will be transported in by helicopter, along with backup teams of ZTS marksmen.

"They are not immune to the disease, so their main function will be clearing hostiles from a distance. That leaves the up close and personal to you."

"Are they letting anyone out?" I asked, trying to imagine the panic of such a densely populated city.

"Evacuation procedures have been implemented, with clearing points at the checkpoints on each bridge and on the freeways. Plans are in motion to deploy Chinooks to airlift healthy citizens out, once we establish a secure perimeter in Golden Gate Park." Paxton stared directly at me. "But we know from experience that there will be a certain percentage of healthy civilians within the quarantine zone when you arrive. We will do our best to make sure these people have a sanctuary within the city, until such time evacuation can be completed or the contagion contained. And to that end…"

He gave a nod to Nathan, who stepped up front and center, pulled out an M4 from a nearby duffle bag and casually shot the female zombie in the head, splattering the wall behind it.

I winced, and Lil gave me an odd look.

"What?" she said. "It's just a zombie. You've killed dozens of them."

I hesitated, trying to find the right words to describe the discomfort I felt. I finally found them.

"Killing them when they're trying to eat me seems a lot more ethical than using them as demo dummies."

Or lab specimens, I thought, remembering the gut-crawling horror I'd felt when Colonel Paxton's predecessor, General Heald, had forced me to go to the labs under Patterson Hall. There I'd seen zombies strapped to operating tables, slices taken out of their flesh like turkeys being carved at Thanksgiving. Heald wanted to persuade me to join the wild cards by showing me what would happen to Matt, my boyfriend-turned-zombie, if I refused.

My reward for being a good soldier? Matt got a swift

and final bullet to the head, instead of being used as a lab rat.

"They're dead," Lil said. "It's not like they're human any more."

"I know." I saw Matt's face in my mind's eye. "But they used to be."

Nathan cleared his throat, and we turned our attention back to him.

"See that crap on the wall? Should be a familiar sight by now. Blood, brain matter, lots of gore. To a wild card it's no threat." He paused for effect, and the theatrics began to bug me. "But to uninfected civilians, it's another story. Any of this gets into an open wound or mixes with mucus membrane, the virus spreads, and we have another zombie on our hands. The lesson, my children, is that splatter is bad."

No one argued the point, so he continued.

"Then there's the question of over-penetration. On a really ripe biter, your M4 round won't find much to slow it down. It'll punch through and keep right on going. Not a bad thing, unless you have a team member or civilian on the move somewhere behind them. That's a lot more likely to happen in densely populated territory, and a risk we don't want to take."

He reached into his duffle bag again and extracted a toy-like rifle in a jaunty shade of metallic royal blue, something I'd expect a Spy Kid to use.

"This is a Marlin Papoose bolt-action rifle."

"It's so cute!" Jamie exclaimed. "Does it come in pink?"

You could practically hear people rolling their eyes—I'm pretty sure mine creaked—but Nathan actually grinned as he replied.

"As a matter of fact, one of my teammates back in the day bought one with a pink stock for his niece's tenth birthday."

Jamie beamed.

Tony gave a derisive snort.

"You gotta be kidding," he said. "You want us to take out zombies with a squirrel rifle?"

Normally his attitude would make me want to slap him, but considering that this was the first voluntary social interaction he'd offered since Kai's death, I didn't say a word.

Nathan ignored Tony and shot the other zombie in the head. The rifle made a small pop, nothing near as loud as the M4. Nothing splattered, but the zombie went limp.

Nathan set the rifle down on the table.

"Here's the point, ladies and gentlemen. The M4 is a superior battlefield weapon under normal circumstances. You've proven that. But sometimes you have to tailor the weapon to the war."

He rummaged in the bag and pulled out a small round.

"This is a .22 Long Rifle cartridge. They are small, underpowered, short range. Mostly good for plinking cans in the back yard. But depending on the circumstances, that may be all you need. A .22 has power to breach the skull, but not enough to exit. The flesh may have deteriorated, but the bone will be intact."

"So no potentially infected splatter, right?" Jamie said, sounding entirely too perky.

Nathan gave her a nod of approval.

"Exactly."

Teacher's pet, I mouthed to Lil.

"A well-placed round to the frontal cortex will do the job—if in doubt, make it two. There is negligible recoil, so it's easy to keep on target, and it won't punish your shoulder over an extended firefight. They're small, so you can carry several thousand rounds in place of a few hundred for the M4. If you're stuck in the field and can't get back to base, chances are you can find reloads at department stores, sporting goods shops, hardware stores... hell, in some towns, even drugstores carry 'em."

"Not in San Francisco," I said mildly.

Gentry laughed. "I'm surprised you can buy knives in San Francisco."

"Only if they're organic, grass-fed, and sustainable," Mack said, eliciting a rare guffaw from Tony. That made Mack beam, considering how few and far between any response had been in the last couple of days.

"So," Tony said, "if we're really gonna use these pop guns in San Fran, does mine have to be blue?"

"No." This time Nathan's magic duffle bag produced a stubby rifle with a thick barrel and an odd drum-shaped thingee mounted horizontally on top. "It'll come in OD Green, and a slightly different model." He hefted the rifle.

"This is an AM15. Basically your standard-issue full-auto M16, but with an aftermarket receiver that takes pan magazines for an American 180 submachine gun."

Okay, this was turning into way more info than my brain could process. Nathan's words were starting to blend into "blah blahblah ammo. Blahblahblahsplooshy blood and gore." At this point, I was ready to stand up and go all Vasquez with, "Look, man. I only need to know one thing..."

"We've added a standard red dot scope, and a full-auto-grade suppressor," Nathan added.

"A suppressor is like a silencer, right?" Jamie chimed in. Miss Hot Topic was turning out to be a combination Ms. NRA and a Hermione for the Zombocalypse.

"That's right," Nathan nodded. "No sense ringing the dinner bell if you don't have to. With this you can slip in, drop your targets, and get out before they know it."

"What's that little drum thingee on top?" I asked, figuring I should at least pretend to show an interest.

"That's the pan magazine. The .22 rounds are loaded into a spiral, and..."

I tuned out again. *Blahblahblah, Ginger.*

"It still looks like a squirrel gun," Tony muttered.

Nathan raised an eyebrow and gave a little sigh. Then he did something to the gun and fired a round into the closest zombie's hoodied head. The only sound was a click followed by the tinkle of a casing falling to the ground. The hood moved slightly, but that was it. Nathan fired three more rounds in quick succession, the sound reminiscent of a kid's pellet gun. Then he did something to make the drum-shaped magazine start to whirl, accompanied by a slight chattering sound.

I wasn't particularly impressed until I noticed the storm of tiny rounds chewing a fist-sized hole in the zombie's chest, followed by a steady stitch of ammo fired into one hip to the other. Then he nudged the body with his foot and it separated into two gooey pieces.

"Any questions?" he asked.

Tony stood up and started to raise his hand. Without even glancing in his direction, Nathan continued, "And if anyone asks how they can get out of this chickenshit outfit, rest assured, I will give them an answer they will not enjoy."

Tony sat back down. Gentry looked over at me, and we both grinned.

Nathan continued.

"Each of you will be issued a rifle and six magazines to supplement your other weaponry. The casings will eject out the empty magazine, but do *not* discard your empties if you can help it; supply is limited for the moment. You'll also get a Ruger Mark III pistol in the same caliber, also suppressed. Consider it a stocking stuffer."

Pleasepleaseplease, no more gun talk.

"And—"

Damn.

"—we'll want a heavy gunner as backup, so—" Nathan nodded at Gentry, who reached down and pulled up a big-ass shotgun. "We'll be sending out two

AA-12 full-auto shotguns." He gave another nod. Gentry grinned and handed the shotgun to Tony.

"Wow." Tony lit up like a pinball machine as he hefted the weapon.

"This puppy fires over three hundred rounds a minute, and has minimum recoil," Gentry told him.

"So we don't get to see Tony knocked back on his ass every time he fires it?" I smiled sweetly as Tony shot me the finger, no doubt also remembering his epic moment in our first firearms training session.

"Not unless he's a lot wussier than he looks," Gentry said with a straight face.

Lil pouted.

"How come Tony gets to use it?"

Nathan grinned.

"Because it fits him. Don't you think?"

We all looked at Tony as he posed with his new toy, looking more alive than I'd seen him since Kai's death.

Mack shrugged.

"When you're right, you're right."

SALT LAKE CITY

"Oh my god, there's another one…"

Steph pointed across the street to yet another family consisting of Dad in a white short-sleeved dress shirt, slacks and a truly hideous yellow-gold tie, Mom with teased hair, heavy makeup, and a long shapeless skirt, blouse and cardigan, and multiple matching blond rug rats—in this case, six— scampering at their side.

Jeff gave a bark of laughter.

"Do they grown them in vats or what around here?" He shook his head. "I swear, this is either total inbreeding, or we've seem the same damn family a half dozen times today. It's like Children of the Damned, *but all smiling and shit."*

"And without the glowing eyes."

Steph snickered and pointed again, this time over toward the entrance of the Temple Gardens, where another almost identical family was walking down the sidewalk.

"I'm voting for cloning vats," she said.

Jeff laughed, the sound merging into a wracking cough. He'd been feeling punk since they'd landed in Salt Lake City for World Horror Con. It seemed like at least half the other attendees were coming down with the same bug. Steph seemed to have avoided it, probably because she carried a bottle of hand sanitizer and used it liberally.

Jeff's approach involved the judicious internal applications of booze, bought at the State-run liquor store a few blocks from the hotel, but after a while, even that hadn't helped. He looked almost jaundiced now.

"You okay, hon?"

"I'll live. But some coffee wouldn't hurt."

Steph consulted the little guidebook she'd grabbed from the hotel concierge desk.

"City Creek Mall is right down the street. It's a mall, so they'll have to have a Starbucks or something, right?"

Wrong.

After walking up and down the length of a very pretty outdoor mall with an abundance of fountains and a man-made "river" running the length of it, they'd found a specialty tea store, but no coffee shops. They'd gotten a lot of stares from the conservatively dressed crowds, though. Salt Lake City didn't seem to have a lot of Steampunk fashionistas.

"I guess coffee qualifies as a Big Bad right up there with alcohol, here in Mormon Land."

"Yeah." *Jeff coughed again, a wave of weakness washing over him. Steph eyed him with concern.*

"You look kind of like hammered shit, baby. I think you might have jaundice."

"No way."

"Seriously. The whites of your eyes aren't white. They're, like, Simpson yellow."

Jeff laughed.

"And this, Steph, is but one reason why I worship you above all other women."

Steph smiled smugly. They really were a match made in geek heaven. But she'd known that the night she'd gone to the premiere of Serenity, all dolled up in a painstaking recreation of one of Inara's outfits. She'd seen Jeff standing in line, resplendent in his brown coat, slightly skinny for Mal Reynolds. But then again, Steph herself was on the voluptuous side, especially when compared to Morena Baccarin.

They'd both captured the spirit of the characters, and more importantly, there had been fucking fantastic chemistry between them.

Jeff coughed again, spasms wracking his body.

"I need to sit for a sec, okay?"

Steph rubbed the back of his neck as they found a bench across from a fountain. This one was level with the ground, with a dozen or so jets that randomly sent sprays of water straight into the air. A little boy, maybe three years old, was having the time of his life playing chicken with the geysers. When the water missed him, he did a little victory dance. When it hit him, he giggled with delight.

"Isn't he cute?" Steph smiled.

Jeff didn't answer.

"You okay, baby?" Steph glanced over at him, then gasped in shock.

Dark fluid ran out of his mouth, while his eyes leaked tears of blood. His body spasmed, and a gout of foul smelling fluid spewed from between his lips.

Steph screamed, leaping to her feet as Jeff collapsed onto the pavement, the fluid running into the fountain area and mixing with the water.

The happy toddler stopped in mid-frolic and stared as Jeff's body gave one final bone-breaking shudder, and stopped.

"Jeff?" Steph's voice broke as she fell on her knees next to him. *"Jeff?"*

A fountain of water erupted next to his body, soaking both of them. The toddler gave a hesitant laugh, but the chuckle died in his throat when Jeff's eyes snapped open, revealing milky white corneas cradled in blood-streaked yellow. Another spray of water shot up next to him. He sat up, oblivious when it hit him in the face, grasped the toddler by an arm… and bit into it.

The little boy shrieked in pain.

Steph yelled in shock and surprise, leaping up at the same time the kid's parents did on the other side of the fountain.

She reached Jeff first, grabbing him by the hair to pull him off the now screaming boy, a chunk of the child's arm caught between his teeth. The parents swooped in, snatching him away, shrieking hysterical threats.

Jeff ignored them, turning toward Steph as he finished munching on the chunk of flesh in his mouth. Steph froze for a millisecond before throwing herself away from him, feet slipping on the slick pavement. She fell, another torrent of water jetting up into her face. Steph sputtered, momentarily blinded, but still possessed of enough self-preservation instinct to continue scrambling away from the spreading puddle of blood.

Poor little guy… he'd been so happy…

Steph choked back a sob as another explosion of water gushed up in front of her. She looked over to see Jeff reach out and grab a man by his ugly yellow tie, pulling the hapless Mormon closer and taking a ravenous bite from his windpipe.

She got to her feet and ran as best she could in her high-heeled boots, colliding with other tourists and locals like a pinball careening off its drop targets. She didn't even try to apologize. She just wanted to get away, back to the hotel, where the horror was fake and manageable.

Emerging onto West Temple Street, directly across the street from Temple Square, she found a horde of white-shirted men, big-haired women, and blond kids being swarmed by gore-drenched doppelgangers.

That sent her bolting to the left, past a knot of screaming children, and sprinting toward the Radisson, a few short blocks away. The sounds of agonized screams dimmed as she left Temple Square behind.

She hit the revolving doors of the Radisson at a full clip, stumbling into the lobby. Her heels slipped on the tiled floor and she fell again, taking the brunt of the fall on her hands and knees. Winded, she lay there for a moment, then pushed herself up to a sitting position, hair falling into her eyes, wondering why none of the hotel staff had come to help her.

She pushed her hair back and looked up, to find a dozen or so fellow Horror Con attendees—as well as the concierge and hotel bartender—converging on her from all sides, their eyes boasting the same horror movie FX of milky white corneas, yellowed whites shot with red. Black, viscous liquid dribbled out of their mouths.

As they reached for her, Steph thought vaguely that maybe this was a publicity stunt for the convention. Then the concierge bit her, and all thoughts were driven from her mind by white-hot pain.

CHAPTER NINETEEN

Whupwhupwhupwhup…

Oh jeez, I was gonna barf. I didn't generally get motion sickness, but then I wasn't generally however many gajillions of feet above the ground in a tin can with rotors keeping it up in the air like some sort of metal insectazoid. So sue me—I always thought helicopters looked like bugs.

And now here I was inside of one, with not nearly enough extra space between me and the sky. At least in a plane you had the illusion of that self-contained environment between you and death. I kept hearing Arnold yelling, "Get to the choppah!" and visualizing the movie poster for *Black Hawk Down*.

We'd been separated into two groups, with me, Gabriel, Lil, and Tony in the helicopter whimsically named Zed One, while Mack, Gentry, and Nathan were in Zed Two, with two ZTS snipers filling out each team. Our snipers, both male with similar angular features and compact muscular builds, looked so much alike that I'd nicknamed them the Gunsy Twins.

Dr. Albert was also with our group, the better for Gabriel and me to keep an eye on him.

"You okay?" Even without the specialized wired earplugs and headgear to facilitate communication, I recognized Gabriel's voice, as well as the feel of his hand on my arm, warm and reassuring. I vigorously nodded "yes" without opening my eyes.

"Liar."

"I hate heights," I replied. I really did. And it wasn't helping that Lil was bouncing up and down in excitement, seemingly okay with the fact that we were in a tin can in the air without even drinks and peanut service. Granted I'd seen too many movies where the helicopter door popped open and someone went into freefall, but damn, she made me nervous. Stomach-wrenchingly, full-on, wanna throw up my cookies nervous.

So I kept my eyes screwed shut and tried my best not to hear anything beyond the goddamn *whupwhupwhupwhup* of the rotors.

"Tell me again why we had to split up the group between two helicopters?"

"Redundancy and diversification," Gabriel said soothingly. "If one goes down, we still have a fully equipped team to cover the mission."

Oh, that's just great.

It didn't soothe me in the least, even though the logic behind the decision made sense.

"How likely are we to go down?" I asked.

"Not likely."

"Are we there yet?"

He chuckled.

"Almost."

"Ash, look!" Lil exclaimed. "It's Alcatraz!"

Ulp. "We're over the water, aren't we?" I said.

"Sort of."

I ignored the laughter in Gabriel's voice. How wonderful that he found my irrational fear so funny.

So I kept my eyes shut.

"Just tell me when we land, okay?"

He patted my arm comfortingly.

"Will do, Ash."

The helicopter dipped suddenly and my stomach

did a drop and roll worthy of the Death Drop ride at Six Flags.

Gahhhhh!

"We're heading in," the pilot said.

Great.

"Where are we setting down?" I heard Lil ask.

"The helipad at UCSF," Gabriel answered. "Pretty much right on top of where the laboratory is located."

"Are we going to conduct the civilian evacs from there as well?" This was Dr. Albert. "Because that would be extremely distracting to me while I'm trying to work."

God forbid that saving lives might interfere with your work, I thought snarkily. Then I thought again, since part of his work included keeping Gabriel human.

Crap, I hated these morally ambiguous *Sophie's Choice* type situations.

"No, those will be done from Golden Gate Park," Gabriel replied. "We need room to land the Chinooks so we can move more than eight civilians at a time. Centrally located, but without the built in neighborhood populations of, say, the Haight or Noe Valley. We have a couple Chinooks coming in with more ZTS personnel who'll secure the perimeter and start lifting people out."

"Are we looking for more wild cards?" Lil piped up.

Good question. I wish I'd thought of it.

"No." Gabriel's voice was regretful yet firm. "We have no way to isolate bite victims long enough—not until we have a safe refuge in the city."

"Until, or *if* we have a safe refuge?" I asked. "Is any place going to be safe? I mean, how the hell are we going to be able to contain this any longer?" I wasn't speaking to anyone in particular at this point, but the silence that met my question got me to open my eyes, despite my fear. I wished I hadn't bothered, after seeing the grim expressions both Gabriel and Dr. Albert wore.

Shit.

"We're screwed, aren't we?" I said.

"Not if we can find the cure," Gabriel answered. "Not yet."

"How fast has it spread?" I asked. "Do we have any new reports?"

Everyone was listening now. Even Lil had stopped her enthusiastic bouncing to pay attention.

"Not good," Gabriel said. "It's been contained in some of the smaller, more isolated areas with natural geographical barriers to augment the manpower. But in places with urban sprawl and no real borders, it's spreading quickly. There's been word of outbreaks originating in Lansing, Michigan and spreading to the surrounding towns and communities. Salt Lake City was hit hard, but so far the DZN have managed to stop it from spreading, with the help of the surrounding mountains and more than a few well-armed civilians."

Holy shit.

"The most recent outbreak reported is in Borger, Texas, with news of a possible spread to Amarillo, but nothing is confirmed yet. And there are more."

There really wasn't anything else to say. The mood in the helicopter was bleak enough.

Since my eyes were already open, I tried to keep them that way as we *whupwhupwhupped* our way over the bay toward San Francisco. I tried not to look out the window to my right, but somehow managed to catch a glimpse of slate gray water frothing with white foam caps, the Golden Gate Bridge further away.

"Wow, look at all those boats," Lil said, pointing away from the bridge to the left.

I looked. There were dozens of boats of various shapes and sizes—kayaks, motorboats, sailboats, you name it—all of them heading away from the city toward the north. Some seemed bound for the relative safety of Alcatraz, which wasn't a bad plan, but the overall aquatic chaos was like the bounty hunter scene in *Jaws*.

"They're all gonna die" popped into my head.

The bridge was clogged with vehicles, but all the cars were headed north, even the ones in the southbound lanes. Military barricades had been erected at points all across the bridge, and it looked like so far they were holding strong. People were milling around the stalled vehicles, gesticulating wildly as they faced off with soldiers in full-on biohazard protective gear.

How could they even know that an infected person—or two or ten or a hundred—hadn't already crossed over to Sausalito on the ferry? What the hell was the point, anyway, since the damn virus kept popping up across the country?

I shut that train of thought down before it sent me into a tailspin of hopelessness, and looked out toward the city of San Francisco itself. What I saw didn't help my mood. Plumes of smoke rose from different points in the city, many in the downtown and tourist areas. I got a brief glimpse of the 1 on the other side of the bridge, backed up as far as I could see until it curved out of sight. Total gridlock.

There was also a contingent of armed guards at the tollbooths, although whether they were there to deal with humans or zombies wasn't immediately clear. I thought I saw the familiar lurching movements of the walking dead, but before I could really focus, the helicopter suddenly jerked in mid-air, forward momentum almost, well, *stuttering*, for lack of a better description.

I sat bolt upright.

"Is that normal?"

"Jeez, Ash, chil-lax!" Tony said.

I was torn between relief that he was talking to me again, and the more familiar irritation. Deciding both feelings were valid, I opened my mouth to tell him off, only to be cut off by another, more violent jolt.

"Shit!"

Wait. Was that the pilot?

It couldn't be a good thing that he'd said "shit."

"We have trouble, folks."

Trouble? No, no trouble—not when we're up in the air, thank you. Not allowed.

"How bad?" Gabriel immediately switched into business mode, or whatever the military equivalent was.

"We're losing fuel, and there's something happening with the rotors. We're going to have to set down immediately."

"Immediately, like in the water?" I squeaked.

"Not that immediately, ma'am." The pilot sounded amused. I would have been offended, had I not been distracted by a loud squawk from the com system.

"Zed One, we've got problems."

"Roger, that," I heard in the headset. From the look on Lil and Tony's faces, they'd heard it, too. We exchanged looks. Lil stopped bouncing and settled into her seat.

"We're setting down in Crissy Field," our pilot said. "Hostiles identified, but nothing we can't handle."

"Roger, that," the other pilot responded. "We're setting down near the Legion of Honor. More hostiles identified."

"Roger, that."

I turned my head to look at Gabriel.

"Is this part of that whole redundancy thing? *Two* 'copters going down?"

He managed a smile, despite his own obvious tension.

"It's going to be okay, Ash." Then he added, "You might want to shut your eyes."

I did as he suggested, my stomach doing major acrobatics as the helicopter dipped and lurched its way toward land. I knew we were gonna crash and burn in one of those classic movie fireballs. I just knew it. I braced myself for the worst.

* * *

The room was purposefully dark in deference to his light-sensitive eyes. He'd never complained about the lighting, of course. After all, complaints were a sign of weakness, and to show weakness was as good as giving up, rolling over and exposing one's belly to the claws and teeth of one's enemies.

He preferred to view the closed shades and dim lighting as a sign of deference from the staff, and respect from his colleagues.

And perhaps some fear as well. He enjoyed being the source of fear, especially from some of the most powerful men and women in the world. Some of their names would be familiar to anyone who read The Wall Street Journal, *or* Forbes, *or followed politics. Others could walk down the streets of any city and remain completely anonymous. For their power went far deeper than any political party or government position.*

They watched the screens—someone always watched them—following the spread of this wonderful new Walker's virus. The mutations had been totally accidental, a combination of greed and oversight that had allowed the vaccine out into the world without adequate testing. Had the vaccine worked as intended, its creator no doubt would have won the Nobel Prize. No one could have guessed the horrific results.

Now that it had been unleashed, however, it was something that could be used.

He loved his country, still did, and was willing to go to any lengths to protect it. That much hadn't changed. The difference now was, ideas he used to view as representative of the enemy, something to be defeated, had become tools that could be used to cleanse the nation of those who didn't show the proper respect for the stars and stripes. Those who were bringing the once grand nation to its knees with apathy and disrespect.

The true *enemy.*

They'd abdicated their right to protection by the military.

He turned his attention to the screen—reality TV in its purest form. An obscure town in Wisconsin overrun by the walking dead, its population either devoured or turned into yet more ravenous corpses.

Citizens of Salt Lake City reeling at the sight of the Mormon Tabernacle Choir, ripped to pieces mid-performance.

So much for magic underwear.

Lansing, Michigan, as the virus spread from the college to the surrounding communities.

Chaos in the Financial District of San Francisco as the ravenous dead joined the happy hour festivities. He suppressed a chuckle. He'd never liked San Francisco. What kind of city made it legal for grown men to walk around buck-ass naked?

They all deserved their fate.

He took a sip of a perfectly blended Manhattan before reaching for a bite-sized cube of red meat, almost rare enough to be considered raw, seasoned with salt and pepper. Thank Christ he'd always been a meat and potatoes man. Made this whole thing much easier.

"What's the status on Dr. Albert?"

A very successful financier, statuesque, blonde, and still impressively sexy in her fifties, checked something on an iPad before replying.

"On his way to the lab at UCSF, along with the wild cards."

He frowned at that.

"He's on one of the helicopters?"

She nodded, looking pleased with herself.

"Measures have been taken to ensure that neither helicopter reaches the lab."

"You do know that we need Dr. Albert and the other—the half-deader—kept alive." His tone was soft, almost gentle, but something in it caused the financier to take an involuntary step backward.

"Y… yes," she replied.

"So it didn't occur to anyone to find out which helicopter they would be on?"

The financier gulped audibly.

"Our contact was unable to obtain that information so

we thought it best to make adjustments to both. We're not expecting any fatalities."

"Well, if there are," he said, "we'll… discuss it later."

She blanched as he smiled at her.

"Any word on Typhoid Mary?" His tone was casual as he enjoyed another piece of meat, washed down by more Manhattan. He smiled to himself as his companions averted their eyes.

"Ah, yes." The reply came from a well-known media figure, famous for his deliberately over-the-top radio shows. There was no sign of his signature self-righteous bluster as he continued, "He's in Los Angeles. He's… been cleaning up after himself."

"That's unexpected. All of them?"

The talk-show host nodded nervously.

"He's been very thorough."

He took another sip of his drink and contemplated this turn of events. He'd counted on Typhoid Mary to spread the disease in his own unique way. He hadn't anticipated the appearance of a social conscience.

Maybe it was time to bring Mary back into the fold, and have a chat about the rules.

CHAPTER TWENTY

They say that if you expect the worst, that's what you're likely to get. I say it's okay to set one's expectations at rock bottom, so you can be pleasantly surprised.

Our descent was reminiscent of the Tea Cups ride at Disneyland. I'd only ridden the Tea Cups once, because it made me violently ill.

The landing itself was actually anticlimactic—mostly on the "pleasantly surprised" end of the spectrum—with no jarring thuds, fireballs, claxons, or any other clichés.

Someone opened the helicopter door, and I stumbled toward the fresh air, so dizzy I would have fallen if one of the nice snipers hadn't caught me and helped me down to the ground, where I immediately collapsed onto my knees, trying my best not to lose my cookies. My best wasn't good enough, however, and once again I worshipped the porcelain god without any actual porcelain.

Once I'd finished emptying my poor abused stomach, I folded onto the ground and just breathed in and out for a minute, letting the nausea pass. Lil handed me a bottle of water, which I took gratefully with a strong sense of déjà vu. I swilled some of it, spit it out, and then swallowed some. Someone else offered me an Altoid. The curiously strong mint helped settle my stomach and made my mouth a place I could live with.

"Why isn't anyone else puking?" I asked resentfully.

"I never throw up," Lil said primly.

"All those video games I play," Tony said. "You oughta try some. Maybe your stomach wouldn't be so wussy."

"Thanks loads, Tony."

"No prob."

I suspect my sarcasm didn't register.

Soon I felt well enough to survey my surroundings. Water to the north, benches and buildings to the east and west, lots of trees to the south. Crissy Field used to be an airfield, but it'd been converted to a flat, hard-packed promenade alongside the bay, with some kick-ass views of the Golden Gate and Bay Bridges. There were plenty of places for picnicking, and some scenic tidal marsh overlooks. A nice spot for biking, windsurfing, hiking, or just to take a gentle stroll.

Or a nice lurch.

The smell of sea and salt suddenly mixed with *Eau de Necrosis*, and the plaintive moans of the undead combined with the sounds of car horns, sirens, and distant screams.

"Uh, guys?" I pointed eastward toward a little snack place called The Warming Hut, where several fresh-looking zombies were staggering around the corner, looking for food that the Hut didn't have on its menu.

The Gunsy Twins unslung their firearms, which looked substantially more high-tech than our "squirrel rifles." They used them with quiet efficiency, taking out the zombies before they'd made it more than a few steps toward us. I caught Tony eying the snipers with blatant gun envy and clutching his BAS—big ass shotgun— even closer. Some people had security blankets, others preferred teddy bears. And then there was Tony.

The flight crew joined us on the ground.

"Any word from Zed Two?" Gabriel asked them.

The pilot, a solidly built Latino in his twenties, hesitated briefly before answering.

"I haven't been able to raise them since we landed, sir. Hal's an experienced pilot, though, so my bets are that something shook loose in the com system when they hit ground."

I winced at the words "hit ground."

"Well, what the hell happened?" Gabriel sounded angry. "Why did we go down in the first place?"

The pilot shook his head.

"We're not sure," he said earnestly. "Fuel tanks started dumping, and the rotor engines went all to hell."

"And the other one?"

"Sounded like the same thing."

The mechanic scratched his head thoughtfully, dislodging the non-regulation Giants baseball hat that covered short red hair so bright it was practically fluorescent. Combine that with at least six and a half feet of height, and he'd never get lost in a crowd.

"Funny thing is," he said, "both of these birds were serviced less than a month ago."

Sounded like sabotage to me. Someone really didn't want Dr. Albert to find the cure. Or, if he did, they didn't want the wild cards or the DZN to have access to it. What I couldn't figure out was what the reasoning could be, although I'd bet it had something to do with money and/or power.

Doesn't everything?

The only consolation was that they hadn't planted bombs or done some other hinky shit that would have brought us down in fiery pieces. So killing us wasn't a priority. Or maybe keeping Dr. Albert alive was more important.

Arrrgh. This sort of Machiavellian shit made my brain hurt. Besides, we didn't have time to figure out all the whos, wheres, whats, whys, and hows of it. That was someone else's job. Team A needed to meet up with Team B, get to the laboratory, make more antiserum for Gabriel, and establish a secure location for everyone from Redwood Grove and the survivors of San Francisco.

Piece of cake.

Gabriel's radio squawked from its holster on his belt. He grabbed it, answered, and walked a few feet away.

"Do you think he's talking to Colonel Paxton?" Lil asked me.

"If it's not, we need to let the colonel know what happened," I said. "And Simone, too."

"I'm sure they're monitoring things back at Big Red," Dr. Albert said with irritating assurance. "She undoubtedly already knows."

He was probably right, but I still wanted to smack the smug right out of him.

Gabriel came walking back, radio in its holster.

"That was Nathan," he announced.

"Is everyone okay?" Lil asked. By "everyone" I was pretty sure she meant Mack.

"Their landing was rougher than ours," Gabriel answered, "but no fatalities. One of the snipers sustained a bad concussion, and Mack took a hard blow on one of his knees when the bird went down."

Lil gasped.

"Can he walk?" Her tone was anxious.

Gabriel nodded.

"They've treated it as well as they can."

"But what if he has to run?"

I patted her on the shoulder.

"He's a wild card, Lil. He'll heal up quickly." She still looked worried, so I added, "C'mon, this is Mack we're talking. He's smart, he's resourceful, and no way Nathan or Gentry would leave him behind. They know you'd kill 'em," I said with my best grim smile.

Gabriel continued.

"Nathan says the biggest issue now is the number of zombies in their immediate vicinity. The one sniper isn't in any shape to do his job, so the flight crew called for an evacuation. If they can get to Golden Gate Park, they can make it out on one of the Chinooks being sent in for general evac."

"How the hell are they gonna control that situation?" I said, thinking of the scene in *Titanic* where the passengers were trampling everyone in sight. Substitute helicopters for the lifeboats, and zombies for the iceberg, and you had a recipe for total chaos.

"Lots of weapons," Gabriel replied without a trace of irony.

"So what's the plan then?" I asked. "Are we sticking to redundancy, and seeing who makes it to UCSF first, or are we going to try a rendezvous, and head to the campus together?" Without a doubt, I was for option number two. I preferred the idea of one well-armed team, with plenty of manpower.

Gabriel hesitated, and before he could form his reply, Dr. Albert jumped in.

"We don't have time to rendezvous," he protested anxiously. "Our primary objective *must* be to reach the lab, so I can continue my research!"

"It seems to me," I said, "that we stand a better chance making it there if there are more of us. I mean, it's a medical facility, right? So the odds are high that there's already a hell of a lot of zombies, not to mention infected civilians."

"And we don't abandon our friends," Lil added.

"Damned straight," Tony growled. "No man left behind, right?" He turned to Gabriel. "Because Gentry sure as shit wouldn't abandon *us*."

Much to my relief, Gabriel nodded in agreement.

"For now both teams are going to head for Kezar Pavilion, the stadium at the eastern end of Golden Gate Park," he said, "less than half a mile from UCSF. We'll head straight there, while Team B will drop the flight crew and the injured at the Bison Paddock, where the evacuations will commence."

The pilot stepped forward.

"What about us, sir? We didn't sign on for a trip into zombie town on foot. This was supposed to be drop-off on location."

"The two of you are welcome to make your way to the evac area on your own," Gabriel said, "but this team needs to get the doctor to the campus and get that lab up and running as quickly as possible. We can't afford even the slightest detour."

"So the other flight crew gets an armed escort, but we have to take our chances?" The mechanic joined the pilot, ready to argue.

Gabriel looked at him.

"The other flight crew sustained some major injuries. They need the help. You don't. Your other alternative is to accompany us to the target destination, help us achieve our mission, and enjoy the benefits of our additional firepower. It's up to you."

He turned to the rest of us.

"Our priority is getting Dr. Albert to the campus in one piece. He knows the location of the hidden entrance, at the back of the medical center." He paused, and then added, "Push comes to shove, nothing else matters." He tossed me a meaningful look.

"You're lucky." Tony gave Dr. Albert a nasty look. "If you weren't important, I'd just feed you to those motherfuckers."

Guess Tony'd redirected his anger to the point of origin.

Dr. Albert gave one of his patented outraged sputters.

"You'd best show more respect, young man," he said. "I may be your only hope for a cure."

Tony just stared at him.

"Like I said, you're lucky."

"That's enough, Tony," Gabriel snapped. "We don't have time to waste on this shit."

As if to prove his point, a discordant chorus of moans rose from behind the buildings that lined the south end of the field. It was hard to tell exactly where they were coming from, though. Maybe they were carried by the wind, which was rising even as we stood there, gusts whipping up frothy whitecaps on the water. The longer we stayed in one place, the more the zombies would hone in on whatever "fresh meat" beacon they followed.

So it was time for us to get the hell out of Crissy Field.

I also noticed sweat beading up on Gabriel's brow and upper lip, a sure sign that his meds were starting to lose their *oomph*—and it'd only been six hours since he'd taken his last dose. It wasn't a good sign.

"So, you in, or out?" I turned and addressed the two-man flight crew. "Because we need to leave. You guys are military, so you stand a good chance of making it to the evac area on your own. But… we could use your help. And it would pretty much be helping all of humanity. But it's totally up to you." I smiled cheerfully.

The pilot raised an eyebrow.

"Wow. You could teach my Catholic grandmother a thing or two about guilt trips."

"My mother instilled the value of a good guilt trip at a very young age."

The pilot and mechanic moved away a few feet and conferred quietly, either forgetting or unaware that the wild cards could hear every word. Turned out the guilt trip didn't carry as much weight as having an armed escort. They also thought their odds would be better at UCSF, rather than with the masses of evacuees in Golden Gate Park.

They were probably right.

At any rate, it was no surprise when the pilot turned back.

"We'll be going with you," he said.

"Good choice." I smiled, and held out my hand. "I'm Ashley."

"Carl." The pilot shook my hand. "And this is Red."

"Seriously?" *Oh, crap, that was my outside voice…*

The mechanic just grinned.

"Seriously, ma'am. I've had this—" he patted his very red hair "—from birth."

"Okay, then." I shook his hand too. He had a good, strong grip. "Carl, Red—welcome to the team."

Suddenly a couple of shots rang out. The Gunsy Twins took out a couple of zombies that had figured out there was fresh meat in the vicinity. In the meantime, Gabriel had pulled out what looked like your basic iPhone and punched a few buttons. I had a feeling it had more apps than Apple had authorized.

"Okay, so there are three recommended routes from here to Kezar Pavilion. All of them skirt along the edge of the Presidio, and take various surface streets. In theory, an easy hour-and-a-half stroll. In reality, we'll run into zombies no matter which way we choose."

"So why are we wasting time talking about it?" Lil suddenly burst out, green eyes flashing with impatience. "Let's do this!"

Gabriel and I exchanged a brief glance. I gave a tiny nod, then gave Lil a quick one-armed hug.

"You ready, Freddie?"

She gave a surprised bark of laughter.

"My mom always says that."

"Mine, too," I said quickly, hoping to head off any angst. "So let's go find the rest of the gang, and kick some zombie ass, okay?"

"Okay." To my relief, Lil returned my hug. Still, it reminded me that Gabriel wasn't the only person in our group I needed to worry about being off their meds.

It took about five minutes to offload our gear, stuffing knapsacks and duffel bags full of ammo like over-indulgent parents stuffing Christmas stockings with candy. Our ammo supply wasn't limitless, but it would last for a while.

* * *

Well, crap.

Mack limped along as best he could, trying to ignore the pain shooting up his left ankle with every step. The medic had wrapped it as best he could before they'd grabbed their gear from the downed helicopter and skedaddled through the golf course, through an ever increasing number of zombies pouring out of the Legion of Honor museum.

Why there were so many zombies at the exhibit was a mystery. Maybe someone with Walker's had been on one of the jumbo tour buses parked in the adjacent lot. Whatever the reason, there were a lot of damn zoms inside the museum.

Maybe they're culture lovers.

Mack chuckled at the thought.

Legion of Honor sure was a pretty spot. He glimpsed the ocean through trees, over the line of cars snaking their way down the back road alongside the top of the cliffs. The air smelled like sea breeze and eucalyptus. Well, and rotted flesh, but he tried to ignore that.

He felt sorry for the people in the cars. Traffic hadn't moved since they'd crash-landed in the golf course next to the museum parking lot—which was jammed. People were trying to drive over the green, which left a lot of cars parked haphazardly where they shouldn't be.

One of the reasons they'd landed so badly was because the pilot had been forced to jerk the control hard to the left to avoid hitting a car that suddenly zipped right into the helicopter's trajectory. They'd overshot the smooth stretch of green and hit a rough patch, sliding into bushes. The rotors clipped a tree trunk, flipping the helicopter onto its side. For a few minutes there Mack had felt like a die in a Yahtzee cup.

They'd barely managed to get everyone out of the downed whirlybird before the zombies had started pouring through the museum doors and down the steps toward them. Some had been diverted by people heading toward the museum, presumably for shelter. Others went for motorists still in the cars, slapping bloody, rotted hands against the windows, trying to gain entry.

One driver veered his or her car off into the trees in an attempt to get away from the madness. The car bounced across the hiking path and beyond. Mack had heard the distant splash as it hit the water.

He winced as his good foot slipped on some damp turf and he landed hard on the injured one. He could do this, though. For the last ten years he'd walked miles on his mail route in lousy weather with a bad back and a gimp knee, and neither sleet nor snow nor zombies would stop him from doing his job.

He glanced over at the injured sniper hanging between Gentry and the medic. He was hurt bad, broken leg at least, compound fracture, and a concussion on top of it. They'd splinted the leg as best they could, but it was a rush job. Sweat poured off the poor guy's face, which was pasty white with shock. The movement had to hurt like hell, but it was either that or abandon him to a grisly fate.

Seeing the sniper's stoicism in the face of such a rotten injury made Mack more determined than ever to ignore his own pain.

"How ya doing there, Postman?" Gentry tossed a glance back over his shoulder.

"Fine," Mack said as another bolt of pain shot through his knee. "Just fine."

CHAPTER TWENTY-ONE

The Presidio, a former army outpost turned national park, was a mixture of residences and businesses set amid a mini forest. The buildings were less densely packed than the areas in the adjacent neighborhoods to the east, and therefore likely to have fewer people, dead or undead.

Our route would skirt the edges of the Exploratorium and the edge of the park until we emerged somewhere in between the neighborhoods of Presidio Heights and Pacific Heights. Then we would make our way south into the upper Haight—since the sixties the home of hippies, tie-dye, and disenfranchised youth.

First, however, we had to get from Crissy Field across Marina Boulevard, one of the main conduits to the Golden Gate Bridge. Normally this would be a quick ten-minute walk. Now, all four lanes—the ones heading to the 101 on-ramp, and the opposite lanes heading into the Marina District—were a Dante-esque river of metal and humanity, clogged with stalled vehicles and foot traffic, all of it northbound.

Some of the cars were empty, left behind as their owners realized they weren't going to be moving any time soon. Others still had occupants who seemed to think laying on their horns would miraculously clear the jam. Police officers and SWAT types moved among the cars, trying unsuccessfully to persuade people to leave them and return to their homes.

The cacophony of horns and shouting shredded away at the nerve endings, making an already panicked situation even worse. A car alarm went off nearby, adding the final craptastic touch. It was one of those alarms with four alternating sounds, and if its inventor had been within arm's reach, I would happily have fed him to the nearest zombie.

We approached the pandemonium slowly, using the cover of the trees that dotted the south end of Crissy Fields to keep out of sight.

"Okay," Gabriel said as we reached the edge of the tree line. "We need to get to the other side of this clusterfuck, and into the Presidio as quickly and quietly as possible. If any of the local authorities get a good look at our toys, it could get ugly."

I raised an eyebrow.

"What, there isn't a secret handshake or get-out-of-jail-free card you guys use in these situations?" I was only partly joking. "I mean, it seems like the DZN would have connections up their super-secret wazoo."

Red snickered. Guess he thought I was funny, which was good, because Gabriel didn't look amused.

"We don't have time to deal with any delays, period. So quick and quiet, got it?" He shot Lil and me a look. "Emphasis on the 'quiet' part."

I almost gave him a one-fingered salute, but maturity won out, and I nodded instead. Besides, he was right. As it was, we would already stick out in our pseudo-SWAT gear. We looked—and were—tough, but we didn't look like we belonged to any official branch of law enforcement.

The A-Team looked more official than we did.

We all had our "squirrel rifles" out—even Tony who had reluctantly holstered the BAS across his back for the time being. I kind of liked the lighter rifle, even though

I definitely had a soft spot for my M4—which was likewise secured in a three-point Kevlar sling across my back. I felt overly accessorized.

Paramilitary Barbie at your service.

We reached the edge of the trees, and paused at the daunting sight before us. There was barely space between the tightly packed cars, and most of that space was filled with people. "Bumper to bumper" didn't begin to describe it. More like one continuous fender bender.

Some drivers on either edge of the asphalt had pulled onto the shoulder, trying to edge their way around the jam, but they found themselves stuck as the on-ramp merged onto the 101 and they ran out of room. Others pulled off onto the side streets, trying to turn themselves around, but there was no joy there either.

A couple of cars barreled off onto the grass in front of us, trying to find another way onto the bridge. I wished them luck as they sped off down Old Mason Street in hopes of finding a back route. Like lemmings, other motorists followed them.

San Francisco had never been a traffic-friendly city, and now it looked like it was well on its way to becoming a forty-nine square mile parking lot. *And a buffet for the hungry dead.* It was only a matter of time before zombies found their way to all these meals on wheels.

This scenario never played out well in any of the books or movies.

"We're going to have to go over the cars," Gabriel said quietly, his expression grim. "I'm on point. Ash, you're Tail End Charlie."

"Rear-guard, got it."

"Dr. Albert, you need to stay in the middle and Lil, you and Tony stick with him. Jones, Davis—" he nodded at the Gunsy Twins "—you know what to do."

They nodded back, vanishing into the crowd like two ghostly commandos.

"Stealth is no longer an option," Gabriel continued, "so go for quick. Once you're across, follow the edge of Lyon Street and keep moving until we get to the back of the Exploratorium. Go."

He dashed out onto the open grass toward the street, followed closely by the flight crew—they both seemed to be in good physical shape. Tony and Lil—Dr. Albert sandwiched between them—were next, with yours truly bringing up the rear. Gabriel vaulted over the hood of an empty Prius which was kissing the back of a Mini Cooper. He slid off the far side of it into an unoccupied patch of asphalt with a grace I couldn't help but admire, even under the circumstances.

Red and Carl were next, following in his footsteps as best they could. Lil practically bounced over the car, while Dr. Albert fussed and stalled, unwilling or unable to climb over the hood. Tony pushed him to the front end of the Prius, making him clamber over the bumpers, then followed him.

As soon as they'd cleared the first lane of traffic, I went for the hood slide, landing heavily on the asphalt just in time to see Gabriel vault over the sloping front of a shiny new pink and silver Smart Car with Hello Kitty stenciled on the side. The driver, a dark-haired girl in her teens, was still in the car and gave a shriek of surprised outrage, audible even over the rest of the chaos.

I shook my head. She had scarier things to worry about than a marred paint job.

Some of the panicking people barely noticed us, while others, seeing our gear, turned to us with varying degrees of anger, fear, and hope. A generically good-looking couple in their twenties stopped me as I pushed my way through the foot traffic—he was dark-haired and tall, she was petite and blonde. They looked like they should be in an ad for a tropical resort.

"What's going on?" the man asked, reaching out and grabbing my arm. "Can you help us?"

Well, hell. I guess I did look kind of official.

"The news said there's some sort of outbreak making people crazy," the blonde chimed in. "We just want to get to my parents' place in Mill Valley."

"You know there's a quarantine blockade, right?" I said.

"Yeah, and on the Bay Bridge and all the main arteries leading out of the city." The man frowned. "But we've been stuck here for at least an hour. Do you have any idea when we can expect traffic to start moving again?"

"Look, I can't help you," I said, trying to keep sight of the rest of the team as they made it over the next row of cars. I saw Lil vanish on the far side of a massive yellow Humvee. "I've got to go," I said, shaking off the man's hand. "The best thing for you and your girlfriend—"

"Fiancée," she said, flashing a ring at me with a shy smile.

"Fiancée," I amended, wondering why I was wasting the time, but unable to help myself. "The best thing you both can do is get off this road. If you live anywhere close, go home. Listen to your local news—they'll be airlifting people out when they can from the Bison Paddock in Golden Gate Park. If you can't get home, find shelter, wait until daylight, and get there as best you can." I glanced down at her feet, encased in a pair of gorgeous yet impractical *Sex in the City* heels. "And trade those shoes for something you can run in."

"Can't you go with us?" the woman asked. "You've got a gun, you could protect us."

"I'm... I'm on a special mission," I said, wincing at how lame that sounded, even as the words came out of my mouth. "I have to catch up with the rest of my team."

Lame or not, it worked. The man nodded as he grabbed his fiancée's hand and started helping her across the road toward the Presidio. I mentally wished them luck, and took off at a fast jog, circumnavigating the Humvee in favor of a more easily negotiated Acura.

Where the hell are they?

I scanned the lines of cars and people, getting jostled on all sides as I tried to hold ground instead of getting swept up in the migration toward the bridge.

Sudden screams ripped through the air from the Marina District to the east, sounds of pure terror that cut through the rest of the noise, even rising above the car alarms.

Shit. I knew what that meant.

I clambered back on top of the Acura and looked east, where I immediately spotted the all-too-familiar disjointed movements of the walking dead, at least twenty of them, converging on Marina Boulevard from all directions. More were sure to follow, honing in on their fellow zombies ringing the dinner bell with their plaintive moaning. People were going to die, and there wasn't a hell of a lot I could do about it.

Even as I watched, two zombies reached the edge of the road, latching on to the nearest living person and bearing them to the ground like rotting lions taking down a gazelle. The screams of the victim were horrifying, and the people nearby started screaming, too, trying to get away from the carnage by scrambling over cars and other pedestrians.

Several zombies honed in on an occupied vehicle. One of them reached into the open back window on the passenger side and hauled out a shrieking child, a little girl who couldn't have been more than five years old.

I couldn't stand it.

Bringing my rifle to bear, I quickly targeted the head of the zombie and fired three shots in succession before it could sink its teeth into the little girl. Its knees buckled and someone pulled the girl back into the car.

The other zombie pushed its fallen buddy out of the way and reached in after the prize. Doors on the driver's side opened and the occupants scrambled out onto the street, a teenage boy holding the little girl in a protective hug despite the terrified look on his face. He followed his parents to the other side of the road, where they vanished amidst the general chaos.

More screams rang out. I turned, looking in all directions. Zombies were coming out of the woodwork.

"Get out of here!" I yelled. "Get inside, lock yourselves in! Get the hell *out of here*!" No one paid me any attention. I thought about firing a few shots into the air, but the whole point of the squirrel rifles was stealth. *Oh, for Tony's BAS.*

"Ash!"

My head snapped to one side as I heard someone call my name. Relief washed over me when I saw Lil waving frantically from the far side of Marina Boulevard, the rest of the team behind her in the tree line. I waved back, letting her know I saw her, and leapt back on to the asphalt.

"Hey, this bitch has a gun!"

Someone slammed into me—hard—causing me to fall backward against the Acura. My head hit the upper doorframe just hard enough to rattle my teeth and make me see stars, but not hard enough to get me to let go of my rifle as the person tried to yank it out of my hands.

I shook my head, told the stars to fuck off, and focused.

"Let go of it and I won't hurt you." But a beefy man in a Giants T-shirt and matching baseball cap shoved his bulk up against me, exhaling beer breath into my face. Guess it'd been Miller time before he'd hit the road.

"You really didn't have to call me a bitch," I growled, putting the side of the rifle against his chest and giving a push that sent him flying back into two similarly reeky guys right behind him. All three stumbled back against the tide of people trying to fight their way onto the bridge. I took advantage of the moment to level the business end of the rifle at them.

"If you're smart, you'll get the hell off this road and

find shelter until the military can get you out of here," I said. "If you're stupid, you'll keep trying to fuck with me, and you won't have to worry about what's coming up that road."

All three of them lunged forward.

Did no one pay attention to the Darwin Awards any more?

I slammed the butt of the rifle into the first guy's jaw. He collapsed, poleaxed. His two friends caught him before he hit the ground.

Now will you give me some fighting room?

A mob of people surged into the space between the Acura and the adjacent line of vehicles, shoving the two jerks forward, right into me. I ended up squashed against the Acura again. One of the beer-infused males took advantage of the crush to grab the stock of my rifle, wrenching it out of my hands. The sling yanked my arm out and up, the sturdy nylon strap wrapped tightly around my wrist. It hurt like hell, but stopped the guy from taking off with my weapon.

He swore and yanked again, trying to get the rifle free and giving me a nice rope burn as the nylon dragged around my wrist. Grabbing a length of the strap with both hands, I yanked back.

As we wrestled for possession of the rifle, I became aware of a new sound—a weird rhythmic crunching thud, as if someone was jumping on a metal trampoline. Both the man and I paused in our tug-of-war as the sound grew closer.

Crunch.

Five cars ahead of the Acura, someone was running on top of the stopped vehicles, barely pausing as he went from car top to trunk to hood, as if each surface was just a springboard for the next point of contact. If Gabriel had made it look easy, this guy made it appear effortless, going from SUV to Smart to Honda without any apparent trouble—despite the difference in shapes and sizes.

"What the hell?" The man trying to wrestle my rifle away from me just stopped and stared.

Almost as if he was aware he had an audience, the guy looked over in our direction as he leapt—graceful as a cat—from the back of a Prius onto the hood of a Toyota. He paused long enough for me to get a good look at him, almost as if he was posing for a picture.

Brown hair flopped over a red bandana knotted behind his head, fair-colored skin flushed red with the exercise. Brown eyes with a crazy gleam in them. Not psycho crazy, but "boy, isn't this just the best fun ever" type crazy, with an exhilarated grin to top it off. Kind of like Lil's "isn't it fun to kill zombies!" expression.

And then he was moving again, hitting three or four more cars before landing on the ground on the Presidio side, and vanishing into the deepening shadows of the trees.

"Who was that masked man?" I said to myself. Shaking my head, I turned back to business at hand. I gave my opponent what a Scottish friend of mine called "a mou'ful o' headies" by way of bashing him in the nose with my forehead. He howled in pain and let go of the rifle.

I followed up with the butt of the weapon to his stomach and turned to the remaining man, who was smart enough to keep his hands to himself.

"Take your friends and get the hell off the streets," I warned him. Without waiting to see if he listened, I pushed past, shoving my way through a totally panicked river of people, scrambling over a Saturn, and finally making my way to the far side of the road, where Lil bounced up and down like Tigger on speed. The rest had already gone.

"Being Tail End Charlie sucks," I said.

"Or maybe you just suck at being Tail End Charlie." Lil's tone was caustic, and I looked at her with surprised hurt. "You're not supposed to stop and help people right now," she snapped. "We *can't* help them. We have to keep moving, or you could die!"

"Well, I'm not dead, and I moved as fast as I could." I kept my voice level. "They were pulling a little girl out of a car, Lil. I had to do something." She turned away from me and I reached out, putting a hand on her shoulder. "You would have done the same thing, and you know it. And I'd be where you are, ripping you a new one for scaring the shit out of me."

"Well… yeah!" Lil glared back at me.

"So we'd better catch up with the rest of the gang, or Gabriel's gonna chew my ass, too. And yours, for letting Dr. Crazy Pants out of your sight."

"Oh, crap." Lil looked guiltily over her shoulder. "You're right. Let's go!"

We darted into the trees. I silently hoped for the best for everyone stuck in the traffic jam, knowing that I could have stayed there and used all my ammo, and people would still die. We had to set up the lab and find the cure if we wanted to make a real difference.

CHAPTER TWENTY-TWO

AMARILLO, TEXAS

"Ohmygod, I am sta-a-arving!"

Ted's stomach rumbled, as if to punctuate his words. Kim's growled by way of reply. They'd been on the road for hours, with only a brief bathroom break at a truck stop somewhere between Albuquerque and the Texas border.

The twins grinned at each other.

"Calico County?" they said in unison.

Calico County in Amarillo, Texas, was a traditional way station on their yearly cross-country drive from Los Angeles to Michigan to visit their folks. Right off the highway, Calico County served home-style southern food including catfish, fried okra, and baskets of miniature sweet and savory rolls. Kim always stole the cinnamon rolls right away, but Ted didn't mind, because the waitress brought refills every time she came to the table. Hometown cooking, smiling staff, and cheap prices. It almost made the twins reconsider their attitude toward Texas.

Almost.

"Are we there yet? Are we there yet? Are we—"

Kim reached out and thwacked Ted on the back of his head, keeping her other hand firmly on the wheel.

"You're dealing with a woman with low blood sugar, who's running on five hours' sleep, max. Do you really want to piss me off?"

As if in accordance with her mood, the threatening thunderclouds overhead made good their promise and started dumping a shitload of rain, accompanied by cracks of thunder and flashes of lightning.

Ted laughed and shook his head.

"Sorry, sis, I—"

"What the hell?"

His reply was cut off by Kim's sudden expletive. She jerked the wheel and the car swerved across the I-40, which was luckily empty behind them.

She brought the Corolla under control, knuckles white on the wheel as she pulled back over to the right side of the highway.

"Did you see that?"

"Huh?" he said. "See what?"

"That thing on the road!" Kim stabbed her finger in an indeterminate direction. "Didn't you see it?"

Ted looked back and saw a lot of rain, and very little else.

"Jeez, Kim, your blood sugar is for shit."

"I'm serious! There was someone in the road. Right in the middle of the fucking highway!"

Ted rolled his eyes.

"Are you going all Jeepers Creepers on me? 'Cause I do not want to have my eyes removed by an underwear-sniffing monster."

"You don't believe me."

"I didn't say that," he replied, choosing his words carefully. "I just didn't see anything."

"Which automatically means I'm imagining things?"

Ted considered his options. If he said "No," she'd ream him for the next hour or two. If he said "yes," he'd have to listen to whatever bullshit she thought she'd seen.

"What exactly did you see?"

Better to humor her than put up with her hostile sulking for the next few hours. No one could sulk with more hostility than his sister. She had refined it to an art.

"A woman crossing the freeway," she said. "Looked like a crack whore."

"So where did she go?"

Kim shrugged, the motion not needing the middle finger to convey the "fuck you" that lay behind it.

"How the hell should I know? I was busy trying to keep the car on the road!"

Ted chose to keep quiet until he saw a sign for Julian Blvd-Paramount Blvd exit, a quarter mile up the road.

"There's the exit," he said.

"Thank god." Kim merged over onto the frontage road, turning right onto Paramount. "Almost there." The restaurant was up ahead on the right a few hundred yards distant, almost impossible to miss because of the two huge signs shaped like canning jars, towering in the middle of the parking lot. The sign on the right depicted canned peaches, the words "Calico County Restaurant" stamped across it, while the second showed canned green beans, proclaiming "Home Cookin' Good!"

No lies there. Ted looked up as they neared the parking lot. One of the two quaint old-fashioned streetlamps on either side of the entrance flickered on and off, and the other was completely out. The restaurant itself looked dark inside.

Ted frowned.

"Well, shit, are they even open?"

"They have to be!" Kim scowled as she pulled into the lot. "It's only eight thirty."

"Maybe the electricity went out," Ted said as another jagged bolt of lighting arced through the sky, followed by a window-rattling thunderclap.

"God, I hope not! Because I would seriously kill for some fried okra."

The man who lurched in front of the car came out of nowhere. The bumper of the Corolla smashed into him before Kim could react. She shrieked in shock as blood splattered onto the windshield. Then she slammed on the brakes hard enough to knock the air out of both of them as their seatbelts did the job of stopping them from going through the windshield.

The car screeched to a halt. Kim turned the key as soon

as she'd recovered her breath, cutting the engine off in mid-sputter. The sound of rain splattering on the roof was suddenly deafening, thousands of leaden fingers tapping the metal above their heads.

Kim unfastened her seatbelt, and Ted grabbed her arm as she fumbled for the door latch.

"What are you doing?"

"I just hit someone," she said. She jerked her arm away and glared at her brother. "I need to see if he's still alive." She opened the car door and jumped out, rain sluicing down and flattening her curls.

Even with the driving rain, Ted got a good look at the man staggering to his feet in front of the car, as the headlights illuminated his torn, blood-stained jeans and Western-style shirt, light reflecting off the shiny buttons. Ted could see how many pieces were missing from his body, and the vacantly hungry look in his milky eyes as he honed in on Kim.

"Oh god…"

Ted shoved the passenger door open and started to jump out, but was halted by his seatbelt.

"Shit!" He fumbled with the clasp, fingers clumsy with fear as raindrops splattered against him. What took a few seconds seemed like the work of hours as he finally disengaged the locking mechanism and stumbled out of the car, still woozy from the jolting stop. Rounding the front of the car, he saw Kim reaching for the man—thing—she'd hit, as it in turn reached greedy hands toward her.

"Kim, no! Get away from him!"

Even as Ted cried out his warning, Kim grasped the man by his shoulders to help him up. The man wrapped his hands around one of her wrists, hoisting himself up even as he sunk his teeth into her forearm.

Kim shrieked in surprise and pain as she tried to pull away from her attacker. Ted wrapped his arms around his twin's torso and yanked backward. He heard an audible ripping sound as a chunk of Kim's flesh tore out, eliciting an agonized wail from his sister.

A low moaning from the far end of the parking lot caught Ted's attention as he half-dragged Kim away from her attacker, who chewed mindlessly on the bloody hunk of meat left between his teeth.

"You mother-fucking bastard!" Ted slammed a closed fist into the man's nose, feeling the bones shatter beneath his hand. The man toppled over onto the ground, still chewing.

"Ted, it hurts, it really hurts…"

He turned back to his sister as blood spurted from the wound on her arm.

"We've got to get you to a doctor, okay?"

More moans sounded from the edge of the parking lot, spread around the entire perimeter. Ted looked up and saw indistinct figures lurching and staggering out of the shadows as the one light flickered on and off.

"What the fuck?"

He started to half-carry Kim back to the car when a flicker of movement in one of the restaurant windows caught his eye. There was someone in there. And they'd have a phone and could call 911 and get an ambulance out here a lot quicker than he could find a hospital in the torrential downpour.

Changing direction, Ted dragged Kim over to the red double doors under the shelter of the overhanging awning, trying to ignore the fucked up druggies slowly heading toward them. Reaching the doors, he grabbed one of the handles and tugged.

Nothing.

He tried pushing, but no success there either. The doors were locked from the inside.

"Shit!" Ted turned back to the parking lot. Their path to the car was now blocked by at least a half dozen of the slowly shambling figures, backlit by the glow of the headlights. Even so, they all looked totally fucked up, some of them looked like they had… pieces missing.

They were moving slowly. Ted thought he could maybe get back to the car, but one quick glance at his sister told him she would never make it. She was losing more blood by the minute, and barely able to stand on her own. The bastard had really done a number on her.

Ted used his free hand and pounded on the doors.

"Help!" He slammed his open palm against the wood. "Let us in! For God's sake, we need help!"

Lightning flashed, the ensuing thunder right on its heels. The figures staggered closer. The storm was right on top of them.

Kim moaned, sagging against Ted's supporting arm. He cursed and smashed his fist against the doors.

"We are going to fucking die out here if you don't let us in!"

The figures were ten feet away and closing.

Ted shook his head, unable to believe how quickly their yearly road trip had turned into this fucked up house of horrors, his sister bleeding her life out as nightmare things slowly and inexorably closed in on them. They would die in Amarillo, Texas, which was just wrong on so many levels.

"Kimmy, we're gonna have to try to make it back to the car," he said. "Okay?"

"I can't... it hurts... it hurts so much."

Kim went limp against Ted's arm, sliding to the ground as his muscles gave out against the sudden dead weight of her body. He staggered and fell back against the doors... and inside the foyer of the restaurant, as both doors suddenly opened behind him. Hands dragged him inside, out of the rain and away from Kim.

His last glimpse of his sister was her prone body as the shambling nightmares in the parking lot closed in on her. Then the doors slammed shut, and locks clicked back into place.

Ted stared up at a half dozen or so terrified people ringed around him, including a family with three stunned looking kids. An older woman with a sagging beehive upsweep, wearing a waitress uniform, stepped forward as Ted got to his feet. His first thought was for Kim, and he lunged for the door.

Two burly trucker types grabbed him before he could touch the handles and dragged him back into the restaurant. They smelled of sweat and fear.

"Dammit, let me go! My sister's out there!"

The woman with the beehive spoke.

"Were you bit?" Her accent was pure Texas.

"Are you people crazy? Didn't you hear me? My sister is still out there!" He fought against the men who restrained him, but they collectively outweighed him by at least a hundred pounds.

"Were you bit?" she repeated.

"No!" Ted shook his head. "No, but my sister—"

"If she was bit, she's dead. And she'll be one of them soon enough." Her grim tone left no room for doubt.

"One of what?" he demanded. "What the fuck is going on out there?" Ted's voice broke, all the fight leaving him. He knew in his gut that his twin was dead.

"Fuckin' freaks," one of the truckers said.

The waitress nodded.

"They're dead, but they get up. And they're hungry."

"But that's—"

"Crazy?" She nodded again. "Sure is. But it's happening."

"What about the police? Have you—"

She laughed, but there was no humor in the sound.

"Bunch of them out there, hon," she said, nodding toward the window. "And they're as hungry as the rest."

"And it's not just here," one of the men added. "Sounds like all of Amarillo is in deep shit."

"Maybe the rest of Texas, too," the other man added. "We've been holed up in here for two days now."

"We've got plenty of food," the waitress said. "We figure we can ride this out until someone gets this shit under control."

Something thudded against the front doors. The men let Ted go and scrambled further back into the restaurant as a face pressed up against one of the little windows. The outside light flashed on and off, on and off, allowing Ted to see his sister's face, the muscles now slack, mouth opening and closing in mindless hunger, eyes milky white.

"Kim?"

The waitress put a hand on his shoulder.

"That ain't your sister no more, hon. There ain't nothing left in there. Now come on and sit. I'll get you some food." She patted him again. "We're safe."

Ted looked at her.

"But for how long?"

CHAPTER TWENTY-THREE

Once we left the madness of Marina Boulevard, things got quiet. Maybe *too* quiet. The screams faded into the distance, the thick canopy of trees and increasing fog swallowing up sounds. Except for the occasional buildings, it was a lot like being in the forest around Redwood Grove.

The air had the crispness of autumn interlaced with a slightly deeper chill that heralded winter. Wisps of mist blew between the trees, and if there was any sunshine hiding in the overcast skies, it wasn't showing itself. Our feet crunched softly on damp pine needles and eucalyptus leaves. I inhaled deeply, my nose wrinkling in distaste as I caught a whiff of decay underneath the fragrance of evergreen and rich, loamy soil.

The deepening shadows and our dark clothing made it easier to move without being observed by the few people we encountered. We slipped through the trees along the back of a parking lot, and then went deeper into the cover of the Presidio woods.

There was a lot of activity at the Exploratorium itself, most likely folks from Marina Boulevard seeking a refuge from the "crazy people." Not a bad place to hole up if you didn't want to be bored—lots of cool science-based games and toys.

I wished them well.

We kept moving, staying as far away from buildings as possible. People moved around in the distance—some running in panic, others as quiet as we were. Others moved slowly and stiffly, not the lurching gait of the undead, but the "kicked-in-the-gut" walk of someone in shock.

I heard muffled sobs as one man supported another, younger man, passing nearby. Had they seen their loved ones die from Walker's, and then resurrect? Or maybe their loved ones had been torn apart and devoured, making them the lucky ones.

It was hard to tell.

We were still dealing with relatively few zombies, but the lethal combo of Walker's and Dr. Albert's flu vaccine were doing their thing. And once those zombies started biting, that population explosion Paxton had mentioned would begin.

"Thank you, Uncle George."

I turned to see Tony standing in front of a sign. I took a quick look—directional arrows pointed the way toward a group of buildings where a statue of Yoda stood out front.

The sign read, "Lucasfilm and Industrial Light & Magic."

Of course.

Lights were on there, as well, the silhouettes of people moving around inside clearly visible. If anyone would be prepared for something like this, it seemed like it would be Lucas. Then again, their zombies would probably be CGI and cutesy.

"We're not here to eat you; we just want to be lo-o-ved!"

Suddenly Gabriel stumbled on something on the ground. He was passing between two close-set trees, the path sloping sharply downward. He swore under his breath, recovering his balance and shaking something off his foot before raising the butt end of his rifle and smashing it down. The crunching sound was all too familiar, so when it was my turn to pass by, I wasn't surprised to see the remains of a very fresh female zombie lying face up across the path, one hand still outstretched.

Even with the damage to her forehead, I could tell she'd been young and pretty, thick red hair splayed out around what was left of her head.

Leave it to Gabriel to get attacked by a hot young zombie.

We kept moving. I decided to retire my squirrel rifle in favor of my katana, figuring I wasn't going to be doing much shooting, for fear of mistaking living humans for zombies. The .22 joined the M4, both snug in their respective slings.

Maybe if I'd accessorized with firearms back in the day, my jerk ex-husband would have treated me with more respect. Or maybe I'd be in jail for homicide.

Justifiable, of course.

Our speed picked up, fewer buildings and fewer people making it easier to glide through the trees in appropriate ninja-like fashion. Red and Carl both seemed at home with the whole stealth thing, and I assumed the Gunsy Twins were still ghosting their way ahead of us. Even Tony—for all his height—managed to navigate the terrain with relative ease.

The only exception was no real surprise. Dr. Albert seemed incapable of taking a step without finding a crackling branch, or of moving more than a few feet without going into a muttering monologue. Didn't matter how many times Lil or Tony told him to put a lid on it, he couldn't seem to stop. Luckily there was enough ambient noise coming from all directions to mask his lack of ninja skills.

Gabriel paused up ahead, waiting until we all caught up. I took advantage of the pause to take a close look at him, both to see how he was doing and, well, to enjoy the view while I had the chance.

So sue me for being shallow.

"We're nearly up to the edge of the Presidio," he said quietly. He pointed to a road winding through the park to our right. "Follow that road until it intersects Pacific Avenue. Follow Pacific to Arguello. We'll be overshooting by a few blocks, but Arguello is a straight shot to Golden Gate Park without any of the weird jinks that a lot of the streets take between here and the Haight.

"If anyone gets separated, just go straight to Golden Gate, stick to the east edge, and you'll hit Kezar. Got it?"

We all nodded.

Soon we could see Pacific Avenue, with well-kept houses that were visible through the trees, and streetlights glowing softly on the other side of the road. People streamed past on foot, some heading west, others darting into the Presidio. I could see yet more cars in the street beyond. These were moving, but very slowly, and even so the occasional crunch of metal on metal could be heard. No gunshots, though, which was either a positive sign, or an indication that San Francisco needed a few more hard-core survivalists.

Not that most hard-core survivalists would feel at home in San Francisco. My dad, for instance, was an interesting mix of liberal environmentalist and self-professed gun nut. He preferred Lake County, where he could grow his own organic, sustainable food *and* have live ammo delivered by mail.

God, I hope my parents are safe.

CHAPTER TWENTY-FOUR

By the time we reached Arguello Boulevard, the sun had set, the lengthening shadows giving way to darkness.

The sound of screams and sirens increased as night fell.

Gridlock was, as I expected, outrageously bad. Where cars had been moving on Pacific, Arguello and the adjacent streets were parking lots, so congested not even a Smart Car could negotiate its way through the city. Hell, a moped would've had trouble getting from one block to the next. And yet people were honking horns as they tried to pull out into the non-moving traffic.

The gated entrance to Presidio Terrace, a swanky private community on the west side of Arguello, was blocked by a very expensive three-car pileup; a Mercedes, a Porsche and… was that a DeLorean?

Threats of insurance and lawsuits mingled with the sound of barking dogs, blaring sirens, and screams.

Most of the cars were empty, though, with the exception of those sandwiched between other vehicles. The unlucky occupants were trapped unless they were agile enough to wriggle out of their windows.

The sidewalks and streets were clogged with foot traffic, people weaving in and out between cars, calling for missing friends and family, or just trying to make their way to some other, safer spot, without having any real idea of where that might be or what they were fleeing from.

Would there even be a safe refuge, if they succeeded in getting out of the city? Or would the country collapse into roving bands of paramilitary types and cults headed by nut jobs with messiah complexes? If they were *really* unlucky, they'd make it to an island inexplicably inhabited by clans of feuding Irishmen with bizarre ideas of training the zombies to adjust their eating habits.

Stop it! I gave myself a mental slap.

Oblivious of my mental digression, Gabriel consulted his jacked up iPhone.

"Looks like no matter which way we hit it, there are going to be crowds," he said. "Just keep moving, whatever you do—don't stop until you've reached the destination."

"What if we run into zombies?" Tony asked.

"Try not to get distracted, but… use your judgment. Just keep moving."

We spread out in a line, Gabriel a block and a half ahead of us. The crowds seemed to part before him, and we all just followed in his wake, trying to take advantage of the opening he'd created before the crowds closed in on us like the waters pouring back on Pharaoh's army.

Some people pulled rolling luggage behind them, others had pet carriers. Dozens of little cheap "bag lady" shopping carts were in evidence, stuffed to the brim with whatever the owners considered essential.

I had no idea what I'd take with me if I were in the same situation—I hadn't had the chance to decide. And I hadn't really missed any of my belongings. So I couldn't imagine how these people must have felt.

"Montana! Come back!" A woman's voice called out frantically as a dog ran by—some sort of cattle dog mix—leash dragging behind it. Before I could do anything, Lil's foot stomped down on the tail end of the leash, stopping the dog in its tracks, jerking it backward.

She immediately grabbed the leash as the owner hurried over, her expression flashing between panic and gratitude as she dropped to her knees and gathered her dog against her in a fierce hug.

"Montana, don't ever do that again!" Tears streamed down her face as she looked up at Lil. "Thank you."

Lil didn't say anything, just handed her the leash, her expression fierce, angry, and distraught at the same time. So I spoke up.

"If you live near here, just get back inside," I said.

"I'm trying to get to the vet," the woman said in oddly apologetic tones.

That surprised a laugh out of me.

"I don't think they're gonna be open."

"No, I work there." The woman patted her dog. "There are a bunch of animals and someone has to take care of them. I'm meeting one of the other techs and we're… we're going to stay and make sure the animals are okay."

Lil's fierce expression relaxed.

"Where is it?" she asked. "The vet's office, I mean?"

Oh, no. Before I could say anything, the woman pointed south.

"Arguello and Geary. Just a few blocks away."

Lil nodded.

"We'll make sure you get there."

I didn't bother arguing. It was on our way, and if it soothed Lil's troubled heart, I was all for it. And yeah, okay, it'd make me feel better too.

I just hope Gabriel doesn't notice.

"Stick with us," I said to the woman. She nodded gratefully, wrapped the leash twice around her wrist, and followed as best she could.

"Are you part of some sort of SWAT team?" she asked, panting as we navigated the stream of pedestrians.

"Something like that," I said. Fortunately, it was enough to satisfy her.

There weren't any zombies at the moment, though we couldn't entirely escape their undeniable scent. I wondered how many people were lying inside their homes, dead or dying from Walker's or a random bite or scratch, and how many of those people would soon emerge to join their fellow San Franciscans on the streets.

We crossed Geary Avenue, threading our way between parked cars to the gas station on the far corner. Vehicles queued up for the pumps, but no one was moving. Fist fights broke out for no reason other than frustration. A couple of enterprising men filled two gallon cans at the pump and ran back toward their cars, but unless they had hovercraft they wouldn't be going anywhere.

"Here!" The woman stopped in front of the building adjoining the gas station, her dog heeling next to her. "This is where I work." She fumbled in her purse, bringing out a set of keys.

"Do you think your friend is here?" Lil asked.

"The lights are on… I hope so. He's supposed to bring the people food and bottled water." Her hands shook, but she managed to insert the key and open the door. Lil and I shielded her from view.

"Good luck," I said.

"Thank you." She slipped in after her dog. "And best of luck to you, too, whatever you're doing." The door shut after her and I heard the definitive *click* of the lock.

"Better now?" I said to Lil as we resumed our path toward Golden Gate Park.

"What about the rest of the animals?" she said.

Guess not.

"I mean, the animals in there are lucky. But are people just leaving their pets behind?"

"Don't think about it." I kept walking. Lil hurried to keep up with me.

"But don't you—"

I stopped so suddenly Lil ran into me. I turned and took her by the shoulders.

"You can't think about it because if you do, you'll go crazy. We can't save everyone, Lil. We just can't. That includes the animals. And it sucks and I hate it as much as you do. But we can't think about it. If we do, we will shut down. We have to count on there being more people like that woman and her friend, people like you and me. Okay?"

She didn't look at me and I shook her gently by the shoulders.

"Look. We went back for Binkey and Doodle, right? And they're safe and sound with Simone and Jamie. There are lots of crazies like us out there. So think about those people instead, okay?"

"What about the pet stores?"

I just shook my head.

"Remember. Crazies like us. Good crazies. We're not the only ones. Just remember that, okay?"

She nodded, still not looking me in the eye—and there was a distinctly mutinous expression on her face. Lil wouldn't make a good poker player. I'd have to keep an eye on her, or she'd be haring off every time she heard a dog bark.

LOS ANGELES

Griff yawned and stretched, a long satisfying movement that allowed each limb to wake up slowly. His hand brushed against a faux fur throw that had ended up thrown against the headboard at some point during the night's activities. Good quality stuff, not cheap. The fur was as soft as a Persian cat.

Griff liked cats. Beautiful and amoral creatures, they gave affection on their own terms, taking it away just as quickly if touched the wrong way. He had no doubt that if cat owners suddenly became mouse-sized over night, their beloved pets would eat them, but only after playing with them first.

Nothing personal, that was the thing about cats.

He'd like to get one—maybe two—for companionship if things ever settled down to the point that he could stay in one place for longer than a few months. Until then it wouldn't be fair. Cats didn't much like change.

Griff thrived on change, on chaos. And variety was, after all, the spice of life.

He glanced at the girl in bed next to him, enjoying the satisfied smile on her face. Giselle, a sweet young thing from Kansas, blonde, blue-eyed, corn-fed. And—wonder of wonders—she didn't want to be an actress or a model. No, Giselle wanted to be a makeup artist, and had made it as a contestant on Face Off.

For that reason alone, Griff had used condoms when they had sex. Who was he to deprive the world of the next Tom Savini or Greg Nicotero? As far as he knew, the amount of infection in his saliva was minimal—enough to bring her back when she died, but not enough to kill her any time soon.

From what he'd seen on the news, heavily censored though it was, things weren't looking too bright and cheery for the United States. If the USA went south, where did that leave Canada and the rest of the Americas? Border fences only went so far. And with modern transportation, international airport hubs... well, Giselle might not have time to see her career rise.

Griff felt something else rise as Giselle gave a little moan, somewhere between discomfort and desire, and wriggled her ass against him in her sleep. Very tempting. Although it would mean getting out of bed to see if he had any more condoms stashed away in the bathroom.

He really didn't want to get out of the warm comfort of his bed, especially with the enticing curves pressed up against him.

Would it be such a bad thing if he didn't bother? Considering the tone of the news he'd been watching, it might even be a kindness on his part.

Before he could make up his mind, the doorbell rang. A cheap generic buzzer, nothing fancy like Big Ben or a chintzy version of Beethoven's Fifth. He glanced at the bedside clock, which indicated 11 p.m.

A bit late for visitors.

"Is that the pizza?" Giselle said groggily.

"Did we order pizza?"

She murmured something that sounded like "with anchovies," and curled back up under the covers.

The doorbell rang again. Maybe they had ordered pizza, somewhere between the second and third bottle of wine.

Giselle made a sound of protest as Griff got out of bed.

"Be right back, love." He was steady on his feet—his improved metabolism was very handy, one of the better side effects. He'd always had a good head for alcohol, but this was like having the entire buzz with none of the downside.

The doorbell rang yet again, a shrill, piercing sound that was really getting on his tits.

"Oh, for fuck's sake…" The pizza delivery boy might not like his tip.

Griff considered pulling on a pair of jeans, but the doorbell ringing yet again changed his mind. Fuck whoever it was if they couldn't take a joke.

He threw open the door, not bothering to look through the peephole first.

It wasn't a pizza delivery boy.

Griff raised an eyebrow when he saw his visitors.

"Oh," he said. "It's you." He let them in and shut the door. He hoped they'd let the girl live.

CHAPTER TWENTY-FIVE

The smell of necrotizing flesh became stronger as we neared Golden Gate Park, and more gunshots peppered the auditory chaos. Lil was back helping Tony corral Dr. Albert, who had started lagging behind. That couldn't be helped—he was neither young nor fit, and keeping up with Tony's long-legged stride would have been a challenge for most people.

Red and Carl loped along at an easy pace a few yards behind Gabriel, while the Gunsy Twins were nowhere to be seen.

What could be seen were a lot more sick civilians, the telltale signs of the amped up Walker's virus clearly visible. Eyes looking like bloody egg yolks, dark fluids leaking from body cavities, and the smell of impending death. A woman in jogging clothes suddenly fell to the ground, body convulsing.

Moans rose in a chorus over the rest of the noise.

"Shit," Tony said. "Time to level up."

He was right. The zombie population explosion had officially begun. They were appearing from side streets and buildings, at first one or two at a time, with the trickle slowly turning into a steady stream.

People could do all the macho posturing they wanted with friends while watching *The Walking Dead*, all "Dude, I'd totally shoot you in the head if you were a zombie."

But when it came right down to it, most people—no matter how many zombie movies they'd seen—couldn't accept the reality of it suddenly lurching into their midst. Which is why so many were bitten within minutes after the zombies appeared.

My head knew we couldn't stop and help everyone we saw along the way. My gut, however, kept trying to convince me otherwise by twisting in knots every time we passed someone who looked lost and afraid. I could only imagine what this was doing to Mack, who felt others' pain with an empathy I didn't envy.

A female zombie wearing a "Team Edward" T-shirt and jeans staggered out from a doorway, reaching for the nearest warm body, which happened to be mine. I automatically shoved the business end of my katana into its left eye, using my foot to brace against Edward's sparkly white face as I pulled the blade back out, really wishing there was a way to do it without the nasty suction sound.

Schlorp.

Ugh.

"You killed Bebe!"

I barely had time to register movement behind me when something smacked into the back of my head, hard enough to knock me into a nearby garage door.

I turned just in time to ward off another blow from a young man, mid-twenties and built like a gym rat, all pecs and biceps and deltoids and possibly steroids, judging from the insane rage in his eyes. Of course, if the twice-dead Bebe was his girlfriend or a relative, I couldn't blame him. But I wasn't going to stand still and take another hit to the head.

He swung and I slipped to one side, his closed fist missing me by a narrow margin. I grabbed his wrist, twisting his arm up and back, driving him to his knees.

"If that was your girlfriend, I'm sorry," I said harshly, holding the struggling, swearing man in place. "But she was dead before I did anything to her."

It was then I noticed the bite mark on his arm, a hunk of flesh the size of an egg gone from his forearm, a putrid smell already wafting up from the wound. This man was already dead, too.

He just didn't know it yet.

I let him go and he collapsed onto the sidewalk, cradling the dead girl in his arms as he started sobbing.

"Bebe, Bebe!"

I stood awkwardly next to him, guilt and anger mixing in a stomach-churning cocktail. I'd had no choice, but that didn't stop me from feeling his grief, or wonder if I should put him out of his misery before he turned and started spreading it. I heard a faint pop, and a hole suddenly appeared in the man's head. He slumped lifelessly across his girlfriend's corpse.

I looked around to see who fired the shot, but none of my fellow team members were visible. Then I looked across the street to see Davis—or was it Jones?—standing on top of a car, rifle in hand. He gave me a little nod before vanishing again. I was just as glad he'd taken the decision out of my hands. And I hoped he and Jones—or was it Davis?—had a lot of ammo.

Golden Gate Park was smack dead ahead of us, less than a block away. A large group of what I'd started to think of as refugees streamed across Arguello on Fulton, the street that ran parallel to the park. They were heading towards the ocean. Babies wailed and children cried in that tired, hopeless way a truly exhausted kid will cry. Voices rose in frustration and fear as families and friends tried to keep their groups together. A woman ran past me.

"Sophia!" she yelled. "Where's Sophia?" A man was close on her heels, with two little girls in tow.

I rarely even thought about the existence of a higher being, but I found myself muttering "please let them be safe" over and over as I watched more and more people streaming past with their belongings, their children, and their pets.

Apparently no one was listening to me. It was the

Shrieks rose in the darkness like a clarion call, from an apartment building across the street—one with an open courtyard. More joined in as several zombies staggered into the grass from the far end, latching onto a family of four—the parents and two kids—each dragging a rolling suitcase behind them.

The little girl had a pink Barbie suitcase, the boy a blue and red Spider-Man one. Both cases were splattered with blood within seconds as the zombies ripped into the kids and their parents before I could react.

I'd missed the disintegration of Redwood Grove. I'd been fighting off the zombie virus and making my transformation into a wild card when the shit really hit the fan, then spent a few days training to hone my combat skills. By that time most of the human population of the town, college, and the surrounding areas were either dead or turned, with a few survivors holed up to wait for rescue.

Suddenly it struck me how lucky I'd been, because I hadn't had to watch the innocent being torn to pieces in front of me.

We're wild cards, not super heroes. I couldn't spin the world backwards on its axis to turn back time. I couldn't save those children or their parents. I tried to remember what I'd told Lil. We couldn't save everyone, but every person—or animal—we *did* save counted for something, and we'd have to let that keep us sane in the face of increasingly insurmountable odds and rising death toll.

At that moment, though, it didn't help. Tears streamed down my face as I forced myself to move, wading into the torrent of humanity on Fulton Street and shoving my way through to the other side.

CHAPTER TWENTY-SIX

Gabriel called a brief stop. Dr. Albert was heaving like a set of clogged bellows. We hunkered down in a sheltered grove of pine trees, caught our breath, and shared some bottled water while Gabriel went off a few feet and pulled out the radio.

Lil looked exhausted, her eyes closed, lashes dark against pale skin. Tony, on the other hand, looked like a typical bored, sullen teen, leaning up against a tree and giving the doctor the stink-eye.

Red and Carl seemed to be holding up physically, but their expressions—drawn and stunned—showed that this was their first actual field experience with zombies. No sign of Davis and Jones, but I had no doubt they were within close proximity.

I took a sip of water, passed the bottle to Carl, and then settled on my haunches against a tree trunk. I closed my eyes, breathing deeply as I did my best to wipe my memory clear of the last ten minutes.

Very quickly, however, I started feeling increasingly twitchy. I had the distinct sensation that I was being watched. Not in a good way either, but in that furtive stalker kind of way. I opened my eyes, keeping the lids at half-mast, and scanned the surroundings. There wasn't anyone obvious, but I was positive someone had his or her eyes on me.

And that was a creepy image all by itself. It reminded me of the quintessential literary grotesquerie, "His eyes slid up her dress."

I tried to get a sense of where the feeling was coming from, but there was too much ambient noise to get a bead on it. Unfortunately, my enhanced senses didn't come with psychic radar.

Although...

Peering between the trees, I looked out over Fulton and caught a brief glimpse of someone standing on top of a car, looking in my direction. Before I could focus enough to pick out any details, the person jumped off the car and into the crowd. It may have been a coincidence, but the sense of being watched vanished along with whoever had been perched there.

Whatever. The feeling was gone, and I had more important things to worry about.

Gabriel finished his conversation, shoved the radio back into its holster on his belt, and motioned us over to gather round. By the time we got there, Davis and Jones had materialized out of the trees.

"Change of plans," Gabriel said. "Kezar is out."

Uh-oh.

Lil sidled up and leaned against me like a little kid or a puppy. It warmed my heart that she would seek me out for comfort. I put an arm around her, and she rested her head against my shoulder. The manic energy had dissipated.

"Attempts to secure the Bison Paddock were a bust," he continued. "So they don't have an evac area."

I blanched, remembering that I'd told the couple on Marina Boulevard to go there when the sun came up.

"Are they going to keep trying to secure the area?" I asked.

"Doubtful," he said, and my heart dropped. "The neighborhoods near that end of the park seem to have a disproportionate number of zoms. All it took was one helicopter landing there to draw dozens to the paddock. The bison freaked and stampeded through the chainlink fence, right about the time Team B showed up. Zed Two's pilot was bitten during the chaos."

Red and Carl both flinched at that.

"Now Team B is holed up at a snack bar near the Conservatory of Flowers, with three injured people, and a shitload of zombies trying to claw their way inside. There'll be more coming, so we have to get our asses over there and get them out."

"The good news," he said, "is that we're not even five minutes away. There's a walkway across the road that'll take us right to the back of the Conservatory." He wiped his forehead again. In the diffused light filtering from a nearby streetlamp, I could see that his face was drawn.

Apparently I wasn't the only one who noticed. Dr. Albert stepped forward, frowning.

"It's only been four hours since your last shot," he said, reaching for Gabriel's wrist. "Let me check your pulse."

Gabriel shrugged off his concern.

"I'm fine," he said.

"But—"

"I said I'm *fine*." His tone left no room for argument. "You can check me out after we retrieve the other team." His voice and expression made it clear that there was no room for argument, as he swiveled the M4 out from around his back.

"Lil, Tony, use your hand weapons."

Tony frowned. Gabriel gave him a half smile.

"Don't worry—you'll have plenty of opportunity for the shotgun. We just don't want to take a chance of anything penetrating the snack bar walls and hitting our people. Same thing goes for you, Ash."

I nodded. I was so ready to slice and dice some zombies about now. Up close and personal suited me just fine.

"Let's go," he said.

We left the grove, stepping back out into the open.

Suddenly a sporty little blue convertible jumped the sidewalk off of Fulton, almost as if it had been lying in wait. It sent pedestrians scattering as it careened into the trees and headed straight towards Gabriel.

He swore and leapt out of the way just in time. The front bumper barely missed him as he hit the ground in a smooth forward roll, coming back to his feet about the same time the car plowed into a sturdy eucalyptus tree.

Branches and leaves fell to the ground and onto the car's roof. Steam rose from the crumpled front end.

I ran over to Gabriel, but he nonchalantly brushed a few crushed leaves and sticks from his Kevlar vest.

"Let's move," he said.

"But aren't we going to see if they're okay?" I looked at the wrecked car. It was a BMW, with a license plate that read "SikeOut."

As if on cue, the driver's side door opened an inch or so, then was stopped by the crumpled frame. The driver kicked the door from the inside—once, twice, and then a third time, sending it flying open. The door immediately rebounded into the driver, who let loose an impressive string of profanity.

He pushed the door open again with less force, and stepped out of the totaled sports car. He was clad in cargo shorts, a red T-shirt, and yes, those really were Birkenstocks. He was tall and solidly built, but as he moved toward us, his knees dipped under the weight of that first step. He stumbled onto one of them, blood dripping down his forehead from under an Aussie-style canvas hat.

Shit. I can't just leave him there. Throwing a guilty glance back toward Gabriel, I hurried over to the man's side, putting a supporting arm around his shoulders and helping him to his feet.

"Hey, you okay?" I said.

"Of course I'm not okay, you dumb bitch. Do I *look* okay? Look at my Beamer. I just had it detailed last week! Now how about doing something useful and dialing 911, while I call a tow truck?" He pulled a cell phone from one of his shorts' pockets.

Oookay. My dad would call this dude a "Beamer Bastard." I used to rag on him for the automotive profiling. I'd have to let him know my perspective had evolved.

"Come on, Ash." Gabriel jerked his head toward our destination.

I withdrew my arm, letting Mr. BirkenBeamer sway on his feet. He clutched his beloved car for support.

"Wait!" he said indignantly. "Aren't you going to help me?"

"That would be a big no," I said.

But I'd only taken a couple of steps when the telltale moan of the walking dead sounded in the trees nearby. I could smell them over the odor of burned rubber and assorted car fluids. *Well, crap.* "But I'll give you some free advice." I tossed the words over my shoulder. "If you want to live, leave the Beamer, and get the hell out of here."

"I'm not gonna leave my car," he spat. He reached in and pulled a handle release. There was a faint *thunk* sound and the crumpled hood popped up maybe a quarter of an inch. He went around to the front and tried to pry it the rest of the way open, blood dripping down onto the blue paint.

You have got to be kidding me. Rolling my eyes, I turned and went back.

"Seriously," I said, "you have to leave now." I grabbed him by one arm and pulled, trying to get him away from the car just as three zombies with biking gear and major road rash stumbled through the trees, making a beeline straight for us.

The guy yanked his arm away, totally oblivious to

the shambling doom heading his way. I tried again, seizing one wrist with both hands and yanking hard. I succeeded in pulling him away from the Beamer, only to have him wallop me across the jaw with his free hand.

"Get off me, you stupid bitch!"

With a single-mindedness of purpose he turned back to his car, just as the zombies reached him. They dragged him to the ground before he even had a chance to scream.

Shit, shit, shit!

I grabbed my katana and took off the head of one of the zombies before it could sink its teeth into him. The man yelled as blood splattered onto his shirt.

One of the two remaining zombies, oblivious to the fate of its former biking partner, fastened onto the man's face, knocking the canvas hat askew as it ripped a strip of flesh from one cheek. The other grabbed a Birkenstock-clad foot with both hands and took a bite out of the ankle, looking like something out of a really sick KFC ad.

Finger lickin' good.

I scrambled away, sickened and angry at both myself for failing, and the fates for giving me the time to try and save someone who refused my help, when I'd had no chance to help those kids.

The angry guilt morphed into an odd sense of detachment as his screams finally faded.

CHAPTER TWENTY-SEVEN

A cement pathway led to the backside of the Conservatory. Gabriel and I took point. Lil clutched her pickaxe and Tony swung Thor's Wee Hammer from one hand, looking eager to use it. Our two ninja-like snipers stuck with the group this time.

The path was on a downward slope, and while the lights were still on throughout the park, there wasn't anything in the immediate vicinity. Red and Carl used small Maglites to illuminate the ground in front of them, while Dr. Albert kept a hand on Tony's back. The wild cards, of course, could see every bump in the asphalt, every raised crack in the pavement, enabling us to move swiftly and assuredly through the darkness.

I could also smell zombies, lots of them. It was no longer an occasional nasty-ass whiff, but rather a constant olfactory pall lingering in the air like the proverbial fart in a phone booth.

Thank you, mutation, for the night vision—but screw you for the stinkathon.

We reached the back of the Conservatory, a wood-frame building covered with thousands of panes of glass. Inside, dim lights only served to accent the darkness, causing the plants to look shadowy and vaguely menacing.

Going around the east side, I found several landscape

lights casting a warm golden glow over the grounds. Beds of brightly colored tulips and other flowers bordered a handicapped parking lot, now oddly empty of cars.

We reached the front corner of the building and peered around. Flowerbeds decorated the grounds in front of the Conservatory, and a wide staircase led up from the grounds to a large cement platform that ran the length of the building. Unfortunately, the walking dead had no respect for creative landscaping. Dozens of zombies—at least fifty, probably more—trampled through the carefully maintained gardens, crushing the fragile blooms into the ground. I'm sure there was a poignant metaphor somewhere in that, but I didn't feel like making the effort. I just wanted to see every one of those walking travesties permanently dead.

The snack bar sat on the platform to the right of the stairs, housed in a small cement-and-wood structure, its back built into the larger Conservatory edifice. It had roll-down metal shutters in the front, reaching down from the roof to about waist height, and a single door visible on the side. It was entirely surrounded by zombies—fresh ones. Hands thumping against wood and metal sounded like a band made up entirely of inept drummers.

One of the park's many restrooms lay beyond in a small auxiliary building. I made a mental note in case I lived to use it.

We ducked back around the side to avoid being seen by any particularly observant zombies, and gathered around Gabriel. He gave the group a sweeping glance, taking in the varying degrees of "oh shit" panic on our faces—especially Carl and Red.

"I know it looks bad," he said. "But we faced much worse odds fighting the swarm at Big Red." I tactfully didn't mention the fact we'd had a hell of a lot more firepower then, like, to the tune of a hundred or so armed soldiers, a flamethrower, cool remote-controlled dart bombs, a wicked snow plow...

Ah, for the good ol' days.

I took a deep breath and mentally told my brain to shut up. It didn't matter what the differences were. Our friends needed our help, and *I* desperately needed to rescue someone about now.

So I listened closely as Gabriel outlined the plan.

"Jones, Davis, take opposite sides of the building and focus on incoming, clear the grounds if possible." He turned and continued. "Dr. Albert, stick close to Jones. Red, Carl—you, too. Use your firearms, do not engage up close. Lil, you deal with any biters that make it anywhere close to within arm's reach."

"Gotcha," Lil said eagerly.

"Davis, you take the other side of the building. Tony, you keep the zeds off of him." He looked at me. "Ash, you and I are going to clear the ones at the front of the snack bar." He paused and scanned the group. "Everyone clear?"

We all nodded.

Lil turned to Jones.

"Please don't shoot me by accident, okay?" she said.

He looked at her, somehow managing to convey astonishment at her words without changing expression.

"Ma'am, I never shoot anything or anyone by accident."

"Guess I won't piss you off, then," Lil said tartly.

Davis and Tony split off from the group, looping around the back of the Conservatory to the west side. Jones, looking like a rock star with a small entourage, hunkered down behind some bushes at the east side of the building. Red and Carl flanked him, rifles in hand, and Lil stood poised for action with her pickaxe.

I was surprised to see Dr. Albert pull out a handgun, one of those little Ruger .22s that'd been passed out like party favors. Even more surprising was that he seemed calm and ready to use it. I'd expected him to cower in fear. It didn't exactly make me admire him, but it lessened my contempt just a little bit.

Jones calmly started taking out targets on the flowerbeds, one shot per zombie head, as Gabriel and I rounded the corner of the Conservatory. Gabriel paused and raised his M4, picking his shots as deliberately as Jones, and delivering them just as accurately. Half a dozen zombies clamoring at the walls of the snack bar dropped to the ground. Others immediately surged forward, ignoring their dead compatriots underfoot, clawing and pounding to get to the fresh meat inside. They were like ants swarming over a scrap of food on the ground, and just as single-minded.

We needed to get some of them away from the snack bar, and spread out enough that I could use my katana without getting dog piled, zombie style.

"Hey!" I shouted, forgoing subtlety by stepping out into the open, waving my arms. Several zoms turned slowly towards the sound of my voice, like sunflowers seeking the sun, as they decided there were easier pickings than the ones inside the snack bar.

More turned to follow.

"That's right," I cried. "Fresh meat, already out of the can!"

Gabriel shot me a look.

"One-liners? Really?"

I shrugged unapologetically, and then turned my full attention to the zombies heading my way.

It's slice and dice time.

I smiled and stepped forward to meet them.

Whack.

There went a little old lady in a flowered shift and pink cardigan, its front smeared with blood and black bile.

Thwack.

I sliced through the skull of a male zombie wearing

an "I heart San Francisco" hat, tugging the blade out and decapitating a couple of undead Bears in matching rainbow pride T-shirts. I pulled my tanto free with my left hand, thrusting the tip into the eye socket of a slender female zombie swathed in layers of purple gauze.

They were all fresh—at least as fresh as something can be when its rotting from the inside out. Most of them were probably at the most two days' dead. One woman looked so normal I almost hesitated before striking the killing blow—it took her hands clawing at my shoulders to snap me out of it.

"Hollow shells," I chanted to myself as I cut off her head. "That's all they are. Hollow, deadly shells. We kill them or we die."

Still they kept coming, and I kept moving, slicing and dicing and finding a weird peaceful Zen inside myself, the horror of what I was doing cushioned by the same odd detachment I'd felt when BirkenBeamer had died. I didn't know if this was a good or a bad thing, but I went with it, immersed in a ballet of death-dealing that developed its own inherent rhythm, and never seemed to end.

Until finally it did.

I cut down a little Chinese grandma zombie and spun, katana poised for the next target, only to find the space around me cleared. I suddenly noticed I was short of breath and sweating like I'd been in a sauna. Perspiration dripped off my forehead, stinging my eyes. I dashed it away with the back of one gore-stained hand and looked around me.

There were prone corpses as far as the eye could see—on the grass, in the flowerbeds, on the stairs, and all over the landing. I turned around in a circle, seeing Tony standing over a pile of corpses, gore dripping from the sledgehammer, his face expressionless. Lil, on the other hand, glowed in righteous fury like the cute, cuddly—and totally deadly—goddess of war that she was.

The three of us looked at each other. No words were necessary as we shared an unspoken self-righteous satisfaction in the necessary slaughter.

Hollow, deadly shells.

I vowed never to forget that fact again.

CHAPTER TWENTY-EIGHT

There was an obscenely loud rattling as the metal shutters on the snack bar rolled up. Gentry leaned out over the counter from inside, and grinned at us. There was a door behind him, built into the wall, and it was ajar.

"Can I take your orders?" he asked.

Then there was a scraping sound of something heavy being dragged, and the inner door opened to reveal Nathan, who looked as unflappable as ever under an impressive coating of gore.

"Glad to see you guys. I don't think this—" he rapped hollowly on the door "—would have held much longer."

I slipped inside, squeezing past a medium-sized fridge they'd shoved up against the door.

Mack smiled wearily up at me from a prone position on the floor, one leg propped up on a small stepladder.

"Hey, stranger," he said. He sounded tired.

Next to him on the floor was a thin Asian man dressed in fatigues and Kevlar, eyes shut, face sickly pale. The injured sniper—it had to be. A heavyset woman with curly Orphan Annie hair and freckles lay a few feet away, chunks of flesh and fabric torn away from her shoulder at the juncture between two pieces of armor. I could smell the necrotizing flesh from where I stood. She didn't have much time left.

Standing guard over her with a rifle was a small,

stocky woman armored up like the rest of us, with a platinum blonde brush-cut, holding the same type of souped-up firearm as Jones and Davis. Evidently this pair of snipers wasn't a matched set. Still, there was something about her that reminded me of the Gunsy Twins.

Lil pushed her way past me and rushed over to Mack's side, dropping down on her knees next to him.

"Are you okay?" she said. "Can you walk?"

Mack patted her hand.

"I'll be fine." The pain in his voice gave lie to his words. She hugged him fiercely.

"You'd better be," she said. "I'll carry you the rest of the way myself, if I have to."

Gabriel stepped inside and frowned at her.

"I told you to stay with Jones and Dr. Albert." His tone was brusque, but Lil didn't even look at him.

"Mack needs me more."

Ooh, boy. I didn't have to look at Gabriel to feel his temperature rising.

"That's not your judgment call," he snapped. "Get back out there and do your job."

"Screw you!" Lil hissed, a flash of rage contorting her face. "I'm staying with Mack!" She buried her head on Mack's chest, arms wrapped around him as if he were the last teddy bear on earth.

Yikes.

Mack and Gentry both flinched in surprise, Mack looking up at Gabriel apologetically, while Nathan gave Lil a slow, considering look before shooting an inquiring gaze my way. Gabriel, on the other hand, was the slowly boiling kettle to Lil's bubbling-over pot. He was holding onto his temper with both hands. I could see the sweat beading up on his forehead, skin yellowish, which meant he needed his vaccine. Stat.

Time for an intervention.

I quickly grabbed him by one arm and pulled him

toward the door. His muscles, tensed under my fingers, felt like steel cables.

"Please," I said quietly. He let me pull him outside as the occasional pop of rifle fire announced that Davis and Jones were taking care of any zombie stragglers headed in our direction. Tony was still at his post over to the right, guarding Davis. Jones had taken up a prominent position at the other corner of the Conservatory. Red, Carl, and Dr. Albert stood in a cluster near him.

Nathan followed us out, close behind as I led Gabriel over to the entrance of the Conservatory. I was grateful for his presence.

"What?" Gabriel snapped. I tried not to flinch at his anger, now turned toward me like a heat-seeking missile.

"Two things," I said, keeping my voice as calm and level as possible. "One, you need your meds about now." He opened his mouth to argue, and I held up one hand. "Remember the talk we had? You know this is the virus kicking in. Just like I know when I've got PMS, right? Think of it as the mother of all fucked up hormonal surges, and just take your medicine, okay?"

A muscle at the side of Gabriel's mouth twitched once, then twice. Then he heaved a huge sigh.

"Okay, yeah, you're right." He nodded toward Dr. Albert, who scurried forward even as he pulled off his knapsack, rummaging in it and extracting a padded pouch. From that he removed a syringe and little glass vial.

"You said there were two things," Nathan said as Gabriel silently submitted to the injection. I waited until Dr. Albert had finished, and then motioned them closer to me to make sure Lil couldn't overhear any of what I had to say next.

"Lil is on some sort of medication," I said, my voice low. "Or *was*. I think she's out of it. I found the pill bottle in our bathroom and I asked her about it a few nights ago and she... well, she kind of freaked out like she did in there—" I nodded toward the snack bar "—but not nearly as amped up."

There. I heaved a huge sigh of relief, grateful to finally get this off my chest.

Dr. Albert raised an eyebrow.

"What medication?" he asked. "Do you remember?"

I frowned, trying to picture the label on the pill bottle I'd seen.

"Something like Chlorophyll or Compazine or—"

"Clozapine?"

I nodded.

"Yeah, that sounds right."

Dr. Albert frowned. "That's an antipsychotic, often used to treat schizophrenia and bipolar disorder. The withdrawal effects can be severe. We'll have to find some medication for her as soon as possible. This... this is not good."

Wow. Understate much?

"We're headed for a medical center," Nathan pointed out. "They'll have a pharmacy."

"Getting to it may be problematic, though," Gabriel said, rolling his shirt sleeve back down and refastening the Kevlar. It was reassuring to see him get back to business.

"The trick may be getting her to take it," Dr. Albert said. "Many people who suffer from bipolar disorder refuse to take the medicine when they're in this sort of manic stage."

"We can always crush it up and put it in her food," Nathan said.

I'll sit on her chest, hold her nose, and pop it in her mouth if I have to. In the meantime...

"Gabriel, can you just let her stick with Mack for now?" I asked. "Switch out with Gentry or Nathan, and have one of them watch him instead." I jerked my chin toward Dr. Albert.

Gabriel took a deep breath.

"It sets a bad precedent…" he replied. I just snorted.

"Since when have Lil and I done anything else?"

He gave a short laugh.

"Point taken. Okay, it'll be easier than fighting her on this."

"Do you want me to tell her?"

"No, I'll do it," he said. "Hopefully I can make it clear that I'm making the change for the good of the mission, and not because she threw a temper tantrum. We need her to keep her shit together."

"I'll see what I can do, too," I promised. "But first—" I nodded towards the restrooms "—nature calls."

"Make sure you clear it first," Gabriel warned. "And have someone stand watch outside."

"I'll ask Davis or Tony to keep an eye on the entrance," I promised. Last thing I wanted was to have some opportunistic zombie crawling under a bathroom stall door à la *Zombieland*. What an embarrassing way to die.

Davis kindly agreed to do guard duty in front of the bathroom so I could do my business in peace. First I checked to see that nothing lurked in any of the stalls. Then I risked a peek in the reflective metal that served as mirrors in most of the park's restrooms. My hair stuck out in dark sweaty tendrils under my helmet and from the tight braid worn in a coil at the nape of my neck. My eyes looked huge in my pinched, wan face, with its splatters and streaks of blood like tribal war paint. I'd fit right in with the cast of an *Alien* movie right about now.

Taking off my helmet, I washed my hands, then splashed water on my face, and used wet paper towels to wipe some of the blood and bits off my skin. I tried daubing at the gunk on my Kevlar and clothing, but quickly gave up. I could only hope for a hot shower and a change of clothing in the near future.

No hugging anyone but wild cards until then.

Putting my helmet back on, I stepped outside, nodding at Davis, who was still standing guard.

"Thanks," I said with sincere appreciation.

"Glad to assist, ma'am," he replied with the slightest lift of the corners of his mouth. Both Gunsy Twins were starting to grow on me, even if they did put me in mind of clones grown in vats somewhere.

Someone shoot me if I start quoting Episode Two.

Back inside the confines of the snack bar, Gabriel gave me a slight nod, which I took to mean that he'd had his talk with Lil, and everything was more or less okay. There was still some residual tension in the air, but it no longer crackled like an electrical storm.

Lil was still curled up next to Mack, who was sitting up now, leaning against the wall, one arm around her. He looked content and it occurred to me that Mack needed Lil as much as she needed him. Looking after her would stop him from thinking about the people he couldn't save. And helping Mack might be what was needed to keep Lil stable.

Someone had pulled pre-made sandwiches out of the refrigeration unit and tossed them up on the counter. There were also cookies and brownies under a glass cover; Tony came inside and immediately made a beeline for the sweets. Sandwiches were passed out without any concern for filling, and I got a very passable roast beef and Swiss cheese on ciabatta. It would have been tastier with a few minutes in a Panini press, but I wasn't about to complain.

I finished up with a bag of Baked Lays and a chocolate chip cookie, grateful for every last preservative-filled bite. The old adage "hunger makes the best sauce" never seemed truer.

Davis and Jones ate their sandwiches outside the building, keeping an eye out and taking care of any incoming ghouls. I found out that the injured sniper's name was Hicks, and the female sniper went by Nicks—"as in Stevie," she told me.

Hicks and Nicks. Okay, maybe they do *come in matched sets.*

Team B's mechanic—a young white guy with messy brown hair, a scruffy beard on the end of his chin, and slight stoner drawl—was Brad, although mentally I nicknamed him "Shaggy." The pilot, now delirious, wound reeking of putrefaction... well, they told me her name and I blocked it out. She was going to die, and knowing who she was would make that knowledge even worse.

Nicks kept a close watch on her.

Nathan, Gentry, and Gabriel huddled in a corner, conferring on our next move. If I'd really wanted to, I could have totally eavesdropped, but just then I wanted to shut my eyes and rest. I stretched out on the floor, pulling off my knapsack and using it as a lumpy pillow. Almost immediately I could feel myself falling into an uneasy doze, lulled by the buzzing of voices around me.

CHAPTER TWENTY-NINE

I was jerked out of sleep by the crack of a bullet echoing in the confined space. My eyes shot open and I sat up to see Nicks standing over the now dead pilot, the muzzle of her rifle still pointing at the woman's head.

Damn.

Shaggy sat next to her, sorrow lining his face.

"She didn't sign on for this," he said angrily. "It should have been a simple drop."

Nicks nodded.

"If I ever find out who fucked with the chopper..." She hefted her rifle in a not too subtle threat.

I got to my feet, still groggy from my impromptu catnap. Red handed me a bottle of water. I smiled my thanks, splashed some on my face to wake myself up, and drank the rest.

There was an occasional gunshot outside. Gabriel was nowhere in sight.

"How long was I out?" I asked Red.

"Maybe thirty minutes."

Outside, the sound of gunfire increased. I stretched, shaking the kinks out of my body, and sidled over to Nathan.

"What's up?" I asked.

"More zoms are finding their way here," he said somberly. "We need to leave now, before we have to fight our way out again."

"Damn, I was hoping we'd be able to take a break—the nap just didn't cut it," I said. "Are we going to try and get into the lab tonight?"

"Doubtful," he replied. "Like you said, we need a break—some of us more than others. We're not all wild cards."

"Since dawn is only a couple of hours away, it makes more sense to find a vantage point and assess the situation. We need to make sure there's a clear path to the back entrance."

Red came up to stand next to me.

"We can't just go through the front?" he asked.

Nathan gave a short laugh, but it was totally devoid of humor.

"This is a hospital," he said. "It'll be several circles of hell filled with hysterical civilians, hungry zombies, and sick people who are in the process of turning, all stuffed into a confined space. And this is an urban facility—there *will* be firearms. No, the risks are too great—we'd never be able to navigate those conditions without losing more people."

He took a swig of bottled water.

"So the plan is to go across the park, get as close to the med center as we can, find a place to hole up, and then move out at first light."

"What about the Conservatory?" Carl asked. "Can't we take a break here?" He had circles of exhaustion under his eyes, and didn't look excited at the prospect of going anywhere.

I answered before Nathan had a chance.

"Look at this place—it's all wood and glass. No way it'd hold for any length of time."

So we prepared to leave, stuffing some extra food in backpacks wherever it would fit. Nathan crammed it into his apparently bottomless duffle bag.

Mack could walk, but his expression showed that the ankle pained him with every step, no matter how stoically he tried to hide it. Lil slung an arm around his waist so he could lean on her. When he tried to argue that he didn't need help, she refused to have any of it.

"You'll heal up faster if you stop trying to be all macho, and let me help you."

Whatever Gabriel had said to her seemed to have worked. The signs of her manic anger had been replaced by a calm competence as she focused on helping her friend.

We'd become a group of fourteen, two of them walking wounded. I did a little mental tally—four snipers, one pilot, two mechanics, five wild cards, one mad scientist, and Gabriel. The injured men and Dr. Albert clustered in the middle of our party, Lil helping Mack, then Dr. Albert with Nathan as his shadow, Gentry and Tony immediately behind, supporting the wounded sniper between them.

Davis and Nicks stuck close to us now, protecting our flanks while Jones took point. They worked with deadly efficiency, limiting their shots to the zombies that came close enough to be a real threat, and letting the rest fall behind.

It was harder to move quickly and quietly, but we did our best as Gabriel led us south through the park. There were cars abandoned on the streets and in the parking lots, a few scattered groups of people hoofing it to whatever safety they could find. The light of a fire flickered through the trees somewhere in front of us, the smell of smoke drifting in with the fog and mixing with *Eau d'Undead*.

I grimaced, flashing back to the fire in the lab.

The inescapable sounds of a city falling apart were audible in the distance, but the park itself was oddly quiet. We passed a clump of zombies feasting on recently killed corpses, several of the hapless victims wearing the ragtag clothing of the homeless. The sight both sickened and saddened me.

Golden Gate Park was, under normal circumstances, one of my favorite places to play tourist. Three miles long and half a mile wide, it held a wide variety of gardens, lakes, museums, hiking and biking paths, a polo field, a buffalo paddock, complete with real bison, an antique carousel that delighted me as a child, and a Japanese tea garden where my parents would take me for tea and cookies—the promise of which was the only thing that got me off the carousel without a tantrum. I had loved wandering the numerous little paths that cut through the wooded areas, always expecting to emerge into some magical land.

Now, however, the park had transformed into a horror maze. The lush foliage and pathways held fleeing refugees, rotting, walking corpses, and their victims. It hurt my heart to see the bloodied, maimed figures of zombies inhabiting a place that once had held such joy. It was kind of like seeing Aslan from *The Lion, the Witch, and the Wardrobe* start mauling Lucy.

Just plain wrong.

As we moved I wondered what time it was. I'd lost all sense of real time once the sun had set. It felt late. My eyes were scratchy with fatigue, and the short catnap had just made me crave more sleep.

We passed tennis courts, statues, a soccer field, and the carousel of my childhood, passing the back end of Kezar Stadium, ending up behind some sort of recycling center. A chain-link fence hung with dark netting separated it from the street and the chaos. It was a weirdly peaceful place, where the sounds of screams, sirens, and the oh-so-familiar moans of the undead seemed far away.

Dense shrubbery lined the fence on the other side, affording us good cover but allowing us to observe the street beyond. The street itself was oddly empty of people, living or otherwise. Most of the block was taken up by relatively new townhouses—three rows of them—built somewhere around the seventies. They were set on terraced ground, so that the doorways stood above the street, at the top of steep staircases. There were courtyards between the rows of buildings, and a driveway ran uphill and disappeared over the top, serving the entire row of houses. The second story of each townhouse boasted a balcony with wrought-iron railings. The ground floor of each had a cement patio fenced with the same wrought iron, effectively cutting them off from their neighbors.

The builders had obviously tried to echo the neighborhood's existing architecture, but the townhouses were sterile and looked cheap, with none of the charm or quality found in the older originals.

On either side of them stood two matching structures that looked like art deco had met a medieval church, and made babies. They both were several stories high, and I could see a plaque on the front of the one closest to us. It read "Circus Center."

I nudged Gentry and Tony, pointing to the sign.

"The possibility of zombie clowns just increased."

Tony hefted Thor's Wee Hammer.

"I'm ready."

There were lights on in some of the units, which may or may not have meant that people were still inside.

"What do you think?" Nathan said quietly, standing side by side with Gabriel as a lone zombie stumbled aimlessly down one of the stairways toward the street. I found it interesting that he deferred to Gabriel's leadership without any apparent damage to his ego, even though he had a decade or two more experience. At the same time, Gabriel didn't seem threatened by the older man's expertise, perhaps seeing it as an asset, instead of a threat. Two mature men instead of a clash of male egos accompanied by the Anvil Chorus.

"Seems like a good choice," Gabriel replied. "Considering we're only two blocks from the UCSF medical center, it seems pretty quiet, too."

Nathan nodded.

"Probably less chance of being noticed if we take one of the middle units." He glanced at his wristwatch, a fancy hi-tech thing, black and chrome with assorted gears and shit. "It's almost four. The sun comes up around seven these days, so that gives us a little time to rest.

"We need it," he added.

"I'll take the watch," Nicks said, nodding. "Don't think Hicks is gonna be up for it, though." She glanced at her woozy partner. He was practically unconscious, leaning against the fence. Dr. Albert cast a quick look at the injured sniper, and frowned.

"I'll see what I can do for him when we get inside." For some reason, that surprised me.

Guess a little of the Hippocratic oath stuck to you after all.

"After all," he added, "we need everyone moving under their own steam, or we won't make it."

Or maybe it didn't.

He was right, though. No way we were going to be able to drag an unconscious man through Zombie Central. I hoped Dr. Albert could do something for him, though, because I didn't think Nicks would be open to leaving her partner behind.

Suddenly Gentry held up a hand, and pointed down the street to our left. The sound of uneven footsteps crunching on fallen leaves could be heard as several shadowy figures moved slowly in our direction. The smell left no doubt.

We all fell silent, moving well behind the concealing bushes as two zombies made their shambling way down the sidewalk, past our hiding place. Both had been older teenage boys, wearing baggy shorts and black T-shirts with marijuana leaves boldly stenciled on the front. Even without the giveaway of the shirts, I could smell the skunky odor of old pot lingering on their clothes, combined with the smell of decomposition.

The one in front looked like he'd died of Walker's, whereas his pal was missing great chunks of flesh from his face, arms, and legs. Odds were good they'd been roommates and the one in front had died, reanimated, and been hit with a bad case of the munchies.

We waited until, moving slowly down the street, Bill and Ted were far enough away on their Excellent Undead Adventure for us to continue our planning.

"We need to find our best point of entry," Gabriel said in an undertone.

"I can just blow the lock off one of the front doors," Nicks volunteered.

"Better if we can gain access from either the driveway or window, then unlock the door from the inside," Gabriel said. "If there are still people inside, we don't want to compromise their safety by leaving one of the main access points unsecured."

Nicks' face reddened.

"Didn't think of that, sir."

"No worries, soldier." Gabriel then turned to me. "Ash, are you up for scouting the driveway with Nathan? It means getting over the gate." He pointed toward one of the darkened townhouses, and gave me a challenging look. Whatever "hackles" are, I felt mine rise.

I raised one eyebrow.

"Child's play," I said.

Competitive? Who, me?

Then I thought about it.

Yeah, okay, it's a fair cop.

I quickly shed my knapsack and left both rifles. My blades would do well enough for this, and I didn't need the extra bulk while shimmying over fences.

Watching me, Gabriel actually grinned, then nodded towards the townhouses.

"Tony, you and Gentry take the courtyard between the units, and see if you can find a way in without compromising security. Davis, Jones, you cover them.

Nicks, you clear any zoms you see coming from the park. I'll stay here with Dr. Albert."

Surprisingly, Lil didn't argue at being left out of the action.

Thank goodness for Mack.

We moved toward the recycling center entrance, and were met by a latched gate—also chain-link—that was secured with a heavy-duty padlock. Nathan took one look at it and shook his head. Whipping out a Leatherman from one of his pockets, he proceeded to quickly snip away a section of the fence itself, large enough to allow me, Tony, and Gentry to squeeze through, one at a time.

Nathan followed, bending the section back into place.

The four of us looked both ways down the street. It seemed clear. Nathan nodded, and we took off, threading our way between cars and trotting to the other side. Tony and Gentry split off into the courtyard, while Nathan hoisted himself over the driveway gate with effortless ease.

I followed, not quite so effortlessly, but I managed to get my butt over the top, dropping down to the pavement with less than catlike grace.

"You check up top," Nathan said, pointing to the peak of the driveway, "and I'll check down here." Without waiting for an answer, he headed into the shadows.

I threw a semi-sarcastic salute to his retreating back and trotted up the slope. As I did so, the noise level increased—a mixture of car horns, people shouting in several different languages, and the ever-present moans of the undead. The incline was steep enough that I had to reach the top before I could see that the driveway ran back down the hill, to the next street over. It ended there with the same sort of gate we'd just navigated, also shut.

Which was good luck for us, since the gate was all that separated us from a sidewalk and street jam-packed with zombies—and yet more cars.

As predicted, the streets around and outside of the

medical center were Ground Zero for mayhem. All the bite victims and people suffering from Walker's had flocked there, and those who had died were reanimating to spread the joy. With the appearance of each new zombie, the chaos increased, until it was like the Zombocalypse in Sensurround.

A female zom slammed up against the gate, a petite Japanese teenager looking like something straight out of an anime with its yellow tights, neon pink mini skirt, and matching go-go boots. It was missing pieces of its cheek and jaw, blood splattering the multicolored layers of shirts. It saw me and opened what was left of its mouth, letting loose an ululating moan which was then echoed tenfold by the other zombies in the immediate area.

Time to get inside, and out of sight.

I quickly retreated downhill, out of Anime Zombie's field of vision and looked for easy access to the townhouse. The only open door I found was the entrance to a laundry room. There were no other doors in the carports—just stairs with gates at the top leading to a courtyard.

Well, crap.

Heading back down, I met Nathan in the middle.

"No luck," he said. I nodded, indicating the same.

We quickly and quietly hopped back over the gate. Nathan kindly gave me a leg up this time, before once again making it look as easy as stepping off a curb.

"Showoff," I grumbled.

SAN FRANCISCO

He watched them from the shadows, paying particular attention to the tricked out babe he'd first noticed on Marina Boulevard. He was perched comfortably on the roof of the same recycling center they'd taken shelter in, and as far as he could tell, they still hadn't seen him.

Interesting group of people, especially the one he'd seen taking down the three dicks on Marina Boulevard. He'd watched her progress into the Presidio, seen her join up with her group, and decided to follow. They had weapons and they seemed to have a destination in mind.

They had to be some sort of paramilitary unit—either that or LARPers who were taking things to a ridiculously realistic degree. Role-playing, he supposed, was one way to deal with a genuine zombie apocalypse, but somehow he doubted an amateur could have pulled off her moves.

He'd never really been interested in the zombie scenario, although a butt-load of his friends would go on for hours about how they'd fortify their residences or where they'd go to hole up when the undead rose. Some even had bug-out bags, and considering the possibility of a major quake or even a tsunami wiping out half of San Francisco, that in and of itself wasn't such a bad idea.

He didn't figure he'd need any of that shit, though. He could move—move fast and cover terrain few others could manage. It was a damned useful skill to have about now, considering how fast the streets of San Francisco had become impossible to negotiate. Within hours of the evacuation announcements, things had gone straight to hell.

This is some fucked up shit right here.

He'd left his car parked on the Golden Gate Bridge, radiator blown after it overheated. Heading out on foot, he'd moved with the crowds of near-panicked people massing up against a seriously scary military barricade at the north side of the bridge. Then he heard little explosions, and if those weren't gunshots, he'd pull down his pants and ask for a spanking.

About then he'd decided to take his chances in the city.

Once he'd made the decision, it took a matter of minutes to navigate the same distance that had taken him two hours in his car. He'd kept a safe distance from what he had to admit was an epic battle at the Conservatory of Flowers, and that's where he'd seen the babe really go to town. She had been like a human Cuisinart with those cool-ass Japanese-style swords.

The little chick with her pickaxe and the tall dude with the sledgehammer weren't exactly slouches, either.

He hadn't been close enough to eavesdrop on any of the conversations, but he'd seen enough to figure out that they were probably the good guys. So he'd decided his best bet was to follow them at a safe distance—they had a couple of kick-ass snipers, and he didn't want to be mistaken for a zombie.

Zombies. It still seemed like bullshit. But this shit, as they say, just got real.

So he'd trailed them to the recycle buildings, where he'd managed to pick up something about their intended destination. Then he'd watched as four of them went across the street—two of them, including Sexy Katana Babe, climbing over the driveway gate.

He shook his head at that. Poor use of energy, all that hoisting and scrabbling. Total waste of upper body strength. He'd show them how it was done... once he had a chance to properly introduce himself.

For now, he settled back to watch and wait.

CHAPTER THIRTY

We ran into Tony and Gentry on the street. Tony wore an expression of quiet satisfaction, while Gentry's grin spread from ear to ear as he gave us a thumbs up.

We had to wait for the good news, however, as more zombies turned the corner on our side of the street, shuffling with painful slowness in our direction. I started to unsheathe my katana while Tony hefted his hammer, but Nathan shook his head and motioned us back toward the courtyard.

The four of us melted into the shadows, crouching under one of the staircases. I wished it was possible to speed up their progress, like time-lapse photography, because those damn zombies moved at a more glacial pace than... well, than a glacier. Finally they passed the courtyard without detecting us.

"Why are we not just killing them?" I whispered, my thigh muscles seizing up from crouching for however many minutes it'd taken the world's slowest zombies to go away.

"To avoid detection." Nathan rubbed his own legs to restore circulation. "One of 'em sees us, it'll start with the moaning, and that increases the chance that more of them will show up before we have a chance to get inside and get some rest."

"Your logic is sound," I said.

"Glad you approve, Saavik."

I flashed him a quick Vulcan salute, and turned to Gentry.

"So what's the good news?" I asked.

Gentry grinned again.

"Our boy X-Box here got onto one of the patios and jimmied a sliding glass door open in less time than it takes you to decapitate a zombie. He came through, and now the front door's unlocked."

I gave Tony a considering look.

"You have a lot of experience with breaking and entering, Tony?" I was only half-kidding.

"My parents used to use a security chain to lock me out if I came home past curfew," Tony said with a nonchalant shrug. "I don't think they *ever* figured out how I got inside."

"Well done," Nathan said. He clapped him on one shoulder, and gave him an approving smile.

Tony turned red, pleasure mixing with self-conscious embarrassment. Nathan didn't hand out compliments lightly, and this was the first time Tony had been on the receiving end. It was good to see him happy.

"Show 'em which townhouse it is, X-Box," Gentry said. "I'll alert the media." With that, he bounded across the street, slipping in between cars like a particularly enthusiastic ninja, and then ducking back through the opening Nathan had made in the chain-link fence.

"Um, it's over here," Tony said, gesturing. He scratched his neck self-consciously and pointed toward the second townhouse on the right. The front door was propped open, and from its silhouette, it looked like he'd used your basic garden gnome, but without the peaked hat.

I raised an eyebrow. Upon closer inspection, it proved to be a garden *Batman* gnome, complete with painted six-pack costumed abs.

"You found this here?" I asked Tony.

"Yup," he said. "On the patio, along with a Heath Ledger Joker gnome, and a really lame Robin the Boy Wonder gnome." He shook his head sadly. "With nipples."

It should have disturbed me that I knew exactly what he was talking about, but it didn't.

Which disturbed me more.

"Was anyone inside?" Nathan sensibly didn't address the gnome issue.

Tony looked embarrassed.

"I didn't see anyone, but I didn't really look. I thought I should get the front door open and let you guys know as quick as I could."

"Good call," Nathan said, and relief flashed across Tony's face.

Maybe our boy is growing up. A week ago he would've been all sullen defensiveness. It just sucked that it took Kai's death to kick-start the process.

"I'll check out the upstairs," I offered, anxious to take this party inside.

Nathan nodded his approval.

"I'll check downstairs. Tony, hang out just inside the door, and keep your eye out for the rest of the team." He drew one of the handguns he always carried—there were times I suspected that he showered with them. I had no idea what model it was—Nathan had his own special toys, doncha know—but I was obscurely proud of the fact that I recognized a suppressor on the barrel, so it was an automatic.

Put me on the cover of the next Girls with Guns. I grinned to myself, unsheathed my tanto, nudged Batgnome out of the way with my booted foot, and slipped inside.

* * *

Something scraped against the faux granite flooring in the entryway.

"Did you hear that?" Becky clutched G's arm, long, lacquered fingernails digging tightly into his bare flesh.

G winced, as much at the unwanted contact as from the fact it kind of hurt. He didn't say anything, though—just held a finger up to his mouth in the universal gesture of "shut the hell up." He had heard the sound, and it scared him with a near paralyzing fear that filled him with self-loathing.

The Dark Knight wouldn't be afraid. He wouldn't be hiding in a bedroom closet with some woman he'd just met, either. The Dark Knight would be outside facing the chaos, saving the helpless, and dispensing justice.

The best G had been able to do was to offer Becky shelter in his home when he'd heard her pounding frantically on his neighbor's door, begging for refuge as madness exploded in the neighborhood. He knew the Haywards were on vacation, and he'd seen what happened to people caught outside in the last couple of hours.

So he'd opened his door and let her in.

She'd sat on one end of his custom black leather couch, clutching a fleece throw he'd given her to stop her shivering, and downing a Sierra Nevada pale ale like it was water. He'd pursed his lips when she put the empty bottle directly on the wooden coffee table, instead of one of the handy coasters, but he didn't want to be an ungracious host. So he'd quietly taken it to the recycle bin in the kitchen, surreptitiously wiping up the ring of moisture with his other hand.

She hadn't noticed.

He'd turned on the television, a truly monster-sized flat-screen mounted on the living room wall. He'd been flipping through the channels in search of news when the power went out. Becky had given a sharp gasp, pulling the fleece throw up to her face.

"Maybe it's just a brownout," G had said uneasily.

A sudden thumping noise out on the patio had brought them both to their feet. The sound of footsteps had been enough to prompt G to grab Becky's hand, pull her upstairs, and duck into the bedroom closet.

Where they now sat huddled close together behind a row of costumes, listening to the sound of footsteps coming up the hardwood stairs.

CHAPTER THIRTY-ONE

Walking into the townhouse was a bit like walking into a comic book store, the kind that catered to pop culture junkies like, well, like Tony and Kai. Tony must have rushed right through without checking it out, 'cause if he'd taken a good look, I doubt we would have seen him for hours.

The first thing I saw was an expensively framed *The Dark Knight Rises* poster, displayed prominently on the entryway wall opposite the front door, the cowled character brooding dramatically in front of a city on fire.

A quick glance to the right revealed the living room, and a truly frightening sofa—black leather with the bat logo emblazoned in yellow across the back. A life-sized replica of the blue Police Box thingee from *Doctor Who* occupied one corner, and there were swords mounted on the walls next to yet more framed movie posters and one-sheets. I spotted *Scott Pilgrim Versus the World*, *The Avengers*, *Doctor Who*, more *Batman* posters spanning the years… and yes, there was the one with Val Kilmer and Chris "Nipples" O'Donnell.

It was enough to make me long for a Thomas Kinkade print. Now *that* really disturbed me.

I made my way cautiously upstairs, my feet creaking on the hardwood despite my best efforts at stealth. If there was anyone or anything up there, I could forget about the element of surprise.

At the top of the stairs there was a carpeted hallway with three doors leading off it. The first door was open, revealing three walls filled with floor-to-ceiling bookshelves, all loaded to capacity. Every book was perfectly positioned. The owner had to be a serious neat freak.

Action figures from comic books, movies, and television shows took up shelves on the fourth wall, all still sealed in their original packaging. The doors of the closet had been removed, and shelves had been installed inside to house yet more action figures.

The next room was part office—with a sleek computer setup courtesy of Apple—and part storage space, with at least three dozen long, thin, cardboard boxes stacked in neatly labeled rows. They were comic books, all alphabetized, stacked against the walls and in another modified closet.

Above the computer was a bulletin board covered with San Diego Comic-Con and Wonder Con name badges, dated from 1998 to present, all bearing the name "G. Funk."

The third room was at the end of the hallway, and the door was closed. I pressed one ear against the thin wood and listened closely. Was that the shuffle of feet I heard? Muffled voices? Or just sounds penetrating the walls from the outside?

Turning the knob, I stepped to the side and cautiously pushed the door inward with the tip of my katana. The cause of Kai's death was fresh in my memory.

"Hello?" I offered.

No answer of any kind.

I entered what was the master bedroom.

Holy Batcrap!

Think bachelor boudoir meets Batcave. The walls were painted and textured to look like cement, and the king-size bed was backed by an oval headboard decorated with a black Batman emblem set against padded gold fabric. The sheets and comforter were also black and gold to match the emblem, but thankfully free of cartoons or logos. I peeked underneath the bed, and didn't even find a dust bunny.

A large mahogany dresser dominated the far wall, a trilby hat resting jauntily on a ceramic Batman bust. On closer inspection, I also found a Bat-satchel, a mobile Batphone, and a Bat-wallet, all lined up neatly on the dresser's surface.

"One bat, two bats, three bats, *mwah, hah, hah…*"

Okay, maybe not appropriate, but I'd take my jollies where I could get 'em.

An open door to the left led to a bathroom, and two closed sliding doors on my right hid what I assumed was the closet. I slide a door open, fully expecting to find a Batpole inside. Instead, an almost disappointingly normal walk-in closet greeted me, with rows of clothing hung on both sides and a sectional shoe rack directly in front of me. A dozen pair of Doc Martens lined up like footwear soldiers.

The row on the left held jeans and T-shirts. Each pair of jeans had its own hanger, something unheard of in my closet. Hanging jeans and T-shirts was an alien concept all by itself. There were at least thirty T-shirts hung on thin velveteen hangers. I'd wager my first-born child that they all bore pop cultural characters or quotes, and were arranged by the relevant show or movie.

The right side held a more eclectic wardrobe selection, pretty much what I'd expect to see from someone who'd attended Comic-Con on a yearly basis.

The faint sound of rustling fabric caught my attention, and I tensed. Turning slowly, I peered at the back of the closet where a dark cape and familiar cowled hood were hanging… with two figures huddled on the floor behind it.

"Um, I'm human," I said, realizing they couldn't see me in the dark.

"Really?" A deep, husky male voice with a thick, indefinable accent rose from behind the cape.

"Yup. And if I wasn't," I added, "I'd be trying to eat you, instead of striking up a conversation."

"Ah, good point." At least that's what I think he said. The accent made it tough to decipher.

The cape was pushed the rest of the way aside, fully revealing the speaker—a man in his early thirties with slicked-back dark hair, his eyes hidden behind dark sunglasses. I wasn't in the least bit shocked to see that he wore jeans and a *Doctor Who* T-shirt.

Behind him huddled a petite blonde somewhere in her twenties, wearing yoga pants and a long sleeved pink thermal top.

The man got to his feet, unfolding lanky limbs until he towered above me, at least six and a half feet tall. The woman stood up, as well, staring at me with wide, frightened eyes.

"We thought you were one of those things," she said, voice shaky with remembered fear.

"Sorry to scare you," I said in a gentle voice, the kind my dad used on skittish horses. "But we had to get inside quickly."

The man raised an eyebrow high enough that it popped up above the frames of his sunglasses.

"There are more of you?" Except it sounded like "Theah ah morr o'ya?"

"Yes, there's a group. We're... we're, uh, with the military."

"What branch?" he asked.

Crap.

"I'm sorry, I couldn't understand you." I smiled at him, not quite—but almost—batting my lashes before remembering that he couldn't see me. "I can't quite place your accent."

"Born in Ireland, raised in Australia from age ten, moved here when I was thirty."

Thirty sounded like "tirty." The rest of it vacillated between Down Under and Ye Olde Sod, all uttered in a husky voice that had to have been influenced by the Dark Knight himself.

"And what branch was that you said?" he persisted. I should have known anyone who'd alphabetize his comic books and hang up T-shirts wouldn't be so easily thrown off course.

"Ash, what's the status up there?" Nathan's voice floated up the stairs.

"Someone else can fill you in," I said quickly.

Buck officially passed.

"Everything's fine," I replied, just loudly enough for Nathan's wild card hearing to pick up on it. "Two civvies, no zoms."

"They okay?"

I turned to my rescues.

"Have either of you been bitten, or had a flu shot recently?"

There went that eyebrow again. He could have given Simone a run for her Vulcan ancestry.

"No to both," he said. "Becky?"

The blonde shook her head.

"I feel fine," she insisted.

Suddenly the lights flickered, and came on. Some ambient light shone in from the bedroom window, and a small bedside lamp flared back to life. The sound of a television drifted up the stairs, cutting off after a few seconds. This brought a frown to the man's face.

"Who did that?"

"Probably Nathan," I said. "We don't want to attract those things with any extra noise." I held out my hand. "I'm Ashley Parker, by the way. We're here to help."

He looked at my hand for a few seconds as if debating whether it was clean enough to touch. Considering the fact that I looked like I'd been dipped in gore, I couldn't blame him. He finally gave me a brief finger shake, surreptitiously wiping his hand on his jeans.

"G. Funk," he said. "I suppose I'm pleased to meet you."

"Becky Stiller." The blonde stepped forward and clasped my hand in both of hers. "I'm so happy you're here." She sounded like she meant it, too. "You say you're with the army?"

"Yes." I said, and left it at that. I turned back to Mr. Funk. "We need a place to rest up briefly. May we stay here?"

He gave it some thought before replying.

"Seeing as you're polite enough to ask, when I probably don't have a choice, then yes." At least that's what I think he said.

Some people should come with subtitles.

We went downstairs to find the others arriving, spreading out through the living room, depositing duffle bags and knapsacks on the hardwood floors, muddy boots leaving footprints on a formerly pristine cream carpet. G flinched when he saw just how many filthy people had invaded his home. His expression grew downright alarmed when Red and Carl came through the front door, Hicks sagging between them. Dr. Albert bustled right behind them.

"He needs to lie down somewhere," the doctor said. "Is there a bed we can use?"

G stepped forward hastily.

"The sofa hawpens int'a beeyad. Heeyah." Which I mentally translated into "the sofa opens into a bed. Here." Sure enough, with a few quick moves, he turned the couch into a convertible bed, which had more than enough space for both Hicks and Mack, who'd limped in with Lil.

"We won't break anything," I said reassuringly. G didn't look convinced.

"I need to wash my hands," he muttered. He vanished into the kitchen, and the sound of running water lasted for a good sixty seconds.

I stepped up next to Becky, who stood shyly behind me, taking in all the people in dark camo and Kevlar, weapons practically dripping off all of us.

"Is G going to be okay?" I asked her. She looked particularly interested in Gabriel, who had just come in through the front door and was closing it behind him.

He glanced around, saw me, and gave the smallest of smiles. It was enough.

"I don't know," she said, her voice suddenly all breathy. "I just met him tonight. I got stuck in traffic up on Parnassus, and saw people attacking each other." She winced at the memory. "I have friends here, next door, but they weren't home. G heard me knocking and let me in."

Her gaze continued to linger on Gabriel as he did a quick recon through the house, checking out doors and windows, pulling shades and curtains, and turning off all but the bare minimum of light needed to see. I couldn't blame her, even though it irritated me. No one pulled off the "I'm too sexy for my gore" look like Gabriel. He made it seem like a fashion choice.

G emerged from the kitchen, wiping his hands on a dishcloth emblazoned with the Batman emblem. About that time Tony joined us, a look of awe on his face.

"Coolest. Home. Ever," he said. "Dude, is this your place?"

G nodded, torn between gratification and near panic as Tony walked up to the Police Box and touched it reverently.

"A Tardis," he said. "Kai would've loved this…"

I had other priorities in mind. So I sidled up next to our host.

"Say, G, does your hot water work?"

CHAPTER THIRTY-TWO

I lay on one of the futons, wrapped in a blue down comforter, a throw pillow under my head, willing my brain to shut down and let me get some sleep before we had to hit the road again.

Despite the role of host being thrust upon him, G had risen to the occasion, offering us food and drink—handed out with coasters, no less. He had even pulled out an assortment of pillows and bedding, including two thick futons and several yoga mats, before vanishing upstairs to his bedroom, muttering something about coffee in the morning and looking as if he'd been hit by an emotional tornado.

The chaos in his perfectly arranged abode was too much for him, poor guy.

The rest of us made do wherever we found a place to throw down a pillow and a blanket. I'd decided to crash upstairs in Action Figure Central, hoping for some much needed privacy. Since this whole zombie madness had started, I couldn't remember the last time I'd had more than a few minutes by myself—and those were usually in a bathroom, like the five-minute shower I'd taken before retiring.

The shower had felt great, although having to put my filthy clothes back on was a bummer. I compromised by wearing the pants, boots, and T-shirt, and saving for later the worst of the gore-encrusted Kevlar and long-sleeved overshirt.

Shutting my eyes for the umpteenth time, I tossed and turned under the comforter. Problem was, my body was willing, but my brain would not cooperate. It was operating on full monkey mode, trying to figure out why the universe had given me time to try and rescue BirkenBeamer, who hadn't wanted my help, yet I'd had to watch those little kids ripped to pieces right in front of me.

When someone knocked softly on the door, it was almost a relief.

I jumped to my feet, padded across the room and opened the door a few inches, fully expecting to see Lil. Instead Gabriel stood there, hair damp. Like me, he'd stripped to pants, T-shirt, and boots, a bundle of Kevlar, weapons, and bedding clutched in his arms. We stared at each other for a beat.

"Can I come in?" He spoke in an undertone. I stepped back so he could enter, then closed the door behind him.

"Not that I'm not happy to see you," I said, keeping my voice equally low, "but did you want something?"

He shook his head.

"I just wanted to check on you, make sure you were okay."

"I'm fine." I sat down on the futon, knees folded to my chest with the comforter pulled up to my shoulders, as he stashed his gear against one wall.

"Good," he said. "That's good." He paused, then held up a pillow and blanket. "Is it okay if I—"

"Help yourself."

He tossed both pillow and blanket on the floor a few feet away from me and stretched out on his back, hands clasped behind his head.

The silence was palpable, stretching out like taffy between us.

I cleared my throat and looked at him expectantly. He continued to stare at the ceiling.

Okay, fine. Exasperated, I wrapped the comforter around me like a puffy cape and scooted over next to him.

"Well?"

He looked at me and gave a sudden laugh.

"With that blanket, you look like the caterpillar in *Alice in Wonderland*. The cartoon, that is. All you need is a hookah."

"Just what every woman dreams of hearing," I snorted. "'Honey, you look like an insect.' Although I wouldn't say no to a hookah about now. It might help me shut my brain down."

He rolled over on his side, head propped up on one hand.

"Trouble sleeping?"

"Total monkey brain," I confessed. "I know we have to focus on the mission. We don't have time to save everyone, we have to look at the big picture, blah blahblah. But—"

"But you're not a big picture type of person," Gabriel finished for me. "Is that it?"

"I've always been more of a 'little things matter' person. Sometimes more than the big ones. Like the whole butterfly effect where something as small as a butterfly flapping its wings can cause a hurricane at the opposite side of the earth."

I took a deep breath, and continued.

"I saw two little kids die not twenty feet away from me, and I couldn't do anything. Maybe that little girl was destined to cure cancer—"

"Ash…"

I held up a hand so I could finish.

"—or maybe she was going to be another Snookie. I know, I know. Either way, she and her brother didn't deserve to die that way. And either way—" I looked at him, my eyes prickling with tears I didn't want to shed "—I couldn't save them."

Gabriel reached up, slipping his hands under the comforter to pull me down next him, where his arms wrapped around me. He moved one hand up to my hair, still damp from the shower, fingers gently caressing my scalp.

I gave a shuddering sigh and relaxed against him, my head resting in the crook of his shoulder, one hand resting on his chest, feeling the beat of his heart underneath. It didn't matter that the clothes we wore stank of death. Not when I could feel the warmth of his body against mine. The warmth meant the antiserum was doing its job, that he was still human, and could still be cured.

In this particular instance, the big picture and the little picture were the same size to me.

"I have a confession." Gabriel continued massaging my head and neck as he spoke.

"I am here to absolve." *Or dissolve*, I thought, as tension vanished underneath his strong fingers.

He gave a small chuckle, was silent for a few seconds, then spoke.

"I didn't really come up here to check on you." Another brief beat. "I just wanted—" He swallowed. "I *needed* to see you. I wanted to spend some time with you before we go out there again. Because—" he swallowed again, as if it hurt "—we may not make it."

I started to protest, then decided to do something against my character and just shut up. I listened, tracing circles on his T-shirt clad chest with one finger.

"It's going to be bad," he continued. "Like the swarm, but worse. And even if we make it to the lab… there's no guarantee there either."

"You don't think Dr. Albert can find a cure?"

"Oh, I think he'll eventually find a cure. It just may not be in time to make a difference to me."

I acknowledged the truth of his words.

And then rejected it.

"Uh-uh. Never give up, never surrender. If we have

to dose you up every ten minutes while he figures this shit out, that's what we're going to do."

"It's not that simple, Ash."

"Yeah, it is."

I rolled over so I was lying on top of him, face close to his.

"I will not give up on you," I said fiercely. "I refuse to enter the dating scene again, okay."

Gabriel wrapped both arms around me again, holding me close.

"You're the most amazing woman I've ever known, Ash."

"Good or bad?" I smiled down at him.

"Both. But either way—" he stared up at me with those amazing denim-blue eyes "—you make me feel human, and give me a reason to keep trying."

He kissed me then, with a long, deep kiss, equal parts passion and tenderness combined. One of ten perfect kisses in the history of the world. It kicked the ass out of Buttercup and Westley, and we very quickly lost whatever G rating we might have had, stripping off our clothes in record time, to lose ourselves in each other's bodies for the second—and what might be the last—time.

Finally, with limbs and bodies still intertwined, I drifted off into a thankfully dreamless sleep.

CHAPTER THIRTY-THREE

I was jarred out of sleep by the sound of Gabriel's labored, gasping breathing.

Sitting upright in a tangle of blanket and comforter, shaking the last dregs of sleep from my brain, I realized Gabriel was crouched next to me, body sweating and shaking as his breathing came in hyperventilating gasps. Even in the dim glow from the streetlights outside I could see the sickly pearls of sweat beading up on skin gone sallow. The whites of his eyes had started to yellow.

Shit. Keeping it together, I put a reassuring hand on his shoulder.

"I'll get Dr. Albert," I said.

"No time," he choked out. "Meds in the bag." He jerked his head toward his duffel, then doubled over as if he was transforming from human to werewolf. It looked like a mega-evil case of cramps, with a migraine on top.

Oh, jeez…

I unzipped the duffel, pawing through it frantically to find the little vials I knew were in there. After what seemed like forever I found them in an inner zip compartment, along with syringes. I pulled one of each out, jabbed the syringe into the vial and extracted the antiserum, wincing as I did so.

"God, I hope I did this right," I muttered as I drummed

up the courage to actually inject him. "What about air bubbles?"

"Just. Do. It," he gritted, sweat pouring off his now totally jaundiced face.

I did it, jabbing the needle into his deltoid and slowly depressing the plunger on the syringe. My face started tingling and my vision grayed around the edges. I didn't quite have a needle phobia, but I'd always had to shut my eyes, whether for getting an injection or watching a scene in a movie that showed a close-up of a needle going into the skin.

Hold it together, girl, I told myself. *Now is not the time to wuss out.*

There. The plunger was all the way down. I grabbed a corner of the blanket and held it against Gabriel's arm as I withdrew the needle, catching a droplet of blood as it welled up from the injection site.

Ugh ugh ugh!

I quickly put my head down face first against my pillow and took a few deep breaths until the urge to vomit passed, all the while listening to the sound of Gabriel's breathing returning to normal. After a few minutes I felt his hand on my shoulder.

"You okay there, Ash?" His voice was almost steady, with just a hint of rasp underneath.

"I'm a liberal arts major, not a doctor, dammit," I muttered into the pillow.

He chuckled quietly.

"At least you didn't throw up."

"I still might," I groaned. "I hate needles."

The sound of breaking glass followed by a blood-curdling shriek brought us both to our feet, adrenaline driving any lingering dizziness out of my system.

"Was that downstairs?" he said.

"Yeah." I nodded. We didn't waste any more time on words, pulling on our clothing in record time. We grabbed our gear, slinging weapons over shoulders, and dashed out the door just as G emerged from his Batcave, still wearing his jeans and Dr. Who T-shirt.

"What was that?" he said in his heavily accented Dark Knight rasp, as the unmistakable noise of zombie moans sounded below, along with frantic cursing and the sound of someone choking on his or her own blood.

A loud *splat* followed.

"That is deep shit," I said, taking the stairs two at a time right in front of Gabriel. I hit the landing, dumped all my gear but my tanto on the floor, and ran into the living room, where Tony had just pile driven the business end of his sledgehammer into Hicks' skull.

Oh shit, he'd died and came back.

Becky lay dead on the floor next to him with her throat torn out, expression frozen in wide-eyed horror, the remains of a Samwise Gamgee lamp lying in shards around her. Nathan kneeled over her as he withdrew a wickedly sharp knife from her skull.

"Oh, no." G came up behind me, taking in the corpses of Becky and his *Lord of the Rings* collectible.

Lil crouched protectively over Mack, wearing a feral expression as he pressed a hand against one shoulder, blood seeping out from between his fingers, face drawn in pain.

"Mack, Lil, you okay?" I asked anxiously.

"I'm fine," Lil growled. "Mack got bit!"

He gave a dismissive cluck.

"It's more a scrape than a bite. No real damage. Not like that poor guy."

A choked gurgle to my left brought my attention to Shaggy, now sprawled against the coffee table, bright red blood pouring out from his carotid artery even as Dr. Albert tried to staunch the flow with a handful of blanket. There was nothing he could do, though. Shaggy died in less than a minute.

Nicks immediately stepped forward with a handgun, but Gabriel raised his hand to stop her.

"Too noisy." He looked at me. "Ash?"

I nodded and took care of things with the tanto, wiping the blade clean on the same blanket Dr. Albert had used to try to save him.

I looked at Red and Carl, both of whom looked totally shell-shocked. The remaining snipers looked shaken as well, under their stoic expressions. They had lost their friends and colleagues.

"I'm sorry," I said, and I meant it. These men and women were risking their lives, knowing that even a small bite or scratch that penetrated their skins was a death warrant, unless they were one of the miniscule percent of the population who were wild cards. And even then, they'd have to survive the transition period of bone-wracking pain and fever, if they didn't die of blood loss or trauma first.

"What the hell happened?" Gabriel gestured at Hicks' body.

"Most likely an epidural hematoma from the head injury he sustained during the crash." Dr. Albert made a *tsk-tsk* noise. "Death can be very sudden."

"He wasn't bitten," Nathan said, sheathing his knife in a practiced move. "So why did he turn?"

"There's always a possibility that infected blood will get into a surface wound," Dr. Albert said, sounding as anxious to convince himself as the rest of us. "Even a scrape would do, if it were deep enough."

"But if that's not the case, then what are we looking at?" Nathan pressed.

Dr. Albert gave him a very worried look.

"Why, then we'd be looking at the possibility that the virus has mutated, and gone airborne."

Whatever reaction we might have had to his potentially catastrophic statement was cut off by a sound so mundane, at first I couldn't figure out what it was. A loud buzzing sounded in the entryway, like a hive full of angry baritone bees.

We all jumped, weapons raised and ready—all except for G, who looked at the front door.

"It's the front bell," he said, then he looked at us quizzically. "Should I get it?" The buzzer went off again, followed by a rapid-fire knocking.

I shook my head.

"I'll check," I said, and I glanced at Gabriel, who nodded his approval. G didn't object as I went to the door and peered through the peephole. Peering back at me under the glow of the streetlight and the first glimmer of dawn, all wonky and out of proportion from the fish-eye lens, was a young man somewhere in his twenties, wearing a red bandana in a paisley pattern that brought to mind amoebas tied around his head. His eyes were brown, no sign of the sickly yellow corruption of Walker's in the whites, and his grin was... well, I'd have to say manic.

He looked familiar. At any rate, he wasn't dead so I unbolted the door and opened it a few inches.

"Yes?"

"Heya," he said, sounding weirdly cavalier. "I'm JT. Thought you all might wanna know there's a bunch of those walking dead things headed your way." He looked to his right, in the direction of the med center. "Whoever screamed pretty much rang the dinner bell."

As if in agreement, moans emanated pretty much from everywhere.

The guy looked around him, then back at me.

"Uh, can I come in?" He grinned. "Just until you all head out. Which should be pretty quickly, unless you want to see a zombie reenactment of the white blood cells swarming the *Proteus* and Raquel Welch's memorable bosom in *Fantastic Voyage*."

At a rare loss for words, I looked back over my shoulder at Gabriel and Nathan. They exchanged a quick glance.

"I'll check the view from upstairs," Nathan said.

Gabriel nodded, then gave me the go-ahead, so I opened the door to admit our visitor. He strutted into the townhouse, as cocky and carefree as Tony Manero. I could almost hear *Stayin' Alive* playing in the background. He wore loose-fitting black pants, like something a martial artist would wear, and a sleeveless black shirt with a white Darwin fish on the front.

He looked around, taking in the decor.

"Nice," he commented with a total lack of irony. G beamed, despite the fact there were three corpses in the middle of his living room. Whatever kept him sane, I thought. Or at least kept him from flipping out.

"Did you say your name is JT?" I asked, trying to figure out why this cocky guy looked so familiar.

"I did indeed." He grinned at me. "You're Ashley, right?"

I frowned.

"How the hell do you know my name?"

He just laughed.

"Bet you never expected a stalker in the middle of this sort of shit, right?"

By this time Gabriel and the Gunsy Twins were staring at JT with deadly intent, weapons ready. He noticed and laughed again.

"Relax, kids. Not *that* kind of stalker. I saw you in action—" he nodded at me "—back on Marina Boulevard."

His face suddenly clicked in my memory.

"You were the guy leaping from car to car!"

"Gold star for the babe with the sword!" His grin lit up his face in a cute—and scary—sort of way.

"So you followed me?" I was amazed—and okay, more than a little flattered—that someone would have been able to keep up with us. "Why?"

"Hot chick in a uniform with a gun?" He shrugged. "No brainer."

Gabriel bristled. JT noticed and rolled his eyes.

"Okay, you all need to take the sticks out of your asses and get going, because right now standing in this room is like being in an all-you-can-slap buffet." He spoke with the stylized rapid patter of a Howard Hawks movie.

Tony, by this time, was looking at JT with the expression of someone who'd stepped in a pile of particularly stinky dog shit.

"Who the fuck is this guy?" he said.

JT ignored him.

"Is there a back door here? Probably a good idea, since things are about to go all *House of the Dead* at the front."

"Video game or movie?" Tony said with a challenging glare.

JT shrugged.

"Video game," he replied. "The movie sucked."

Tony shut up, unable to argue.

Nathan reappeared at the foot of the stairs.

"Pack up, people. We need to move."

CHAPTER THIRTY-FOUR

Whatever Nathan had seen from the upstairs window had lit a serious fire under him, and it spread to the rest of us. I've never geared up as quickly.

G watched our preparations with bemusement.

"You're leaving?" he finally asked me as I shrugged my knapsack onto my back.

"We have to go," I said. "And—" I felt like shit, but I had to say it "—if you want to live, you need to come with us. I'm sorry," I added, hating the stricken look on his face. "But they know you're here now. And that's our fault. But if you come with us, we can protect you."

I felt even shittier for saying that, knowing I couldn't guarantee anything of the sort.

"But…" G's gaze flickered around his home, pausing on each of his beloved collectibles. "Everything I own is in this house." I had no trouble translating this time.

I put a hand on his shoulder.

"And when this is all over, it'll still be here. But you won't be if you stay."

"But I—"

JT popped up in front of us.

"Look. I admire your taste in decor and all," he said to G, "but if you don't get your shit together, I am going to dickslap you so hard, it'll leave a mushroom print on your forehead."

"Right then." G nodded as if coming to some agreement with himself.

He vanished upstairs.

I glared at JT.

"Really? Did you have to be such a jerk?"

"Don't worry, he'll be back."

Before I could argue the point, G loped back down the stairs, wearing a black hooded jacket, and a Bat-satchel slung over one shoulder. He pulled a pocket watch from an inner pocket, checked it, and vanished into the kitchen, where we heard water running.

The water shut off and G reappeared, drying his hands on a hand towel.

JT grinned at me as if to say, "See?"

I ignored him.

G put the hand towel down on the entryway table.

"I'm ready," he announced.

Our only problem—and it was a big one—was that there wasn't a back door. There was the sliding door that opened onto the patio, and the front door. Both faced the main courtyard that lay between the townhouses, where a veritable shitload of zombies was now shambling down the stairs.

In the five minutes we'd taken to pack up, dozens had found their way in from the Carl Street entrance, funneling in like cattle in a slaughterhouse chute. JT pointed his thumb to the moaning swarm cascading down toward us.

"Yeah, those are the ones I was telling you about."

"We need to create a distraction," Gabriel said. "No way we're fighting our way through that many without losing someone."

"I got you covered," JT said.

Gabriel ignored him, consulting his iPhone maps. Nathan, on the other hand, folded his arms and looked at JT as though he'd discovered an interesting new bug.

"Oh, really?" he said.

"Sure." JT swung his arms back and forth as if warming up the muscles. "So where are we all headed?"

"A super secret government laboratory up Medical Center Way," Nathan said. He did it with a straight face too.

JT's eyes lit up.

"Secret government lab… no shit?"

I nodded solemnly.

"He shits you not." That elicited an appreciative whistle.

"That is *sooo* cool." JT frowned for a moment, working out some mental navigation, then said, "Okay, no problem. Tell you what I'm gonna do. I'll distract this bunch, lead them downstream, towards the Haight. You guys go around the corner the other way, up Arguello to the UC parking garage. Then take a left and a right up Hillway. Got it?"

Gabriel looked up from his iMaps and regarded JT thoughtfully.

"Good route."

It was my turn to frown.

"Um, yeah, but what about him?" I said, nodding my head in JT's direction.

"Awww, she worries about me," he said to Gabriel, then he grinned at me. "I'll catch up with you on Hillway. Won't take but a minute."

"How the hell do you propose to perform this miracle, without becoming zombie chow?" I asked with an admirable lack of sarcasm.

"It's quite simple," JT said. "I will compel them with my deliciousness, then confound them with the speed, grace, and power of Urbobatics. Follow… and observe."

He bounded up the stairs. Nathan and I looked at each other, then at Gabriel.

"Go ahead," he said. "See what he's got in mind. I'll work on plan B, just in case."

So Nathan and I followed JT to the second story

balcony, off of the master bedroom. Still ahead of us, he stepped outside and looked down at the zombies.

"Over here!" he yelled, and he spread his arms as if he was Evita addressing the masses.

"He's crazy," I muttered to Nathan. We went to the balcony doors, keeping out of sight of the hordes below.

Then I gasped as he lightly vaulted over the railing, planted his feet against the bars, and leaned out, posing like a ship's figurehead for a moment before he threw his head back and gave an operatic howl that drove the zombies crazy with hungry expectation. They swarmed the narrow courtyard until there was a thicket of horrid, outstretched arms clamoring below him, all clawing the air in frustration.

Then he simply let go of his grip.

The crowd of the dead moaned as he tumbled toward their ravenous mouths. I almost screamed before his tumble turned into an expert backflip and he touched down, feet first—right on top of a solidly built zombie, one that looked like it'd spent most of its time at the gym.

The walking corpse crumpled under the impact and JT tucked and rolled down the sidewalk, before he popped up again to his feet, all "Ta-Dah!" and none the worse for wear.

"Come and get me, you undead pussies!" he yelled at the milling horde, waving his arms and jogging backward. The members of the Z cascade jerkily shambled and tripped over one another to get to this new meal-on-the-go. He whistled and pogo'd and smacked his own butt, saying, "Mmm, don't you want to eat that tender ass?" all to lock in their attention, leading his would-be predators down the street like the Pied Piper of the Dead.

Nathan gave a low whistle. "Well, I'll be damned."

"That," I said to Nathan, "has got to be the most effectively irritating distraction in the history of the world."

"Damn straight." He nodded. "Now let's take advantage of it."

CHAPTER THIRTY-FIVE

Nathan and I hit the first floor at about the same time. I gave Gabriel the thumbs up as Nathan barked, "Let's move!" Obediently we barreled out the front door, Gabriel and Nicks on point and the Gunsy Twins bringing up the rear. Both Lil and Gentry supported Mack, and the rest of us made sure Dr. Albert and G were sandwiched in the middle for protection. I traded my tanto for the katana, chopping off the hands of a female zombie in a blue hospital gown as it reached for G.

I saw JT rounding the sidewalk onto Frederick so I dashed ahead of Gabriel and Nicks just in time to spot him sprinting towards the Haight, most of the horde swarming after him. The rest of the group joined me, all of us pausing to watch what was an amazing display of athleticism and pure chutzpah.

Every time it looked as though the zombies had him within reach, he would sprint ahead again, bouncing up and off walls, vaulting over debris and barriers, and swinging around streetlights and traffic sign poles as carefree as Gene Kelly singin' in the rain.

Even Tony looked impressed.

"Dude knows parkour. Total *District Thirteen* shit."

JT waved at us and flashed us thumbs up just before launching into a shoulder roll onto the hood of a burned out car, and then leapfrogging over the top.

He didn't come up again.

We waited as a tide of zombies closed in around the trashed car.

"Something's wrong," I said worriedly.

Suddenly a hand came up. JT laboriously pulled himself up onto the hood like he was scaling a cliff.

"Shit! Is he hurt?" I strained my neck trying to see.

Then he raised his head and looked at us.

"Fly, you fools!" he yelled, and he dropped again in a dramatic fall before leaping to his feet and hauling ass further down Frederick, leading the horde further and further away from us.

"*The Fellowship of the Ring*," G said in vaguely pleased tones.

"Oh, my god," I snapped, "this is *not* the Bridge of Thulsa Doom and—"

"Khazad-dûm," G corrected.

"Whatever," I growled. "This is not a movie. Let's move!" With one last glance at the zombie swarm, I wondered if we really would see him again. There was no time to worry, though—we had problems of our own. There were still plenty of undead stragglers emerging to investigate the ruckus. More than likely, there wasn't a square block of the city left that wasn't crawling with enough cadaver power to mount a decent-sized swarm.

We had to move fast, before the next one could come together.

So we slipped down Frederick Street, staying close to the residential buildings. Knots of stray ghouls continued to shamble through the maze of dead cars and emerge from the trees of the park. The snipers conserved their shots to clear a path in front. The rest of us dealt with our flank on a case-by-case basis, skewering or crushing the cranium of any zombie that came too close, and leaving the rest behind.

We rounded the corner of Arguello Boulevard and faced a slight hill. At the top was a multi-story parking structure for the University of California. It looked downright medieval—like a fortress wall. One end was all thick slabs of grey concrete with dark patches of carports. There was a rounded stone wall pierced by a series of narrow windows that looked like arrow slits. A band of crossbowmen could set up shop here and do very well for themselves, I thought. Too bad there weren't any there now, since this street crawled with the walking dead.

"Hug the walls and keep up, folks!" Nathan hollered from his position as Tail End Charlie.

Up ahead Gabriel and Nicks were moving fast, and the Gunsy Twins were staying tight behind them. Nathan, Tony, and I ran interference for the rest. We had to keep our forward momentum now, because another horde was slowly growing larger in our wake. I began opting for quick katana strikes to the knees and thighs—striking at the weakest points—and as a result several of them were downgraded to crawlers, crippled and still moaning. Meanwhile Nathan was using the butt of his rifle to good effect on any undead face that came within striking distance.

We shot, hacked, and mashed all the way uphill to Carl Street, where Gabriel and Nicks rounded the corner, and immediately began backpedaling. The shock on their faces did not bode well for the immediate future.

Well, shit.

"Hold up!" Gabriel called.

He sank into a crouch, waving me and Nathan up to the front.

"We've got a problem," he said in a low voice.

I hazarded a look around the corner.

He wasn't kidding.

The block ahead was a complete roadblock. A massive fire truck lay directly across our path—it had smashed right into the apartment building, and its ladder jutted out into the air at a crazy angle.

Adding to the mayhem was a maze of clusterfucked

ambulances, trucks, and cars that had poured out of the UC's parking structure in a panic to escape, only to become mired like mammoths in a tar pit. Some of them were smoldering, the grimy black twists of smoke making it hard to see a way through, and tingeing the whole scene with an air of wartime and doom.

Most of the firemen and drivers were still milling around the stranded vehicles in an undead daze, as if trying to swap insurance information.

"Is there any way through it?" I asked.

Gabriel and Nathan both scanned the ugly mess. Gabriel then pointed to the fire truck and shot a "what do you think?" look at Nathan.

"It's not the best option," Nathan responded, "but we should be able to go alongside the truck, and then cut through the middle."

Gabriel nodded.

"My thought exactly. I'm just not sure if it's open all the way through. We may have to do some crawling in order to get to the other side, or climb over the top—but it's a little Z-heavy for that."

"It's not pretty," I agreed, "but it's either that or go back the way we came. And that route's pretty much fubar'd at this point."

As if to prove my point, Nicks abruptly turned to fire off a point-blank hip shot that blasted an opportunistic zombie's face and sent its corpse tumbling backwards.

"Right." Gabriel nodded and turned to the rest of the group. "Straight line, single file. Stay low and follow me. Let's go!" He set off in a crouching run, gunning down a pair of ex-firemen, and disappeared into the smoky maze of gridlock. I let the snipers advance ahead of me, unslinging my M4 in order to help Nathan with the rearguard effort. The others moved swiftly past as he and I opened up on the horde coming up behind us.

Red was the last to pass. He tapped us on the back, shouting to be heard above the roar of our suppression fire.

"Everyone's through!"

I waved Nathan on, and he ran ahead, with Red and me close on his heels. We made it past a curtain of smoke to the big red wall of the fire engine, slipping into and out of the cab of the ambulance that had crashed into it, and finding ourselves stuck in a cramped triangular space. Another ambulance had crunched into the fire truck alongside the first, walling us in with no visible exit.

I could hear more zombies coming up behind us.

"Crawl underneath!" Nathan yelled, dropping and vanishing into the dark.

Red and I looked dubiously at each other, and then sucked it up and squeezed underneath. It was a tight, uncomfortable fit, and the rough asphalt was slick with something wet and sticky.

Mud? Oil? Blood?

Probably all of the above, I thought, suppressing the urge to gag.

There was barely enough light to see, and we would have to crawl beneath several vehicles before we could emerge again, I was guessing about eighteen yards or so ahead. I could just make out Nathan moving through the gloom ahead of us, and wondered if Red could see anything at all.

We both scrambled as best we could to catch up, but it was slow, painful going. About a third of the way through, Red suddenly cursed.

"Shit. I'm stuck!" He struggled to free himself. I tried to inch back to help, but found myself getting snagged when I tried to retrace my way under the vehicle.

There was nothing I could do to help him but stay by his side, while one agonizing second after another ticked by. Was it just my imagination, or was the smell of gasoline getting stronger?

"Fuu-*uck*!" Red growled, trying to free himself. "This was a bad idea."

Movement nearby caught my attention even as the

stench and hair-raising groans announced the presence of a trio of hungry crawlers, all with wide, toothy grins.

"Red! We've got company!" I tried not to sound panicked, but pretty much failed as I tried to get to any of my weapons while the zombies crept closer. I went for my tanto, but couldn't get enough space between the ground and my body to unsheathe it.

The nearest one scuttled up, trying to get a big juicy bite of my face. I could smell rot wafting out of its mouth and choked back bile.

No more puking, fer crissake.

I head-butted the thing as hard as I could, my skull slamming into its teeth before it could get a chomp in. Once, and then again. Its rotted gum-line crunched with a sickening sound, and I managed to grab the nearly forgotten Ruger from its holster, jabbing the barrel under its chin and blowing a hole through its head.

I capped the second zombie point-blank in one eye as it closed in for a face bite of its own. I couldn't see the third, but I could feel it pulling my leg into its jaws. I fired blindly around the first corpse. One shot went wild, but the next two hit just as I felt its teeth sink into the back of my calf. The fabric of my pants protected me, so it didn't break the skin, but damn, that hurt!

"Ash!" Red yelled, flailing to get free.

"I'm okay!" I called back, trying to ignore the pain lancing up my leg. I was more concerned at the thought of more zombies finding their way under the vehicles, attracted by the ruckus. Moans and gurgles sounded to my right.

"Come on, move it, Red!"

He cursed again. There was a ripping sound as something gave way.

"Okay, I'm loose," he grunted, careful not to yell again. "Go! Go!" I didn't need any more encouragement than that.

We scurried as fast as we could. I paused briefly to

look back and put bullets in the skulls of two of the faster zombies crawling after us.

We passed two cracks of light from the narrow gaps between cars. I could hear shouts from the other team members, calling our names. Where were they? I couldn't believe we weren't in the clear yet. Could we have veered in the wrong direction?

Red had fallen behind.

"Ash!" he shouted.

I turned back to him. My wild card vision picked up on his wide-eyed look of fear.

"Ash? I—"

He never finished.

The darkness gave way to the flash and the roar of a blast furnace. Red disappeared in the fireball, his scream abruptly cut off even as I was thrown forward by a deafening wall of sound and heat as fire raged around me. Buffeted by a killer wave that tumbled me around, I watched as the car above me spiraled up and away. I heard the crash as it landed.

Then I found myself on the ground under open sky, lying in between burning vehicles. I was dazed, deafened, shaken, and my pants were on fire. I rolled and beat at the flames until they were extinguished, then staggered to my feet, realizing how completely and utterly lucky I had just been. If poor Red and the bodies of those zoms hadn't shielded me from the worst of the blast, I would have been completely barbecued.

My head spun and ached, and my ears were ringing. I looked around, trying to get my bearings. I'd made it to the other side of the clusterfuck, although apparently I had taken the scenic route. Gabriel and Carl ran over to me from the sidewalk beyond, as Lil called my name in joyful disbelief. Gabriel looked at me in equal parts relief and amazement.

"You are just frickin' death-proof, aren't you?"

Carl looked beyond me, though.

"What about Red?"

I shook my head, and his jaw tightened.

"Damn."

"I'm sorry," I said, meaning it. Gabriel put a hand on his shoulder.

"We have to move before the rest of these cars go up." He looked at me. "Are you good to go?"

Ignoring the ringing in my ear, I just said, "Which way?"

Gabriel jerked his head back toward the steep side street ahead of us.

"Up that hill, and we're nearly there," he said. "Let's move."

We reformed our ranks and pushed our way up the hill. The explosion seemed to have stopped up the undead bottleneck behind us, but as always, there were plenty more on the welcoming committee ahead, with still more continuing to trickle out of the woodwork.

A piercing whistle from somewhere overhead caught my attention. In spite of everything, my face split into a wide grin as I saw JT poking his head out from the top of an apartment building on our left. He gave a shout and leaped to the fire escape, then swung and dropped himself like a pachinko ball down the face of the building, swinging from one precarious leap to another.

Finally he launched through the air and caught hold of a telephone pole retaining wire, grasping it like a trapeze artist. He lowered himself in a gentle, lazy spiral descent, hitting the ground with bended knees, then sauntered over to the rest of us, grinning from ear to ear.

"How'd you lose that horde?" I asked him.

"Noisy and flashy going out, silent and ninja-like coming back. My standard M.O." He sniffed the air. "Hey, what smells like fried chicken? It's making me hungry."

Carl glared at him.

"I lost my friend back there, asshole."

JT looked at him, grin fading away.

"I am truly sorry to hear that," he said.

Carl turned without a word and walked rapidly up the hill.

JT turned to me.

"I really am sorry."

"I know," I said. "Let's just clear out these damn zombies and get up this friggin' hill."

CHAPTER THIRTY-SIX

We were a grim-faced bunch as we reached the foot of Medical Center Way. Several large trucks crisscrossed the entrance, one lying on its side, steam still trickling sullenly from the engine, another rammed up against the first, effectively blocking off the road to any automotive traffic. Both trucks bore the logos of pharmaceutical companies—whether by coincidence or design, I didn't even want to hazard a guess.

Beyond the trucks, the road curved up a hill into a nature reserve filled with hiking trails. It sprawled behind the medical complex, which lay on the right. On the left was a slope overgrown with ivy and autumnal colored foliage.

I've hiked those trails, I thought, suddenly struck by how surreal it all was. *Never knew it was a Men in Black branch office.*

Then again, the same could be said of Redwood Grove.

The good news for us was that the barrier also limited the number of zombies in our path. We needed all the breaks we could get, after the hell of the last few blocks. Mack was red-faced and laboring with each step, even with Lil and Gentry's help. His shirt was dark with blood from the bite he'd sustained. I'd lay odds on it being worse than he let on.

G was struggling valiantly to keep his cool. He stayed

with Dr. Albert, checking his pocket watch periodically, muttering to himself like a thickly accented White Rabbit. Dr. Albert was also muttering, punctuated by huffing and puffing as he struggled to keep pace with Tony and Nathan, his two protectors.

Our progress took us uphill, and I was feeling the burn myself, more than ready to collapse in a heap somewhere, preferably in a place that was free of zombies.

I'd had enough, thank you.

JT was the only one who seemed unaffected by Red's death, and for that matter, the rest of the carnage. It was as if he carried an unlimited source of energy, like an Energizer Bunny on crack. Every wall, building, and object, instead of being an obstacle, provided another opportunity for acrobatics. The world was his trampoline. He would have been a joy to watch if not for the circumstances.

Right now it seemed too much like dancing on a giant grave.

Speaking of the acrobatic devil, JT suddenly dropped his speed and settled next to me.

"So what's the deal with the older dude with the bite?" He spoke in a normal tone. I held up a finger and turned down an imaginary dial.

"Do you mean Mack?" I lowered my own voice accordingly.

He shrugged.

"I mean the older dude with the bite," he said, nodding in Mack's direction. "I haven't been formally introduced to anyone yet, you know."

He had a point. I tried not to let that fact irritate me.

"What about him?" I said as we hurried past a driveway that sloped down to some loading docks. They butted up against three different buildings, and the area was crawling with zombies—so many they looked like a cluster of cockroaches.

"I've seen people get bitten," he responded. "They die.

Then they come back, unless someone with triple-digit IQ points takes out their brain, right?" We moved past a phalanx of electrical transformers. "He's obviously not feeling great, but he's not sick. What gives?"

What the hell, I thought. He'd risked his life for us, and we'd gone way past the point of a cover story involving Ebola and an escaped lab monkey.

"He's a wild card," I said. "He's immune to the virus. So are Lil, and Tony and Nathan and Gentry." I pointed to each person as I named them. "And so am I."

JT looked intrigued, but not particularly surprised.

"So basically, you're saying that you guys could get chomped on like a turkey leg at the Renaissance Faire, and you'd be fine."

I gave him a look.

"As long as we don't bleed out or lose a vital organ, yeah, pretty much."

JT considered this.

"How do you know if you're immune?"

"It's simple," I said. "You get bit the first time, and you don't die." I shivered as I remembered the feverish, agonizing pain of the zombie virus coursing through my body as my immune system fought it. "It hurts," I added. "A lot."

"Huh." JT thought about that. Then without a word he bounded ahead, springing up onto a metal railing and rebounding off the side of another phalanx of transformers with no apparent effort. Pausing briefly, he eyeballed a series of progressively taller aluminum storage sheds, and his muscles tensed.

"*No*," I hissed. He looked at me like a cat getting yelled at for planning to jump on the counter—you know, fully prepared to ignore the yelling and do it anyway. I could just imagine the hollow metallic booming his feet would make on the aluminum siding.

"Noise!" I added in the same frantic hiss, pointing at the sheds.

That got through to him. Instead he veered to the side and leapt onto the top of the low raised wall that bordered the foliage on the left.

If he's this hyper normally, I'd hate to see him on a sugar rush.

The ground sloped upward on our left, toward the hospital building. Thankfully the hillside was clear. I dropped back next to Lil, Mack, and Gentry.

"You hanging in there, Postman?" I asked Mack, trying not to sound too concerned. He gave me a wan smile.

"Hanging in there, Ash."

"How about you, Lil?" I asked. "You need a break?"

"No!" she snapped. "I've got him."

Over her head, Gentry and I exchanged looks.

"Yeah, Lil and I can handle the mail," Gentry said.

"Hah, hah," Mack huffed.

Suddenly shots cracked off to our left as Nicks took out several zombies, all wearing scrubs, wandering down the bottom flight of a wooden staircase that zigzagged up into the hill above. Pretty staircase, beautiful scenery… ugly zombies.

More came trickling down the road—these looked like hikers who'd been in the nature reserve when the shit hit the fan.

Pop. Pop. Pop.

Three headshots from Jones, three dropped zoms.

Moans rose from behind us. I looked back, and saw the zombies that had been milling around the cargo bays. Alerted by the gunfire, they'd found their way up to the road and were gravitating toward our group. There were a lot of them, and more kept pouring sluggishly from around the corner of the driveway.

"Lots of incoming behind us," I yelled. No point being quiet any more.

"Double-time, people," Gabriel hollered. Sweat poured down his face, whether from the exertion or his condition, I wasn't certain. How long had it been since he'd had his last injection? An hour? Two?

Ahead on our right was a blue sign with white lettering. Dr. Albert saw it and brightened visibly.

"We're almost there," he panted, trying to hurry up his pace.

The sign identified the "Center for Regenerative Medicine."

Now that's *subtle.*

Nicks and Nathan dropped back, turning to face the hungry mob heading up the hill, taking out those in the lead and creating stumbling blocks for those behind. It wouldn't stop them, but it would slow them down a little bit. The sound of branches breaking and the crunch of leaves underfoot alerted me to several wobbling down the hill with an unsteady but determined gait. I started to swivel my M4 around.

Pop, pop, pop.

Jones beat me to it.

Alrighty then.

We reached a point in the road where it began curving around and up further into the nature reserve. A glass-and-metal-enclosed platform stretched ribbon-like across the hillside, improbably balanced on steel trusses and supports, framed by eucalyptus trees and fog. Suspended from the north facade were exterior ramps and staircases. The result was a building that was a work of practical art.

A steel-and-glass bridge—sort of an enclosed catwalk—ran from the new hi-tech structure to a pair of bland and much older multi-story buildings, hitting about the ninth floor. The catwalk itself was bisected by a giant metal shaft resembling a square grain elevator, rising in between the old and new buildings. A sign proclaimed it to be "Elevator 35," which made me wonder where elevators one through thirty-four were located.

"There." Dr. Albert pointed at the elevator. "We go in there."

You've got to be kidding.

"That's the super secret lab?" I said. "That thing out of *Architectural Digest*?"

"Seriously," JT chimed in. "That's about as conspicuous as a secret lab could be."

Dr. Albert tapped one side of his face and smiled mysteriously.

"Much like Patterson Hall, there is more than meets the eye. The elevator is just the entrance."

Unfortunately the entrance to the elevator lay at the base of a long wide drive that dipped down a steep hill. Between us and said entrance were more loading docks, trucks parked at odd, inconvenient angles, and dozens of zombies.

Nathan turned to Tony.

"Now's the time for that big-ass shotgun of yours, kid."

Tony's eyes lit up so you would've thought it was Christmas.

"Cool," he said.

Well, as long as someone's happy…

CHAPTER THIRTY-SEVEN

Nicks and the Gunsy Twins spread out along the top of the hill next to the drive and started picking their shots. In the meantime, the group following us up Medical Center Way grew closer—too close for comfort—so Tony made use of his BAS, blasting away as enthusiastically as a kid playing a first-person shooter.

Gabriel surveyed the situation, and shook his head.

"This isn't going to work. We need to move."

Nathan nodded his agreement while coolly dispatching several of the zombies closing in on us from Med Center Way. Then he looked at JT.

"You game, kid?"

"You guys need another distraction?" JT's eyes gleamed as he studied the struts, supports, and other opportunities all around him.

"It would help."

"Tell me your heart's desire," JT said, "and it shall be yours."

Nathan actually grinned at that.

"I doubt you could deliver, but how about we settle for you drawing enough of those zoms away to clear the elevator entrance."

Dr. Albert took a moment to understand, then smiled. "Ah. We have to go up—" He pointed at the catwalk. "—and then back down again."

"Secret elevator entrance?"

Dr. Albert nodded.

"Coolio," JT said, then turned back to Nathan. "I'll meet you up there in five or so."

Nathan gave him a thumbs up.

"We'll wait for you."

JT grinned at me. "But will *you* wait for me, baby?" He pinched my cheek, dashing off down the drive before I had the chance to swat him.

"If he doesn't die, I might kill him," Gabriel muttered. Even so, he looked impressed at JT's gravity defying progress, as he used trucks, walls, loading dock ramps, and zombies to make his way to the base of the Regenerative Medicine building, hooting and hollering all the way like a drunk at Mardi Gras.

And once again, it worked. The zombies shifted their attention and gravitated toward the noise and motion with a comfortingly Pavlovian response. A few still focused on some tasty treats they'd found at the top of the drive, but most stumbled after JT as he led them away from the elevator shaft entrance and toward the grounds under the Regenerative Medicine building.

Once there, he scaled the first twenty feet of the struts as if his feet and hands were made of particularly sticky adhesive.

"He's like fucking Spider-Man," Tony said, reluctant admiration in his voice.

"Well, we don't have time to enjoy the show," Gabriel said firmly. "Let's move, people!"

We ran for the elevator. Nicks stayed in front, clearing any strays that weren't off chasing JT, while the Gunsy Twins covered our retreat by taking care of the ones closing in on our flanks. I stuck close to G and Dr. Albert, right in front of Lil, Gentry, and Mack, katana once again replacing my M4.

Gabriel reached the elevator first, hitting the call button with his fist. A loud hum reverberated through the air as the car slowly moved from the catwalk down toward ground level.

We're gonna make it, I thought, just as I heard a scream of terror. Hands dripping with blood and bits reached out from the front bumper of a truck and seized Dr. Albert by his knapsack. He vanished around the front of the trunk.

Shit!

I rounded the corner in time to see a gore-rimmed mouth bite down on the canvas just below the doctor's neck.

Dr. Albert shrieked as if his flesh had been pierced, struggling frantically to shrug out of the knapsack even as the zombie—a female in skinny jeans and not much else—tugged on it, trying to reach the more edible parts.

I chopped down on its wrists with the katana just as Dr. Albert wrenched his arms out of the straps. Dead hands and knapsack fell onto the asphalt.

"My knapsack!" he cried.

"Run!" I shouted as he hesitated, reaching for the fallen knapsack even as two more zombies, both in cheerful purple scrubs, staggered toward us. "I'll get it!"

He ran as I dispatched Skinny Jeans with a merciful decapitation, and then hamstrung the two scrubs zombies. I snatched up the knapsack, turned, and found myself face-to-face with a trucker in jeans and flannel who looked as if he'd eaten everyone of his meals at Big Texan, "home of the free 72-oz. steak."

Trucker Zombie grabbed me by the shoulders before I could do more than gasp, its grip like a vise as it pulled me towards its gaping, stinking mouth. I tried to swing my katana up and around, but the zombie's sheer bulk made it impossible to get any sort of angle or leverage.

Shit, shit, shit!

A plug of flesh and blood exploded from the front of its forehead, spraying me with the mess as its hands loosened, letting me slip free. I looked around and saw Nicks across the way, grinning at me. I gave her a grateful thumbs up…

…just as her forehead exploded in a similar manner as that of the zombie she'd just shot. Her expression shifted from the grin to surprise as she crumpled to the ground, rifle falling from suddenly limp hands.

What the fuck?

I hit the ground just as a bullet smacked into the hood of the truck.

"We have enemy fire!" I hollered.

More shots cracked in the air. I heard a hoarse yell and flipped over on my back in time to see someone in fatigues falling from one of the support struts under the Regenerative Medicine building. Whoever it was hit the ground with a fleshy thump and was immediately swarmed by opportunistic zombies. By the sound of the screams, whoever it was hadn't died on impact.

I just wished I'd been the one to take them down, for Nicks' sake.

Coming up into a crouch, I hugged the bumper of the truck and did a quick scan of the underside of the building and surroundings. I sheathed my katana in favor of my M4.

Jones took aim, fired, and another body dropped down to the ground from the far end of the building. He waved at me from one side of the elevator shaft. Davis was on the other side as the rest of the team ran for the now open elevator car. Gabriel was using his body to keep the door from closing.

"Come on, Ash!" Gabriel shouted.

Taking a deep breath and mentally chanting "serpentine," I snatched up Dr. Albert's knapsack and zigzagged my way across the rest of the open pavement to the elevator. A bullet smacked into the asphalt next to me, and then another hit Davis in the shoulder, spinning him around into the waiting hands of two zombies that had crept up from behind.

I veered away from the elevator door and smashed the front zombie in the face with my rifle butt before it could sink its teeth into Davis's face. Getting the barrel up, I shot the second in the head. Grabbing Davis, I shoved him toward the elevator door even as another bullet narrowly missed both of us.

Jones was right behind us as Gabriel finally let the doors close.

There was a gentle hum of gears and pulleys as the elevator slowly began ascending. The smell of sweat, blood, and cordite filled the car as we all squashed together, pressed for space. Mack's face looked almost green in the artificial light that came from the top of the car.

"Why do we have to go up to go down?" I asked. "Is this like *The Poseidon Adventure* where death is down at the top and life is up at the bottom?"

Dr. Albert looked at me, head cocked to one side.

"I think you're in shock," he said.

"You may be right," I agreed. "But seriously, what's with the up-to-go-down business?"

Dr. Albert pulled a key out of his pocket.

"We wanted to make sure the lab couldn't be accessed from the ground level," he explained. "There's another elevator car, but it can only be accessed from the catwalk level, and then only if you have the key."

"That's fucking convoluted," I said. "Why not just have a secret keypad access at the bottom? Why go up to go down? Why does it all have to be so… so James Bond?"

Underneath my random irritation was a very real and justified fury. Too many good people had died to get us here. And most—if not all—of the deaths had occurred become of some assholes who had a secret agenda that included preventing us from reaching this lab.

Weren't flesh-eating zombies enough of an obstacle?

Dammit, we're trying to save *people*.

I shut my eyes and leaned against the elevator wall, trying to ignore the fact that every muscle in my body ached, and that the smell of roasted flesh and gasoline still lingered in my nostrils.

The elevator gave a gentle lurch and came to a halt.

The doors slid open.

That's when all hell broke loose.

CHAPTER THIRTY-EIGHT

As the doors opened, a rifle stock slammed into Gabriel's jaw, knocking him back against Nathan before he drooped forward and fell half in, half out of the elevator, unconscious.

Someone else drove another gunstock into Davis's midsection, doubling him over in time to receive a crack to the head. Before the rest of us could react, we found ourselves looking down the barrels of several nasty-ass, hi-tech looking weapons, the kind Nathan collected. The kind you didn't want to argue with.

The firearms were held by two men in basic black camo uniforms, large Ray-Ban style sunglasses obscuring the top half of otherwise expressionless faces like bargain basement ninjas. A trio in forest camos stood behind them to our right, similarly armed.

The man who'd just cold-cocked Davis looked in at the rest of us, studying our faces. He nodded at Dr. Albert.

"You. Step out."

Dr. Albert sputtered with indignant fear, but did as he was instructed. Then the same man jerked his head down toward Gabriel's prone body.

"That's the other one," he said. Two of the men in the background reached down and dragged him the rest of the way out of the elevator. Then he was half-dragged, half carried down the catwalk toward a pair of doors that led into the two buildings a hundred feet or so off to our right.

Dr. Albert was hustled along right after him, led by the third guy in camos.

I started to lunge forward, but someone, probably Nathan, jerked me back before I could move more than an inch or so.

"Don't," Nathan whispered into my ear. "Not now."

The lead guy waved his gun at us.

"Everybody else, drop your weapons," he said, "and step out of the elevator. *Now.*"

We all set our assorted firearms, swords, pickaxes, and such on the elevator floor, then piled slowly out onto the catwalk, where we were herded to the left by the two ninja wannabes. The one in front reached in and hit a button, pulling his arm out as the doors slid shut and the car slowly descended, our weapons inside.

"You two—" The man motioned to Lil and Gentry. "—move away from him. He can stand on his own."

"And if he can't, well, too bad," the other man said with a laugh.

I looked quickly at Lil, hoping she wouldn't do anything stupid. Amazingly enough, the fury of her glare didn't burn a hole in the asshole where he stood.

The first guy spoke again.

"Do it or I'll shoot him," he said. "I don't have orders for the rest of you, one way or the other. I'd just as soon not waste bullets, but I will if you piss me off."

"It's okay, hon," Mack said. "I've got this."

Lil growled under her breath, but stepped away from him, as did Gentry. Mack swayed on his feet, but managed to stay upright—most likely out of sheer stubbornness.

G muttered to himself. On total autopilot, he reached into his jacket for his pocket watch.

You idiot! I thought. *No!*

Guns swiveled toward him with a chorus of clicks. G woke up and pulled his hand out as if something had bitten it.

"It's just a pocket watch, you son of a bitch," I said softly. No one bothered to answer.

The other men vanished into the front building with Gabriel and Dr. Albert.

"No fucking way. This is *not* going to happen."

The man in front cocked his head to one side and looked at me.

"You don't think so?"

Crap, did I say the quiet part loud?

Yeah, I did.

He stepped directly in front of me, looking me up and down. I could see myself reflected in his sunglasses, my face smudged with smoke, blood, and grit.

"You must be Ashley Parker," he said.

He knew my name. That could not be a good thing.

He smiled. That made it even less of a good thing.

"I have a present for you, from an old friend," he said, and pointed his rifle at my head.

Lil screamed—the sound reverberating through the enclosed space—and rushed forward, knocking the barrel of his rifle down as he pulled the trigger. There was a metallic ping as the bullet ricocheted off the metal floor of the catwalk. Nathan and Gentry rushed him, wrestling the rifle away before he could fire again.

The second man's face grew ugly as he raised his weapon, but before he could fire it, something dropped from the metal struts in the roof above, and landed on him like a spider monkey.

Or Spider-Man... It was JT.

His feet hit the gunman square on the back of his neck, sending the man down on his knees, hard enough to make the entire catwalk shudder. The guy lost his grip on his rifle, and it clattered to the floor.

Should've used a sling, asshole.

JT hit the ground in a shoulder roll, popping back up to his feet with a little bow.

"Miss me?" he said with that manic grin.

"Maybe just a little," I said. "Thanks." I grabbed the fallen rifle and swung the stock down at the gunman's head as hard as I could, pulling the blow at the last second so I wouldn't kill him. Not that I had any ethical issues with killing the asshole, but we might need to get information out of him.

In the meantime, my would-be assassin was on his knees, hands clasped behind his head as Nathan covered the bastard with his own weapon.

"Where are they taking them?" he said in a tone that managed to convey a world of hurt without raising his voice. Before the man could reply, yet another gunshot cracked in the enclosed space. His eyes widened in momentary surprise as the back of his head exploded.

One of the men in forest camos stood by the open door to the right, aiming his rifle. A second shot sounded and the man I'd knocked out twitched once, as a bullet took him in the skull.

"Down!" Nathan yelled.

We all hit the deck—all except JT, who hit the side of the bridge interior, using walls, struts and floor to cover distance between him and the gunman. He was an impossible-to-hit moving target and after two shots, the gunman stopped trying. Instead, he suddenly opened the door to the left.

Then he vanished through the one on the right, closing it after him. JT dropped to the ground with a puzzled expression.

Almost immediately zombies started pouring out of the door on the left.

CHAPTER THIRTY-NINE

JT immediately took to the ceiling as undead hands reached for him, swinging his way back toward us and dropping back down in front of the elevator.

"Son of a *bitch*!" Nathan tossed Jones the rifle in his hands and slammed his hand on the elevator call button. "Ash, give your weapon to Gentry—he's a better shot." I didn't argue, doing as he said. "Everyone else, get ready to grab our gear as soon as that car gets up here."

He immediately turned to a panel next to the elevator doors and pulled a key out of one of his vest pockets.

"Is that—"

He nodded.

"We had copies of the key made before we left Redwood Grove." Flipping the panel cover up, he fit the key into a little slot and rotated it. Another little panel popped open, revealing a dark blue button. Nathan pushed it, then retrieved and pocketed the key.

Jones and Gentry aimed carefully, taking out the zoms in the front of the hungry queue, trying to create a barrier of corpses to slow down the ones behind. They were all dressed in hospital gowns, and I wondered if they were spryer in death than they had been in life.

As before, it worked to some degree, but determined zombies kept pushing their way through much in the way little old ladies with shopping carts managed to negotiate the local Wal-Mart on Black Friday—with total disregard for anyone or anything in their path.

I dropped down beside the dead gunmen and dug through their pockets. Nathan gave me an approving nod as I triumphantly held up a half dozen spare cartridges, handing them to Jones and Gentry as they ejected the empties.

Meanwhile the first elevator car slowly groaned its way back up to the catwalk. From somewhere deeper in the shaft, another car also begin its ascent toward us.

Zombies continued pouring out the door, their corpses piling up, but a few were making it through despite Jones and Gentry's best efforts. And they were on the last two cartridges.

Jones ran dry first. I put a hand on his shoulder.

"I'm immune," I said, "and you're not." He handed me the rifle, which I flipped over to use as a bludgeon just as Gentry ejected his last cartridge. Looking at each other, we gave a simultaneous battle cry and charged, cracking little old undead skulls for all we were worth.

A rush of adrenaline hit me in a wave. Suddenly this was for every time I'd had my foot run over and knees bashed by one of those aforementioned psychoseptuagenarians. Did it make me a bad person that I enjoyed it?

At that moment, I didn't care.

The first elevator car reached the catwalk. Tony and Jones were inside even before the doors finished opening, tossing out bags and weapons until the car was empty. Lil shouted my name, and I turned as she tossed me my sheathed katana.

I dropped the rifle, caught the katana by the hilt, and unsheathed it in one smooth movement I probably couldn't replicate if I practiced it for hours. Lil dashed up beside me, pickaxe a blur of movement as she scythed through zombies like Death through a battlefield. Between the three of us, we built up quite the pile of corpses, and the zombies still emerging from the open door slowed to a trickle.

"Having fun yet?" I said to Lil as she paused to wipe blood off her cheek.

"You bet," she said, face alight with the glee of battle.

"Sorry to interrupt, ladies," Nathan said, "but it's time to go."

A cheerful "ding" sounded as the second elevator car arrived, doors parting smoothly. Lil and I backed slowly away from the zombies that were still reaching for us, weapons ready as the rest of the group tossed the gear in.

"What about them?" Jones nodded at the dead gunmen.

"Leave 'em for the zoms," Nathan said coldly.

The *whupwhupwhup* of rotary blades sounded overhead. We looked up to see a helicopter—much like the one we'd crash-landed—taking off from a helipad somewhere in the med center complex.

Gabriel, I thought. For a moment, time froze.

Then G cleared his throat, and we looked over to where he and JT knelt. Mack was sprawled against the catwalk wall, face gray with shock. Blood soaked the right side of his uniform under his armpit and into his shirt.

Lil cried out and ran over to him.

"Get him into the elevator," Nathan barked.

With G and JT's help, Lil got Mack into the car. Blood trailed behind him on the walkway as they dragged him in. I followed, chopping down one last persistent zombie.

There were only two buttons on the control panel: UP and DOWN. Nathan hit DOWN with enough force to shake the walls of the car. The doors slid shut. The car descended with a gentle hum.

Nathan immediately dropped down next to Mack.

"What happened?" he asked gently.

Unbelievably, Mack smiled.

"When that jerk tried to shoot Ash... When Lil... I think... I think the bullet..." He nodded toward his right side.

Oh Christ, I thought. *The ricochet.*

Nathan gently lifted up Mack's right arm, exposing a bullet hole in the armpit of his shirt, where he was totally unprotected by our Kevlar armor. The entire right side of his shirt was now soaked, bright red arterial blood still pumping out of the wound.

"Oh, Mack..." I said.

"Do something!" Lil demanded, and she turned to Nathan.

Nathan shook his head.

"It's the brachial artery," he answered. "He's lost too much blood."

"No! That's not right." She turned to me, her eyes asking for a miracle I couldn't supply. "He's a wild card, right?"

Mack gave her a gentle smile.

"Even wild cards can die, hon."

"Not you!"

"Even me." Mack smiled again, reached out and touched her face softly. Then his hand slipped down and fell to his side.

Lil's cries of grief started as she buried her head against Mack's chest, then rose into a keening wail when she lifted her head, looking at me with incomprehensible pain. I wrapped my arms around her, my tears mingling with hers as she rocked back and forth with sobs so violent I thought they'd break her in half.

The elevator doors opened, revealing white walls and metal furniture. Lil continued to sob inconsolably, unaware that we'd reached our destination. A tall— very tall—woman in her thirties, chestnut brown hair neatly skimming the shoulders of her white lab coat, stood a few feet away, looking at us. A Hispanic man in his twenties, also wearing a lab coat, stood behind her, flanked by several armed men and women in fatigues, weapons leveled at us.

"Who are you?" the woman said sharply.

"We're from Redwood Grove." Nathan stepped forward, mindful of the weapons trained at his head. "Simone Fraser sent us. We're with the DZN."

The woman scanned all of our faces with a look as precise as a laser. She frowned.

"Where's Phineas?"

Around the world in eighty days? I thought, about to drop where I stood.

"Phineas," she repeated. Seeing our blank faces, she elaborated, "Dr. Phineas Albert."

"Someone took him," Nathan said, tension radiating off his body. "Along with another member of our team."

"That would match what we saw on the monitors, Dr. Arkin." The man in the lab coat nodded. "Two men were taken away at gunpoint."

I stared at him in disbelief.

"You mean you people saw what was going on up top—" My voice rose with an anger I couldn't begin to quantify "—and didn't do jack shit to help us?"

He looked at me quizzically, as if truly confused by my anger.

"We couldn't risk compromising the security of this facility." He offered the explanation as if it would make everything clear.

"Whatever," I snapped. "We have injured people here." *And dead.* "We need help."

The woman gave a nod to the armed personnel.

"Come in," she said as they lowered their weapons.

We all stumbled out of the elevator, our blood-spattered clothing and gear standing out in sharp contrast to the sterility of this new environment.

G pulled out his pocket watch and checked the time.

"Is there a bathroom?"

The woman pointed to a door.

"Down that hallway to your left, second door." She nodded to the man standing behind her. "Josh, make sure he doesn't get lost."

G nodded his thanks and hastily beelined towards the door. As Josh followed him, his coat snagged on one of the uncomfortable looking chairs lining the wall. He yanked it free, but not before I noticed the butt of a handgun sticking out from his waistband.

I got to my feet, one hand still resting on Lil's shoulder.

"So you know Dr. Albert?"

She looked at me as if I'd wasted her time by stating the obvious.

"I should say so."

"Who, exactly, are you?" Nathan asked, sounding as weary as I'd ever heard him.

"Dr. Marianne Arkin," she replied in precise tones. "Dr. Albert and I developed the Walker's vaccine together."

CHAPTER FORTY

I sat on a chair next to Lil, who lay sleeping on a cot in a small, utilitarian room, much like the ones hidden away under Patterson Hall, as if all DZN labs were thought up by the same boring interior designer.

I found the similarity both reassuring and creepy.

I'd had a quick shower in a gym locker-style facility and been given some clean clothes—more fatigues—by Josh, who introduced himself as Dr. Arkin's assistant. If there were any other people in the facility, I hadn't seen them, and I hadn't asked. I had far more pressing issues on my mind, the first being Lil.

Dr. Arkin had slipped her some sort of sedative in a glass of water that had effectively knocked her out. I tucked the green wool blanket around her shoulders, brushing a stray lock of hair back from her pale forehead. Her eyelids were red and swollen, even in sleep.

I desperately needed some rest myself, but was afraid to leave Lil's side, in case she woke up. I didn't know what she'd do if left by herself. So I sat there, forcing my eyes to stay open even though they drooped with exhaustion.

There was a knock on the doorframe and Nathan entered, two steaming mugs in his hands. He handed one to me and I smelled the ambrosial scent of hot coffee.

"Thanks," I said, taking a restorative sip.

"I spoke to Simone," he said without preamble.

"As soon as we clear out enough hostiles and secure a perimeter, they'll be moving the rest of our operations here." He reached out unexpectedly to touch Lil's face. "All of them. Including Binkey and Doodle."

I gave a wan smile.

"Someone's been monitoring our communications," he continued, "so it'll be a few days until we can guarantee secure channels."

"Yeah, I figured that out," I said. "Why did they take Gabriel?" I inhaled the steam rising off the coffee, trying to make sense of things.

"I don't know," Nathan said. "Probably for whatever fucked up reason they screwed with the 'copters and ambushed us here. Whoever it is has been one step ahead of us. But we have an advantage they don't know about."

"What?"

"Microchip." He grinned at me. "Implanted in Gabriel's arm."

"Seriously?"

He nodded.

"You've got one too. All the wild cards do. Except me," he added almost as an afterthought. "I dug mine out years ago." He raised his arm so I could see underneath, and there was a strange, misshapen scar I hadn't noticed before.

I stared at him. That was just creepy, no matter how you looked at it.

"So are we going after them?" I asked, not sure I wanted to know the answer. Because I knew that, no matter what he said, I'd have to go.

He nodded, and I exhaled.

"Simone is convinced that the answer to a cure for this whole fucked up zombie virus is somewhere in our blood—all of the wild cards—and in Gabriel's as well. Dr. Albert may be a megalomaniacal narcissist, but he's come closer than anyone else to understanding how the thing works."

He took a sip of coffee and continued.

"The good news is that Dr. Arkin is indeed familiar with Dr. Albert's research and assures us she can continue his work. What's more, Dr. Albert's laptop and samples of the antiserum and the vaccine were left behind with his knapsack, and that's a major stroke of luck for us—not to mention a real kick to the balls for the assholes who kidnapped him."

"Them," I corrected, then I sighed. "We made it here. That's something, right?"

"More than something," Nathan said. "We've got another chance to stop this."

There was another knock at the open door. I looked up and into a pair of hazel eyes framed with dark lashes. Feminine eyes set into an undeniably masculine face, with thick, wavy chocolate brown hair that begged to be touched. He wore jeans and a dark green T-shirt almost this side of too tight, showing off subtly sculpted muscles.

The guy was a walking case of bad-boy sex appeal, and I'd bet my last cup of coffee that he knew it.

"Can we help you?" I said coolly.

"Dr. Arkin told me to introduce myself to my fellow wild cards." He stepped into the room and held out his hand to Nathan, saying, "I'm Griffin." Nathan gave his hand a cursory shake before dropping it.

Mr. Too-Sexy-For-His-Pants then turned his attention on me. Looking me up and down, he flashed me a smile I instinctively distrusted.

"But you can call me Griff," he said.

LONDON, ENGLAND

Danny coughed, a deep wracking cough that shook his entire body. It pissed him off, but also struck him as a just punishment for abandoning his wife and three kids in Boston, three days earlier than his trip to London actually required.

He'd told Grace he'd had prep work to do before the big annual LP meeting, so he needed to leave sooner than expected. He'd neglected to clarify that the prep work would involve the pneumatic body of one of his colleagues, a Swedish VP of Research and Development who was also attending the meeting. They both worked for the same multinational corporation, though in different sectors.

He was venture capital, and liked to imagine himself a Gordon Gekko for the modern age, but with better hair than Michael Douglas's character. He and his associate had enjoyed similar exchanges of vital information whenever they'd gotten the chance to dovetail their travel schedules.

Danny knew he should feel guilty, especially for leaving Grace during what looked to be a total snot-fest. Chuckie, the youngest, had brought Walker's Flu home from daycare, passing it on to Celia and Bonnie in the space of just twenty-four hours.

But hey, he needed to be healthy for his presentation. No way would he impress the bigwigs—the guys with the money and the power—if he had to blow his nose every few minutes.

So he'd bailed on his wife and three kids, telling her to bring in their nanny if she really felt she couldn't handle things on her own. As soon as he said it, he knew Grace would handle it on her own, just to prove to him that she could.

He could play her like a familiar old keyboard.

Of course, he preferred to play with new ones, too, now and again.

Another bout of coughing wracked his body as he turned to Nita, his very lovely and intelligent colleague, who sprawled naked on the 500-threadcount Egyptian cotton sheets provided at the boutique hotel they'd both "coincidentally" booked for the trip.

"You sound like shit," she observed, charming in her lilting accent. "Did you get a flu shot this year?"

"No," he admitted with some embarrassment. "I sort of forgot." Truth be told, he'd never had any use for them, and had frequently given Grace a hard time when she insisted on getting the kids vaccinated.

It turned out that Nita was also a huge proponent of them, and given her scientific background, he'd actually listened to her, and had intended to follow through this year.

Nita made a tsk tsk *noise.*

"This is what happens, see?" she said. "Promise me you'll get one when you go home, yes?"

He nodded, burying his head between her breasts.

"Sure, babe. Whatever you say."

Oh well, *he thought.* I made it through the presentation and even the reception without more than a few sneezes now and again. *He'd probably spread a few germs, what with all the handshaking and backslapping. Hopefully if and when the honchos came down with the grunge, they wouldn't connect the dots back to him.*

Never knew what could queer a promotion these days.

ACKNOWLEDGMENTS

I hate writing acknowledgements. Not because I don't like thanking people who have helped me, but because I'm terrified of leaving someone out. So caveat #1: if you were listed in *Plague Town*, consider yourself listed here (although there will be repeats). Caveat #2: there will be blanket acknowledging. Caveat #3: please don't hate me if I forget to name you!

Starting with the amazing Team Titan: Nick Landau, Vivian Cheung, Katy Wild, Cath Trechman, Miranda Jewess, Tim Whale, Selina Juneja, Sophie Calder, Hannah Dennis, Chris McLane, Jessica Gramuglia, with a loud shout out to Martin Stiff for the awesome cover design, and extra special "I love yous" to Tom Green and Katharine Carroll for being so fun to work with on publicity. I am officially spoiled rotten, especially by Steve Saffel, my Dark Editorial Overlord. A very extra special thanks and "oh my god, we got through the second book!" squee of joy to Steve.

To all the booksellers and bookstore owners who helped me promote *Plague Town*, you are amazing, generous people. Special thanks to Patrick Nichol with Indigo Books, Maryelizabeth Hart with Mysterious Galaxy, Del and Sue with Dark Delicacies, Jack with Dark Carnival, and Alan and Jude with Borderlands Books. Also, I am so grateful to Sisters in Crime NorCal, Lurking Novelists, Writing Wombats, and all of my fellow authors who've given me so much support. Special thanks to Kat Richardson and Jess Lourey for their extra time and love, along with Joe McKinney, Jonathan Maberry, Mira Grant, Loren Rhoads, and Lisa Brackmann.

A huge thanks to all the bloggers, reviewers, and assorted website hosts who've been so supportive and enthusiastic, and gratitude for every reader who has taken the time to read my work. And those emails you send? Those make a bad day good, and a good day great!

So many people helped with research. Therefore to all of my wonderful Facebook friends and family members, of which there are far too many to list, a heartfelt thank you! Special thanks go to: Captain Michael Castagnola with the San Francisco Fire Department; Major Marcy Meyer; and Peter "Indiana" Allison in the areas of setting fires, all things military, and parkour. Hell Ocho and T. Chris Martindale, you two continue to provide me with research material and some of the coolest ideas—with permission to use. I adore you both, and always will.

To my "let's help Dana get some sleep" support group, especially Shantal and Ona, you saved my sanity.

Anne Stevenson and Jane Gutierrez-Thornton, your generosity and huge hearts saved both my sanity and my bacon! Aldyth, Brad, Maureen, and James, you also get sanity saver stickers for your ever-supportive friendship. Rick and Jen, bad movies and your company were high notes in a low year. A special hug of thanks to Linda Schrade—mom of Allie, my real life Lil—for my zombie-head necklace with hand-beaded blood and veins! Mom and Bill, thank you for knowing when *not* to ask how the writing was going.

And biggest thanks this time around goes to David Fitzgerald. Without his constant love, daily encouragement, and willingness to view endless zombie movies, I would still be huddled over my computer, rocking back and forth and muttering, "It'll never be finished… it'll never be finished…" Me too you!

ABOUT THE AUTHOR

Dana Fredsti is an actress with a background in theatrical sword-fighting, whose credits include the cult classic *Army of Darkness*. Her favorite projects include acting alongside Ken Foree (*Dawn of the Dead*) and Josef Pilato (*Day of the Dead*). She has been a producer, director, and screenplay writer for stage and film, and was the co-writer/associate producer on *Urban Rescuers*, which won Best Documentary at the 2003 Valley Film Festival in Los Angeles.

She has written numerous published articles, essays, and shorts, including stories in *Danger City* (Contemporary Press, 2005), and *Mondo Zombie* (Cemetery Dance, 2006). In addition she's published *Murder for Hire: The Peruvian Pigeon* (Rock Publications, 2007) and several books and stories for Ravenous Romance. She has served as the president of the literary organization Sisters in Crime, Northern California Chapter.

Through seven-plus years of volunteering at Exotic Feline Breeding Facility/Feline Conservation Center, Dana has had a full-grown leopard sit on her feet, been kissed by tigers, cuddled baby jaguars, and had her thumb sucked by an ocelot with nursing issues. She's addicted to bad movies and any book or film—good or bad—which includes zombies. Her other hobbies include surfing (badly), collecting beach glass (obsessively), and wine-tasting (happily).